The Ivory Stretch

Coerte V. W. Felske, noted Zeitgeist chronicler of the skin-deep and shameless age, flits, flaps, flutters, stretches wings, and struts with his fifth novel, *The Ivory Stretch*. Frenetic, idiosyncratic, bedazzling, and uniquely original, this wild ride of a narrative showcases protagonist Billy Sixkiller who seizes the reader's imagination and uses him to gaze boldly into the heart of the American psyche in the great literary tradition of Twain, Kerouac, Kesey, Thompson, and McCarthy. Through Billy the author launches a revenge tale steeped in the Native American ethos to create a vivid snapshot of conflicted America in the 21st century. Aptly named Sixkiller—a modern-day Odysseus if not Moses himself—is a larger-than-life anti-hero who takes dispirited road companions on an adventure of a lifetime of his own design, a postmodern Vision Quest of spiritual renewal and self-discovery. "Billy Six" slices through the breathtaking settings of the Southwest in a supercharged elongated car made of curves, white beyond white, blasting wide the eyes of his unsuspecting roadies—reluctant accomplice, the Parisian orphaned Frenchy, and his suicidal captive Roland. Billy initially kidnaps the dead-souled novelist for a past crime, but a curious relationship develops between the two men, which is the beating heart of the story. Along the way the emotionally recessive prisoner develops an amorous bond with sheltered, spiritually starved Frenchy, Billy's former lover. This ever-shifting three-way and unlikely clashing of personalities and blend of intimate motivations staves off predictability and the narrative not only retains its oxygen, but surprises the reader as it reinvents itself at every turn. When the trio are together taking to the highway in the stretch limo the novel zooms into high gear comprising one of the great road trips to be found in American literature, rife with unconscious echoes of Least Heat-Moon's *Blue Highways*, Pirsig's *Zen and the Art of Motorcycle Maintenance*, as well as Thompson's *Fear and Loathing*. The dramatic ironies compound as the charismatic, dazzlingly unpredictable Billy, seeking to exact revenge on Roland for a past crime, ends up giving his emotionally voided prisoner a new appreciation for life. Billy hauls him across three states' worth of deserts, forests, and Indian lands for five sleep-deprived days, in an effort to peel away a lifetime's layers of disillusionment, anguish, and guilt and blow the winds of life back into the man's lungs. Because only by having his captive embrace living again can Billy truly have the power to take something of value away from him, that is, the man's life. Why? To give his revenge value and meaning. Which brings us to the grandiose, complex, and magnificent rendering of the Sixkiller character. Perceptive though manipulated, profane yet sacred, gentlemanly but diabolical, and like a bomb going off in a fireworks factory, Billy explodes onto the page spouting his vast artillery of language like shrapnel. His prescient, savvy, irreverent, fuel-injected rants border on the Whitmanesque and his outlaw spirit at once embodies *and* contradicts the journeying aspect of the American character; a contemporary equivalent of the searching characters in Kerouac's *On the Road* and Kesey's *Sometimes a Great Notion*. Almost as uncommonly, the pouty-sexy-feisty Frenchy, Billy's thirsting sidekick is another full-bodied, unique personage who evolves before our eyes and learns to more than hold her own against him. Simultaneously thrilling, *noir*ish, crackling and detouring, the electric prose masterfully seasoned with philosophies, historical asides, tribal customs, letters, diaries, metaphors, and individual paths to enlightenment gives the tome a heightened reality, at the same time remaining true to the enchanting milieu of L'Amour and sensibilities of McCarthy to forge a new kind of western. Felske, who previously lasered in on modern fast lane culture, has gone lyrical, poetic, even classic here, with his boldest and most significant work, shepherding a cast of characters who start out searching for external validation, but find internal truths instead. The author expertly transports his eye for detail and innate curiosities on a different kind of "dolce vita" that is equally sweet but twice as spicy. Like a gun barrel to the small of the back, *The Ivory Stretch* forces the reader to contemplate the vulgar and divine, entwining sex, lyricism, violence, and spirituality to inspire deeper epiphanies. With its author's mythic vision of a southwestern death trip that transforms into something decidedly more life-affirming, *The Ivory Stretch* claims its place as a vital part of the American literary tradition and Billy Sixkiller joins the pantheon of great fictional character creations, certainly to be one of the most talked about in recent memory. Conjuring hints and evoking whispers of some of literature's finest *The Ivory Stretch* sets the imagination ablaze with an unforgettable, high-octane, adrenaline rush ride which haunts the psyche well after the story's climactic conclusion.

— *Kenneth Nichols*
Professor of Playwrighting
State University of New York,
Oswego

"**Tom Wolfe rewrites American Gigolo**. Felske, a veteran of the New York fashion scene, makes a fiction debut marked by sheer chutzpah and this satire commands attention. Behind every tottering runway diva, every pouting cover girl, every buffed swimsuit babe, the author would have us believe, there's one guy who sleeps with them all. Here it's narrator Nick, who loves the breed of woman he calls "Thing," that rare Amazon who renders civilian females hopelessly schlubby by comparison. Astride his Harley, a copy of *The Letters of Vincent Van Gogh* jammed in a pocket, the chest of some Scandinavian demigoddess pressed against his leather-jacketed back, Nick knows he has a leg up on the average male. Mercifully, Felske makes almost no effort to redeem this fool for sex. Cruising Gotham's fashionable haunts in search of fresh material, Nick is more an artist of physical pleasure than the misogynist he at first appears to be; nevertheless, he receives his overdue comeuppance in spades by book's end. Though Nick jets to Miami's South Beach on a brief detour of debauchery, his story is fundamentally one of New York days: the flashy parties he promotes, the circuit of trendy enclaves where people pose fabulously and smoke a lot, the whole scene populated by a pumped-up tribe of neo-Cheeverians endlessly in search of love. By minimizing Nick's obsession with his mother's untimely death, Felske avoids the Jay McInerney first-timer's error of laying too much blame for the indiscretions of an American rude boy on the altar of family and Nick's unrepentant offensiveness carries things on. Fun stuff."

— Kirkus Reviews

"**Boys In Babeland**. No scruples or psychological doses of saltpeter daunts the narrator of Coerte V.W. Felske's *The Shallow Man*. This novel's hero, Nick Laws, is a club-hopping hedonist who exclusively targets models as bedmates and makes no apologies. Rather than waste time with names, he refers to each of his model-dates as Thing. After greasily chomping on nubiles and discarding them like spareribs, the narrator flirts with the prospect of maturing and settling down, a momentary lurch which takes the form of an affair with a non-model. The frustrating interlude leads him to decide, The hell with it—real women are nothing but hard work. The novel is crass, entertaining, slangy, egotistical, and reeking of sun bronze and the fresh turnover of fleshy delights makes the narrator's decision to become an aging roué instead of a responsible adult seem like an honest, if not admirable, choice. He's willing to go with the flow even if it leaves him stranded. Where *Zoe* belongs to the sadder-but-wiser category, *The Shallow Man* ends up neither sad nor wise, which seems right. The novel is prefaced by a remark from Oscar Wilde—'Only the shallow know themselves.' Felske writes like a gigolo and treats seduction as a dirty sport. Ambitious-minded literary types fasten on models as subjects and objects because their smooth blankness and mute mystique (the silencing effect of a beautiful woman entering a room) allow so much space for inscription and speculation. The bodily landscape becomes a sacred scroll. The model, reduced to abstraction, becomes Other: exotic animal, extraterrestrial, goddess, cyborg, or billboard archetype. Unlike Felske's Shallow Man, Jay McInerney knows what he wants to be when he grows up: F. Scott Fitzgerald, bugler of lost promise. But McInerney is a case of arrested development. His new novel *Model Behavior*, an urban safari of superficial people saying superficial things in a superficial culture, seems like an attempt to squeeze the last bit of wattage out of *Bright Lights, Big City*. Bret Easton Ellis's *Glamorama* with its supermodels, terrorists, and globetrotting story line, is an absurd escapade that's smirkingly aware of its own glossy anachronisms. The 'angry feeling' Ellis nurses about models reflects a deeper aversion to women, who are pretty much chopped liver in his fictional universe. Perhaps the biggest letdown of model fiction is that, aside from *The Shallow Man*, its boyish irresponsibility doesn't explode into sexy fun. The writers seem to have hangovers before they've even gotten looped. Who knew going to all these fictional parties would be such work?"

— James Wolcott, *Vanity Fair*

"**Model Citizen**: the story of a man who never met a stunningly beautiful woman he didn't like. Love, H.L. Mencken said, is the delusion that one woman differs from another. Nick Laws, a marginally more enlightened fellow, claims that one in every 50,000 is quite different from the other 49,999: she's drop-dead gorgeous, and he's determined to sleep with her. Nick, who narrates Coerte V.W. Felske's amusing first novel, "The Shallow Man" is 30 years old, lives in Soho and works by day as a hand model, by night as a party promoter for clubs with names like Café D&A. He knows how to ask "Would you like to take a bubble bath with me?" in 10 languages, and he has committed to memory the Victoria's Secret 24-hour toll-free number. With the exception of his Harley, all he cares about is what he calls collectively, "Thing": "Fashion models, beautiful women and general hotness." He happily acknowledges his obsession right from the start. When Nick contemplates "the sweetest joining of limbs known to man," his company is agreeable. But during the couple of weeks he tangles with his brother, his confidante, and of course, models' boyfriends, all of whom demand he re-evaluate his life. By his own account, he is neither very bright nor very witty, and a dullard's earnest ruminations can only be dull—or, as Nick would put it, as exciting as York Avenue. Before long, though, he is back to his old, unreflective self, proving that the unexamined life is well worth living. To Nick, everything resembles conjugating the verb, and if your mind works in similar fashion, you'll probably understand his ruling passion. One feminist writer has used the term "penised humans" to refer to men. Mentally, at least, Nick Laws is as penised as a human can get. When he awards Audrey Hepburn the crown for "pinnacle hotness," it is only because Mr. Felske has nodded. Nick detests the beach but this novel is perfect for it. "The Shallow Man" is also perfect for shallow men. On the other hand, women may think the title is redundant."

— David Kelley, *The New York Times Book Review*

"In his first novel, *The Shallow Man*, Coerte V.W. Felske spins a clever tale of the narcissistic world of fashion modeling. In this comic send-up, Nick Laws is the shallow man whose every thought and word reflect his sole interest in life: boffing models. From the late-night clubs of Manhattan to the art deco bars of Miami, Nick searches for beautiful women to take to bed. He's so perfect, he's hilarious. Is there a man with a soul so noble that he has not entertained this fantasy? In real life, no one could stand around all day in his motorcycle jacket and sunglasses, purring platitudes to curvaceous dimwits. But Nick's relentless, self-conscious pursuit is very funny. Nick reminds us, "Never judge a book by its contents." Certainly not this book. *The Shallow Man* is fun, flash, and filigree—a sexy, witty spoof of the Nineties."

— Digby Diehl, *Playboy*

"**Shallow Waters Run Deep**. This stunning, but unreflective man knows a lot more than you think. Behind those big blank eyes and that deep tan is … well, something that women find hopelessly tempting: a healthy disdain for thinking too much. Since he can't be bothered connecting the dots, he maps out the politics of the jejune and Gitanes with an easy straight line. Reading the quick-witted prose, one begins to think less about things and more about Thing, the Shallow Man's tag for the women he dates: gorgeous, seemingly unattainable models. Nick Laws is like Hamlet without the mental baggage, tumbling Ophelia by Act II. So what if behind all that cigarette smoke and charm lies a lean mentality. Felske's *The Shallow Man* makes a case for the unexamined life."

— *Esquire*

"I may not have been the king of Generation Face," proclaims hipster Nick Laws, invoking his superficial peers in screenwriter Felske's first novel, "but I was definitely one of its princes." Nick can't get enough of "Thing" his catchphrase for models and other impossibly stunning women; his every waking moment is devoted to bedding them and their friends—as long as they're not Civilians (regular-looking women). It would be easy, but inaccurate, to dismiss Nick as a misogynist. For one thing, his acidic classification system extends to men too. "Guys can be Dialtones," he concedes. Spiked with original Nickspeak and hilarious dialogue, Felske's depiction of the physically elite is so clever in its anthropological detail that we can forgive his protagonist for just about anything. Besides, *The Shallow Man* harbors a few glimmers of Nick's humanity. You just have to dig to find them."

— People

"Coerte V.W. Felske's novel *The Shallow Man* turned the fashion world on its head—and introduced the term 'modelizer' into the collective consciousness. One of Nick Laws's dictums is "don't judge a book by its contents" ostensibly delivered in support of his 'beauty = truth' theorem. The novel is presented as a comment on our society's obsession with models, and therefore its cultural relevance outweighs any criticism of its craftsmanship. It's a notion that had its day during the genre of the hip urban novel of the 80's, a genre characterized by its most prominent literary agent Amanda Urban as, '*and then they fucked.*' *The Shallow Man* fits in perfectly with this body of work. It's an entertaining book, a pleasant diversion. Like its protagonist, *The Shallow Man* doesn't take itself too seriously, and it urges you to do the same. It's a fantasy, a lark, a good time. The Shallow Man has his moments of doubt and pain, wherein he questions the basis of his existence, but they are brief, and far from mending his ways he vows to indulge in as many in as many places for as long as he can, in retaliation for all the 'politically correct bullshit' he's been assaulted with. And, in a way, after several years of that 'politically correct bullshit' *The Shallow Man* is refreshingly moral-free."

— Detour

"Deep thoughts from a hand model, *The Shallow Man,* by Coerte V.W. Felske, humorously portrays Nick Laws, a model and club promoter who's happy to let "Thing" (the allure of beautiful women) dictate the conversation if not his life—to the point where he's mastered how to say "Would you join me for a bubble bath?" in every language spoken by supermodels. Aware that his lifestyle annoys "dromes" (average-looking people who resent the beautiful), Nick argues that it's not his fault that "4-B girls" (beauty, breeding, brains, and bank account) were created, or that men are compelled to pursue them. He frequently hauls out his tattered copy of Van Gogh's letters to prove that history's purest artist was also a model muncher. Set up by a "catsuit feminist" (one with beauty and brains), wary of "donuts" (male models who are stuck on themselves), a too-frequent partaker "the Dracula nap" (sleep all day, come out at night), Nick is a lot of laughs even as his promiscuity takes on the aspect of an addiction passed from father to son. Fans of Jay McInerney and P.J. O'Rourke should be amused."

— Glamour

"Cruising Manhattan's young and beautiful scene on a Harley Davidson, Nick Laws is on a desperate search for supermodels or, as he puts it, "Thing." Whether throwing parties or that one in 50,000 who is "hot, Thing hot," fending off "Civilians," (everyday girls with everyday looks) or convincing Thing to dump "Guy" (everyday boy, everyday looks), Nick is driven by Thing—how to get it and how to enjoy it. Though the world Felske paints is self-consciously hipper-than-thou, he holds his portrait of it in check with a ribald sense of humor and an understanding of the limitations of Nick's ways. Tight prose and smooth dialogue impel the story along, while the names of so many trendy New York night spots dot the text that hipster wannabes can use it as a guidebook. This first novel captures the gloss of its characters with a smart shine of its own."

— Publisher's Weekly

"Make no mistake, Coerte V.W. Felske's literary Lothario Nick Laws, the Shallow Man, is no ordinary ladies' man. He is an uberstud for the '90s, otherwise known as a model hound, modelizer, beauty junkie, or, as fashion insiders prefer, model fucker. Is this an accurate depiction of modelettes and the men who pursue them? While the book may be fictional, the modelizer phenomenon most definitely is not."

— Details

"**Move Over, Jay McInerney**: Coerte Felske, the author of *The Shallow Man*, wants you to know : he is not his title character. The narrator of his forthcoming novel, he says, is a composite of a number of men whose antics he witnessed on the model circuit. 'I used to live with a fashion photographer,' he explains, 'and these characters would show up at all the fashion shows. They'd fly around the world. They could be lawyers, restaurant owners, party promoters.' Felske says he himself doesn't even date models. 'OK,' he admits, 'I have gone out with a few, but only very briefly. All my girlfriends, though, have been Catsuit Feminists.' This is Felske's term for women who are both intelligent and gorgeous. He introduces a number of such swell terms for young women in his book, which he says he wrote in five weeks. For example, Civilian Girls (anyone not fortunate enough to be a model) and Dialtones (women so stupid they might as well emit one each time they open their mouths). 'One of the challenges of the book was keeping the shallow man from being too smart,' says the Ivy League-educated Felske, who until recently lived in Hollywood writing screenplays, including one for Mickey Rourke he'd rather not discuss. "The shallow man doesn't care to be deep. He's introspective but tries to avoid it. *The Shallow Man*, Felske insists, is a book for the nineties. 'It's different from the eighties,' he says, 'when money and power were the big things. Now glamour is eclipsing substance even intelligence in a lot of ways, rightly or wrongly.' In any case, Felske asks, 'what's wrong caring about beauty? The shallow man thinks it's life-enhancing.' As Forrest Gump might have put it, shallow is as shallow does. The *Bright Lights, Big City* of the 90s."

— Buzz Magazine

"**Shallow Waters**: This is where **Coerte V.W. Felske's** protagonist wants to be—sandwiched between the most beautiful women in the world. Surrounded by the most life-enhancing supermodels there are. Amid *hotness*, as his anti-hero Nick Laws would say. Felske is a native New Yorker and author of *The Shallow Man*—a book that details one man's pursuit of sleeping with that one woman who is agonizingly, physically superior to every other. I would hereby like to make Felske's book required reading this rainy summer, and, at the same time, inform the author that, in writing the book that I always intended to write, he basically devastated me. I am not applying for a job with the Kirkus Reviews, but I do think the book is important enough to describe and appropriately gush over certain parts. The Shallow Man is narrated through Nick Laws, the hand model/club promoter who refers to all models as *Thing*, friends who get you closer to *Thing* as *Conduits*, guys who are bitter over never being able to land *Thing* as *Dromes* and women who possess both brains and beauty as *Catsuit Feminists*. Some people are calling *The Shallow Man* the new *Bright Lights, Big City*. Others say as soon as Felske's agents find a film home for his tome, it will be the 'Shampoo' of the 1990s. In fact, as we speak, **Johnny Depp**, **Brad Pitt**, and **Keanu Reeves** are being pegged. 'The whole this is mind-blowing,' Felske told me. 'I always liked books where you can climb into a character's obsessed head and see what drives him. In this case, what drives him is his quest for these beauties.' Sadly, I hear area party promoters are laying claim to the book's title character being modeled after them, but Felske shoots that down. 'That's absurd. It's no more based on me than it's based on those guys,' he said. 'I was born in Manhattan. The 70s, the 80s. I was at Club Area and Nell's and M.K. I moved to L.A. in 1991, but still way before these tourist promoters started working the scene.' Still, it's all pretty heady stuff for the author. Just last week at a book signing party at L.A.'s Monkey Bar, Felske was floored when **Jack Nicholson**, **Harvey Keitel**, and **Kiefer Sutherland** all asked for his John Hancock. But the better story comes from a book bash in the Hamptons last weekend when a woman waltzed past doormen without an invite. 'I don't need one,' she said. 'I slept with the Shallow Man when I was 16.' Felske confided, 'She was right.' To his credit, Felske is not a kiss-and-tell guy, so there was no chance he and I were going to compare notes on, perhaps, at one time chasing the same *Hotness*. He also didn't care to battle feminists who might get frosted at his character learning the phrase, 'Do you want to take a bubble bath with me?' in eight different languages. Some will call that shallow. I call it being prepared. Meanwhile, Elite supermodel **Frederique** is not surprised at Felske's success. The supermodel told me she was his designated first-draft reader—and the woman he based his Catsuit Feminist on—and knew the book would blow everyone away. 'I am honest and direct,' Freddy said. 'There were so many recognizable moments that I saw from the personal end of modeling. And, for the most part, he's right, and women should not be upset with it. There are women who are *Dialtones* (a less than eloquent lady) and there are women where you get an answer. But ours is one of the few businesses where you can get work if you're just a *Dialtone*. This book says more about the way men think and feel than *Bright Lights*. And Coerte is not the Shallow Man himself. He's a voyeur …' ''

— A. J Benza, *"Downtown," The New York Daily News*

"**Useful New Word** (from the novel *The Shallow Man* by Coerte V. W. Felske): 'Dialtone'—a girl or guy who is so stupid, the sound of a dial tone hums in their brain and comes out their mouth."

— *Vogue*

"**Generation X's answer to *Less Than Zero*.** The (anti) hero is shallow. Nick is a New York party promoter and part-time hand model, simply so he can shag as many models as possible. Only one in 50,000 girls reaches his standards of 'pinnacle hotness' and the rest are 'Civilians' and 'Dromes.' He never recalls names, so models are 'Thing,' as in, 'I thought about the imminent arrival of Spring thing fresh from Europe. Then a new sea of Baby Thing would come along in the summer.' Nick never got over Robert Palmer's 'Simply Irresistible' video and this book would bring Naomi Wolf out in a nasty rash. If Jay McInerney had written the expose Model, it would read a lot like *Shallow*. Our hero also fantasies about a time when the world will be one big stretch of black tarmac—suitable for his Harley—and zoned for a 7-Eleven every 10 miles. It is not so much politically incorrect as politically indecent and I loathe Nick—but I love the book, which is worth it for the jargon alone. It is probably Generation X's answer to *Less Than Zero*, although Nick, of course, doesn't believe in Gen X. There is only Generation Face. And Thing."

— *Sydney Morning Herald (Australia)*

"In Deep With The Shallow Man. Linda and co. might not get out of bed for less than $10,000, but the vainglorious, model-toting Nick Laws of *The Shallow Man* won't climb *into* bed with anything other than the one woman in 50,000 who is hot. Nick, a hand model and party promoter, is drawn to hotness like a heat-seeking missile. In his shallow life, models are 'Thing's and are 'Thing hot.' If he is having a *very* good day, he'll meet a '4B' model—with beauty, brains, breeding, and bank account. 'I never met a model I didn't like,' he proclaims. With the rest of us, he's not so generous. There are Dromes (men who have Hotness Deficiency Syndrome and an inability to land 'Thing'); Civilians (women with real looks and real personalities—read average face and ordinary figures); Donuts (male models, because … well …); and Dialtones (the mentally challenged). With *The Shallow Man*, Felske skims along the glossy surface of club glamour, exposing the ugly facts of an industry where beauty is truth. A first novel for Felske, who was a scriptwriter on Mickey Rourke's 'Homeboy,' it's funny, brutally clever and, when the shallow man gets deep, can also be surprisingly insightful. And not a politically correct sentiment on the page."

— Elle (Australia)

"The book world's preoccupation with megamodels and glamazons continues with this New York-based tale of nipples and nightclubs. The man drooling on the end of the catwalk is Nick—also known as Dick—Laws, the kind of guy who checks out the trim of his lovers' privates before allowing sexual progress. He's a real character, which is why you might enjoy seeing what happens to him at the end of the story."

— Cleo (Australia)

" 'I never met a model I didn't like.' That still makes Nick Laws choosy, because he can only go for one woman in 50,000. Not a 'civilian,' but a girl who is on a model agency's books and who has that *je ne sais quoi* that Nick, with more economy than elegance, calls 'thing.' Nick is a model himself and a philosopher in his spare time, sharing with us his thoughts on life, love, the letters of Vincent Van Gogh and the significance of being asked to hold a girl's lipstick. Slick, self-consciously funny, occasionally sentimental, *The Shallow Man* by Coerte V.W. Felske is a modern morality tale."

— Marie Claire (Australia)

"*Vogue, The New Yorker, The New York Times, W* and *USA Today* don't usually turn out for parties to mark the publications of first novels by unknown authors. But they made an exception for a recent bash in Southampton, N.Y., for Coerte V.W. Felske's 'The Shallow Man.' A sendup of society's obsession with superficial beauty and glamour, the novel chronicles the life and times of Nick Laws, hand model, club promoter and lover of Thing; his name for all exceptionally beautiful fashion models. Just published by Crown, it is knee deep in good reviews: *Playboy* lauds it as 'fun, flash and filigree,' *The New York Times Book Review* calls it a perfect beach read,. and *Buzz* concludes that it 'very well may be the 'Bright Lights, Big City' of the '90s.' But rave notices weren't the only attention-getters at the party hosted by department-store heir Ted Field. As anyone who's flipped through a fashion magazine or turned on MTV's 'House of Style' knows, the media are as drawn to Thing as Nick is, and on hand were Sports Illustrated swimsuit models Ingrid Seynhaeve and Daniela Pestova, and fashion stars Yasmeen Ghauri and Gail Elliott. 'The model phenomenon is absurd. These girls could be running for office at this point,' says Felske, 34, referring in his candid, politically incorrect style to models as 'girls.' On the telephone from his home in New York's Upper East Side, Felske denies . that he's anything like his fictional hero. 'Every interview, certainly the question comes up, 'Are you the Shallow Man?' I only have one thing to say about that—absolutely,' he says, laughing. 'Not really. The whole idea came from thinking of a new Marvel Comics hero, the Shallow Man, who just appears on the scene like Batman. I just thought it was funny.' Amusing. and appalling, Nick Laws makes his appearance in the novel with the lines: '*I never met a model I didn't like. The revelation came to me early one morning when I was in that dreamy state, beyond the point of sleep but too comfortable in the Ocean of Love to get up. ... Since I don't have a great attention span, I thought about this for a short while, then went on to other thoughts.*' The novel follows Nick from SoHo nightspots to a Miami modeling agency, through the small world of hipsters, photographers, bookers, designers and stylists that revolves around models. What plot there is involves Nick's relationships with his best friend, a woman who is both beautiful and smart, whom he refers to as the Catsuit Feminist, and some unresolved issues from his childhood. It's a milieu Felske knows well. A former denizen of the club scene he documents, he counts as friends photographers Peter Beard and Richard Bailey and model Frederique Van der Wal, all of whom are noted in the novel's acknowledgments. He says he got his first exposure to the world of the fashion model when he was growing up in Quogue, N.Y., and a neighbor was Eileen Ford, the head of Ford Models Inc., the pioneering modeling agency that represented Christie Brinkley, Cheryl Tiegs, Lauren Hutton, Jean Shrimpton and just about every other big name in the 1960s and '70s. After studying romance languages at Dartmouth College, he attended Columbia University's Graduate School of the Arts in the film division. For several years after college, he labored in the other big glamour industry—the movies—as a screenwriter. But after a frustrating experience writing four drafts of a script called 'Homeboy' for Mickey Rourke, he turned to the novel. 'The Shallow Man,' written in six weeks in May and June two years ago, was his first. It comes on the heels of 'Model: The Ugly Business of Beautiful Women,' an expose of the modeling industry by former New York Times reporter Michael Gross that hit the best-seller lists this spring. Felske says his focus is less on supermodels and the fashion and beauty industries than on their effects on the rest of the population—especially men. 'The new trophy has been advertised and she's the fashion model. It's like the new Corvette or the new beautiful home in the Hamptons,' he says. Felske sees the rise of the model as linked to the boom in cable and its nearly insatiable appetite for programming. 'So the media thrusts these girls' faces in your living room and you end up wondering, who are they? People have been asking that question for a while and it just fed onto itself,' he says. 'I also feel that while you have the pressures of society out there, people seek out whatever flecks of beauty that are left—whether it's a van Gogh, a beautiful piece of literature, Proust, or a beautiful face. It takes you away from the dehumanization that's part of contemporary life.' "

— Orange County Register

" 'I never met a model I didn't like,' goes the opening line of 'The Shallow Man,' the first novel by **Coerte Felske**, the 33-year-old screenwriter who has met a few himself. The book is about a man obsessed with covergirls. His best friend, the Catsuit Feminist, is said to be loosely based on **Frederique**, the Dutch beauty who decorates those Victoria's Secret catalogues. As for the title character? 'He's a composite of all the shallow men I know.' The book won't hurt their feelings. 'Most of them will never read it,' Felske said, 'because they are too shallow.' "

— "Page Six," The New York Post

"**Chandler for the 90s:** ***** There are two reasons to write a Hollywood novel, and they're both the same: everyone will shell out for a peek backstage. Some Hollywood novels—Jackie Collins's oeuvre, for example—exist to perpetuate the fiction that stars' lives are as glamorous off-screen as on. Others are written, with equal commercial savvy, to expose the shocking vice and greed of the industry. Ultra-glam or ultra-scum; we love to read about either, and the very best back lot potboilers dish out both at once. Coerte Felske is an ex-screenwriter and he seems to have dug enough dirt during his time in the industry to fill several bookshelves. His hero in *Word* is Heyward Hoon: a failed screenwriter whose hobby is Hollywood anthropology, observing the local Wannabeasts, 8x10s, Noguls, Starmen, and Muffin Heads, and so on. Girls, though, are Hoon's real area of expertise—all 2,000 of them that he happens to know. When lonely studio magnate Sidney Swinburn sees him stagger out of a bathroom with four lovely Bullets on his arms, Hoon sees the perfect opportunity to sell his years of research for a slice of success. It's an old story, and in a way this is an old book. The flicks and chicks may represent 90s excess, but the style of *Word* is pure 40s cool, all choppy sentences and dry wit. It's a pastiche, but no more than anything else these days; people are getting used to judging authors on what they borrow rather than what they create. And if you like the original—in this case, the work of Raymond Chandler—the throwback can be terrific fun to read. Felske knows this and has gotten his chosen style down perfectly. Whole paragraphs swing with voiceover rhythms that put Harrison Ford's famous Blade Runner monologues to shame. 'He told me work was totally uncommercial. Sure, I'd heard it before … But I was damn good at producing work that didn't sell. So why ruin a good thing? He told me I should look for new representation. I told him he should look at my tallest finger.' It's all good, punchy stuff and Felske never falters. Beautiful babes, New York wasps and sleazy zillionaires all flit through *Word*, larger than life and twice as interesting. The only bit of Chandler that Felske has chosen not to pilfer is the labyrinthine plot, which is a pity in a way: a long, zippy book like this could use a few more twists and turns. In the end, though, *Word* is lovable for the addictive dry wit of Felske/Hoon: 'As I massaged number 4 into her back, my mind drifted from its search of all that is original, and plopped splat on the cliché.' Can you blame him?"

— Carrie O'Grady, *The Guardian (England)*

"**Magnificent Obsessions:** *Word* is the book Bret Easton Ellis didn't write. It's a satire of Star Camp, USA, Felske's term for the movie colony. His narrator, Heyward Hoon, is a winning and wicked Ivy League prepster trying to conquer Hollywood. He's a screenwriter, and things are going miserably except for his not-so-little black book of gorgeous L.A. women. Felske does a great job with female characters, and his playful language introduces Strugs (struggling actors), WAMs (waitress-actress-models), and Noguls (wannabe movie moguls). Felske also has one eye on the screen, still, sometimes a book is meant to be just a good read, and we're grateful for it."

— Christopher Napolitano, *Playboy*

"**The return of *The Shallow Man!*** His first novel turned the fashion world on its head—and introduced the term 'modelizer' into the collective conscious. Now, with his tough-talking *Word*, Coerte V.W. Felske is back, red-eyeing it over Tinseltown's turf, but navigating much of the same Faustian topography. Catch a ride on this tale of a street-savvy screenwriter who sells his soul—but meets a lot of 'Wams,' 'Fundies,' and 'Mom-I-Got-the-Part girls'—on his trek toward the fabled Hollywood sign."

— *Detour*

"*Word: The Talk of L.A.:* By page 3 of this sharply funny send-up of all things Hollywood, you will agree that author Coerte V.W. Felske shares his lead character's talent for language. While threading his way through the Tinseltown jungle, Felske's wannabe screenwriter Heyward Hoon desperately tries to maintain his sanity. You will be patting yourself on the back for having discovered Hoon's story before *Variety* announces its inevitable arrival at a theater near you."

— Marie Claire

"**If We Gave Out Book Awards:** Great Read Gift Guide; Edgiest Girl, *Bridget Jones's Diary*, Edgiest Boy, *Word* by Coerte V.W. Felske. Felske's hero, an out-of-work screenwriter who calls himself a 'Blip' on movieland's radar, hilariously manages to find some beating hearts inside the hippest Hollywood hyphenates."

— Glamour

"*Word* is Coerte V.W. Felske's second novel. Like Peter Farelly's *The Comedy Writer*, Michael Tolkin's *The Player*, Peter Lefcourt's *The Deal*, *Word* belongs to the growing genre of Hollywood novels in which idealistic would-be screenwriters and filmmakers experience disillusionment as they come up against the madly illogical Hollywood system, in which liars, con artists and charlatans occupy almost all of the positions of power. In *Word*, the hapless seeker of the Hollywood jackpot is Heyward Hoon, scion of a privileged WASP family of declining fortunes. Many tales of American success involve a person of Jewish descent changing their name and trying to pass themselves off as WASP. In Hoon's case, however, he determines that he may best get ahead by blending in and not provoking envy of his upper-class WASP background. So he dies his blonde hair black and changes his name to Hoonstein. When we first meet Heyward, he has written 13 unproduced screenplays. What he does have command of, though, is his perspective on L.A. and its inhabitants, whom he has minutely categorized and labeled with hundreds of buzzwords. Hollywood, for instance, is "Star Camp." "Strugs" and "8x10's" are struggling actors, "Wams" are waiters/actress/models, while "Starman" and "Stargal" refer to those who have crossed over into success. (A specific star can be reassured to by a quality that made their reputation, such as "Starman Steroids.") "Thickies" are the omnipresent bodyguards that escort Starman and Stargals. "Noguls" are overly self-important producers who lack the one thing that would make them genuinely important—the power to greenlight a film. All agents are called "Agent Orange." A "Storage Guy" is a man so uninteresting that you feel safe leaving a beautiful woman with him at a party when you go to get drinks. A "Stowaway is a woman you can call up in the middle of the night for steady no-strings-attached sex. In addition to his general categorizing of the L.A. scene, Heyward has made what he calls a science project out of the study of individual women in L.A. In his attempt to fathom the mysteries of the female sex, he has catalogued and made a computer file of hundreds of L.A. women. A part of the key to his success at unraveling their secrets is that he has willfully chosen to remain "inactive," or celibate, thus making it easier for him to gain women's trust as they surmise that, unlike most men, he is not after sex. Wall his mastery of the L.A. scene, we are taken by surprise to discover, fifty pages into the novel, that Heyward's primary income comes from his day job as a temporary filing clerk. However his fortunes soon begin to change when, after crashing a party at the Bel-Air mansion of genuine mogul, Sydney Swinburn, the head of Novastar Studios, Heyward is taken under Swinburn's wings. Swinburn is impressed by Heyward's social ease with beautiful women, and he makes a pact with him. In exchange for lessons on how to successfully score with women, he will allow Heyward stay in a bungalow on his estate and encourage him as a screenwriter. The only rule: He must keep his hands off Teal, the beautiful woman who also lives on his estate and who, of course, is the only woman Heyward really wants. The more Swinburn learns from Heyward, though, the less he begins to feel he needs him, and Heyward soon finds he may have unwittingly entered into a pact with the devil. The more he becomes aware of Swinburn's deceitfulness, the more his struggle becomes whether he can voluntarily choose to end an association through which he feels he might gain so much potential Hollywood status."

— USA Today

"Language is what this novel downloads—a torrent of L.A. buzzwords and insider cynicism unmatched since Odets and Lehman's 'Sweet Smell of Success' took on Manhattan's nightlife. As with Tony Curtis's Sidney Falco, Felske pumps Heyward Hoon with so much film babble he's ready to burst. Insecure but WASPish Heyward, who's written scripts on spec, with not one green-lighted, tars everyone around him; leading men dismissed as 'Starmen,' struggling actors as 'Strugs,' and pretty faces with few goals, '8x10s.' When Heyward, accompanied by his beautiful but alcoholic arm piece, Baby Garbo, meets mega-mogul Sydney Swinburn, he sees a way of perhaps getting his masterpiece, the script of his 'Age of Astonishment,' sold at last. A wonderfully literate script, Sydney says, but, sadly, uncommercial, and he is in the business to make money. Still, he sees in Heyward a bookish ladies' man who can bring into this boorish super-producer's life just what he needs to fill a void: intimacy with the type of woman he has always challenged himself to attain. They strike a Faustian bargain to help each other as Sydney attends Heyward's charm school. Heyward, however, must not pursue Sydney's sought-after and mysterious Teal. When Heyward and Teal find each other irresistible, Sydney, the fearsome dark lord, assures Heyward's destruction in Hollywood. Cynics may snap their fangs at that big-bucks ending, but for film lovers the Hell-A hypechat will flick all of your fuses."

— *Kirkus Reviews*

"Heyward Hoon is yet another brilliant, but uncommercial and unproduced screenwriter careening around L.A. looking for a life amidst the clichés. His tale? Hollywood newcomer strikes a Faustian bargain in exchange for entrée into inner circle. It's winningly told, with often ferocious humor, including a fresh, funny argot (e.g., 'Wams' are waitress-actress-models). Recommended for fiction collections."

— *Library Journal*

"Flashy and dark, this energetic Nathanael West retake offers a rich Hollywood menu of pandering, ambition, power, and retribution. Narrator Heyward Hoon—30-year-old Ivy League New Yorker, creditless screenwriter, friend to a thousand Wams (waitress-actress-models), self-described 'wannabeast, a fame-seeking hound' and compulsive social taxonomist—hates L.A. but examines it closely. In company with some of the women he calls 'the Bullets' (the best of the L.A. party girls), he crashes a party where he meets Sydney Swinburn, mega-mogul studio head. Divorced after a long marriage, Swinburn seems humble and naïve, looking for female company. He and Hoon make a deal: Hoon will introduce him to attractive, available women, and Swinburn will improve Hoon's non-career by setting him up with a powerful agent. This turns out to be a Faustian bargain—with none of the upside for this Hollywood patois-spouting Faust, who gets into hot water after he moves into Swinburn's luxurious guest house and meets beautiful, mysterious Teal poolside. Sexually ante-diluvian and with the sharp wit of recent tinsel tales like Bruce Wagner's *I'm Losing You*, Felske's second (after *The Shallow Man*) is bright, bitchy fun and it's up to date with name-dropping local atmosphere and cutting edge jargon. *Author tour*."

— *Publishers Weekly*

"In a vicious story of the Hollywood lifestyle, Coerte V.W. Felske transports the reader into the movie-driven anathema of depth that is L.A. Struggling screenwriter Heyward Hoon narrates our journey through 'industry' parties, dinners at the hippest eateries, and sexy encounters. A gaggle of questionable characters inhabits this story including 'Wannabeasts' (fame-seeking hounds), '8x10's (all look, no content), and various other movie types that exist in this insular, elitist community. This story about aching for success and the price of achieving it in Hollywood is good, fluffy fun that will remind you why you live in Northern, not Southern, California."

— *San Francisco Metropolitan*

"His latest tale, *Word,* is a jazzy, ironic appreciation of writing, filmmaking, and chasing skirt. In two of those arts, at least, downtown novelist Coerte.V. W. Felske seems more than passingly adept. It's an unexpectedly hot, sticky night in late November, and though the police are trying to persuade the hundreds of revelers gathered around the iron gates of Joe's Pub to move along, inside the three-week-old Lafayette Street club a wild party is in full swing. Pink and red spotlights swirl over the sunken dance floor as models in backless dresses dance to Abba with the men who love them—arch-rivals Donald Trump and Roffredo Gaetani, photographer Sante D'Orazio; tank-topped club impresarios Jeffrey Jah, Mark Baker, and Nur Khan; and a couple of well-known gossip columnists. An open-shirted Kevin Costner takes a breather in a banquette with Chuck Pfeifer, Bob Shaye, and Peter Brant; from their table nearby, Emma S., Kara Young, and a few more models edging over 30 wriggle their fingers seductively in greeting. A movie premiere? A supermodel's birthday? No, it's a book party. But one befitting Coerte V.W. Felske, the author of 1995's *The Shallow Man* and the upcoming *Word,* both of which are taut, clever character studies centered on this posse of older roués and slightly over-the-hill models—all of whom the author considers close friends, the kind who come over for late-night glasses of port in the SoHo apartment he shares with gallery director Michiel van der Wal, brother to Frederique, and whichever South African or Dutch or Italian models are passing through town. That is, when he's not in Quogue playing tennis with Taki, or in St. Tropez with his new Czech-Croatian girlfriend who lives in Switzerland, or hanging out in L.A. at Monkey Bar with his old friend Jack Nicholson, who helped arrange for the filming of *The Shallow Man* (for protagonists, Felske's thinking 'Pitt, Penn, Downey, DiCaprio, or Cage'). With his surfer's patois, a mellow constitution that he chalks up to being a Libra, and a practiced way of speaking similar to Mister Rogers's, Felske is beloved by all: a guy's guy and a model's guy, whose novels neatly refract their own lives through a highly ironic prism. He does take his shots at pony tailed, Vespa-riding, mannequin-addicted, SoHo-loft-living thirtysomethings who are hand models by day and party promoters by night. But Felske sympathizes with the dudes at the end, attributing their flaws to societal shortcomings and a general millennial ill will. In Felske's world, models are called 'Thing' (young ones are 'Baby Thing,' stupid ones are 'Dialtones'); the rest of womankind are 'Civilians.' His girlfriends are 'Catsuit Feminist's, and we, 'Generation Face,' all live in the notoriety-obsessed 'Age of A' (for Astonishment). His characters often think in these terms; what's more, their feelings are italicized: '*No one wants to be sentenced to life at someone else's table … I want the reservation in my own name. I want my own table and I want to fill it with whomever I fancy.*' Less self-consciously writerly than other colleagues who are concerned with this tribe, like Bret Easton Ellis or Jay McInerney, Felske confides that he writes his books in only a few weeks. 'It's all about the voice,' he says, often, as if it were a mantra. Just tonight, Felske comes up with a theory he calls the Ten-Year Window. 'Women only have the years from 20 to 30 to really make it happen,' he says, taking a seat at the bar next to Joaquin Phoenix. 'For some, maybe 24 to 34.' How to take this comment, delivered, to all appearances, by a guy who's apparently spent a little too much time with Things and not enough with Civilians? Auditing women's-studies classes while a grad student at Columbia's film school, he tells me, qualifies him as a feminist—yet he suggests that women are different from men because they're "ruled by the moon." As a samba band tunes up onstage at Joe's, a sunglasses-wearing Ralph Lauren model named Zofia jumps up on a table near the D.J. booth. 'God, do I adore Coerte, he is so wise,' she announces, narrowly avoiding the approaching gang of Felske's high-school buddies, who smother him with bear hugs and painful-looking noogies. 'This dude,' gurgles the beefiest one, grabbing him by an Armani lapel, 'was so popular with chicks in high school that cheerleaders from the other team were asking for his number.' Sipping an Amstel Light with three or four undone shirt buttons revealing dark tufts of chest hair, Felske runs a hand through his white-blond, shoulder-length locks before jumping onto a conga line between Mark Bavaro and Daniela Pestova, his five-foot-eleven stature greatly diminished by their hulking figures. He leans in close and confides, in utter mock seriousness, 'I'm the Mad Hatter.' Over the din at Da Silvano's a few nights earlier, Felske takes gulps of San Pellegrino and looks over the crowd—David Duchovny, Helmut Lang, and, to his delight, Robert De Niro eating penne with his family at a corner table: the perfect setting for what he wants to discuss. 'See, the most important businessmen, bankers, film producers, and studio heads often don't know anything when it comes to women,' says Felske, winking indiscreetly in De Niro's direction. That's what Word is about: the Faustian bargain struck between a film writer struggling for credits and a 50-year-old studio head trolling for dates. It's a relationship not unlike Felske's with Ted Field, the fiftyish head of Interscope Records, who is rarely seen without a woman hovering around legal age ('Ted has no problem getting dates,' Felske retorts, denying buzz that the character is based on Field). Not to mention Felske's friendship with Mickey Rourke, with whom he lived for five months while rewriting Rourke's boxing movie, *Homeboy*. 'I only got respect once he realized that I knew pretty girls,' says Felske. After dinner, Felske suggests a trip to Lot 61—'I hear it's the hot joint'—but I beg off. He asks if I have a boyfriend, and walks me home. Running his fingers through his mane he has one last thing to say before stepping off into the night: 'So, what's going on with my hair?' "

— *New York Magazine*

"**The word on *Word* is all good**. No sophomore slump for **Coerte Felske**. The young author has followed his well-received first novel 'The Shallow Man,' with 'Word,' which is due next month from Warner Books and already is getting good reviews. Plus, Felske just sold his third book, 'The Millennium Girl,' to St. Martin's Press. Pretty good for an Eastern-raised screenwriter who was banging his head on West Coast studio walls a few years ago unable to get much of anything going. The protagonist in 'Word' happens to be a good-looking young screenwriter himself, who happens to make friends with a powerful studio executive who in some ways resembles **Ted Field**, the Interscope mogul who was close with Felske for a couple years. Kirkus Reviews found 'an insider cynicism not matched since [Clifford] Odets' and [Ernest] Lehman's 'Sweet Smell of Success' took on Manhattan's nightlife.' Publishers Weekly calls it 'flashy and dark,' and said 'This energetic Nathaniel West retake offers a rich Hollywood menu of pandering, ambition, power, and retribution …bright, bitchy fun and up-to-date name-dropping, local atmosphere and cutting-edge jargon.' Detour was so taken by Felske's lingo, the glossy is publishing a glossary to go along with its excerpt of the book. Among the terms are modelitis: 'a fashion model's personal self-corrosion and character contamination as a result of her beauty. Affects her mind and behavior.' And model repulsion: 'a severe distaste and dislike for fashion models due to galactic maintenance behavior and prima donna needs.' "

— *"Page Six," The New York Post*

"**How to Catch a Man at the Century's End:** This happens to be written by a man, the novelist-journalist-screenwriter Coerte V.W. Felske. It's a face-to-face encounter with 'diggers,' women who troll resort towns in search of the perfect millionaire. *The Millennium Girl* is based upon Felske's own research. We all know women like this exist, but until now we didn't have all the gory details. Our heroine is a nubile 28-year-old named Bodicea, who dies her hair incessantly and has a wicked habit of giving her fellow diggers nicknames like 'Operation: I Do,' and 'Ellen B. Generous.' We go on tour with the charming Bo as she uses men and vice versa, and along the way she dispenses various nuggets of self-analysis like 'if women weren't so jealous of one-another, we'd be the rulers of the planet.' The book is hilarious and sympathetic and even stops to examine a gay man's search for the perfect mate in the midst of all its heterosexual sex scenes. Bo gains her humanity and has a real soul which is perhaps the surest indicator that this is fiction."

— Melanie Rehak, *The New York Times Book Review*

"*People Are Talking About: Books*; **Novelist-cum-boulevardier Coerte V.W. Felske explains how to marry a billionaire.** The outtakes from the life of Coerte V.W. Felske teem with glamour: the portrait of the novelist as a young man by good friend Peter Beard; a snapshot with model Frederique Van der Wal; another with his book party hosts director Peter Berg and Janice Dickinson. To Felske, whose previous book launches were held at Joe's Pub and Lot 61, the velvet rope simply does not exist. For tonight's out-on-the-town interview, Felske suggests we start with drinks uptown at Fifty Seven Fifty Seven ($110). From there, perhaps we'll move on to dinner at Harry Cipriani ($500) before finishing up with nightcaps at Au Bar ($175). An evening with Felske is enough to make a girl's Prada habit seem positively economical. By 7: 30 P.M., Felske is stretched out at a table in the cavernous bar, ready to talk about his new novel and what inspired it. He runs a hand through his shaggy Caesar cut, cocks his head forward, and tries desperately to be heard above the din. 'It's a good night, Wednesdays,' he says, surveying a room of Armani-clad tycoons, endless martini glasses, and the high-pitched laughter of well-dressed women. 'The men have finished their business day; maybe there's a meeting tomorrow, but now they have a night or two before they have to go home to their wives. And you get everyone here—Europeans, South Americans, everyone. It's prime Digger territory.' A 'Digger,' mind you, is Felske's term for a woman who targets wealthy men like a heat-seeking missile. And Diggers are at the center of *The Millennium Girl* (St. Martin's Press), Felske's much-buzzed-about new novel, a fictionalized account of his gimlet-eyed social observations. *The Millennium Girl* takes the reader through the marriage market of the nineties. His heroine, Bodicea, is determined to land herself not just a husband but a husband who meets a strict set of financial and social criteria. According to Felske, it's women's lib for the nineties: Bodicea's point of view takes a quick tussle with the fifties (for that perennially chic retro feel), spins through the eighties (for a dose of glamour), and lands firmly in the next century—the goal is still the same (landing the guy), but the white picket fence has morphed into a classic six, several vacation homes, and a Gulfstream V for the commute. The difference is that these women, like Bodicea, approach finding a husband with the steely-eyed acumen of a CEO: Wine and dine at Le Cirque 2000, shop at Gucci and Manolo, summer in the Hamptons, and winter in Aspen. Beyond having the money that allows them to traffic in global finery, these women are looking for men who can spend it with style. But *The Millennium Girl* is not just another collection of insider's jargon and 'Page Six' gossip. Felske is the real thing: He knows his territory, and he writes about it with wit and style. *Girl* may have taken him only a few weeks to write, but he's been steeped in its culture since childhood. He grew up in New York City and on the Eastern Shore of Long Island, navigated his way around Manhattan from a very early age, spent his undergraduate years at Dartmouth, and then did graduate work at Columbia University's film school—after which he co-wrote *Homeboy* for actor Mickey Rourke. Then came two novels that, like *Girl*, glitter with a diamond-sharp deconstruction of modern life in the fast lane. Both got solid reviews, including *The New York Times*'s: both are being produced for the big screen by New Line Cinema. 'It's all about the voice,' Felske says, describing what makes his novels different. 'I believe the book is honest. It's not an indictment, rather, it's in praise of women, in a reverse angle way, women who are trying to better themselves, empower themselves any way they can. To not be dependents, but independents. Occasionally, you write a certain piece of music and people respond to it, and I think *TMG* strikes those universal chords.' "

— Dana Wagner, *Vogue*

"His debut novel, *The Shallow Man*, introduced us to Manhattan 'Modelizers.' His second novel, *Word*, brought us Tinseltown's 'Blips,' 'Bullets,' and 'Strugs.' Now, in *The Millennium Girl*, pulse-of-the-Zeitgeist author Coerte V.W. Felske sets his sights on 'Diggers,' a.k.a. the globe-trotting hotties on the hunt for 'Walletmen,' the ultra-rich men of their dreams."

"**Let's Hear It for the Girls:** They're baaaack, and in the latest reads, they rule the world. So much for that un-p.c. term 'girl' becoming as obsolete as 8-track tapes. It's back with a passion. Who are these lit It Girls? The Millennium Girl, by Coerte V.W. Felske …'I'm not a hooker … but I do live off men,' says the title character. 'Why shouldn't I take what I can while I can?' Bodicea is a 28-year-old knockout with lips she's tattooed an even deeper red. Her work alias is 'Digger'—she globe-hops in search of filthy-rich 'Walletmen,' some to be kept by in high style, and one to marry before she turns 30. I wanted to hate her, but I couldn't: She was too shameless and too hilariously over-the-top."

"**Prolific Pen: COERTE Felske** is alive and well on a 49-foot ketch in Barcelona. The author of 'The Shallow Man' and 'Word'—quite the man about town in the 90s—vanished when he fell in love and had a daughter with a gorgeous Swiss woman. Without the distractions of Gotham, Felske, now repped by CAA, has finished two more novels: 'Scandalocity,' the speed it takes for a disgrace to turn you into a star, and 'The Dolce Vita Diaries and the Final Phantasmagoric Flight of the Ivory Stretch Limousine into Freedom and Destiny.' Meanwhile, **Heather Graham** is planning to produce and star in 'The Millennium Girl,' and **Morgan Freeman** is slated for 'Wild Blood.' "

"Another from the resourceful and amusing Felske, whose satire of the fashion industry, *The Shallow Man*, and knifing of Los Angeles, *Word*, are both in the pipeline at New Line Cinema. His latest topic is international gold diggers, the sweet lovelies more shark-like than Anita Loos's or Truman Capote's who speak of Walletmen (fat cats of Fortune 500 and Forbes 400 fame), of Chanel, Bulgari, and Armani, and of the seasons of Gstaad, Cannes, Nice, and Ibiza. Felske's narrator, Bo (Bodicea), has jade-green eyes, has had her lips tattooed deep red for a strong lip line, changes hair color every six weeks, and has just gone off-Tour and arrived in Manhattan to see an English sugar daddy whom a fellow Digger (Travels With Men) has asked her to entertain. Bo, part Native American Zuni, builds the ego of her Walletmen with wise words lifted from astrology columns, and, since seeing *Dances With Wolves*, she nicks all her fellow Diggers with names like Earns Every Penny and Every Little Bit Helps. She has a Ten Year Window, from 20 to 30, to hit the Mother Lode, a Walletman she can mine for lasting, lifetime security. For the time being, she lives in a cute two-bedroom on the 34th floor of Trump Tower (rent: $4,800 a month) that she shares with her best friend, the snowman (that is, gay) budding psychologist Napoleon Dieudonné, to whom, as his only patient, tells her steamy life story: her pursuit of the Rich Rebel, Bradley Lorne-August; her tie with late sister Vicky's daughter, Maximilia; and her own rise to true self-empowerment. Felske laces every page with a masterful cynicism that Bo sees as he own Millennial Smarts while still charming all. A novel with legs."

"Meet Bodicea Lashley, 'the millennium girl,' living by her wits, and various other attributes, as a 'digger'—a species of jet-set hooker who gets paid for her tricks in clothes and rent instead of cash. She travels an annual circuit from Gstaad to Ibiza and points in between, following the money in hopes of catching some crumbs from some generous older gentleman. Bo fills us in on the tricks of the trade as she relates the story of her twenty-eighth year. The digger jargon is kicky, as is the device of giving fellow diggers pseudo-Native American monikers a la 'Dances With Wolves': Travels With Men, Earning Every Penny, Smiles to Your Face. *The Millennium Girl* is based on a magazine article Felske wrote in 1997 about young women hustling in Aspen. As a novel, it is snappy fun, a box of candy wrapped up with a black latex bow."

— Booklist

"Bodicea Lashley has definite goals. She is a 'Digger,' a woman who makes her living sponging off of supremely wealthy 'Walletmen' and an active participant on the 'Digger Tour.' The tour takes her all over the world, from Gstaad to St. Tropez, Palm Beach, and Aspen, to trade her feminine wiles for wearables from Prada and Gucci and for cold, hard cash. The goal of the Digger Tourists? To marry a Walletman, and Bo is trying her hardest to land the big one. A likeable character despite her excesses, Bo speaks in catchy phrases and, for her compatriots on the Digger Tour, finds hilarious nicknames like the Three Minute Princess and At these Prices. This is a strong follow-up to Felske's previous novel, Word, which delved hilariously into the Hollywood screenwriting scene. Here he uses his trademark insight and detail to peer into the lives of sassy but sad women. Learning how Bo got started in her line of work and observing encounters with the richest of the rich is a complete hoot. Sexy, hard to put down, and 100 percent fun, this is recommended for all fiction collections."

— Library Journal

"Of the slew of new single-girl manhunt novels, Felske's (*The Shallow Man, Word*) third novel scales new heights, aiming to describe the art of gold-digging women and the folly of their prey: wealthy, high-living "walletmen." Bodicea Lashley, hailing from a small factory town in Ohio, relocates to New York to pursue a career as a Digger, a woman who lives off well-heeled lovers, hoping to lure one into marriage. Her perfect body, satirically described, provides the bait. After dumping two-timing multimillionaire Giles, Bo decides to marry Napoleon, a gay friend who can access his family's considerable fortune if he weds. But while visiting Napoleon's family in Palm Beach, Bo takes up with Bradley Lorne-August. Bradley's attentions wane and Bo resumes with former lover Warren Samuels, America's 11th-richest man whose tastes run to sex in airplanes, religious role-playing and sadism. During the Aspen leg of her Digger Tour, Bo falls for a young journalist and keeps tabs on her ailing sister and niece, both living in poverty back in Ohio. Bo realizes that all that glitters is not gold and decides to become independent. Clever Bo invents cute nicknames for her fellow Diggers: "Travels With Men" and "Operation: I Do." Bo's discovery that wealth isn't love is unrelieved; sex scenes mix with lessons for Digger survival—'Don't depend. Independ.' The acidic jibes at upper-class hypocrisy are good for chuckles and the novel's stabs at satiric revelations of vision and subject."

— Publishers Weekly

"Fast Lane: *Coerte Felske's new book shows that life is no stranger than fast track fiction.* **Latest Felske Fiction:** *Millennium Gold Digger.* 'It's not a Gary Cooper-Jimmy Stewart world out there. I don't write fairy tales,' says Quogue native Coerte V. W. Felske, author of *The Shallow Man, Word,* and, out this month, *The Millennium Girl.* Mr. Felske will be reading excerpts from his new book this Saturday, October 9, at Book Hampton (20 Main Street in East Hampton) before departing on a book-signing tour of major U.S. cities. His new book—his third in a loosely constructed trilogy devoted to exposing the grit-behind-the-glitter lifestyles and moral ambiguities of those who would make their way among the rich and famous—marks a departure in tone and voice from his two previous works. Last week, Mr. Felske took a few moments before heading out to Los Angeles for film meetings on his first novel to sit down over lunch at the Blue Parrot in East Hampton to discuss this shift in tone, along with his past, present, and future. *The Millennium Girl* is the story of Bodicea, a nice girl from Fort Lowell, Ohio, who happens to be a quarter Native-American, quarter English, quarter Brazilian, and a quarter Eskimo. Bodicea's primary attributes, 'nice full breasts and an ass that's high, tight, firm, and about the size of a grapefruit,' have allowed her to slide smoothly from a broken home and onto the Digger Tour, the fast-paced world of globe-trotting gold diggers chasing the fat cat men of their dreams from party to party against a backdrop of fashionable vacation destinations. But Bodicea is not all evil or cold calculation. Her heart's in the right place, if her values aren't quite there yet, and she's on the path to enlightenment. As written in the first person by Mr. Felske, Bodicea is possessed of a wry sense of humor and an eye for detail that sustains the narrative. She's a sympathetic character (with a love for Chanel) who Mr. Felske insists is emblematic of the sort of 'conflicted modern people who interest me.' Throughout *The Millennium Girl*, Bodicea picks apart her own insecurities and those of the other girls on the tour. And, in the end, Bodicea manages to raise herself above the fate of her cohorts— amusingly referred to as Travels With Men, Earning Every Penny, Never Flies Coach, and For Your Wallet Only. 'This is an odyssey about female empowerment,' Mr. Felske explains, adding that he finds women inherently more interesting than their male counterparts. 'It's about getting to a position of strength and the opportunities available to women today. *The Millennium Girl* title is a loaded one, particularly ironic, but about how women should be addressing themselves to empowerment, given the societal restraints of their peak years and today's societal pressures.' But above all, it is the 'double-sided nature of human beings' that has drawn Mr. Felske to map the morally dubious interiors of characters who live on razor's edge of scruples. In *The Shallow Man*, Mr. Felske examined the life of Nick Laws, a celebrity-obsessed, supermodel-pursuing rake. *Word* presented Heyward Hoon, a writer of substantial but commercially non-viable screenplays, who procures women for a producer. And, Bodicea, Mr. Felske's millennium girl, follows in their tradition: decent people trying to make the best of the outrageous situations in which they've found themselves. Although Mr. Felske insists his work is not a case of art imitating life—'I wish I had had as good a time as I wrote about," he says—he is no stranger to the worlds he documents. From 1990 to 1994, he was a resident of Los Angeles, living the life of a struggling spec writer, churning out script after script, all highly praised but never made into movies. Now however, the likes of Jack Nicholson have proclaimed him 'the voice of the late 20s to early 40s group of people.' After the success of *The Shallow Man*, published in 1995, Mr. Felske moved back east, where he finished *Word*. But it was when he was sent by *Esquire* magazine to write a feature story on the above ground gold digging happening on the hills of Aspen that Mr. Felske discovered the material at the heart of his latest oeuvre. Granted two weeks of access to the parties that cap the social year in the famed Colorado mountain resort, Mr. Felske says that he found it difficult to get any women to open up until after New Year's. Then, 'they gushed. A purge took place when they were disillusioned, when they hadn't gotten their man.' Eventually published in *Manhattan File*, Mr. Felske's piece revealed the secrets of real women on the real-life husband-hunting circuit— mind boggling proof that fact is far stranger, and dirtier, than fiction. Mr. Felske, 39, writes in a style that mixes Brett Easton Ellis's precise obsession with designer labels with Dominick Dunne and Louis Auchincloss's insider looks at the over-the-top, rarified lifestyles of the super rich. 'It is what it is,' says Mr. Felske who sees himself as something of a documentarian and, at the same time, a writer who 'likes to play with, and invent, language.' Mr. Felske uses his 'literary anthropology' in hopes of 'allowing a reader to come into one of my stories and get a sense of the world, even if they are not familiar with it.' Mr. Felske's blond, unpretentious good looks, his laid-back approach to life (he carries his wallet, business cards, pen and paper in a fanny-pack) and gregarious, California sun-drenched personality seem to have served him well in the shark-infested waters of the movie business. He has just put the finishing touches on the script for *The Shallow Man* to be produced by New Line Cinema and directed by Gary Fleder ('Things To Do In Denver When You're Dead,' 'Kiss the Girls') and casting for the movie begins soon. He's also been teamed with the writer of 'Things To Do In Denver When You're Dead' and 'Armageddon' to develop a script based on *Word*. Film offers for *The Millennium Girl* have already started to come in. But Mr. Felske is a cautious optimist who'd rather wait to see the reviews of his book before committing to any deals, and he does not consider himself on top of the world. He feels simply that, 'I've been fortunate in a lot of ways. I'm having fun. I'm doing what I love. I make my own hours.' Appreciative of the 'less-touched' ocean vistas at the end of Long Island, Mr. Felske plans to divide his time between a house in Montauk and his apartment in SoHo. His next book, tentatively entitled, *The Bossa Nova Diaries*, is about the Hamptons in the 1970s. He will also publish next year, under a pseudonym, a 'traditional, classical' literary work set further back in time. 'The most significant aspect of my writing is the voice,' Mr. Felske says, explaining his productivity. 'Once I can get that, everything else falls into place.' For *The Millennium Girl*, finding Bodicea's voice was 'my biggest challenge. But when I had it, I had it.' After one draft, he submitted it to his agency, William Morris. After a 'mild, two-day modification,' the book was sent out to publishers and quickly sold. In the literary world, where authors are known to labor for days on sentences and years on books, this kind of productivity marks Mr. Felske as a rare bird indeed. With five more novels already planned out and plans of purchasing a house in the South of France or Tuscany, Mr. Felske seems poised to document a good deal more of pre- and post-millennial, American high life. Although he speculates about someday settling down and having children, right now he says, 'my books have been my children. I've given them all my attention. I travel extensively and write as I go. It's a pretty nice life.' "

— Nick Snyder, *The Southampton Press*

"**The Millennium Girl:** Coerte V. W. Felske. Despite its portentous title, this novel about a gold digger's calculated search for love is more than a racy rehash of *Pretty Woman* or any number of similarly old-fashioned hooker-with-a-heart-of-platinum tales. That's not to say it isn't great trashy fun too. Felske who covered the 'digger' scene in an investigative article for *Esquire*, clearly knows the turf (New York, Aspen, Hong Kong). Female empowerment, a having-it-all ending, a pampered husband hunter, and a flaming gay sidekick perpetuate these pages."

— *Entertainment Weekly*

"**Sugardaddy Sinderellas**: *Author* **Coerte V.W. Felske** *mines America's goldigger circuit in his new novel* The Millennium Girl. **Bill Powers** *learns why honey makes the world go round.* At a high-profile fete in Manhattan, Coerte V.W. Felske was once introduced to **Christy Turlington** as 'the man who never met a model he didn't like.' Just recalling the incident is enough to give him chills. 'It's stuff like that that really makes me cringe,' says the scribe, taking three steps back as if to punctuate via pantomime, 'but I guess it sort of comes with the territory.' When your first novel is *The Shallow Man* and follows the antics of an urban model hunter leading a barely examined life, there's some inherent baggage an author must learn to accept. Nevertheless, his 1995 debut put Coerte's name on all the right lips, including those attached to **Jack Nicholson,** New Line Cinema, and *Esquire* magazine. That winter, the men's glossy assigned Coerte an investigative feature on Aspen's yearly Christmas break influx of goldiggers. The $18,000 expose was ultimately killed due to changes in *Esquire*'s editorial leadership but

Coerte's encounters with these 21st century courtesans on the slopes of Colorado's toniest ski town left a lasting impression. Eventually they would serve as foundation for his latest tale of woe and dough entitled *The Millennium Girl*. Coerte recalls his Rocky Mountain excursion over a round of St. Pauli Girls at the Time Hotel in New York: 'I interviewed about 25 or 30 girls. At first no one wanted to talk and, really, what woman in her right mind would want to draw this kind of attention?' he asks with the annunciation of a TV anchorman. 'Then after New Year's Eve it was interesting, the women who hadn't managed to land their guy sort of felt this need to purge. I promised I wouldn't use their names and they gave me the full rundown. That's when I heard about girls studying the names on the *Fortune* and *Forbes* lists. Some girls were going to Brunei the next week. They just disappear for a while—tell their family that they're going to model in Europe or something—and wind up making $25,000 a week. It's a totally viable financial undertaking for a woman. I mean, there's no question what they're doing is prostitution, but they get paid incredibly well.' The assembled anecdotes have been fictionalized into the life of *The Millennium Girl*—a twenty-eight year old Digger named Bodicea—who lives in Trump Tower with her gay best friend Napoleon. Bo is looking to get off Tour permanently, meaning no more St. Moritz in March, June in the Hamptons, July in St. Tropez. She's tired of constantly chumming the bigwig waters hoping to get hooked on the purse strings of unreliable, though often generous, Walletmen. But, she's also wary of settling down. To paraphrase a rhetorical pondering of Bo's: Why have one guy who treats you like shit when you can have 20 who treat you a Goddess? 'Many of the girls I spoke with think a woman should get what she can,' says Coerte. 'Let's face it, survival is where it's always been at and some women are more hard-nosed than others. There's a very low success ratio [when it comes to golddigging] and if they play *the game* too long, these women often end up making compromises they never would have in their youth. In this modern age, as things get more stressful and Darwinian, people start doing things they never would have found acceptable back when life was a little more homespun. My whole thing was to show the warmer side of these women so you that you know where that money gravitation comes from. Ultimately Bo prevails and gets what she wants on her terms, but it's definitely a low-percentage racket.' "

— Bikini Magazine

"*The Millennium Girl*: Coerte V.W. Felske's novel is a *Breakfast at Tiffany's* for the year 2000. Bodicea Lashley, a former poor girl from Ohio, is a gorgeous twenty-something fortune hunter who does the circuit—Gstaad at Christmas, Aspen at New Year's, February in Palm Beach—hunting for what she calls "walletmen." But as the 20th century draws to a close, Bodicea begins to take stock not just of her finances but her way of life. A totally titillating read."

— Woman's Own

"**BEAUTY THRILLS**: Main Street in East Hampton was invaded by particularly beautiful people the other day for **Coerte Felske**'s book-signing, sponsored by Hamptons.com, of his thriller 'Scandalocity.' Felske—recently seen on 'Real Housewives of New York City' kissing **Countess LuAnn de Lesseps**—was flanked by models **Irina Shayk**, **Jessica White**, and **Eugenia Kuzmina**. Shayk graces the cover in a photo taken by **Peter Beard**. 'Scandalocity'— defined as 'the speed at which scandal, measured in velocity, can turn you into a star'—features a hero named Harry Starslinger, an online gossip columnist who becomes embroiled in the police investigation of his girlfriend's murder."

— "Page Six," The New York Post

" 'People Are Talking About: Books,' Favorite Novel: *The Shallow Man* by Coerte Felske which begins with the line 'I never met a model I didn't like.' "

— Candace Bushnell, *Vogue*

"**PLAYBOY CENTERFOLD DATA SHEET**, 'Favorite Book: *The Shallow Man* by Coerte V.W. Felske. It's about a very shallow man and his involvements with models.' "

— Priscilla Lee Taylor, Miss March, 1996, *Playboy*

"**COERTE:** generous son—James Joyce and Ernest Hemingway never got plugged the way **Coerte Felske** just got plugged. Readers who plowed through the biographical data provided by Playboy's Miss March, **Priscilla Lee Taylor**, on the flip side of the centerfold learned that her favorite book is **Coerte Felske**'s *The Shallow Man*. But Felske, who's in Miami finishing up his second novel, doesn't seem too eager to meet the buxom blonde. 'I'd like to introduce her to my dad,' the shy writer tells us. 'He's had a dry winter.' "

— *"Page Six," The New York Post*

"A Model Wordsmith."

— *New York Magazine*

"**A STRETCHED TITLE**. **Coerte Felske**, who wrote *The Shallow Man* and *The Millennium Girl*, went for a longer title on his latest novel: *The Dolce Vita Diaries and the Final Phantasmagoric Flight of the Ivory Stretch Limousine into Freedom and Destiny,* which the author describes as 'an abduction story which takes place in the southwest.' The manuscript is generating buzz as it makes its way through publishers and talent agents who think it could be a vehicle for **Tom Cruise** or **Brad Pitt**. The novel is being compared to Ken Kesey's *Sometimes a Great Notion*, Jack Kerouac's *On the Road*, and **Robert Parsing**'s *Zen and the Art of Motorcycle Maintenance*."

— *"Page Six," The New York Post*

"That classic opening line from *The Shallow Man*, 'I never met a model I didn't like,' defined an era. Coerte V.W. Felske has given us a run of texts which skillfully chronicle the skin-deep and shameless age with laser-like precision. There are pretenders to the throne of the genre, but this resourceful and amusing novelist has it down. Like the late Stanley Elkin, Felske masters the pedantry of various trades and milieus, then creates a joyous poetry of jargon to float his novels on, setting sail on an ocean of buzzwords which continue to creep steadily into the daily vernacular. At the same time, he's not merely an inventor of neologisms, rather, a sorcerer of language and the written word, lacing each page with a masterful cynicism. I suspect we'll be talking about this author as the one who captured certainly the Nineties best. He one-upped fashionista literature with *The Shallow Man*, bested Nathaniel West with *Word*, and took Capote a step beyond with *The Millennium Girl.*"

— *The Guardian (England)*

The Ivory Stretch

The Dolce Vita Diaries and the
Final Phantasmagoric Flight of the
Ivory Stretch Limousine into
Freedom and
Destiny

Also by

for

The Shallow Man: 20th Anniversary Edition
Word: 15th Anniversary Edition
The Millennium Girl: 15th Anniversary Edition
Scandalocity
Three Sleeps to Double Happiness

Chemical / Animal
A Touch of Noir

Coerte V.W. Felske titles for The Dolce Vita Press are available
at the author's Web site coertefelske.com, thedolcevitapress.com,
Amazon.com, BN.com, e-book distributors, and
independent book stores worldwide

The Ivory Stretch

The Dolce Vita Diaries and the
Final Phantasmagoric Flight of the
Ivory Stretch Limousine into
Freedom and
Destiny

Coerte V. W. Felske

The Dolce Vita Press, Inc.

New York

Copyright © 2016 by Coerte V. W. Felske

Front cover calligraphy and back cover photography of by Peter Beard by permission of the artist; back cover shot on Giant Polaroid in New York, produced by CVWF

The Ivory Stretch graphics and cover layout by Christian Toms for Red & Jacket or chris@redandjacket.com and cover design by CVWF for The Dolce Vita Press

The Dolce Vita Press series cover concept and logo by Jackie Merri Meyer for MeyerNewYork@aol.com and CVWF for The Dolce Vita Press

THE DOLCE VITA PRESS is a trademark of The Dolce Vita Press, Inc.

Manufactured in the United States of America

Library of Congress Cataloging-in-Publication Data

Felske, Coerte V. W.

The Ivory Stretch / by Coerte V. W. Felske—lst ed.

1. Title.

PS3556.E47259S53 2016

813'.54—dc20 94-47947

ISBN 978-0-9840786-2-2

10 9 8 7 6 5 4 3 2 1

First Edition: July, 2016

For Bodicea

Acknowledgments

I would like to thank the following individuals for their inspiration, friendship, and guidance now and through the years.

Alex and Jacob Agam, Muhammad Ali, Alessandra Ambrósio, Bad Company, Ana Beatriz Barros, Peter and Nejma Beard, Bill and Sally Beatty, Alison Blume, Clint and Mary Blume, Bono, Brad Branson, Helen Breitweiser, Tim Carbone, Jayma Cardoso, Chris Cooney, John Cooney, Billy Corgan, John Donne, Albert Einstein, Anneke Felske, Norman Felske, F. Scott Fitzgerald, Milos Forman, David Greeff, Douglas Greeff, Gabriel García Márquez, Grace Holland, Richard and Sessa Johnson, LuAnn de Lesseps, Courtney Love, Lisa Mazzucco, Raphael Mazzucco, Sascha Mazzucco, Alexandra Michler, Roger Moley, Kenneth Nichols, Stevie Nicks, Chuck Pfeifer, Peter and Patti Riordan, Nora Sabrier, Waldo Sanchez, Irina Shayk, the Good Ship Sköl, Ellen von Unwerth, George Wilson, Cameron Winklevoss, Tyler Winklevoss, Diamond Felske, and Bodicea Felske.

I give special thanks to Peter Beard for his creative cover magic, Christian Toms for his graphic artistry, and Jackie Meyer for her design concepts.

I offer thanks as well to Dave Carson and Jamie Sams, the authors of *Medicine Cards*, and James Rado, Gerome Ragni, and Galt MacDermot who wrote the lyrics to "Aquarius/Let the Sunshine In." I credit Burt Bacharach and Hal David for the lyrics to "The Windows of the World." I credit Lenny Lipton and Peter Yarrow for the words to "Puff the Magic Dragon." And, of course, I thank Stevie Nicks for lyrics to "Rhiannon" and "Nightbird." I would also like to thank the late Ronnie Van Zant and Allen Collins of Lynyrd Skynyrd for lyrics to "Free Bird." I credit Bob Dylan for the lyrics to "I Shall Be Free No.10" as well as for years of my own personal inspiration.

To friends and fallen soldiers, great souls and spirits taken too soon, you will always be remembered and I'm honored for the time we shared: Alan Beeber, Noel Behn, Joe Cole, Doug Cummins, Frank Daniel, Robert Hattersley, John Kennedy, John Rassias, Dr. Thomas and Nan Rees, and Billy Way.

Lastly, I feel the deepest gratitude toward my father Richard Norman Felske who has always fought the good fight, never given up, and who taught me about honesty, generosity, and family integrity, qualities I am honored to pass on to our own.

I dedicate this book, as I do all my work, to my treasure and guiding light, Bodicea.

We all are conceived in close prison. And then all our life is, but a going out to the place of execution, to death. Nor was there any man seen to sleep in the cart between Newgate and Tyburn—between prison and the place of execution, does any man sleep? But we sleep all the way; from the womb to the grave we are never thoroughly awake.

John Donne
1572-1631

Crash and burn all the stars explode tonight,
How'd you get so desperate? How'd you stay alive?
Help me please burn the sorrow from your eyes,
Oh come on be alive again, don't lay down and die.

Courtney Love, Billy Corgan
"Malibu"
2003

… Me, we …

Muhammad Ali
Harvard University Commencement Address
1975

Dedication

To my friends Roland Manakajeh, Benji Jones, Tribal Elders Bob and
Clayton, Blaine, Dmitri, Rafael, Leota, and Tim "Two Feathers"
Uqualla of the Havasupai Nation,
James Begaye and Carol Draper of the Navajo Nation,
and Wil and Faron Sulu of the Hopi Nation:
It was an honor to have been hosted and welcomed by you and I
remain in awe of your nobility and grace. I thank you for introducing
me to the Great Spirit and I offer thanks to Father Sun, the Earth
Mother, and the Great One for allowing our Earth Walks to cross and
our Medicines to meet on the Good Red Road.
I know my Walk has been made better for it.
Hañ-gyu.

1

In Chandler, Arizona, a southern suburb of Phoenix, Billy awoke in his hotel having slept well the night before it was all to happen, primarily because of the nocturnal vision he'd had. His dream was a recurring one and it had always bade good fortune. All the pretty butterflies had come to him while deep in slumber, dancing in the air above him and below, so colorful and bright they made him smile as he lay there. This nocturnal gift, the Spontaneous Flight of the Butterflies, was a recounting of a tale from the ancients, the story of Iitoi the Papago tribal Elder and how the glorious creatures had come into existence on the Earth Mother.

As Billy Six dreamt it, springtime had returned to the desert; the flowers were blazing with color and the children were playing in the cornfields. Yet Iitoi could not shake the sadness in his heart knowing these beautiful children, like all living things, were destined to grow weak and old and would eventually die. The flowers would wilt, the leaves would fall, days would grow short, and the nights would become very cold.

When a gust of wind blew a leaf past the tribesman in the bright light of the sun, the idea came to Iitoi, a way to brighten the children's spirits and make their Earth Walks more joyous and fulfilling.

Iitoi decided to collect all the faded and dead petals of the flowers and the fallen leaves from the trees and gathered them in a burlap sack. He sprinkled in pollen, corn dust, the green needles of pine trees, and added sunlight. From the birds singing in the trees, he placed some of their songs in the sack, as well.

Iitoi approached the children and offered the brown sack to them, instructing them to mix the contents. The children took turns shaking it. As tiny fingers clutched the sack and opened it wide, much to the children's delight, the first butterflies flew out. It was a miracle. The creatures possessed the vivid colors of the flowers, leaves, pine needles, and pollen, and they shone as brightly as the sun. The butterflies resembled brilliant, resplendent flowers dancing in mid-air

and they made the children laugh as they flew all around, singing songs to them.

Admiring the spectacle, the birds sought out Iitoi and complimented him on his beautiful creation, but thought it unfair the butterflies had also been awarded their songs. Iitoi agreed.

Before Billy woke, he was reminded how it is today the butterflies dance in the wind freely and vibrantly, but they can not sing, they remain silent, yet still bring joy to the world and brighten spirits whenever children see them.

When Billy concluded his slumber that late October morning he had a smile on his face. He felt strong and energized and understood the dream had been a proper omen. He knew this day was the day, the exact day to accomplish his duty. He uttered a prayer of thanks to Elder Brother Iitoi for coming to him in the night and comforting him, reminding him of the beautiful butterflies and how they were created.

"Hañ-gyu," he finished the prayer with, the term for giving thanks in Supai, the language of the Havasupai Indian tribe.

His uniform was laid out on the extra bed; his black slacks, the short-sleeved white button-down, the calfskin gloves, laboriously shined shoes, his black cap with patent leather brim, and black leather briefcase. Billy had prepared everything the night before and the articles laid flat against the whiteness of the sheets. He'd rented a room for the night as he wanted everything clean, precise, and findable. His apartment in Mesa was too cluttered with the overwhelming trappings of his life. Things could hide there and he could get sloppy. But in a motel room with twin beds and blankets drawn for a white sheet backdrop, nothing could get lost. Contrast, containable. Billy wasn't forgetful, rather a perfectionist in every sense. If there was anything he wanted perfect, it was his preparation for this day.

He took a shower and shaved the deep shadow that had only needed the overnight to assert itself. He dressed and checked his watch; it was seven-thirty. He'd checked out the night before and he had time, but not enough for a chatty, caffeine-bolstered swivel stool breakfast.

Billy left the room key on the dresser and stepped outside, briefcase in hand, adjusting the tilt to his aviator rims. He didn't bother closing the door. He crossed the street to the Mustang gas station and poured one dark and straight that tasted just bitter enough to match his mood.

Milk and sweeteners were symbolic gestures of softness, with implications of surrender; not the way to start the day. The man was a purist.

The taxi swung into the motel as he crossed back over the street; his timing was perfect. Billy was not one for waste. He was tremendously Zen that way. He didn't waste steps, physical gestures, or gratuitous looks, assigning a time clock for each task, a special instinct and talent. He slipped into the awaiting taxi. "32nd and Broadway," he directed.

"Sounds like New York," the driver piped good-naturedly in his own Bronx dialect. Many New Yorkers had moved to Phoenix, elderly folk especially, seeking out the arid climes to soothe arthritic conditions and ailments.

"Damn straight, pumpkin loaf."

"Say *what*—?" The driver peeked back in the rear view, wondering if he'd been insulted. "All the same to me," he mumbled.

It wasn't all the same to Billy Six, however. He'd been wrapped up too long, mummified for years, in fact. Starting today, he would express himself, he would speak his mind and what came to it and a seemingly pointless barb cast at the lackadaisical driver was right on schedule.

The address Billy sought was in an industrial section of the city south of the airport. After ten minutes of slow silence, the rumbling car pulled up to what seemed the middle of nowhere and Billy got out. The driver surveyed the line of dusty brown warehouses and gray storage structures, and then once more eyed his passenger curiously. Billy handed the man a twenty and added a vague smile. The cab half-sped off.

The blocks ahead appeared deserted except for a slow-rolling hauling truck down the road. Billy strode along the asphalt path to avoid dusty wind twisters. He passed the row of gray buildings that housed private storage units, and he turned in at one, drawing a key from his pocket. He inserted the key, twisted the handle, and raised a shrieking metal door.

The fresh blast of sun into the dark space shimmered off the enormous purple silk cover and gave it an elegant regal sheen. Eagerly, the man unsnapped the fasteners at the corners. Then he gracefully swept the cover away like a magician unveiling his latest reveal of the inexplicable.

There she was.

Shiny, ivory white, exponentially long, delicately waxed and buffed, the gorgeous vehicle had been impeccably cared for like a baby. It was an HX Chevrolet DeVille Custom Stretch from 1971, Billy's favorite year for them, and he took her in like a proud papa while carefully folding the cover as if seeing her for the first time.

She had lived most of her glamorous life in New York City and he was proud of that. There had been other models in other cities he'd had his eye on, but when he heard this one had been docked outside Madison Square Garden on March 8, 1971, the night Joe Frazier fought Muhammad Ali in the Fight of the Century, the deal was sealed. He'd found his prize through a car broker and traveled to New York to test drive it and ship it west. The vehicle was in immaculate condition as it had been locked away in a garage for thirty years and had only twenty thousand miles on it. It was a flawless design with elegant lines and curves for a limousine and he considered her the sexiest lady on the planet. She was several shades beyond white, creamier and closer to vanilla. For this reason he called her The Ivory Stretch.

He slipped behind the wheel and filled his lungs with the soft Florentine leather smell. The briefcase was placed on the seat and he traced an index along the dust-free dashboard. He gave the ignition a twist and a short fierce growl erupted, easing to a poised and steady hum, the mellifluous song of a specially-designed custom engine. Reclining back, he listened to the unfaltering, pleasing music as he'd done many times and the corners of his mouth turned up. This was the car. This was the day.

Billy Six removed his eye shields, bowed his head, and uttered another prayer to his Native American Master. "I come humbly Great Spirit at a time of unrest, with wars of religions and the world confused. But I give thanks for all you have given us, the sun of day, moon of night, and strength of purpose. Guide me on my Walk on Earth, our Mother, whom you generously place in the hands of men, not to destroy and possess, but to love, cherish, and protect. I pray I am doing right.

"I pray for Frenchy too, a young spirit seeking answers. Please help her understand what I'm hoping to accomplish and the difficult challenges that lie ahead. I ask you to watch over us in our hour of need, Great One—"

Billy folded his hands and meditated a dozen minutes.

"*Oof-mah,*" he chanted intermittently, the native Supai call to ward off the evil spirits.

The man possessed dark, almost black hair cropped in a Caesar cut with delicate, premature sideburn frost and a silver birthmark patch at the widow's peak. He was thirty-three, but appeared decidedly younger. At quick glance, he was strikingly handsome, even in a matinee idol way, but further scrutiny would yield the disquiet. There was a severe doctrine in his errant eye, the one spinning slightly inward, which betrayed the tempest, the crack; a veiled charge of darkness. Something sudden, slashing, brutal, and exact lay beneath and if confronted, provoked, or even teased, this could prove problematic and for that reason only the most vigilant apply. It was fossilized in his psyche that he had nothing to lose, perhaps less than nothing. The man was born of a unique strain of pathology, a figure so configured, so emboldened, he could root in deep, gestate, and appear on the landscape out of nowhere seasonally and repeatedly like clockwork with devastating front-page fervor; the uncompromising and unyielding dedication, the preparation, the protracted silence, then the mayhem.

Billy Sixkiller was the most dangerous of men.

The great car eased out of the garage and it came and kept on coming. Elongated beyond domestic limousine proportions, the car had been redesigned, widened, and fortified. The chassis was reinforced with steel and roll bars had been added to the roof. The outer sheet was layered with Kevlar panels and the electronics were state-of-the-art with complex global positioning systems and radar. Sophisticated radio equipment was hidden behind panels and in the trunk. To designate the Ivory Stretch as loaded was understatement. The vehicle was genotypically unlawful, not even close to street legal.

The mechanical overhaul had been performed over the years in the storage facility that served as a private auto body shop. Billy was an expert mechanic, electrician, and engineer. A self-taught craftsman, he had taken the car apart dozens of times and there was not a screw for which he did not know the pressure exerted in the fastening. The only task left to others was the paint job, the choice of ivory inspired by his beloved mother's childhood house back in Montgomery, Alabama. All that remained was a paint chip that Billy saved and used to produce the proper shade of white to replicate it.

A tiny Alabama state flag—the crimson cross of St. Anthony on a field of white—fluttered from the rear and was placed there in homage to Diane Randall as well.

After the engine warmed, Billy took a casual swing down Broadway to check how she was running. Once satisfied, he motored onward and opted for the onramp to the Papago Freeway known as the I-10 en route to the airport. The vehicle sped along evenly and the driver tested its acceleration, torque, and quick-stop braking capabilities along the way.

Check.

The Ivory Stretch took hold of the freeways easily, but her driver encountered traffic on the Maricopa that threatened his schedule. On his two-way he ascertained a jackknifed truck had crosscut four lanes near Tempe, backing up the freeway for miles. Normally, Billy would have endured the wait as he appreciated events of a chaotic nature from an expressionistic even artistic standpoint. He was known to chase down car wrecks, fires, floods, and all types of tragedies and disasters to record the devastation. He would photograph or videotape events or put them to paint in an interpretive way from memory. But not this time. He needed precision, he needed to be on time, though he did ponder missing a "good one" perhaps as one regrets missing an exciting sporting match.

Billy took the off-ramp at University Drive and backtracked, the maneuver nearly preserving his to-the-minute schedule. It got him to Sky Harbor International at eight forty-five, a full sixty minutes before zero hour. He'd phoned ahead and the flight was on time.

The driver avoided the taxi lineup and docked the Stretch off and away beside a pink sandstone ramp with a Sonoran gecko scampering across it in raised relief. From beneath the seat he drew the car service placard, placing the nameplate beside him.

"*Oof-mah*," he chanted again. It was all really happening.

And what was happening for the chauffeur had begun two days earlier for Billy's scheduled pick-up, the soon-to-be passenger.

2

Beneath the wild whispers of the Hohokam gypsies long since perished to join the Great Mother in the Big Sky, a determined arroyo tarantula inched its way across the pink track of the Apache Trail hoping for favorable timing. The winds were shooting fast through the canyon, pounding the cholla cactus into submission, and forcing the creature to dig delicate extremities into the burning red sands for support. The challenged maneuvering was its own brand of dash, but the westerly thrust impeded progress and odds of survival severely diminished if it flipped. The nasty glowing green Mojave with its lightning spring and deadly distilled poisons, or the cruel, yellow-eyed coyote, the tarantula couldn't decipher cause, but knew death would come quickly. Yet the oppressive Sonoran Desert sun was punishing all it hit, keeping predators hidden and danger at bay even this late in October, when most American cities welcome shaved temperatures. But not Phoenix. At scorching levels, the sun was merely getting ready to assert itself.

Lucky spider.

Forty miles west, it had miraculously poured rain the night before and the air was filled with the sweet smell of creosote brush that enveloped the city. Roland Polsonby was driving the navy Mercedes sedan attending to duties, devoid of complicated thought. He had several errands to run, then he would be done.

Heading east on Camelback, Roland passed the underwhelming Motel 6 and glimpsed Miguel Sanchez inside behind the check-in desk. Sanchez knew Roland well as his patron secretly spent nights there when life at Luna Plata became difficult. It was always room 412, located in the rear parking lot so his car would not be seen. Roland could afford better of course; his wife and he were among the most affluent in the state. He didn't go there for the pampering, but for a relaxing of the pressure. The Biltmore could not offer him that, not in the same way, not on your life. Roland wanted to be around no one and nothing, certainly no familiar faces.

Roland took 42nd Avenue and rode the curve into Paradise Valley, swinging into the Country Club driveway. He got out of the car and took the detour through the locker room to the back entrance leading to the golf shop. He owed for a putter Adele ordered him, one he never used and decidedly left out of his bag.

Avoidance techniques were shattered when he passed the practice green and Lanny Pilcher, the club pro, was standing there. A standout college player, Lanny was handsome and comfortably dim with worked on white-tiled teeth that smiled easily and too often. With his strident tapered build, clothes fit him snugly, too perfectly, and his sexual preference was often questioned in cocktail whispers at the golf course's halfway house. It was perhaps the most interesting thing about him.

As Roland attempted to flee, Pilcher broke into the requisite backswing tutorial, as if to justify and subtly campaign for his position to an empowered club member who could affect his tenure. The family of Polsonby's wife, the Griffiths, had been founding members of the club back in the thirties. Roland offered a vague smile for the impromptu pointers, a polite enough pose of veiled disinterest.

Watching the man fade away, Pilcher leaned on the chrome stick with which he earned his living, the six-G smile gleaming, and he thought to himself, *Odd. Looks at you, but doesn't hear you. Wonder if he knows what his wife is up to? Tragedy cracks people. Can't tell with that one. Strange guy …*

Now it was October 26th and a different sort of day for Roland. There were details to which he needed to attend. One errand had been taken care of. Arthur Strange, his Park Avenue attorney, informed him he'd located Bliss Parker and the letter he'd written her was on its way.

Old Bliss, he thought, and left it at that. It was enough attention awarded before the irrevocable recession, before the what-if melancholy and ensuing debilitating chasm of thought. Old Bliss, "old" everyone, was the trained dash panacea which allowed for disposability and relief.

Roland pulled into the Bookman's outlet in a mini-mall. He came upon the used musical cassette section and to his surprise found it, *The Grateful Dead at the Mars Hotel.* He nearly curved a smile. He purchased the tape, but chose not to play it in the car. He didn't care to delve into the nostalgia the music would conjure. He still had more errands to run.

Roland's next stop was the bank and he veered into the parking lot, slotted the car and stepped inside and up to a teller who recognized him. He withdrew three hundred thousand dollars in cash and had to wait longer for a denomination of that size, longer than he'd hoped. He placed the thick stacks of money in a metal attaché case and returned to the parking lot where he locked the box in the trunk of the car.

He checked his watch. There were a few hours left before he had to dress for the awards dinner at the Biltmore. He'd given up formal functions and had it been any other event, he would not have attended. But Adele was one of the honorees that night. Of course, he would attend out of respect for her.

As he reversed out of the bank lot, he noticed Eugene Phelps, their personal wealth manager surveying him through a side window. Roland wasn't known to make large withdrawals and never in stacks of hundred dollar bills; yet he had needed to tend to this now without any consultation or interference. He still had one more thing to do that afternoon and it was not an errand.

3

Gonzalo and Fernanda Encarnación

On the northern mesa beyond the city, Gonzalo Encarnación cursed himself as he eased the pickup up the snaking dirt drive that rose over the parched landscape. The mesa was abundant with choked vegetation. Rows of prickly pear and sturdy saguaro stood like desert sentries, their trunks peppered with holes, doorways to generations of resident owls. Like most Sonoran ranchers, he knew each bump in the terrain and drove aggressively, but never too fast up the mesa. He was Catalan by blood from a family of sugarcane farmers in the hills above Barcelona. A reverent and dependable man, when he traveled the ridge top he took his time as a show of respect for what was up there.

On this day he was late and he gave the pedal a little more weight than usual, but not much.

Escalera al Cielo, or "Stairway to the Sky," was the private cemetery of the Ribroths, Adele Griffiths-Polsonby's celebrated family, located atop the mesa. On Adele's mother's side, the Ribroths were one of Arizona's "four families," the original mining fortune clans. They were originally from Jerome that, at the turn of the century, boasted the largest copper mine in the world. When the mining business became less profitable, Adele's great-grandfather cashed out and started a railroad that would join Santa Fe and Phoenix. This route initiated the modern boom and the subsequent expansion of the city.

The Ribroth cemetery was part of an enormous tract owned and controlled by the industrial giant clan for over a hundred years. There were rows of headstones and rectangular slabs. An above ground vault made of smooth charcoal marble towered over the rest.

Gonzalo got out of the truck and approached the cemetery, removing his beige short-brimmed Stetson. A sudden gust kicked up as he slowed to a halt. Before him rose the tower vault erected for Gerritt Droheim Polsonby, Roland and Adele's son, inscribed with the heartbreaking lifeline: *2002-2007*. Gonzalo wiped his brow and offered the sign of the cross.

Gonzalo and his wife, the lovely and exceptional Fernanda, had worked for the Polsonbys the eight years Roland had been in Phoenix.

Gonzalo's father had been caretaker of the Griffiths ranch in Payson where Gonzalo was raised. When the Polsonbys built *Calle de la Luna Plata*, "Way of the Silver Moon," the sprawling estate on the hillside above Paradise Valley, they asked Gonzalo to join them. Gonzalo brought his young Native American wife eighteen years his junior.

Gonzalo was responsible for the estate's security, as well as maintaining the gardens. He was a loyal and spiritual man whose faith was matched by his wife's. Fernanda ran the household, but more importantly she was Adele's personal secretary. Adele had a frenetic social calendar of fêtes, soirées, and charity events to attend. The Ribroths had always been philanthropic. Adele had taken over the tradition and was a frequent fund-raiser and chairperson.

Though Fernanda managed the consuming affairs of Adele, she sought to monitor Roland's well being, taken by his soft fragile quality. Fernanda's greatest gifts were her uncanny powers of perception. Though Roland rarely spoke to her, she could feel his every move and cadence of emotion. Disheartened by his shaken spirit, she constantly offered her assistance careful to not let on she perceived something wrong. She took down his bed at night as husband and wife slept in separate rooms. She'd read the books he'd authored more than twice.

From the flats atop *Escalera al Cielo*, Gonzalo craned back and spotted the car advancing up the ridgeline. He carefully laid the flower arrangements beside the tower and returned to his truck. He eased the pickup down the earthen track so as to not kick up too much dust and proceeded through the iron gates. As he approached the Mercedes, he offered a short wave. Roland Polsonby returned it. After the Benz passed, Gonzalo cursed himself. *"Imbécil!"*

He hadn't wanted to be there, not when Mr. Polsonby came. It was Gonzalo's supreme honor to place flowers at the base of the grave each day. He retrieved them from the nursery in the early morning once they were freshly stemmed and had them up on the mesa by eight o'clock; but not that day. The flowers had not been prepared in time. Still, the man determined there was no excuse.

Though Mr. Polsonby had never requested unburdened privacy, Gonzalo was determined never be seen at the garden. This courtesy was observed to make his employer feel the flowers grew there year-round, that the colorful, non-desert species survived the heat and hadn't been imported or delivered, to give the appearance they sprouted around the boy's grave like magic. For this reason, Gonzalo was upset with himself as he bumped and rocked down the ridge. He had failed his duty.

As Gonzalo's pickup disappeared in a haze of dust in his rearview, Roland gave thought to his dutiful ranch hand. He'd become more generous with his reflections on this day as each encounter had been an unspoken farewell. Gonzalo was a good man and he had not known any who bested him. He seemed a throwback personage to another century when honor and loyalty was not considered a luxury, but an inalienable duty. Gonzalo was perhaps his only friend now and the man was humble enough to not even know it.

Roland was not oblivious to the warmth extended him by Gonzalo's wife. Had he been more egocentric, carefree, and less principled as in his early years, he would have pursued her, and not for a carnal triumph as in kindling to the hearth or even a savored memory. Deep down he sensed he could have lived his life with this woman. Yet those were decade-old sentiments. Feelings of the sort no longer registered on him. There was no emotional reserve left for anyone, except his little boy.

The light was failing and winds blew through him as he stood there before Gerritt's monument. He spoke to his boy often, but never about his plan. He thought it might scare him and he would never do that. For this reason he never mentioned it.

He stayed up there that last afternoon in his solitude with his little boy beside. They were alone, the two of them.

And the man never thought to sit down.

4

She was standing alone in her bedroom before a full-length mirror spying her naked body before deploying the first layer of defense. The form had shifted from coveted dimensions of yesteryear when it was deliberate and hard, curving perilously, surging with immobilizing hints and devastating wild promise; desired beyond dreams and despised. Now Adele Griffiths-Polsonby held little appreciation for what her body and shape had become and even less, the way she had come to look.

Hers was a recurring mantra, a debt she'd incurred after years of bludgeoning the competition and the privilege her beauty afforded including the societal free pass and global passport. For all the advantages bestowed upon her, time had caught up and here it was, the payback, delivered to her doorstep and her perception of it was the truth even if it wasn't true.

Adele heard Fernanda step lightly into the bedroom.

"What about the Valentino burgundy backless?" She often consulted Fernanda on the evening's wardrobe selection.

"That will be memorable," the capable one said genuinely.

"Nothing is memorable," Adele sent back bluntly. "Just repeated. Over and over again."

Fernanda knew to choose her words carefully as the tragedy was all around them and the woman was in a perpetually fragile state. "You are not excited about tonight?"

"-*Ish*. Can't you tell?"

"It should be a pleasant occasion."

"The Senator is coming," she threw, an enthusiasm barely sparked.

"It will be a tremendous night. I have prayed for it."

"Thank you, Fernanda. I'll need it."

As silken hose were stretched and snapped in place, Fernanda stepped forward to help guide and lower the dress over the woman's shoulders. She assisted with the tiny buttons and zipper and retreated back to Adele's side and they both took her in fully in the mirror.

"Too much?"

"Stunning. Very elegant."

"Think so?" She was shifting sideways and back.

"Truly," her employee confirmed, but the woman didn't hear it.

Adele sighed and then seated herself on the vanity table ottoman and lit a cigarette. She crossed her legs as if she was already at the banquet table. "Maybe we should try again," she proffered.

It was in the air, it was always in the air, not talk of the future, but what had happened in the past. It lingered in the rooms of Luna Plata like the smell of charred embers to a once-raging fire. Fernanda understood what was being proposed, but feigned ignorance and chose not to be deceptive, rather, dignified.

"What are you referring to, Mrs. Polsonby?"

The woman wouldn't verbalize it. "Sometimes I do," she said and quashed the cigarette. "And sometimes I don't."

It was a loaded proposition, especially given the consistent hearsay of all the society woman's alleged dalliances and indiscretions.

"Giving it time is always a step forward," Fernanda offered deftly like a warm throw blanket.

Adele trapped her own reflection stone-coldly in the mirror as if she'd never seen the face before. Remaining frozen, she spoke absently. "Right, Fernanda; give it time."

The woman fastened her diamond-drop earrings, rose, gathered her evening purse and moved off, her stockings whishing provocatively. She may have lost a tightness and a step, but only in her mind.

Fernanda followed, floating paces back. Her stomach was upset. She had not sung for days, having sensed something was terribly wrong. She was afraid for everyone, including herself and her husband. The tarot cards suggested it, too.

Roland was seated in the living room, gazing through the sky lights of the angled modernist ceiling. It was a starry night, clear and desert evening cool. He was thinner than when he'd bought the tuxedo at Brooks Brothers ten years earlier. The jacket was oversized and the cummerbund needed adjustment. His legs crossed thinly and his shoes barely pressured the terracotta floor.

When Adele advanced from the corridor to her wing, Roland set himself in motion to the cuing clicks. She slipped in front of him at the front portal and he followed her out the door, a tired and mindless ritual they could perform in their sleep.

The sedan coasted down the hill and turned onto Roosevelt Drive, Roland driving a steady forty miles an hour.

"Gus called," the woman said.

The news, if in fact there was any, was left hanging there to die.

"Oh?" he sent back neutrally. The passive return volley offered her the option of informing him further, but Gus Griffiths and his life mattered little to Adele. They'd never gotten along. When he called, it was usually about the same thing; what disgruntled siblings usually call in for. Money. She let it rest and so did her husband.

Along the front drive to the Arizona Biltmore, a row of white-shirted, black bow-tied valet parkers were standing at attention before the long troughs of scarlet geraniums. The glorious "Jewel of the Desert," completed in 1929, was influenced by Frank Lloyd Wright and was constructed with special concrete blocks featuring the geometric patterns of palm trees. The magnificent structure was alit for twilight and the pink and mauve-streaked sky served as a tasteful watercolor backdrop for the elegant occasion.

A thousand of the Southwest's social elite were on hand to attend the annual YWCA Women of Distinction gala and three deserving women had been chosen for the award, including Adele Griffiths-Polsonby for her generous contributions and tireless charity work in the state.

The Polsonby's vehicle was met by a brace of valet support and flashbulbs popped as Adele emerged from it. Of all the honorees it was Adele after whom the press flocked as she possessed a local celebrity quality that invited intrigue. Though raised in the Southwest, she was schooled at Columbia University in New York where she met her husband. Upon graduating, she worked for Condé Nast and by virtue of her intellect, comely appearance, general affable nature and in part because of her financial standing she was soon recruited by New York society's grand dames to serve on the boards of major fund-raisers for the Met, the Library, the Whitney, and other prestigious charities. Her years in New York served to develop and refine her tastes and shape her unique sense of style. Though Phoenix was more dressed down and low key than elitist Manhattan, one needn't tell Adele Griffiths-Polsonby. When she emerged for an outing she was exquisitely put together as if attending *Vogue*'s annual Met Gala. She rarely disappointed photographers and the publications hiring them and certainly did not that evening. Ever radiant, she glided up the carpet as Roland stayed a deferential step back and to the side.

The MacArthur Ballroom was a fabulous space with lofty ceilings, chandeliers, copper inlays, and wall sconces. The furnishings were mission-style; the textiles were desert palettes of beige, sand, and cream. Lamps from the thirties enhanced the charming western decor.

The program for the evening included cocktails and dinner, then the presentation of the awards and dancing to a twelve-piece band.

Roland checked their coats as Adele stood by the entryway to the ballroom to receive congratulations from wellwishers. As they proceeded inside, Adele cut a path right around the tables and Roland moved sharply left, making his way to their table situated prominently in front by the podium. He remained there, seated alone, as was his preference to keep personal interaction to a minimum.

The Polsonbys were sharing a table with country club friends Tom Stafford and his wife Maydell, a former beauty queen from Midland, Texas. Roland found Tom pleasant, uncomplicated, and not too inquisitive, the precise social formula for maintaining even the sparest of contact with him. Tom's wife was less discreet with frizzy and puffed red hair which gave the impression an animal was residing somewhere in the midst.

The cluster of table guests arrived after having made their rounds of social grazing. Lily Matthews, a young widow, joined and the Lutzes at the table's end. Trudy Lutz was a childhood friend of Adele's; her husband Lawrence was a pediatric physician with a private practice.

"Roland?"

He swiveled in the direction of the voice and simultaneous tap on his shoulder. The man before him appeared unbraced and skittish.

"Hello, Dale," Roland said.

"You look great," the man tossed vacantly with the urgent follow-up. "Have you seen Adele?"

"Not in the last ten minutes."

"I'd like to ask her, uh, something about an upcoming event—"

Dale Widger was also a friend of Adele's, but a different sort and Roland did not know him well. He seemed unmanned at present, however, and the man scurried off atwitter, which was a relief. Roland didn't care to envision the demi-surrendered lives of others now, to be granted that window into their private defeats and suffering. He wanted it thin and breezy with little or no attention to detail.

Behind the ballroom's large pillars Adele was enjoying a private conversation. The object of her attention was a tall, distinguished-looking man: Parker Prescott. The man's aroused glow was unmistakable and the energy between them raw and certain, embarrassing too if you knew the Polsonbys or the Prescotts.

In the midst of the social whirl, a pleasantly disheveled man with a handsome youthful face sashayed through the room with the smooth confidence of a court prince. With chestnut shoulder-length hair, a rumpled dinner shirt, and askew tie, Brandon Slaughter was late, but his attitude indicated everything was quite all right, he was on time to his own clock and that he looked pretty damned razor. He was thirty-two, it was his Saturday night and he derived his confidence from an assumption no one in the room had anything on him no matter how accomplished as he was peaking in a blaze, he was the shit. He had a talent that wagged tongues and yielded contracts and women fell in to place accordingly in bouquets or single stems. Years of privileged schooling at the tops of his classes and a plethora of professional awards and citations all conspired to grant him the generous opinion of himself.

He called on a waiter for his table assignment, but his arm was gently intercepted and clasped by a galactically beautiful woman with diamond-fired drop earrings. She spun into him gracefully and so very close. "Brandon?"

"Yes?" he returned grinning expectantly.

"I'm Adele, remember?" Her expression was sparkling.

"Of course," he fibbed. The young man was struck by the vision, even pained to have been deprived of a look at this terrific woman at that supposed prior occasion.

Barely breaking stride, she interlocked his hand with hers. "Come with me," she instructed cozily, offering no chance for a rebuttal; nor did he care for one. He was being towed by a magnetic personage known the room over. Her pace was a soft delicate glide, yet experienced and her gorgeous burgundy gown flowed regally. The woman floated forward with an air of sophistication he'd only read about in literature from the Jazz Age.

Adele was equally pleased to escort the *wunderkind*. Allying with the city's latest golden boy she was clutching onto the cutting edge, perhaps preserving what she could no longer find in her full-length. It was the architect who was being made the star, however, and he took immense satisfaction splitting the room apart with this charismatic woman all too aware the eyes of the room were upon them, including Dale Widger's. Low-toned commentaries passed through the societal landscape as they joined the Polsonby table.

"Friends, I'd like to present Brandon Slaughter, the 2015 DuPont Architecture Award recipient. Mind you, I had the distinct pleasure of presenting it to him myself—even though he doesn't remember me!"

"Not true!" he protested with an anguished laugh.

Brandon shook a row of welcoming hands. The smiles belonging to bobbing heads doused with spirits were warm, gay, and delightfully uneven.

"Congratulations, again," Adele said to him semi-privately, drinking in his eyes with a skimmed intimacy. "You're sitting next to me." He didn't argue the point. "And this is my husband Roland—"

The man politely rose up and they shook hands. "Hello, Brandon."

"I read your book in college, Mr. Polsonby. I liked it," he said generously. "It was more than tolerable."

"What a review!" Adele teased, playfully aghast.

"I mean the story turned, that sort of thing," he tap-danced.

An event coordinator swept behind Adele and whispered in her ear.

"Senator McCain can't make it," she announced to the table.

There were scattered boos until the table hushed dully.

"Where did you get your start, Brandon?" Tom asked, tending to the silence.

"Right here at Taliesin West," Adele supplied for him, referring to the prestigious graduate school of architecture founded by Frank Lloyd Wright in nearby Scottsdale. "Tell us about Taliesin. It has such a delicious cult-like reputation—"

"Is it true you build your own homes to live in?" Trudy posed.

"They're huts made from personal designs, yes, but that's in the second year. For the first year you live outside in tents."

"For what purpose?" Dr. Lutz enquired.

The young man relished the attention and reveled in it. He'd heard them all by now and found no one to pose a challenge to his intellect or table supremacy. The one person who could no longer cared to. Duly prompted Slaughter would deliver his tour de force albeit canned line. "To drink in the environment and taste the nature."

Adele drew in closer to him within whispering range. "You spend a year in a tent? And pay for it?"

"Actually you learn about waste, the inefficient way homes have been built in the area and still are—"

"Just take a drive down Fernwood Way," Trudy concurred.

"I'm not talking aesthetics. Homes are mass-produced by builders who ignore the environment. The desert is tricky. When asked what religion he practiced, Mr. Wright used to say, 'Nature is my God.' "

Roland's interest was piqued a first time as the young man had referred to the master architect and school's founder as "Mr. Wright." It demonstrated a capacity for respect lacking previously, a touch which could have made him like the young man more in former days, perhaps.

"Those awful adobes in Scottsdale are completely inefficient," Slaughter continued.

"They're peeling them off like hotcakes," Lily countered.

"And they are. They heat up like saunas and need AC to keep them cool, they're poor function, poor design, and depend on raw electricity to bail them out, hence the power shortage in Phoenix ..."

"Have you seen Adele's home?" Trudy followed up, a staunch admirer of everything Adele.

"It's to *die* for," Maydell added, the drawn out Texas version of the colloquial cliché.

"Only in pictures. I know Doherty's work," he added.

"We'll have to audition it for you," Adele ribbed. "As long as you're absolutely honest, I mean brutal, with your appraisal."

"I always am," the young man sent back, further peacocked.

The interplay was weighted to the keen observer, if you knew what to look for. Roland did, but the exchange also provided the lull he'd been waiting on. He excused himself and faded from the ballroom scaling down the grand staircase. His departure brought to mind his childhood on the eastern shores of Long Island when he'd routinely ask to be excused from meal tables. His mother misinterpreted his behavior as a quirky obsession with bathroom layouts. The ritual was more a desire to escape the gray cloud of family disunity, a reprieve also from his father's angry watch as he became increasingly embittered with each scotch. Restroom pilgrimages had been desperate excuses to get away.

He continued his stroll across the tiled terrace and drifted on to the Paradise Pool. He hovered at the edge a while gazing freely into the depths which were illuminated for night with a dazzling, fluorescent aqua glow. Pools had meant much to him when he was a boy, symbolizing freedom more than anything, sweetened honeysuckle air, reunions with summer friends, blonded hair, hot-shower rainbows, pretty tanned girls, skinny-dipping, those first romances in the dunes, and so many more pleasant image systems.

He wiped an eye and cut short the meditation. He didn't care to remember. He was just relieved to have left the table.

After a brief terrace run-in with Tom Stafford and an informal chat with the celebrated retiring Sheriff Harlan Graves in the bar, Roland returned to the ballroom as dinner was being served. The awards were then presented. After Adele received hers, he congratulated his wife one last time and pecked her good night and good-bye. He exited the ballroom again and left the awards gala, not to return.

Adele stayed on at the table for a dance and returned home at three in the morning. She chose not to sleep in her bedroom, but opted for the guesthouse. She kept her promise of an audition to her home, however. She even awarded herself a prize. She fucked the young architect until the sky resumed its pale red-orange. When the man dozed off, she removed the long thin strands of chestnut hair stuck between her fingers and buried herself beneath the covers quietly wailing in between deep heaves.

An hour later, Roland Polsonby was on his way to the airport.

5

He was thirsty again. He was always thirsty. He'd lived most of his life dehydrated. Roland was not a water drinker; even as a kid, he experimented with every brand of pop to avoid drinking it. Later he lived off the sap provided by coffee, juices, and fruits. His general practitioner complained of the bright hue of his samples. It no longer mattered now. Dehydrated was the way it was going to play out.

The passenger was on the tarmac at Sky Harbor International on board Southwest Flight 1165 to Tucson awaiting takeoff. He had his own seat in business class free of neighbor. He was clean-shaven, his hair combed tightly across his forehead. He was wearing the charcoal suit. Though he appeared healthy, his insides were churning. He'd wrestled with his plan through the night. Not that he was having second thoughts; worse, he feared it may not work out.

Roland declined an offer for coffee. He calmed himself by putting his head back and embracing the present, a catechism he'd adopted to live singularly in the moment. It helped lift him from his unnerved state. When the plane touched down in Tucson he felt better. Before deplaning, he made a trip to the bathroom. The mirror image reflected was a reminder and his resigned but resolute eyes were the proof he was doing the right thing.

The Director pulled into the airport's arrivals terminal on time at eleven forty-three in a silver Audi sedan. Roland waited beneath the taxi stand's overhang and observed the ebb and flow of shuttles and vans retrieving passengers.

The Director sprung from the car and spotted Roland and they exchanged pleasantries. "I'm Rolf Stammbach," he stated. "The company Director." He had an austere Swiss-German accent and he opened the trunk to place the carry-on inside, but Roland decided against it.

It was a scorcher of a day and heat waves danced above Interstate 40 as they drove along. Roland eased his grip on his bag and tried to relax, but the Director needed to discuss arrangements.

"The charter plane will make the pick up tomorrow," he said. "The flight is at two o'clock if that meets with your approval."

"Yes." He had always liked Fridays, he thought. Throughout his life, they'd held a certain form of promise and that was positive.

"They're anticipating sun and clear skies—"

Roland wasn't sure what the man meant, but left it alone. He would avoid verbal communication whenever possible.

"They'd like to know if there's a certain town you prefer."

The comment threw him again so he was forced to speak up. He could not risk any confusion. "Excuse me, sir, what are you referring to?"

"Is there a specific place, village or beach or region you have in mind, or is it just the French Riviera in general?"

"I'm not following—"

"It is what you requested, isn't it?"

"What request?"

Director Stammbach angled over sharply at him. "To have your ashes spread, sir, over the south of France—"

"Wait—" he interjected. He was desperately trying to remain calm, to not get agitated, but he couldn't any longer. "Do you have the right person? *Roland Polsonby?*"

"Yes, Mr. Polsonby."

"No!" he blasted. "Those were not my instructions! I signed up for a charter back to Phoenix. I am to be placed in the above-ground vault on the Ribroth family plot next to my son!"

"It says in my folder—"

"I don't care!" he snapped. He hadn't been emotional in such a long time. "It's not what I requested and it's definitely not what I want under any circumstances!"

"There must be a mix-up—"

"—for chrissakes—"

"I'm very sorry, Mr. Polsonby."

"How could you mix up something as," the riled man searched for words. "As *personal* and *delicate* as this?"

"Don't worry, sir. We'll get it straightened out."

Roland's heart was racing; they'd been planning to cremate him and take him to France instead of his private cemetery in Arizona. Could they get it more wrong? This on his last day no less!

The Director placed a call on the hands-free phone and picked up the handset to explain the situation to a colleague. After some discussion, the issue seemed to be resolved.

"It's all taken care of, Mr. Polsonby," Stammbach announced to assure him.

"Everything's in order now? *Perfect* order???"

"You have my word. I'm very sorry for the misunderstanding."

The Director waited a moment to let his client regain his composure and then reached beneath his seat to draw out the clipboard.

"This is the authorization form for the transportation back to Phoenix, for you to sign—"

Roland hesitated then took hold of the pen and signed the document. He was sweating profusely.

"I expect the rest of my business with your company to run smoothly."

The man said it would.

Roland's heartbeat eventually returned to normal rhythms and they drove silently the rest of the way.

The doctor's office was stark white, its chairs modern and not comfortable. The reception area was dark and gave way to a lit-up examining room further back. A doctoral type stepped out in a white coat. He was blond with a youthful face. He seemed in his thirties.

"Hello, Mr. Polsonby. I'm Dr. Frye," he greeted. "Did you receive my letter?"

"Yes. Thank you."

Roland was led into the examining room and the doctor gave him a short, required physical. Upon completion of the exam, the doctor perused the file.

"Have you made preparations with the city?"

Roland was daydreaming, still somewhat shaken. "Sir?"

"Your plans for burial."

It annoyed him to have to answer the question. "Director Stammbach has taken care of it." In fact, it astounded him the doctor didn't know—how an enterprise of the sort could be lacking in basic communication on a day he needed no surprises and already he'd experienced major ones.

"The registration form indicates you have a request."

"I filled out the questionnaire and reiterated it to the Director, yes. I hoped to discuss professional football over coffee … with milk."

"I see," the doctor said, seemingly taken unaware once more. "Again, Director Stammbach has made the arrangements?"

"I hope so," Roland threw cynically.

Planted there in the brightly bulbed room, surrounded by the shadowed outer office Roland felt on stage. He checked his watch and for the first time it struck him how little time there was, how little time he had left.

"I am confident of my decision, Doctor, but I am curious. Do some people lose their nerve?"

"Not often. Most welcome the day, especially when the pain is overwhelming. But there have been cases …"

"I hear it is getting more difficult—"

"We're under scrutiny; the Death with Dignity Act protects us, but with the rise in suicide tourism, we don't know for how long. Some officials don't like the reputation the city is getting, but in my opinion, if someone is drowning he must be rescued regardless the color of his passport. Or state of issue of his driver's license."

Roland nodded and rewarded himself with a long deep breath. He was comforted for the first time that day.

"The Director will pick you up at thirteen forty-five."

"1:45?" The doctor nodded. "Guess you use military time."

"It's actually European time. Perhaps you know we're a branch of the Swiss assisted suicide and euthanasia concern called Dignitas."

"*Dignitas*," he repeated for himself. "Better than RIP.com, that's for sure. America loves its acronyms."

Roland left the building and checked his watch again. It was 12:45. He had another hour of what could be considered free time. He decided on a stroll through El Presidio Park and paused to read the bronze plaque that told the history of the Spanish fort constructed there. He advanced across the green, taking in the impressive twin towers of the Spanish-style St. Augustine Cathedral with its imposing sandstone facade and intricate desert-fill carvings.

Inside the ornate structure, Roland found a pew and knelt before the pulpit and an exquisite marble figure of Christ on a gold cross. He prayed to be escorted to Heaven to join his boy, to hold his hand and guide him to light if he was lost. He thanked the Almighty for the time he'd had on Earth. His last prayer was for Adele, in the hopes she would find happiness, a happiness he'd tried to, but could not provide for her.

"I'll be seeing you soon," he whispered openly to Gerritt.

The sun slapped him as he emerged from the church and his eyes adjusted to the brightness. It was a hundred-plus degrees and the high heat made him take refuge beneath a willow tree where he settled on a park bench. He pondered fanciful things and avoided stabs at introspection. There was no questioning his decision.

He recalled the only time he'd been to Tucson. He tabulated it had been exactly twenty years before, in 1995, when he was twenty-five. He allowed the memory to flow freely. Like a furious source long waiting to be tapped, the floodgates were opened, the pressure released, and the reminiscence of that strange episode cascaded in a torrent.

Several summers after graduating from Dartmouth, he'd taken a car across the country and traveled for six months. A pretty older woman he'd met in a local bar took him home and slept with him, inviting him to stay on a week with her that he did. He would learn later she was the wife of a low-level organized crime figure who'd been sent away to prison. One day a couple years later, the woman phoned out of the blue and asked him if he'd like to meet "his daughter," the one he'd fathered with her during his visit. Astounded by the news, he returned to Tucson and met the little girl. They had lived as a family; he was twenty-seven, she was thirty-six. By the end of six months, however, he'd felt from deep within the child was not his. Though he'd come to love the girl just the same, the mother never denied her deceit and he left never to see them again. He wondered where they were now.

Roland shifted on the bench beneath the blazing sun. He reflected on his career then, considering less the novels he'd written and more the ones he'd planned to write, but now never would.

The man raised his regard and saw Stammbach's car swing into the gate to the park. He checked his watch that said 1:30, thirteen-thirty, indicating the director was fifteen minutes early. He contemplated the fifteen minutes and how his time was being cut short. Yet he didn't want to get emotional, not now. He needed peace.

Roland rose up and faded over to the car and got in.

They took West Alameda to Grenada Avenue to the outskirts of the city and the silver Audi swept into the drive of an industrial building renovated for commercial offices at thirteen forty-seven.

The office had been converted into a sparsely furnished two-room flat with a kitchenette, small refrigerator, assorted wine glasses on the shelf, and a wall poster for *The Outlaw Josey Wales*, an old Western movie starring Clint Eastwood. The main room was larger with two beds, a table, and a window that overlooked the city. There was a stack of canes in the corner along with walkers and wheelchairs.

Roland immediately spied the collection and sent the director an inquiring look.

"Remains," Stammbach provided in earnest, the implication no less macabre.

Roland sat at the table prompted to ponder those who'd preceded him in the apartment. It would seem many had been elderly and incapacitated.

"And my football discussion?"

"I'm sorry, Mr. Polsonby, we couldn't find anyone knowledgeable enough to discuss it with you, but I could still try—"

"You had trouble finding someone in America to discuss *football*?" Roland had to question it; he was incredulous.

"The problem is, we're a European outfit. We had someone, but he was knowledgeable in European football which is—"

"Soccer," Roland volunteered morosely. "Another mix-up."

But he had to let it go. He did not want to be irritated the remainder of his time.

Moments later, a thin elderly nurse with limp white hair in casual dress stepped through the door. She introduced herself as Mildred and Roland noted the dreary sound of her name.

"Would you like to hear your music?" the Director posed and Roland handed him the Grateful Dead cassette he'd purchased.

As the Director commenced with the formal procedure, Roland sat on the couch and listened to his music, relieved the process was taking place now, exactly as he'd been briefed, with no additional surprises. The nurse was keeping minutes on a clipboard and at fourteen-twenty, the Director asked him formally to initiate the process. "Are you absolutely certain you wish to do this?"

"Yes," he said, his voice unwavering.

At fourteen twenty-three, Roland signed the "Declaration of Suicide" which affirmed he'd made a "reasoned and rational" decision to end his life. As he held the pen his hand stuck to the paper. He felt a fresh nervousness as he wondered what was waiting for him over "there" on the other side. Was there even any "there" there???

The Director rose up, went over to him and shook his hand. Then, following protocol and procedure, he left the room.

"Would you like a candle?" the nurse asked him thoughtfully.

"No, thank you; I was never a candle person."

Roland refocused on the music and pleasant memories from college and the early years in New York before he'd been published passed through his mind. He even mouthed the lyrics to "Unbroken Chain," a song that he used to play over and over again.

At fourteen thirty-one, the nurse dropped an anti-nausea tablet in a tumbler and explained that the medicine prevented vomiting of the extremely bitter barbiturate. When the tablet was fully dissolved, she walked over and handed him the glass.

He contemplated Nurse Mildred then and tried to envision her life. She seemed a lonely sort, but gratified, perhaps, that she was helping people.

"You do this often?"

"No," the nurse replied. "A couple times a week. It takes twenty minutes for it to take effect."

"I'll be able to listen to side two," he said, noting the small mercy. Roland downed the contents of the tumbler quickly in one haul.

"You can move into the bedroom if you like—"

He held off as he was enjoying anticipating the notes of the Jerry Garcia guitar solos, the ones preserved in his memory from long ago.

At fourteen forty-six, the nurse stepped into the kitchenette and emptied the lethal barbiturate into a glass of Evian water.

The sun was easing up on the city, giving the space a yellow-orange glow and Roland moved to the bedroom and sat at the edge of the bed. The twenty minutes had passed and the music was still playing. At fourteen fifty-two, the nurse appeared with the fatal dose, placing the glass on the bedside table. Roland waited for the song's chorus to finish. Then he held the glass up and uttered a final prayer for him and his boy. Roland Polsonby imbibed the contents to end his life and he did it rapidly. He sat there a moment before lying down.

The nurse was not watching him, but it was required that she remain in the room. Still, he felt he was by himself.

As Roland lay motionless, meditations came in waves. He gave thought to his mother who'd tried to understand him, but had so only tangentially; and his father: an embittered man. He remembered the silly social climber's town they'd chosen to live in on the eastern shore of Long Island. He concluded then that his parents had done their best with who they were and what they had.

He recalled Gerritt's tiny starfish hands and how wonderful it had felt to hold them.

He tried to anticipate Fernanda's reaction when she opened the metal attaché case, concerned she may feel insulted by the offering. He hoped the money would be enough.

Roland didn't second-guess himself. It was right; it was time.

Then all of a sudden he started to feel alone. His psyche began to weaken and then erode. He got panicky as room sounds became fainter and the sunlight seemed to fade.

He was comforted when the nurse came into focus above him at fifteen zero-three. "Mr. Polsonby," she said, "your family is here. Your wife, Gerritt, Gonzalo, Fernanda, your father and mother."

The Director must have gotten in touch with them, he thought.

"Shall I send them in?"

He could barely hear her now and had to read her lips.

Moments later, they all appeared from above looking down at him. They held his hands. He was glad they were there.

The lights were dimming, the sounds increasingly muted. He was losing consciousness fast. He was shutting down.

At fourteen-zero-five, Roland Polsonby slipped into a coma.

The nurse noted the time of death at fourteen-zero-five, and at fourteen-fifteen, she used her mobile phone and selected her speed dial number for the Tucson Police to formally announce the death of Roland Droheim Polsonby. She requested an ambulance within the hour.

Director Stammbach re-entered the room just then and that seemed strange. Roland remembered him saying he would not be present. The director began discussing the funeral arrangements while he still lay there on the table and though in a coma, he could still hear him.

The Director mentioned "Charles de Gaulle Airport" and the flight time and "Air France" and "the south of France," and "just pick any beach, he'll never know the difference."

Horrified by the exchange, Roland tried to scream at the top of his lungs—*"NO!!!"*—but he was inert and his parts would not move. "Listen to me! *You've got it all wrong!!!* "

He had no muscle memory, no power in his limbs. His vocal cords would not respond either; no one could hear him, but he yelled anyway.

"I am to be placed next to my son! In Phoenix! In the Ribroth plot! The big vault! Next to Gerritt my boy, dammit!!! Not France, *PHOENIX!!! Do you hear me???* "

Terrorized, he screamed his son's name and where his body should be laid to rest and he repeated it until he felt movement, a tapping and shoving at his shoulder. Someone was above him coming into view, just barely, and he tried to read the nametag, but it was blurry. He spotted a breast pin logo, a Southwest Airlines logo, and he couldn't understand how or why someone, perhaps a flight attendant, would be trying to wake him.

"Excuse me, sir—" she said, nudging him easily which had no effect. "Sir!" she exclaimed forcefully.

Another business class attendant dashed up the aisle and informed her, "His name is Polsonby." He was squirming and the attendant leaned in calling him by name, "Mr. Polsonby, wake up. Mr. Polsonby!"

His dried eyes unsealed, sticking then snapping open. His carriage vaulted forward and he jerked a look around at them and the three attendants took in his frightened, haunted expression. He fell back against his chair rest.

"He's still out." They shoved him gently. "Sir, wake up!"

He shifted again and his shoulders sunk into the chair. The fog cleared and then it dawned on him what had happened.

"I-I-I'm awake …"

"Get him some water—"

"You were dreaming—"

He fastened squarely on the woman. It had felt like nothing of the sort to him.

He was handed a cup. "Thank you," he said, his heart slamming his ribs.

Over the flight intercom it was announced the plane would be landing in ten minutes. Roland never stopped glaring straight ahead and didn't say another word, not even when they reminded him of his carry-on.

Once in the terminal he was ambulatory, but still shaken and disoriented. He checked his watch and reasoned he had enough time to take a table at a franchise restaurant. He tried to collect himself and eventually ordered a cup of coffee. He prayed for everything to go smoothly now.

Five minutes before the designated time, he maneuvered outside to the passenger pick-up area. Five minutes passed. Then ten and no sedan showed, so he scanned his mobile phone for messages. There were none. He phoned the company, but a recording indicated the number was not a working one; directory assistance, however, assured him the number was correct. He avoided calling Margaret. He did not want to involve her in his plan any more than he had to.

A half hour passed and Roland grew very concerned.

After forty minutes, he called Margaret at the office and she didn't pick up. Phoning her mobile, there was no answer.

A few minutes later, he decided to take a taxi directly to the company's office, to the address listed on the documentation they'd sent him. The R.I.P. concern was located on Speedway Avenue in the southern section of town.

The biracial driver was desert indolent and his uninspired driving extended a ten-minute trip to twenty. It put Roland further on edge.

"Tourist?" the man put to him. "Well, if you got the time head over to Old Tucson. S'where they made all them movies …"

The passenger decided not to respond and lose focus.

"You seen most of 'em, least I have, like *Outlaw Josey Wales*. You see that? Made it right there at them studios in Old Tucson."

Of course, the mention of the movie was striking. Roland had seen the poster for the movie in his sleep, which was strange.

The cab slowed to a halt at the street corner as he double-checked the address. He eyed the number tacked to the building. Slipping inside he scanned the in-house wall directory. *Rip.com* was on the third floor in Suite 312. He rode up the pre-war clunker of an elevator, the indicator lighting a "3," and the door spread for him.

He knocked on the office door and when it opened a short, bespectacled man wearing a yarmulke stood before him.

"It's Mr. Polsonby," Roland blurted. "Is the Director in?" He looked sweaty and troubled, the perspiration soaking through his shirt.

"Director?"

"I've been waiting an hour for him; he was supposed to pick me up. I'm not happy about it, considering the circumstances—"

"But sir, what are you here for? Are you a client of ours?"

"Of course I am!"

"Who handles your account?"

"The Director, I said!"

"Sir, there is no director here. We have three thousand clients. Who was assigned to you?" Roland looked at him dumfounded. "Which accountant?"

"Accountant?"

"Yes, who does your taxes?"

Roland gave him a look of absolute disbelief. "*Taxes???*"

"This is an accounting firm, Mr. Poolingsby."

"This isn't RIP.com, the Internet company?"

The man's face sobered considerably. "Uh, no," he said awkwardly. "They left the premises over a month ago. The wall directory hasn't been changed. I'm sorry—"

Roland stood there devastated, his bag tumbling over to its side. "They went out of business?"

The accountant perceived the desperate man's plight with empathy as he was apprised of the business of RIP.

"When the dot-com bubble burst, they ran out of money. Non-profit organizations and companies set up like theirs were first to go. They lasted longer than anyone thought on an overseas grant—"

"Are you sure?"

"Quite. We did their taxes."

Roland was shaking now. "How could this happen? Does anyone need sponsorship for a damned phone call?"

The accountant remained planted not knowing what to say.

"Is the Director still in," Roland searched for words, "the business?"

"I don't believe so, but I may have a contact number for him."

As Roland tried to calm himself, the accountant wrote a number on a piece of paper and handed it to him.

"I'm sorry, sir," the harried man apologized. "It's been a rough day."

"I understand. They should have notified you."

Roland inspected the piece of paper. "808? Where the heck is that?"

"Hawaii, I believe."

"Sure, Hawaii," Roland muttered. "Sounds like someone's on vacation—for good."

Back on the street, Roland tried the number in Hawaii, but was greeted by a mechanized answering machine voice. They must have been informed he'd canceled, he thought, or perhaps they'd sent him a letter and Margaret tossed it as junk. There was no other explanation for the gross insensitivity.

His predicament initiated a nosedive into a morass of debilitating thought, an hour-long stream of morose meditations. He'd never considered this turn of events and had no back-up plan. The initial shock endured, but eventually gave way to rational thought and he decided to research other associations that performed the service. A taxi dropped him off at a mall where a bookshop manager allowed him to borrow a laptop.

He went online and checked Oregon first, as physician aid-in-dying was legal in the state. He contacted the first P.A.D. clinic listed and attempted to book a termination appointment for later in the day, but he was told they could not comply with his request. They needed to see medical records first and schedule an interview. He confessed he was not ill, it was his wish to end his life and he was not a depressive who'd attempted suicides. They informed him no assisted suicide group in the state would perform the procedure without an urgent medical reason: as in a terminal disease or an advanced HIV condition and provided also that he had less than six months to live. The case was the same in Montana and Washington, the only other states where physician-assisted death was legal.

Roland became distraught. There he was trying to leave the Earth graciously and with dignity, to join his boy in Heaven, and it would seem it was absolutely not to be. He could not believe the injustice.

He considered doing it himself. He'd contemplated it numerous times having never admired its implication. It seemed too desperate, the maneuver of the mentally ill, which he did not consider himself. More importantly, it was not the proper example for his boy. But perhaps this time he would have to; there seemed to be no other way.

He combed a miracle mile in another taxi attempting to devise a plan when he spotted a Motel 6, a familiar franchise in a city foreign to him. At the modest chain's outpost in Tucson, he hoped he could find peaceful refuge and weigh his predicament with no further setbacks or surprises.

He phoned his office, after checking in, but got the machine again and another attempt at Margaret yielded the same lack of response.

Roland Polsonby was holed up in a Motel 6 having failed at his assisted suicide attempt. He considered his dream which had been a veritable nightmare, one from which it took an entire flight crew to wrestle him, the patient records mix-up, the director showing early, the botched "football" discussion, then the topper, the horrific "living coma" with faulty burial arrangements. He wondered if it was an omen, that perhaps he was doing the wrong thing.

Roland slipped into the bathroom and checked the bathtub that seemed comfortable enough with a sloped end. He eyed the hairdryer on the wall then twisted on the bath water and adjusted it to lukewarm.

He phoned the front desk and asked for a shaving razor that was delivered by a sprite teenage girl with a spouting ponytail. She was pretty, blond, her expression eager enough to indicate she hadn't been on the job long and that it wouldn't be a lifelong career. There was also clarity of speech in her diction and brightness in her eyes and she radiated a special confidence. She was likely making extra money while attending the local state university.

"Sir?" Her hand remained extended, her palm suspended with the yellow-capped stem of a single-edged blade atop it.

Just seeing her standing there he realized he couldn't do it, not to her, someone so young and fresh to the world. He would not make her witness to a scene of the sort; he wouldn't provide that horror, not on her watch. "No."

"No?" She was still smiling sweetly, hoping to please.

He shook his head. "I found one, thank you."

It hit him all at once what he had to do.

An hour later, lying on the wide bed in his preferred chain of budget motels, Roland Polsonby watched television almost peacefully having resolved his predicament. He would travel to Phoenix in the morning where he would pick up medical records specially prepared for him. At noon, he would return to the airport to fly to Portland where he had an evening appointment scheduled to conclude his business once and for all.

6

And here it was.

Billy Sixkiller quickly dashed inside the terminal and scanned the board of incoming flights. Flight 87 from Tucson was landing presently, so he returned to his vehicle and waited for the flow of arriving passengers.

A refreshed, but hurried Roland Polsonby emerged from the terminal dressed in his suit, his small bag in tow. Billy instantly recognized the advancing figure and rose out of the car holding aloft the name placard. He purposely stayed away from the cluster of hired drivers and taxis.

Roland eventually located his name card held high and his face showed momentary relief. He quickened his step toward the man.

"Good morning, Mr. Polsonby," Billy initiated amicably from the distance.

"Great," Roland responded thankfully. "And you're—?"

"I'm from Metro Limo."

"Metro, did you say?"

"Yes, I'm your driver. Margaret phoned us."

"Good. Did she fax you the itinerary?"

"She called it in, sir. Scottsdale, then back to the airport."

"Right, okay," Roland said with a sigh, an additional measure of calm registering on his face.

"Any bags?"

"Just the carry-on. I'll keep it with me."

"Come right this way—"

The two men sauntered along to the end of the landing. Roland remained paces behind. Up ahead he spotted the lone vehicle they seemed to be closing in on and he took in fully the enormous fancy white car. He paused and slowed. Billy continued to stride right up to it and opened the trunk to place the placard within.

"That's some car—"

"Thank you. We like to think so."

"Is it yours?"

"Only to drive. It's the company's, sir."

"I usually take town cars—"

"They're all out already. If you prefer we can switch perhaps—"

"No," the man countered quickly. "That'll be fine—"

In fact, he was just relieved the car had been there, he'd been through such hell. As the driver opened the door for him, Roland hesitated and straightened. Still, he didn't want to take any chances.

"Do you mind if I call my office?"

"Not at all—"

"Just need to check in." Roland stepped away from the car and paced a slow circle, waiting. He got the answering machine again.

"Hello Margaret, just double-checking about my car here; Metro Limo is the outfit, the driver mentioned your name. It's a limousine, they're out of smaller cars, I guess. He does have the itinerary, thanks. As you know, I'm making more stops. Call me when you get this—"

The man wheeled around and saw Billy positioned dutifully by the rear door, spreading it wide. "You know the first stop?"

"The Pima Medical Center on Hayden."

"Right, then we're coming right back—"

"To the airport," Billy filled in. "Yes, sir."

Roland settled his frame into the backseat and wiped the film of perspiration on his brow, his torso remaining pitched forward. He was still jittery. "My flight is at noon I'm pretty sure—"

"Yes it is; you're flying Delta, Flight 1204."

"Yes, Delta," the man said. The pointed and detailed repartee proved the driver's specific knowledge. More at ease now, Roland leaned back and let out a wedge of air from his pressured chest.

The driver started up the engine and maneuvered into the flow of exiting traffic.

"To Portland," Roland volunteered, sparked with a fresh confidence that things were working out. After the disturbing sequence of miscues in Tucson, it was crucial for him to regain this peace of mind. A cool breeze thrust at him from the air conditioner and felt soothing against his face.

Roland examined the car's interior and noted its luxurious decor. The seats were upholstered in red velour that gave it an almost Parisian nightclub look and the soft cushions were easy on his tired limbs. There was a widescreen HD television inset behind the front seat and a stereo panel overhead that the passenger could control with a remote. The bar had crystal decanters filled with spirits.

The partition separating the driver from the rear motored down.

"Would you care for some water?"

"No, thank you."

"It's there if you need it along with a wide range of soft drinks and the open bar. And ice, of course. There is cable TV and satellite radio and extensive digital music and movie collections."

"Thank you," he said. "What did you say your name was?"

"Metro Limo."

"No, you. Your name."

"I didn't say my name, sir." Roland angled up at him, surprised by the answer. "But my name is Billy."

"Okay, Billy," Roland said and he even forced a quick smile.

The Ivory Stretch motored up the exit ramp from the airport and Billy could see the Maricopa Freeway ahead was still running bumper-to-bumper.

"There's a truck accident on the freeway, Mr. Polsonby. We would make better time if I took the access road—"

"Whatever you think is best," he said. "*Quickest*," he emphasized.

Billy took the right fork away from the freeway on-ramp and swung down low to a designated trucker's route that ran parallel.

"Is the 60 backed up too?"

"According to the shortwave. I'll take Baseline, then turn up."

Roland was pleased the driver showed knowledge of the city and had the proper technology. He decided on a can of Sprite and settled into his seat, noticing the limousine was now coasting freely down the access road.

The partition slid down once more.

"Would you like to hear some music, Mr. Polsonby?"

"Not right now—"

"Do you mind if I play some?"

He was paused temporarily having just finished telling the man his preference, a clear decline. But the man was doing a competent job and Roland valued that. "Go ahead," he tendered.

From the dashboard control panel Billy accessed the digital player that held a catalog of ten thousand songs. He knew many of their numbers by heart. "I enjoy rock and roll—" he sent back offhandedly.

Roland didn't respond as the song came on, early Rolling Stones, "Monkey Man," an up-tempo rocking cut from *Let It Bleed*.

"—'Because it gets through to you,' " Billy quoted, projecting cheerily over the music. "Keith Richards said that in an interview in *Rolling Stone* some years ago, 1982, that rock and roll 'gets through to you.' But John Lennon said it before him, also in *RS*, the 1971 interview with Jann Wenner, February, to be exact."

Still, there was nothing from the passenger. He was not encouraging a chat.

"You like rock and roll?"

"Yes," the man said briefly, pondering whether to communicate a preference to be left in peace.

"Right? There's no fluff, no bullshit. I must say when it gets late, I mean midnight and beyond, I have to hear techno—"

"I'm not much of a conversationalist," Roland returned as an exchange-stopper.

It seemed effective as Billy was not heard from again though he'd whispered, "And that's what kids respond to—the no-bullshit clause."

The car continued coasting along, but when held at the next stoplight, the driver studied Roland in the rearview and broke the silence again.

"Shame we didn't see that jack-knife, sounded like a good one …"

Roland was daydreaming and hadn't heard him and realized he should remain vigilant so there would be no surprises. "Excuse me?"

"That accident was four lanes across, fire trucks, smoke, shattered glass, and a line of dominoskis. Must have been beaucoup blood—"

Strange remark, the passenger thought. Inviting the driver to speak had been a mistake. Roland hoped now to be left alone. For calm he gazed out the window and took in the poor residential section of south Phoenix, an endless row of stucco bungalows with parched scraps for front lawns.

"Sometimes a scene like that can be inspiring and very beautiful. Like a Monet sunset. Wouldn't you agree?"

The man in back would remain silent now.

"I mean it's not the tangential horror, the tragic aspects, the wet hankies, or the effect on individual lives that get you. But the creative dimensions and force of it, the form and the framework, the twisted metal, the disposition of the bodies, the majestic nature of the visual. It has the potency to completely unlock your valves of sensation and leave a memory trail. For years to come. The blood is helpful, naturally. Scarlet rivers that meander or make a dipping pool. Or web out and patternize as they find the lone drain and such—"

The passenger couldn't believe his ears. "Excuse me, Billy—"

" 'Cause let's face it, Mr. Polsonby," he steamrolled, "and *I'm sure you'll agree*, the history of mankind, or, man-'not-so-kind' is one of desperation, misinterpretation, and waste. With the exception of a few superior individuals like Galileo, Leonardo, Picasso, Darwin, and Einstein, the entire glacier of human flesh is riding on the coattails of these few exceptions that have hauled this other crap forward over the centuries. So I say we better take any fortuitous beauty and piddly little thrills whenever we can—like a healthy and stimulating stack of auto dominos."

"I do not wish to be rude to you," the passenger said resolutely. "But I'd prefer it if you closed the divider so I can rest—"

Not only did the driver fail to comply, but a twisted curve came to his mouth. " '*I think we all died a little in that damned war*,' " he spouted.

There was a break in the exchange, but the man behind the wheel spied the rearview waiting for a reaction that never came. "*Outlaw Josey Wales*," he offered instead, supplying the answer to the cinema dialogue pop quiz he'd secretly launched.

There was another pause. " 'Dokie, Mr. Polsonby. I'll put a lid on it." But he did not motor up the partition.

This chauffeur seemed unbalanced certainly to Roland and yet the coincidence was staggering. Again it was that movie, the one he'd dreamt of, the one mentioned again by the Tucson taxi driver. It made him consider things he rarely did such as coincidence, synchronicity, and the predetermined nature of events. He was uncomfortable once more and a deep feeling of concern took over him. He could smell a sudden rank perspiration wafting up from his armpits.

"Holy moley!" the driver suddenly called out. "You see that?"

The passenger had no idea what Billy was referring to and didn't respond.

"That hottie? In the whisper mini? Must have been twenty, tops. Know how I can tell? The butt flaps. If you see tiny folds, meaning creases carving beneath the globes of a girlie pumpkin as they get tugged to earth by gravity's cruel pull—it's mid-twenties. Pronounced folds—thirties-plus and so on. No fold, well that's pure Twinkie sugar. And you be nice to that. If you want that sugar to pour. I can usually tell within a year. It's all in the butt flaps …"

Roland nervously mopped his brow again. Just then the car slowed and veered across the opposing lane ducking beneath the shade of an off-ramp overpass where it came to a halt. There were no other vehicles in sight and the passenger's pulse quickened. "Where are we?" he called out, spiked at the edge of the seat.

"We seem to be running a little hot. I'm going to have a look at the radiator and check fluid levels—"

The driver reached beneath the dash and yanked the hood release.

"Damned Mercury retrograde is what it is," he threw loud for the passenger to hear. "And eccentric Uranus opposing the New Moon bringing out Virgo's edgy side. Sends everything into a tizzy—"

Billy got out of the car, sunglasses riding his face. He popped the hood and raised it, shielding him from view. "A high-intensity, emotionally-charged lunation that keeps us jumping like fleas—"

Roland hurriedly drew his phone and finger-pecked it with a fury.

"The two outer planets Uranus and Pluto are the most subversive, each an expert in demolition. They can cause deep rumblings in the psyche. More committed to change than comfort, I'll tell you that—"

As the man pressed a seventh key, in a flash, the rear door of the limo was flung open and the phone was snatched from him. In a frightful display, Billy swiveled, wound up, and hurled the instrument against a concrete girder of the off-ramp support smashing it and sending plastic shrapnel flying.

"What the hell are you doing?" Roland leaped from the car.

Without saying a word, the driver lunged and cracked him, a punishing blow directly to the face. He'd blackjacked him with the metal gun butt and the snapping sound of cartilage was unmistakable. It sent the man careening back against the car and down to the ground.

The passenger's nose exploded with numbness. He angled up and was facing the barrel of the weapon that struck him: a Glock nine-millimeter semiautomatic handgun.

"Get up!" the driver roared.

Roland rose slowly, unevenly, as though he'd forgotten how. His face was throbbing and blood trickled over his lip.

"I don't want any trouble," he said, attempting a neutral and controlled tone.

"Get in the goddamn car!"

Roland stumbled and obediently moved to the opened door. He eased himself into the car's interior, the sparest movements causing pain to his nose, bones in the face, and ribs.

The driver stood at the rear door, hovering menacingly.

"W-what is this about?" the passenger posed, still feigning calm, but his voice quavered erratically.

The man was planted before him with the gun, eyes hidden behind the shields. Roland couldn't know what the man would do next and he was terrified. As an answer the door was closed in his face, but delicately so. The car door locks then snapped shut from a remote device.

Moving swiftly to the rear, Billy spread the trunk and snared rolls of silver duct tape and a ring of rope from within. He reopened the back door, spearing the barrel into the space. As Roland's mouth parted to call out in terror, the driver whacked him in the face once more.

"I'm not much of a conversationalist either," Billy snapped, sarcastic.

The passenger wiped his nose in careful increments and teetered there, expressionless. He was in shock. There was a deep maroon blot to his shirt and his hands were smeared in blood.

While delivering phrases in native Supai Billy wrapped the man's crown with duct tape from back to front. He covered his mouth then bound his feet together, winding them thickly in a tight brace.

The passenger was forced to lay face down on the limo floor, hands taped behind his back. Billy secured them with additional rope and knotted his hands to his feet with the slack. When the hogtying was complete, he sat still eyeing his prisoner.

"*Oof-mah,*" he released again.

Billy hauled Roland's body out and impressively lifted him over his shoulder and carried him to the trunk. He released the hatch again and piled him onto a thin mattress spread within. The spacious and meticulously arranged trunk was equipped with books, a portable shortwave radio, more electronics, and camping gear. The man organized the contents to make additional room until the passenger's body extended the length of the bed's interior. It was then the captor delivered his declaration, the precise verbiage and phrasing refined and sculpted over time.

"Mr. Polsonby—in October of 1995 in this very city you murdered my parents in the middle of the night as they were sleeping. Naturally, they didn't have a chance. Twenty years later, I've come to return the favor. Not to offer you any more or any less. You will be handled precisely the same way. So my justice is pure. I will kill you, but not until your faculties are in the requisite alignment and you're in the proper state. That is, unconscious and asleep, the identical state of my unsuspecting parents. You may consider these your final hours."

"It's simple," he added. "Stay awake if you want to stay alive ..."

The prisoner's eyes blazed up at the man and he did not attempt to speak and couldn't if he wanted to. Billy's regard was one of disdain and disgust and he closed the hatch albeit gently so again.

Up front the captor changed out of the chauffeur garb and went with a wife-beater V-neck, jeans, and snip-toed snakeskin boots. He caught a glance of himself in the rearview long enough to see the contented if not triumphant expression. He'd waited so long for this. He turned over the motor then and gave the pedal some weight.

7

Mélodie "Frenchy" de Charlebois :
The Dolce Vita Diaries 1

I am taking sun. Billy gave me a tube of 45, but I didn't use it. I want to get very dark. The way I did that time in Beaulieu Sur Mer with my mother (before she died). I am so excited he is coming. I can't wait to hear the surprise. Last time it was a Hula Hoop. Cheap! What do I want? An Austin Mini car, the green one with beige leather seats! But I would never ask for it. Because he would buy it! Even if he didn't have the money! (and so how would he get it? uh-oh!!!) I think it's a bicycle. He thinks I should exercise. But I'm French! We smoke! If we are sexy French that is what we do! Be sexy! A sport by itself! Haha! Bitch! I can be such one ...

The longer he takes to get here the more I go crazy! (And the longer the dirty old men watch my titty-tits) They're so cute. It didn't used to be like this. I have beautiful tits, yes. It's a fact. (Bitch x 2!) But I think after Viagra they all think they have a chance! To get some! It's soooo cute (the male ego)!!! It kills me!!!

My medicine cards today were scary. I pulled the reverse Dragonfly card, meaning it came upside down. The Dragonfly (right side up) deals with the illusionary parts of life. If you take in the medicine of the Dragonfly it helps break illusions you have and helps you move on. And the reverse Dragonfly card suggests you may be caught in an illusion. This may weaken you. And get in the way of your abilities. I know what Billy will say. "Reading those cards IS the illusion!" (Even though he gave the cards to me!) It's part of Native American spiritual philosophies. I am just learning. It seems very powerful. Each animal offers its own medicine. And message for life. I do feel the animals. I feel them better than human beings. I have always liked them more than human beings. I feel close to them. Their simplicity. And the "no bullshit," as Billy says. People, human beings, are deceivers. They do not have to be and maybe that is naive. But I do know we should listen to the animals. It would make us better people.

I believe the troubles of the world are because people don't have faith in something. I am searching, trying to find mine.

After "ten-clock" in "Billy-time" (as he'd dropped the "o" in his incessant desire to streamline), the Stretch turned onto the 60, the

Superstition Freeway, named for the mountain range rising steadily east of the city. The car off-ramped in Apache Junction, continuing north. It turned in at the main gate of a sprawling recreational vehicle retirement community, the Whispering Palms Resort.

The car slowed before a security shack fronting the entrance to a wide sweep of trailer home units. A white-haired man with a sweat-stained hat and gold badge attached to it slid back the plastic window. "Jesus, Mary, and Josephine: Billy Six—"

"*Ungawa*, Marty! You don't look so good—"

"She's up to it ag'in!"

"What?"

"I keep tellin' her she can't carry on like that. I know she's a Frenchie, but damn. 'Specially after all that Eye-rack stuff—"

"Sarkozy took care of all of that. He married a model. Can't get more Americano than that. Frogs have been with us ever since …"

Marty didn't know to whom or to what Billy was referring. "Yeah, well, these folks ain't read a newspaper in ten years!"

"So what's the problem? Where is she?"

"Pool! Where else?"

"Let me park." He slotted the car down a side alleyway out of view from passersby. He stretched the custom-fitted purple silk cover back over the chassis and with a small duffel in hand he ran back to where Marty was awaiting him in his golf cart. He hopped on and Marty put the pedal to the floor, the cart humming past tiny streets with tribal names—Blackfoot Avenue, Chippewa Way, and Havasupai Drive.

"EZ-Boy's still running good," Billy appraised.

"Thanks to you—"

"No, '99 was the best year before EZies went plastic fantastic."

"Ever since you fixed them brakes she been working like a charm. But ol' Ned, he's got some problem'r other. You still in business?"

"Sixkiller Quadruped Transportation Management? Damn straight we're in business and it was a banner frickin' year! Serving the greater metro area and we've expanded, got the RV wrecking yard, too—"

Billy had a facile way of speaking to folk; less a chameleon and more a student of human nature and master linguist who could adapt to different dialects and slang as well as the rise and fall of intelligence quotients.

"You don't say—"

"Whatta ya think? I went inheritance boy on you? Gotta make the buckaroonis too …"

The cart passed through the village. Each plot held a single RV unit with a driveway and tiny concrete yard boasting eclectic outdoor decor; everything from barbeques, to walkers, to Astroturf gardens. Golf carts were suspended on blocks for those traveling. The homes themselves were adorned with strip mall bric-a-brac—cutesy signs, desert creature figurines, howling coyotes, baby deer, lizards, hanging bells, chimes, and bird feeders, all from the home furnishings inventories of Wal-Mart and Target.

Marty's cart drove swiftly along the Fifth Hole fairway of the pitch-and-putt golf course and turned up Seminole Street. Ahead, Billy spied what appeared to be the flashpoint of commotion. A row of canopied electric quadrupeds were docked beneath the palms aligning the pool fence, their drivers aged anywhere from sixty-five to eighty, all peering from beneath the canvas cart lids. Those on foot craned out from behind trees. The subject of keen interest was a tanned and curvaceous young woman lying poolside in the distance—topless—on a chaise lounge with a hardcover spread and jotting into a notebook, seemingly oblivious to all the fuss. She had an exceptional figure, for sure.

I started writing a journal because it's medicine suggested by the cards. Billy thinks I am writing to record everything we do. Meaning everything HE does! He calls it the Dolce Vita Diaries. He thinks everything he does and says is worth writing down. He's so mignon that way. And such a big ego! One of his power animals is the Mountain Lion. He is a leader. That is true, he is a born leader. Guru? Maybe, but of what I don't know! Of me?

Even though it's called The DVD, I am writing the journal for me!

Do I really need change in my life like the Dragonfly card says? Am I too dependent on a man? Perhaps, but a life without Billy terrifies me.

Here he comes! With that old geezer man on the cart … Billy my love! "No good-byes, only hellos!" HELLO!!!

"What is this?" Billy called out to the peepers. "A casting call for 'Dirty Old Perverts?'"

They all craned around, some slower than others.

"Billy Six!" one croaked.

"Don't be scarin' me like that, boy," another scoffed. "Make my heart go hippity-hop!"

Suddenly a golf ball whizzed through the air, striking a cart with a gong. Everyone twisted around and blue-haired Annie-Alice Overlake was standing there menacingly beneath her blue flamingo awning.

"Lloyd, git yer keester back here!" she hollered. "Oughta be ashamed. I see you Clem hiding behind that tree—just cause Janet's in the infirmary don't mean you should be out carryin' on like James Dean! *Lloyd???* You got two minutes!"

Lloyd, a stout man with a hearing aid waddled off sheepishly, tugging down his Ocotillo Gold golf cap brim, slumping and defeated.

"Giv 'em hell, Lloyd—"

"Do yourself a favor—turn yer volume down!" another quipped.

The young woman had long honey-blonde hair, topaz blue eyes, full hornet-stung lips and a facial pout that was her natural expression. She was sunned deep brown and oiled and from her neck hung a turquoise bear claw talisman. The pale peach string bottoms were barely there and the peach shade made for nudity at twenty paces especially to eyes that were failing. If that wasn't enough, her breasts were full, round, and pointed skyward, years away from any time-slide. The rest of the body was erosion free, the vision slotted for prime time July Côte d'Azur. For the retirement community the spectacle was overkill with a baseball bat and the uprising it caused wasn't a first time. Mélodie "Frenchy" de Charlebois was the most talked-about subject on a daily basis. Since each day boasted high desert heat and sunshine, for the men of Whispering Palms, it was a question of whether or not would she show; unquestionably, the most exciting part of the day.

Marty whisked the cart up and they were greeted by the swarm of elderly peepers. After hearty salutations, Billy made his way through the throng charging past the recreation hall and billiards room, across the patio, then through the pool gates. The gate's metallic click broke the girl's concentration as she was penning away at a decent clip.

And there he was. "Beelly!" she cried out in jubilation. She clapped her volume shut and dashed across the lawn hopping over sprinklers, vaulting into him, legs wrapping his torso and arms clamping his neck. "Where were you? I was waiting here since—"

"Since when? It's just after ten-clock—"

"Well, I've been waiting seence ten!" They both laughed at the oversight. "But I'm so glad you're here!" she exulted smooching his neck. "You were gone *sooo* long. How long was it? Ten days?"

"My little Mistral," he said neutrally. "See the chaos you're creating with these Q-tips?"

She cast an eye on the snowy-haired gawkers unfazed, the mischievous smile following along harmoniously. "*Je sais*, aren't they cute? I put baby oil on for them today. I like the leettle theen one with the taxi-man hat …"

"You know we are on *theen* ice here," he stated, returning her Franglais.

"So what? Why not give them a leetle fun? They'll not be here forever. Look what the poor babies go home to. *Bulldogs!* Have a heart!"

He appreciated her rebellious spirit and refreshed himself by diving into her irresistible swimming pool blues, further enhanced by the glow coming off the pool and Jacuzzi. There was nothing in doubt here aesthetically; she was a shimmering Riviera treat. "*D'ac*, you're hard to argue with."

"Don't even try—"

"Want a ride back to the house?"

"Let me get my journal," she said, sprinting back to the chair.

" 'The DV Diaries' ?"

"It's not dolce vita—it's my personal journal!"

He ignored it. "How the 'Diaries' coming along? Am I in them?" he posed artificially, fully convinced he was the star of the manuscript.

"No!" she teased, still on the run.

Billy eyed the run of stoops and screen doors, noticing three snowbirds sending grim, vituperative looks. The widowers were still spying the young woman as she pranced across the grass, performing a dancer's flying split over the last spitting sprinkler. Approaching Marty's buggy she stretched a sheer glittery linen tank over her chest, the deep maroon eyeballs peering out still and leaving little to the imagination; a final gifting.

"*Bonjour*," she offered, breaking a flawed one, her special brand of insincere shame.

"Bahn-chore," Marty responded, still flustered.

The young ones howled in unison and hopped on. Marty spun around and they sped off noiselessly down Zuni Drive, a row of interior curtains repositioning house-to-house as they passed.

"Darn-it-all, it's damned funny 'n all that, but the board put it to a vote. They're asking you two to leave the premises, no jokes—"

"They've been saying that for two years—"

"Now they're serious—with minimum-age requirements at fifty-five. Don't forget, we slipped you through special, your 'grandfather Lem Atkins' and all, who gave it to you in his will—"

"You're looping, Marty—"

"Then you done good things for folks, cart mechanics and stuff, 'n no one asked no questions—but you ain't been around, some need carts fixed, couldn't go golfin', and with Frenchy doin' her striptease, agitatin' the wives, someone went on the snoop—"

"Who?"

"That hairnet set—"

"Doc Turner?"

"The mouse wife with *cheveux bleu!*" added Frenchy, disgusted.

"When?"

"Recent-like—found out you wasn't no relation to Lem, found out more too and I don't know what's true, but they're sayin' things, plum fed up."

"Okay, Marty."

"Told ya to lay low, go about business in a low-key way, but—"

"I said okay!" Billy blasted, a crack like an engine backfiring, a frightening display.

Marty angled one over to Frenchy, but she twisted off and his disapproval died silently. Silence was the only chance at quelling Billy Six's temper.

On Cheyenne Drive, the cart slowed before a silver aluminum-sheeted unit. The screen door was topped with a hand-painted "Versailles West" sign above. The two leapt off the cart.

"*Merci*, Marty," Frenchy said, pecking him on the cheek. He nodded, saying nothing more, and coasted off down the lane.

Versailles West was a modest space with a tiny kitchen, dining area, living room, and bedroom beyond. The color scheme was peach explosion with aqua trim as Frenchy was in her second act of the palette's period. The furnishings were hippy statester meets Latin Quarter red-light French with a sprinkle of Balinese, an unavoidable dash of Arizona cowboy, and to complete the globe's circle, Native American artifacts—Hopi kachina dolls and feather rings.

"Why did you do that? He has a job. He's been very good—"

"If you kept your damned tits in your shirt this wouldn't be happening—"

"Oh yeah?"

"But you're doing it on purpose, twenty-four going on eighteen ..."

"*Quoi*? Don't geeve that young theeng Bee S—I'm an old soul! And it's a poor soul that needs to be fed—"

"Tell me the Denny's Grand Slam isn't nourishment. Two saucies, two strips of hickory smoked and a stack of buttermilks—"

"I need other things too—"

"Like what?"

"Guidance, a spiritual adviser."

"Religion?"

"I'm a seeker. On a quest—" she shot back, exaggerating now. "I'm investigating; there's Scientology, Landmark, and a man named Moon."

"Loonies. You don't need religion, you've got me."

"Yeah, Billy religion. You're a guru, a Svengali!"

He was silently intrigued, even impressed. He'd never heard her speak this way, but didn't let on. "Say what?"

"I read about them. Bo Derek had one: her husband. It's the Religion of Man and they all want the same thing—the puss-puss at home een a box tweedling thumbs while they go bang all the beavers!"

"So you're getting your spiritual guidance from *People* magazine again—"

"Old *People* magazines in the rec room! *C'est vraiment* peetiful."

Billy took in her crestfallen look; the disillusionment distilled in it he could tell was genuine and absolute.

"I know it's no life for you baby, you want out. But this is temporary; always has been, I promise—"

Reaching to wrap her, he gave her an enduring squeeze.

"I can't stand it here," she whispered, pulling from his clutches and another note of sympathy would have drawn her to tears.

"Me neither. I'm sorry."

"My life is passing by. I should be out having fun, going to parties, dancing the lambada, kissing and making love to cute guys ..."

"How challenging; don't you get the Tiffany kidney bean."

"I don't want a kidney bean. I don't want any beans. I'm sick of beans. Black beans, red beans, rice and beans, all beans!!!"

"Keep your titty-tots on," he teased.

He nearly pulled her out of it. "They're on! Can't you see?" She arched and boosted her chest higher.

"Yeah, me and every other octogenarian within ten miles."

"Jealous?"

"Only when we get kicked out on our ear—again!"

"You stop showing off your brain, I stop showing off my tits—deal?"

She extended her hand, clasping his. Instead, he toppled her thumb with his, pinning it. "Got you!"

"Not a thumb wrestle, a deal!" As she closed on his mitt again, he snatched it away. "See? You can't do it—"

"Bad business—take away your mammaries, you still have an excellent mind, that hottie 3-D mug, and a perfect pumpkin. We take away my smarts, what have I got?"

"*Buh*—" she spat French-ly. "That car, maybe!" she cracked in a burst. "Not to take away your brains, just the show-off part—"

He fell suddenly silent.

"That male ego," she said while combing through his hair. "That's okay, use it, it's a gorgeous mind, it's how I fell in love with you."

He sent his hands up her shirt and palmed her breasts. Her eyes melted and slid closed as he traced each nipple.

"These are so nice," he said. She was quiet and aroused as he fondled her. "Do you mind if I interview them?"

"Beelly!" she fired, strangling his hands and escorting them from the premises. "Don't make jokes and play with my body at the same time, I don't like it!"

"Doesn't 'no' mean 'yes' in French too?"

" 'No' means 'no' in any language!"

"I say *Hannah Montana* reruns: *NOT* just for kids—"

"You're a pig! Either that or it's Merv the Perv talking—"

"Merv the Pedophile Perv with a whistle lisp, don't sell him short! Now where were we? Oh yeah, your lumpies. What did I call them?"

On cue they blurted it simultaneously, *"HANS AND FRANZ!"* breaking up hysterically. They were the names Billy had given them.

"And I remember Hans is bigger than Franz!"

"Good memory."

"Good mammary!"

They dissolved into each other, cuddling. Soon however, Billy sounded off his best Rod Serling accent, a professional impersonator's rendition.

"*Billy Sixkiller and Mélodie 'Frenchy' de Charlebois: two desert drifters caught in a tangle of love, fate, and destiny—as family, as friends, as lovers, for better, for worse. Bonded by a past which linked them forever and haunted them into eternity; Billy and Frenchy—*"

"This is not *Zee Twilight Zone!*" she interjected. "It's our life!"

"The sweet life!" Picking it up again he played, "*You're in the driver's seat, you pass the signpost up ahead, your next stop: The Dolce Vita Zone!*"

"Want to hear what my medicine card was today?"

"Not exactly."

"Reverse Dragonfly—"

He jumped on it. "Precisely! Illusions, just like the cards!"

"I knew you were going to say that—I wrote it in my journal."

"Yeah, well …"

"Maybe I am caught in an illusion, I need to change." Frenchy weighed it seriously while studying and micromanaging a loose cuticle end.

"Not necessarily—it could mean a dream you possess is a pipe-dream, hollow without purpose, just depends on your interpretation." He huffed to divert her. "You didn't ask about the surprise—"

"The *what?* " she repeated, her eyes widening, overly dramatized.

"Don't act like you don't remember, I told you—"

"Did you?"

"Frenchy—" he challenged, appealing to her honesty.

"I love surprises," she said reluctant to cave, "especially yours because you're so crazy. Crazy people make the best surprises."

"Like bipolar people make the best love?"

Her eyes narrowed. "What bipolars have you been fucking?"

"Last chance—"

"Okay, okay. I thought about it all day!" she exploded. "What is it? *Tell me! Tell me! Tell me!* "

He raised the duffel and drew from it a wrapped box with pink ribbon. He extended it to her. She thrashed it open and her face lit up. "*Mais non!*" She held it up. "Billy, it's beautiful!"

The slender short dress was white and covered in colorful sequined butterflies. The butterfly was Frenchy's favorite living creature and she saw them as having special powers. The Butterfly animal card had been chosen by her as her totem animal and they were absolutely sacred to her.

"*C'est génial!* I looooove it. *Mais non*, I'm going to cry!"

" '*The skies are filled with butterflies,* '" he recited in verse, " '*That flutter here and there/Like flying flowers they flit for hours/and dance upon the air.*' Iitoi has been coming to me, the 'Dream of the Butterflies,' and when I saw the dress I had to get it—"

She wiped welled eyes and shot to a stand, pinning the garment to her shoulders. "It's everything a woman could want, low cut—"

"Sheer—"

"*Trés* sexy—"

"And potently symbolic—"

"The gift dream!" she twisted up. "Can I wear it now?"

"Wait, I have a double surprise—"

"A double surprise? Beelly, you shouldn't have!" she fibbed, dive-bombing right down beside him again. "What?"

"This one's especially good—we're leaving."

"Leaving?" Her eyes brightened, not yet convinced of the news.

"You heard me—"

"Leaving Apache Junction? The butthole of America?"

"That's the buttonhole of America, don't be glib."

"When, Billy, when?"

"Tonight."

"*Tonight???* " She was exultant. She stuck fingers in her mouth and unleashed an ear-piercing whistle, the way she used to cheer the Paris-St. Germaine soccer team as a schoolgirl in France, before her mother died and her evil aunt took her in prior to running away to America.

"The folks of Whispering Palms can kiss my whispering ass!"

"We are leaving, really leaving? For good?"

"Change the address on the *Paris Match* subscription, we're movin' on up! I told you baby, in the words sung by Paul Rodgers lead vocalist for Bad Company: 'Our rainbow is due!' "

She let go of her finest roller coaster shrill, "*Weeeeeeeee!!!*"

Billy extended his hand and they slow-danced to country music playing in the distance, emanating from a neighbor's unit. After several revolutions, it hit her. "So where are we going?"

"I ray, you ray, we all ray—"

"*C'est pas vrai!* Ouray???"

"The Switzerland of America!"

"No way! You are such a beautiful man!"

Ouray, Colorado was the place Frenchy had been yearning to go all her life and she had reasons for that and Billy had been promising to take her there for years. She delighted, easing into him and entwining herself around him, her eyes thinning. She tugged him down to the couch and from a distance of noses touching she nodded suggestively, pointedly.

He shook his head with equal intent. "No, *petite*—"

"If you have any guts you will—"

"I'm curious yellow then."

"You and your mixed-up philosophy. What if you're wrong?"

She rarely aired her true beliefs and sentiments as he routinely confounded her with a bombardment of philosophical and lawyerly logic. She'd unquestionably learned from him, but now prepared, she would express herself.

"We had those moments—wonderful moments—and we can have them again. When you're old, that's what you remember. It's the cement that keeps people together. No cement and the building falls apart. One day I will have to find that—and I will have to leave you."

It struck her then how important her journal was. It gave her courage. She'd just written this and now she was articulating it.

They could hear the distant whir of a lawnmower now, the music having faded. It was strangely quiet and Billy lay there absolutely still.

"That's from the 'Diaries,' isn't it?"

His intuition was keen and she would not refute it. She wanted him to know also. "We've wasted time—time we could have been making beauty."

That was her thing, her sacred mantra in life, *making beauty*.

"We do make beauty together, don't we? Every day."

She clutched his shoulders to make him face her. He resisted until she held his chin and forced his head to angle her way, revealing his

flooded eyes and the sight melted her. "Oh, Beelly," she said cradling him. "I'll never leave you, I could never leave my little baby boy."

Unbeknownst to them a handsome ten-year old boy, Genesis Giones, half-African-American, half-Mexican, was poised at the screen door. Word had quickly spread through the RV village that the boy's cherished friend had returned. Genesis loved Billy, but more than that, he revered him.

The boy had taken his Mexican father's adopted American name Jones, a man he'd never met and asked Billy to give it a gangsta-rapper's handle. Billy thought "Genesis Jones" sounded cool and thereby only altered the spelling. The boy lived part-time at his grandparents' place in the retirement community while his mother Belinda worked in Mesa, a secretary to a real estate attorney. Belinda had no formal education, but possessed fading *Ebony* magazine looks. Her boss was a smarmy, hypersexual Lothario who paid her as much for her womanly gifts and she was on call for office couch sessions when dates dried up or new seductions stalled. In addition to a regular salary, Belinda Jones received hand-me-downs from her employer's kids like the white Lacoste shirt the boy was wearing.

From the living room neither of his friends noticed Genesis looking through the screen door and he patiently watched them doze for minutes on end.

Billy's eyes bounced suddenly to a crashing disturbance. A Siamese cat had knocked over a bowl of Friskies nearby, startling him. Lifting himself from the couch, he opened the refrigerator and grabbed a bottle of water, then scratched a note before quietly slipping outside.

"We leave at midnight!" the scrawl read and a breeze nearly blew the paper from the table, but the sweat from his palms helped tack it briefly in place.

Frenchy enjoyed waking up in new places and undiscovered locales. It was always a thrilling reveal and surprise for her. Billy knew she'd be overwhelmed with delight soon with holiday fervor. Instead of dashing from bed to unwrap gifts beneath a tree at Christmastime, a custom she barely remembered, there'd be a sparkling, fresh lan.dscape to explore. They took to the road at night for this reason. That way each new day would seem like Christmas morning.

8

Surreptitiously, he drew back the silk cover stretching across the elongated chassis. With pistol raised at the ready, he silently teased the key end into the trunk lock and gave it a slight twist. In a flash, he spread the hatch placing the barrel to the prisoner's temple. But the man's eyes were already wide open, nearly white and now ablaze with terror.

"Not napping? Had you for a goner already—"

The captive's mouth showed foam trails at its corners and Billy began to cut away the duct tape covering it. He twisted off the cap of the bottled water and held it to the man's mouth.

"Ninety-four out here—how's it in there?"

The man quaffed the bottle aggressively. He was not only dehydrated, but also deathly scared, his bodily sap levels diminished and failing.

"Shouldn't be too bad; she stays cool on the hottest days—"

Roland gulped away until the captor snatched the bottle from him, offering a first opportunity to speak. Instead, the prisoner quickly averted eyes from the powerful sun. Spotting the sunglasses laying there, Billy matted them to the man's face to spare him the assault. Then he recapped the bottle and proceeded to quote verbatim, his special gift beholden to a near photographic memory.

"In 1815, at Black Buffalo's funeral Big Elk, Chief of the Omahas, said, " *'Do not grieve. Misfortunes will happen to the wisest of men. It is the command of the Great Spirit and all nations and people must obey. What is past and cannot be prevented should not be grieved for. Misfortunes do not flourish particularly in our path. They grow everywhere. Death will come and always out of season.'* "

After a brief pause he issued his own grim sequitur. "I may be back in an hour, I may be back in six; it's called random consciousness-testing, Mr. Polsonby."

Re-taping the man's mouth, he left the water bottle to roll to his rib cage and then carefully shut the hatch.

As Billy sauntered up the street, Frenchy stepped out the door of Versailles West sporting her shimmering new butterfly dress.

"Hottie-hot!" he scored it.

The little figure stepped from behind her. "Look who's here—"

"Genesis Giones—my man!"

"What up Billy? *Ungawa!!!*" He'd adopted his idol's patented Swahili greeting as Billy-speak was virulently contagious to most who met him.

The boy tore down the cement stoop and they batted forearms and knocked fists and matched snaps and wiggled finger fries until Billy snared the boy's limbs to twirl him in airplane flight formation. Genesis giggled in ecstasy as he flew around and around. When he laid him down the boy was dizzy, dazed, and disoriented, gleefully so.

"Hot shot wants to go for a ride in the Stretch. Say we go see the ostriches?"

"Not zose smellee birds—"

"Can we, Billy? I'm down, dog!"

"Soundin' more like a hip-hop scenester every time I see you. Don't tell me you been thuggified!" he teased. "What up muthafucka!" He play-boxed him too.

"Come on Frenchy! It'll be dope!"

The boy wouldn't see them much now she appraised and the loss would sadden him terribly. "Okay, *on y va!* But I have deebs on the car—to stay een eet!"

"Done! Plasmatics for the frog—"

Billy went to retrieve the big car while Genesis and Frenchy thumb-wrestled. When the car pulled up they piled three across in the front. Genesis positioned himself between the two, his favorite place in the world to be. Billy played Bad Company and they sang in unison, " '*Give me Silver, Blue, and Gold/ the colors of the sky I'm told/ my rainbow is overdue-a-whoo-hoo! …*' "

"*J'adore* his voice—"

The driver's accent suddenly went "Okie" as he dipped into Murph the Blue-Collar Roadside Cafe Trucker of America, one of his many invented characters. "Now you get Journey, Kansas, Styx, and Foreigner in concert, that's one helluva hair spray convention—"

"It's Murph!" Genesis identified. "On point!"

"All with zee bad hair."

"They ain't got no hair no more!"

The boy was in heaven and laughing from deep in his belly. It was a reprieve from the profound hurt he couldn't define and wouldn't for years with a mother away too often and a father he would never know. This tiny worm carving its way steadily into his soul was totally forgotten as long as he was in their company. "Billy—"

"Lay it on me, hot shot—"

"What do you think about the Scorps?"

"That south Phoenix gang? The Boiled Scorpions?"

"Straight up—"

"Why?"

"Been talkin' to some of the guys … They kept it real funky, telling me I should join up when I'm old enough—"

Billy wouldn't take up the discussion today and disturb the boy's present joyfulness. "Let me think about it," he said in a clipped and neutral way that offered no incentive for rebellion.

"Can we manufacture some nonsense? The Italian clothes guy?"

"*Sergio?*" Billy spouted back. "The Sleazy Euro Fashionista Designer Suit at 70%-off Salesman on Madison Avenue?"

"*Oui,* Sergio!" Frenchy piped.

"And I'm the 'Special Friend,' " Genesis signed up for.

"*Allez!*" Playacting was their cherished sport.

On cue, Billy broke into Sicilian-accented pizza English as he parodied Sergio, the scaly, unctuous salesman who'd say anything to secure a sale.

"You! Little man in the white shirt, you can't be seen wearing tiny reptiles on your nip-nips!"

"My Mom gave it to me, straight up!"

"No class! Besides, they bite!" He pinched his nipple on the Lacoste alligator, Genesis yelping.

"Come, my Special Friend!" he hammered. "Admire with your very own eyes my new collection just arrived from donkey train in Milan! The wrapping still fresh! This beige suit the color of Moroccan kings, pure wool from the finest milk-fed sheep in Tuscany, doesn't wrinkle or crease, you can cough on it and it doesn't stain …" *COUGH! COUGH!* He blasted and his audience howled in laughter.

"It is formal, yet casual; it's tasteless, yet utterly sophisticated, completely ordered, but with a whiff of chaos, naughty and yet prudish, it's déclassé yet it reeks of chic, it's conservative and yet it screams of risk, exclusively for the day, but you can wear it at night, and expensive too, but utterly affordable!"

The two chimed in.

"Fresh, yet you've seen it before!"

"Finely-tailored and yet seamless!"

"Cuffed and yet not!"

"Controlled, yet it shrills of anarchy!" Sergio added. "And I give it to you, my Special Friend, for a Special Friend Price of eighteen thousand dollars! Speak about giving it away!"

They were laughing hysterically, the parody becoming sillier.

"Predictable and yet, utterly original!"

"It's handmade, yet factory-woven!"

"It's black, yet delicately off-white!"

"It's a suit and yet it could be worn as a dress!"

"Come, little man, step up to the register!" Sergio cried. "We take all major credit cards and yet, we only want *CASH!*" He rifled a hand into the boy's pockets looking for money. It became an assault on his sensitive points—underarms, neck, and ribs—as Genesis was ticklish. The boy giggled in half.

"We are going to adopt you," Frenchy declared as she always did, and there was nothing Genesis loved to hear more.

The dust bowl ostrich farm was on the route to Globe. The terrain was rugged and a special odor greeted oncoming vehicles if windows were opened and Billy made sure of it. Pulling into the uneven dirt drive the two got out and Frenchy held her nose, repulsed. "Shut the door! Queeck!" She stayed put a moment then decided against it and got out and dove into the back of the limo wincing at the terrible smell.

Old Creek Ostrich Farm was in its own league for local charm and lore. The Farm was run by a mutt cowboy, Luis Gomez, a native southwesterner who had a mix of Spanish, Apache, and Mexican blood. In the twenty-acre pen, hundreds of ostriches were nestled in clusters, some high-stepping in the sands further out. As the pair approached they heard piercing squeals. A baby javelina charged from behind the house, disappearing into a thick of catclaw brush. The wiry Gomez dashed after, his slingshot raised, its rubber hose stretched back, set to fire another round.

"Hey Luis!"

The call distracted him enough to pause then postpone the quest.

"Fellas," he greeted. "Porker know me now," he piped proudly, his lip stuffed with chaw. "Want a dip?" He shuffled up and extended a tin of tobacco, the uneducated man speaking like a panhandler from the 1850s.

"No thanks. You plug him one?"

"Hell yes."

"What do you use for ammo?"

"Whatever I got—rocks, nails. That there been a marble. Yep, he knows me," he repeated eyes sparkled. "They git into my garden, eat all my 'tuss."

"That's tuss?"

"Lettuce. And tow-mats too. Don't want to hurt him none, just sting him so's he can eat still, but not my crops!"

"When I was sheepherding in the mountains of New Zealand, we had to keep the wolves out," Billy tossed, eyeing off in the distance.

"You been to New Zealand? Straight up?" Genesis asked.

"We'd set traps; no one likes to kill the beasts, but if they're culling your herd, that's money; each head is money."

"So what bring ya out to Old Creek?"

"Hot shot here wanted to see the action—"

"Don't got action, got birds. Want one? Make fine burgers."

Billy dropped out, suddenly reflecting on a potentially loaded situation back at the car. Leaving Frenchy alone may not have been wise.

"Came to see how you're doing," Billy reiterated, but Luis didn't bat an eye at the clumsy loop in dialogue.

"Fine—was up there on the ruhf at four-thirty this mornin'."

"What were you doing up there?"

"Ruhfin'," he spat flatly. "Couple leaks, so I was brushing tar. Gotta do it early when it's cool; tar git hot, you betcha …"

Billy knew the man well enough. The year before, he'd repaired his vintage transport truck. Luis was over sixty and a war veteran. A tunnel specialist, it was his special duty to go deep into the vast network of underground tunnels the Viet Cong had dug to flush the enemy out; a dangerous assignment. Tunnelers may have lacked qualities, but courage was not one of them, and Luis saw as much hell as any soldier should ever endure. "Killed more people by the time I was twenty-one than Billy the Kid done his whole life," he often repeated.

"Can we see the ostriches now?" Genesis spouted anxiously.

In the car's rear cabin, Frenchy was tuned into Court TV on the HD screen. It tickled her to witness the dramas of what she considered the underprivileged masses airing oddball grievances before a television judge to get some "US justice," Billy's term for no justice at all. The episode featured a woman accusing a male neighbor of angling cameras at her shower, though he claimed to have been recording a jet plane air show overhead.

As Frenchy lay there transfixed, a sudden thump resounded in the car. There was a follow-up noise, then the unmistakable sound of water leaking. She jumped out to investigate. Peering beneath the car, she located a thin trickle of fluid falling from what seemed the trunk. It flowed for seconds and then stopped as suddenly.

After another brief interval a third thud was heard.

She gasped. "*Mais non …*" was mumbled under her breath.

The fearful woman advanced on the trunk cautiously one step at a time. After a pause she tapped once quickly on the fender and stepped back.

Immediately her tap was returned. She swallowed with difficulty. After three more communicative taps, three heavy bangs were returned. Her face contorted and then she screamed it. "*BEEELLLY!!!*"

The man was already sprinting down the dirt drive and when he came within thirty feet, she bellowed, "*Who is in there???*"

"Frenchy—" he cautioned, eyeing her steadily.

"Tell me!"

His face hung to a swollen, stupid regard and remained there.

"It's him."

Her eyes froze momentarily before rolling back in their sockets and the winds of life released from her lungs. From where she stood, she reeled then collapsed to her knees lifelessly like a rag doll and with no resistance from her leg joints; she spiraled further and flat to the ground.

"No, no, no," she repeated, rolling on her back, sobbing uncontrollably.

Billy bent low beside, almost stroking her. "It will be fine."

"*Mais non*, Billy. It's definitely, definitely *not fine!*"

"You know—"

"I know the damned story!" she blasted. "Your damned story!" she shouted louder. "How could I forget? Didn't you learn your lesson? They will lock you up and eat the key!" She crumpled back helplessly, sprawling, her malapropism making it all the more painful to witness. "This is your idea of *making beauty?*"

She was innocent of his affairs; this was his business, his nasty revenge business, his and only his business—and he knew it. He was getting her involved in something he shouldn't. She was so young and already a victim to her own troubling past. He was damaging her and it came to him clearly and starkly he'd been dead wrong, not about abducting the perpetrator, but by trying to bring her along, to keep their family of two together, selfishly so.

He crouched close trying to console her.

Raising knees high, she bowed her head against them. Her crown shook, the "no"s repeated, barely audible.

"It's all my fault," he avowed. "I promised to take you to Colorado. I mixed it with my affairs. It's my cross to bear and only mine. It was a mistake, Frenchy, and I'm so damned sorry."

The brutal sincerity of his rare apology produced another extended silence.

Eventually, she angled up and asked him soberly, "You have the right guy?"

He nodded, his eyes freshly aflame with conviction.

"How do you know?"

"Frenchy, I know."

She said it resolutely. "Then do it."

"What?"

"Do it, Beelly—"

"You mean now?"

"If you are absolutely sure, do it now and get it over with. Drop us off and drive off far away into the desert and do it."

"I can't."

"You can't? What do you mean you can't?"

"You know—"

"Yeah, I know," she snarled, shooting to her feet. "*Tu es fou!*"

"—It wouldn't be honorable—"

"It is killing!" she roared. "Killing is never honorable, Billy! It never has been and never will be! It is taking life! Read any book of faith! Worldwide! Any one!"

"I have read them—all."

She counted off on her digits. "The Ten Commandments, the Koran, Buddhism, the Bible, the Great Spirit, they all say it's wrong, it is a sin, the biggest sin! There is no honor in it, Billy!!!"

"There is—"

"*Tu parles!* For those who make their own codes to suit wrong and evil ways. They're not heroes or warriors, they're not seeking justice, they are killers, cold-blooded killers! Everything that makes me wish I wasn't a part of this damned world!" she bawled, dropping to the ground again, her arms scraping the dirt.

He knelt beside her as if genuflecting in a pew. He spoke piously. "I have prayed for it. It is my destiny."

The tears flowed from her dripping into her lap soaking a once-white butterfly dress. Blood trails curved at her elbow.

"I know," she allowed. "But not mine."

With that declaration, a chip was taken from his face, but he would not try to persuade her, not ever again.

"Not this time," she underscored rising up. With a composed and graceful combination, she floated forward to the car, but her toe snagged a jagged rock, stubbing it. *"Merde!"* Frustrated, she swung open the passenger door and got in, slamming it.

Genesis had been feeding the birds grain pellets, but was now bored and missing his friends. Tossing off what remained in his palm, he dashed down the dirt track. Billy gazed upon the Superstitions that were piling mightily and painted in that late afternoon golden-green hue. The weakened sun had receded and he took in the preliminary purple-pink tracers of the Southwest's billion-dollar sky.

"He let me feed 'em!" the boy cried out.

"You don't say," Billy droned. "Let's go."

The drive west on Highway 60 was void of conversation and noticeably tense. Genesis sensed the discord, but it didn't prevent him from at least trying to incite more shenanigans with his friends.

"Billy—? Can we do the funny foreign ones?"

He sighed. "All foreigners are funny, last I knew—"

"The Frenchies—"

"Claude and Justine—?"

"Yeah, them!"

"Not today, hot shot." Drained of spark, Billy was repenting still.

Genesis knew where to file his appeal. "Frenchy? You be Justine and start it off—"

Gazing upon the passing desert expanse dejectedly, she'd withdrawn, mired in all the troubling meditations.

"What do you call 'em, Billy?"

He roll-called it off, devoid of any enthusiasm. " 'The Desperately Wealthy Excessively Bored Eurotrash Romance.' "

"That's it! And they live in New York, right? Sittin' at those fancy tables drinking coffee, smoking lots of cigarettes—"

"In Soho, Cipriani Downtown on West Broadway," he supplied again, feeling for the boy. "They smoke Gauloises …"

"And sit all apart and don't look at each other, their legs are crossed with buggy sunglasses and they hate America—"

"Fine recall, Gionesy."

Spying the boy secretly and his freshly brightened smile redirected Frenchy from weightier matters. She envisioned the full scope of his life and its shortcomings and how uplifted he seemed now. Time spent with them was uniquely nourishing to his spirit, a temporary pause from the hardship and disadvantage. In an elitist Parisian dialect from the 16th *arondissment* she charitably initiated the Franglais parody chat.

"*Woof,* Claude," she labored. "*Quel ennui*, I'm so bored—"

Billy lit up a cig, heartened Frenchy was engaging. "*Bah-oui*, Justine," he followed. "I cannot stand eet, but what are we to do?"

"These damn *Américains!*" she scoffed in disgust, her harsh pronunciation of "Américains" making Genesis burst out every time.

"They are so *primitifs!* " he returned, with more contempt.

"*Voilà!* And no class! *Tu as un feu?* " she posed while he reacted, miming to light her up with a match.

"I meess Paris—the ceety of love, culture, and romance," he said.

Justine turned away from her lover, puffing her own imaginary cigarette. Claude was angled off also, pretending to pinch the tiny handle of an espresso. "Where are we going this summer, Claude?"

"*Buh* … Cap Ferrat, Porto Cervo. As long as we get away from these damn *Américains!* "

"They are so crude!"

"And without the *bon goût!*"

"With their Starbucks and Geico and Beliebers and Burger King! *Quel horreur!*"

"But my leetle *oiseau* Dodo?"

Frenchy chuckled herself, increasingly amused. "*Oui, ma petite?*"

"When are we going back to Paris—ze ceety of love, culture, and romance?"

"Our friends have all left, *tu sais?*"

"Zere are no Parisians left?"

"Zay call Paris 'Little Morocco' now!"

"I've heard New Tunisia! Ees that like New England?"

"Little black mustaches are een, *tu sais?*"

"*Mais no! C'est pervers!*"

"*Mais oui!* Just like when Adolf visited Paris—the city of love, culture, and romance. Ah, the memories," she said, dipping into nostalgia. "All those handsome blond men," came out as if unintentionally.

"Justine!" he snapped, jealously.

"*Nein*, I mean, *non*, just thinking about when I had my hair like Marlena, I mean Marilyn, *chérie.*"

Genesis ate up the skits, his head twisting back and forth. He didn't understand the politics or particulars involved, but took it in no less joyfully.

"Ah ya," she sighed, colossally bored once more. "And thees autumn?"

"*Buh.* Maybe Punte, maybe Rio."

"*Chérie*, this espresso ees too small—"

"Should we go get a real cup of coffee—?"

"Een a beeg cup!"

"And we know where! Where zay write your name on zee cup!"

"Where we first met! Starbucks uptown!"

"No it was Starbucks on Spring Street!"

"*C'est vrai!*"

"Let's get the hell out of this place and all these damn *Américains!* They are so *primitifs!*"

"And *dégolas!*"

"*Chérie?*"

"*Oui?*"

"I heard zere are Starbucks een Paris now—"

"*Mais non!*"

"*Bah oui!*" she sang. "Near Odeon even!"

They said it simultaneously. "*C'est pervers!!!*"

"Tooey!" Claude mock-spit.

"*Alors petite*, zen we steell have somezing to go back for!"

"*Voilà!*"

The two players exploded, drawing the curtain on their absurdist theater.

"Dope!" Genesis clapped and cheered. "Damn, Billy, how do you speak French?"

"I lived in Paris back in the eighties, on Rue Dauphine right off the Seine. It's in the Sixth—"

"Straight up? Damn. Where haven't you lived?"

Frenchy admired again the passing vista as the sky glowed increasingly purple with mauve, pink, and orange streaks.

"Travel is fuel for the soul, hot shot—the best fuel. Become a Road Scholar like Frenchy and me …"

"I want to speak French too—"

"Ask Frenchy, she's an original. She's from Mante-La-Jolie!" he said teasing. Genesis laughed, it sounded so strangely funny.

"Am not!" she shot back. "*You* are from Mante-La-Jolie!"

It was Billy's running joke. Mante-La-Jolie was an economically depressed, predominantly French-Arab ghetto suburb of Paris. Translated, it meant "Mante the pretty," but in reality, it was not considered safe and was anything but pretty.

"I am from Vernon—"

"Right by Mante! And she summers in Riverhead—it's in the Hamptons, but not quite!" he ribbed. "Frogette's from all the hot spots!"

"Vernon is close to Giverny where Monet lived and Monet was a *real* genius," she countered pointedly. "And it is very beautiful."

"Now how sexy does that sound? When she says 'bew-tee-full?' Come on, hot shot, you gotta hear that. Say it again Frenchy—"

She boosted her lips beyond their normal hornet-stung swollen, exaggerating it. "*B-YOO-TEE-FULL!*"

The boy was speechless and didn't know why. She gave him a wink.

"Are you two going to get married?"

"Billy doesn't believe in it."

"You don't, Billy?"

"I am married. To Frenchy. We're life partners."

"*Woof!*—in your mind. More Billy religion."

"By the way, I'm not a guru. I'm a wizard."

"Okay, *Merlino*, whatever," she said, noting she'd opted for the Italian version of the famous sorcerer's name.

They pulled into Whispering Palms and Genesis ran off to his grandparents place on Cherokee Drive. He was late and his mother was just leaving her job in Mesa. She would go home and watch television and steam through a pack and sigh, contemplating the following day when she would pick up Genesis after work. She was looking forward to seeing his little button face; it had been a week already.

At Versailles West, Frenchy poured Billy an iced tea and he downed the glass in one gulp. He then stepped outside and she joined him to see him off. They strolled silently and sadly down the alleyway.

"Which way are you going?"

"North—"

"I won't ask where, I know you have it worked out." She eyeballed him penetratingly, as mysterious a woman's look as she'd ever given to him. "Are you going to call me?"

"I'll fax you," he said, teasing.

"Be careful, Beelly." She redirected her attention to the car, focusing on the rear of the chassis. "So eet's really heem—"

"Double-downed."

She moved in, squeezing him, and water seeped into her turquoise pool blues. She pulled back to study his eyes. They were aglow with traces of white; perhaps it was the reflection of the sky. She couldn't be sure, but something was there and it was almost angelic. His traits were contradictions and they confounded her, as did much about him still. She whispered it. "*Je t'aime*, Beelly."

"I hope, baby doll. I need it."

Fading back from him, she spun and ran. She didn't look back and he was stuck there waiting for at least some further sign of the significance of the moment, if not a full reversal of decision, but she never turned around. He kicked the asphalt only to smooth it over as if it was grass.

Billy maneuvered the vehicle to the security gate of the resort and vaulted out. He hauled Marty from the shack and gave him a full Comanche hug. "You know the deal," he said conspiratorially.

"Yeah, I ain't seen you—like usual." Though he wouldn't show it Marty loved Billy Six. He was the most electrifying person he'd ever encountered, his wacky stunts reminding him of his own high-octane days. The elderly man caught it first over Billy's shoulder. "You forgettin' somethin'?"

Billy pivoted.

She was advancing unevenly, her face puffy from crying, lips swollen, expression determined, exhibiting that indomitable Frenchy spirit. She was dragging a suitcase covered in peace signs on rollers behind.

"Baby—"

"Beelly!" she cried, dropping the suitcase and sprinting to him. She sprung into his arms. "I had to come!"

"Little Mistral—" He squeezed her with all he had. "My favorite playdate has come back to me—"

"I would never live with myself if something happened to you!" It was true; she feared this trip, deeply to her core.

"I'd never let you forget it—"

"My life is—" And she couldn't complete it in words.

"With me?"

"Shucks, I'm gonna cry," Marty piped, lifting his sweaty cap.

She heaved again. "I'm having my period," he added to discount the sentimentality though Marty didn't pick up on it. She blew Marty kisses and piled in the car. In the rearview she spied herself. *'Woof!* Look what the *chat* dragged een—"

Billy stored the suitcase in the rear cabin while giving Marty instructions to show Versailles West to prospective buyers. Then he burnt rubber out of the retirement community, never to be seen again.

"*Merde!* I forgot all my toilet things!"

"S'what *Caffè Sette-Undici* is for." It was Billy's Italian coining for 7-Eleven.

Up the road Billy pulled the Stretch into the rear of a local gas hop, shielding the car from sight. Frenchy grabbed water, tampons, and Tex-Mex chips. While waiting in the queue, she reviewed a mental list, relieved she'd remembered and packed her most coveted possession, which was a comfort.

"Howdy, Frenchy," the decrepit clerk croaked, identifying the local starlet instantly, while his grin buzzed with a peeper regular's enthusiasm. He was about as old as water.

"Hi," she returned sweetly, not recognizing him at all.

9

The Stretch penetrated ten miles into the meandering Route 88, the Apache Trail, cutting past the Superstition Mountains home of the Apache Thunder Gods and the man-made lakes. The Trail had been used by Indians for centuries and later stagecoaches and covered wagon trains of new settlers west, the cavalry, too. The receding range gave way to golden hills rising and falling steadily with tall saguaro perched spottily on the lookout, the failing light transforming the rock canyon walls from rust-red to a pale yellow-green.

"Did you give him anything to drink?"

"Water—"

"It spilled." He reacted sharply. "But Billy, I don't want to see him, I want nothing to do with him." And she was adamant.

"You won't have to—"

"I don't want to be a 'whatever' if you get caught."

"An accomplice? You won't be. And I won't get caught—"

The Stretch veered sharply off the route, hard-charging directly into the rough landscape. As the vehicle crosscut the Sonoran granular, deserts dusts, red, purple, and yellow, shot up from behind.

"What are you doing?"

"Sit tight—"

The off-road tactic was performed in switchback and only the desert savvy need apply for the detour. The sharp rocks could slice a tire in seconds, but Billy's custom steel radials were designed to take the punishment. The man knew the terrain; he'd grown up on it and lived off it. The Sonoran Desert had been his home, his own private playground.

The seven hours Roland Polsonby had been held captive on that blistering October day, he'd had the time to consider his predicament. His plans had been upset once again in a most bizarre and extraordinary way. His attempt to leave the earth was perhaps not meant to be, at least the way he'd planned it.

Who was this man and what did he really want? Was he attempting to scare him while waiting to secure a ransom? Or did he truly believe Roland was responsible for the murdering of his parents and was exacting his revenge? Roland had been in the southwest in Tucson at the approximate time of the crime; he'd calculated that. Oddly, he'd rehashed the memory in his dream the day before. Was there a legitimate mix-up?

There were unique features to the desperate situation as well. The temperatures had been torrid outside, yet the trunk's interior remained cool indicating his captor had had the forethought to install a superior cooling system. The abduction therefore had been likely planned either to avenge the killing of his parents or something else, but it seemed wholly premeditated with perhaps deadly intent.

The prisoner could overhear conversations through the air ducts, but he was less certain that had been allowed intentionally. He'd absorbed the banter, skits, and "manufactured nonsense." He'd listened in on the quarrel outside too, which implied the captor had performed an abduction once before having fingered the wrong guy. In a perverse way he couldn't help but be intrigued by this disturbed man. Gifted in his ability to memorize quotations, pass in and out of foreign languages, domestic accents and dialects, the man had enough of a keen sense of world events and cultures to satirize and present them humorously, theatrically, politically, and—off the cuff. The dialogues were brilliant; the prisoner had even laughed twice. This man Billy was learned, charismatic, and funny.

The strange respect, even appreciation, he held for his abductor fell to the outskirts of rational thought as he'd been through a hell of an ordeal, traveling for two days with little sleep. He'd been beaten twice now, his nose fractured, the physical punishment considerable, the emotional letdown undeniable. Yet Roland found himself not fatigued, rather, on pins and needles, energized and listening intently as he tried to extract more information from this uncommon, dangerous, and psychopathic man and the predicament he'd placed him in.

At the bottom of a desert valley, the car was docked beneath a rolling thick of creosote brush that formed an overhang, shielding the vehicle from all vantage points. The trunk snapped open suddenly and the gun barrel was pressed to the captive man's temple again, Billy's finger feathering the trigger. He'd again anticipated the man succumbing, which was not the case.

"Okay, Polsonby, vacation's over."

He belted the gun then and drew out a serrated knife, the prisoner's eyes alighting. "It's not for you," the captor said. "I'm not like you, unceremoniously breaking contracts—I keep my word …"

Roland eyed him, more than a touch confounded. Not even his wife knew he'd broken with his publisher. The man had investigated him thoroughly.

Billy cut the tape away and unpeeled it, taking precaution not to rip skin or snag hair. "Heard you had a spill—"

Free to speak now, the captive only nodded, balking at another invitation to respond verbally.

"Or was it a pee? You can confess …"

Though the man was sharp, the prisoner recognized his unpredictability. A remark taken the wrong way could get him hurt, even offed. That was his ultimate fear and cause for trepidation; not the act of murder, but what the man would do with his body. His plans of being laid to rest next to his boy might never be realized and he'd never be able to guide Gerritt through the darkness. That was his gut-wrenching fear.

Billy disappeared momentarily, returning with a water bottle. He gave it to him and the prisoner downed nearly all of it.

"Conserve, you're in 'the nasty'—that's slang for deep desert," he said, eyeballing him as he lay there. "I can understand you being shy, you're in shock. It lasts a few hours. Don't mind if you express yourself, but no yelling; that cuts everything short for you, you follow?"

The captor hung on a reaction and Roland offered a short nod, wondering if it was better to speak and thwart any potential flashes of unpredictability. He was walking a thin line.

On curious delay, Billy proffered, "I think it's too formal. Reminds me of a schoolteacher I had, Mr. Potts. Hated his guts. Mind if I call you Roland?"

Polite, even respectful now, the man appeared almost fragile; and if the prisoner didn't know better he'd think Billy was enjoying this, if not his company in particular. The man had been absolutely brutal with him, but was now acting peaceful and reflective and not the maniac who'd belted him to a red gush.

"No," Roland uttered hoarsely, communicating for the first time.

Billy angled over sharply. "So you do talk—"

With the gun still tucked in his belt, he severed the wind of tape binding the man's legs and gestured for him to get out. Roland struggled awkwardly to right himself without a free hand. When his legs finally spilled from the trunk, he fell to earth like a sack of grapefruit.

"How about 'Rollie?' Anyone call you that?"

Panting, he cleared his throat. "No one. Ever."

"I like Rollie; mind if I call you Rollie?"

He decided then it was the proper moment to initiate a dialogue and glean information if he could. "May I ask you a question?"

"S'what I'm here for—"

"Why did you say 'the vacation is over?' "

"Coulda been the sleeping Disney dwarf for all I knew … You take a nap?" He shook. "Too bad; was your last chance to recharge. Now I'm going to watch you—"

Billy Six's powerful arms raised him to a stand, the prisoner's hands still bound. Then he rummaged through the trunk.

"Not making a run for it? Desert would eat you alive anyway, someone with your makeup—"

He dared it. "And what is my makeup?" As soon as he said it he wished he hadn't. It was an attempt to pick the man's brain, but it came off as challenging. The captor didn't appear to take offense, however.

"Soft," he sent back. "Cowardly. Nine handicap NARP kind of guy. Puffing ultra lights in the Geronimo Room of the P.V. Country Club." Billy was now wielding a pair of shiny antique silver handcuffs inlaid with mother of pearl. "Know what I'm saying?" he finished tauntingly.

"Narp?"

"An acronym: Not a real person. That's you." Roland was reminded of the acronym term in his dream. "Unless you feel like killing someone—"

In that instant the captor's mood changed from amicable to dark and deliberate as he pushed behind to cuff a wrist. Roland spun it for comfort's sake and it came off more a tug. Just as fast, Billy had the serrated hunting blade tickling the man's throat.

"Just a whisper of an excuse to slice your straws is all I need—"

Roland stood there trembling. He remained frozen and still.

"Save me a lot of premium gas pesos—"

Billy took a few deep breaths to calm himself, then severed the mass locking the rings to his wrists and—snap! "Pack up the palominos, Rollie, you're ridin' in style now—"

"Oh?"

"Happy days, I'm your driver. Just like old times—" He shoved the prisoner toward the car. "But I'm gonna have to silence you. Anything you want to say 'fore I do? Confession, maybe?"

The captor stepped in close and delivered it strangely intimate.

"Come on, Rollie, right under the gentle desert moonlight, the twinkling stars, like Miró's constellation series. Remember the 'Diamond Smiles at Twilight?' "

Billy's pupils had expanded now, nearly fully dilated. The prisoner would become familiar with this uncommon attribute as he listened cautiously, still terrified and in shock.

"You must know Joan Miró, the greatest modern Catalan artist—next to Gaudí and Picasso. Sorry, Joan, but they did you one better. And Dali, except for his house in Port Lligat, he was the Dennis Rodman of the bunch. You know Dennis and Dali have the same birthday? May 13th. But I'm champion of the underdog and Miró is a prime example. He invented a fresh pictorial language, a communion of the heavenly and the terrestrial achieving a transcendent poetry through visual means," he projected professorially as if to a lecture hall crowd, his hand gesturing high to low, from the sky to earth.

"Miró once said, *I have always valued the poetic content according to its visual possibilities, the xoc inicial is of prime importance.*' It's all in the initial shock, shock spelled with an 'X'—it's Catalan. Kinna the way you're feeling now, Rollie—dazed by the initial shock. And that's okay, more than okay, it's totally understandable."

Billy craned up at the midnight blue sky. His eyes spun back and were now as black as eight balls. "It's all ready for you, twilight, inching in on blackness of night, a blacktop backdrop. Use primary colors and Miró's alphabet, the moon, the stars, some birds, the sun. That's the language, make it memorable, Miró-memorable. Be the artist, Rollie, and give it to me. Your confession. Some initial shock on a blacktop backdrop—and don't you forget the diamond smile."

Roland assessed he'd just witnessed his first glimpse of the real man. He was starving, starving to be heard and more. He chanced it a second time.

"Who are you?"

"Who am I? The better question is, *who are you?* " His eyes were not only burning black, but aglow as though he was possessed. "And I'm here to tell you, until I get bored, of course—"

Billy swiveled away then, turning his back on the man.

" 'Eccentric' … 'Odd' …" he commenced. "Those were the words Phoenicians used to describe him. The city may not have been top-tier cosmopolitan, but it knew what it liked and held its own unique pulse to America's heartbeat. Unquestionably it knew 'odd' when it saw it and if you knew him at all he was an offbeat figure; but from the outside it seemed there was a measured twist beyond that. Roland Polsonby, if nothing else was a strange bird."

The man's delivery was noteworthy, offered in past tense as if written and memorized. Roland was immediately captivated.

"To look at him you wouldn't perceive anything wrong. He was forty-five, but looked ten years younger. His hair dark, he had all of it and from frosted temples, a sharply-angled hairline sliced back like that of a forties movie star; his carriage erect, the shoulders slumping, but not overly so, and thick legs which made him a tough tailback to tackle in high school. Physically, he was in decent enough shape, the genetic luck of the draw, but if you got behind his sunglasses you found the difficulty; not the creases commensurate with middle age or the distinguished crow's feet—it was in the beams—the hollowed gaze, the pain, the loss, the guilt and surrender. That was if you got behind the eye shields. They never left his face."

Still angled away, Billy directed his oratory to the oncoming blackness of night, addressing a no-doubt mesmerized audience hidden somewhere in the desert undergrowth. His delivery was energetic and consumed and it came off like a story, a novel perhaps, and the most remarkable aspect: it was not fiction, not any of it.

"What can be said is, everything led to it; everything led from it. The man could not escape it nor did he even attempt to fight it. He'd have it no other way. Roland Polsonby no longer gave effort; giving effort was for those who hadn't found out yet.

"He'd had his moment, having achieved his acclaim, but when it got tough, and it stared at him straight in the face with hotly contesting eyes, a mounting pressure ready to devour the insecure and conquer the underequipped, he eyed the challenge with nothing to give, the glossy glaze to a capitulated gaze, without flame, without fire.

"The move west was the beginning of the end. He hadn't planned it that way; he'd assumed new parts of the world, new stories to uncover, new books to write. Money made them comfortable, but Polsonby never ran his life according to sums of money. He wasn't frugal, he just was not material, money had not been his undoing, he'd simply let it go.

"If you inquired, he had the smooth intelligence to swirl you a taut, meaningful answer concerning the topically significant subject matter to his latest work replete with literary buzzwords like 'pathos,' 'long second act,' and 'parallel narrative,' and a high-brow title like, 'Until the End of Now,' and protagonists 'Elias' and 'Pilar' too, offering the impression he held a passion for his southwestern historical tome still; but really they were crafty, conversational techniques of an experienced yet untested demi-raconteur, perfected over years on the Manhattan gala charity circuit, Hamptons country club porches, the finest dress up and get extraordinary Fifth Avenue cocktail soirées …"

He'd uncovered his undecided names of characters also and the prisoner remained planted there, incredulous.

"This is not to say he couldn't turn a beautiful phrase or didn't possess a gift; he'd never had the guts to use it, spending the last years coasting along with little professional resistance except what it took to press a primary-colored tee into the earth and making sure higher octane fuel was pumped into the Benz. Sure he had 'friends' and an office and a secretary named Margaret Hardardt, but they were exercises that blew his bangs back and little else—" The man twisted around suddenly. "Sound familiar?"

Billy's face had lost its captivated glow as though the subject had become a burden, boring him more than anything. He then spouted off quickly like a soldier in response to the prisoner's initial query.

"Billy Sixkiller, born 'Dennis Roy,' adopted member of the Havasupai tribe of the Havasupai Nation, Supai, A-Z, that's postal code for Arizona—" Rolling back his sleeve, he displayed proudly the multi-colored tattoo with its tribal shield and "Havasu Baaja," the tribe's name written in Supai.

"I'm part Native-American, part Irish, part Bad Company, and part Confederate—a dedicated champion of the little guy, and mom and pop business. And limousine liberal. And I fly the crimson cross … I don't mind telling you because you will be gone—"

"What does 'adopted member' mean?"

"Don't get all Mount Gay and tonic-chatty with me—"

"They know what you're up to now, Mr. Sixkiller?"

"Does who?"

A second glimpse of the man was coming through. He was regressing to earlier form and seemed absolutely unbalanced. Roland played it cautiously.

"The tribe."

They glared at each other and not hatefully. The regard was something different, perhaps substantive and charged, but its energy was vague and confused, perhaps paradoxical, or not. In fact, neither of their advanced masteries of psychology could put a finger on it. Billy wasn't used to being appealed to in this passively judgmental, but no less paternal way. Frenchy was his only confidant and as she was either adoring or rebellious, she was not reliable in her criticism. They were too close. Yet this man placed under extreme conditions was appealing to him, to his moral code, or perhaps something else, something more profound. Billy had a moral code, a proud one, though the man couldn't know that. Or did he?

"Billy—?" the voice cut in from the black of night behind.

Frenchy was standing by the passenger door awaiting his response intimidated by monstrous silhouetted shapes of piling desert brush and darkness and only then did Roland see her a first time. She didn't appear as he'd imagined, she was taller and decidedly more attractive as in, stunningly beautiful.

She wheeled around and posed, "Did you finish pee—," but noticing the prisoner she gasped and hurriedly ducked back inside the car. *"Merde!"* was shouted from within.

"She's French," Billy offered wryly. "Little snooty about traveling with you. Too bad because I know what a fine conversationalist you are—"

"I understand the French part."

The captor stiffened at the sardonic comment lobbed back and without warning he marched up and cracked the man across the face. Roland fell to the ground, a sanguinary stream reappearing at the corner of his mouth.

"Don't get cute, Rollie. Your temple is looking slug-friendlier by the minute." He drew in a deep breath. *"Oof-mah,"* he released.

After spreading tape across the captive's freshly bloodied mouth again he piled him into the limo's rear interior. He looped the wire lock fastened to the door through the cuffs, locking him inside.

Billy got in and turned over the motor as Frenchy remained silent. It left them with the buzz of the shortwave radio and the low rumble of the engine. She caught him eyeing her in her side-view, prompting her to shake her head disapprovingly. Then he sped off. The Sonoran cave bats flew, jackrabbits hopped in flight, and field mice scattered as the car tore through the thick and fast blackness enveloping the after hours desert.

10

The Dolce Vita Diaries II

I don't like writing when it is my time of the month. I become mushy, gossipy and too emotional. I like to make observations about life, but not as a child pouring a heart out. Like a sponge being squeezed and all the dirty water pouring into the sink. It's dégolas. Some things you leave alone and don't write. Or even whisper.

If I write everything I am feeling I will become too upset. That man is here and Billy is in danger. I have spontaneous tears.

The Apache Trail had been designated an historical landmark by preservationists and federal edict ordered that it remain unpaved dirt track for twenty miles. There were runnels, bumps, and potholes in the dusty road and the car wound down it roughly and steeply. The vehicle shook and vibrated as it hugged the dangerous pass through Fish Creek Canyon, the same thoroughfare used by racecars in the early 1900s. Many deaths in the interest of sport had been caused by its treacherous drop-offs.

"Turns are making me sick—"

"Almost done," Billy put to her. "Any requests?"

"I'm hungry … And I need a *femme* stop—"

Passing the Reavis Trailhead and Apache Lake, the car motored onward to the Roosevelt Dam completed by President Teddy in 1911. Billy purposely veered past the touristy Inspiration Point parking lot which offered a scenic view. Frenchy knew not to use a public bathroom, as this road trip was different from their previous excursions. When she returned from her nature's call she seemed even more downcast.

"Looky down there—" he said, indicating the dam. "Where Phoenix gets all her juice for your blow dryer—"

"I don't use a blow dryer," she huffed. Once again he'd forgotten her personal habits, which was always annoying to her.

"When you want Stevie Nicks hair, you do."

"That was Halloween."

"Yes'm, the 'One-Winged Dove' which was the shit. At the haunted hotel in Jerome, 'member?"

He eased the Stretch back onto the road. Perceiving her funk, he hoped to wrestle her from any further dip in morale. It would make the coming hours easier.

"It's nearly upon us," he cast forth.

"What?"

"The golden age—of Aquarius, that is. Technology and innovation will take over ... Already has." He waited on a reaction, but she offered none.

"We're Aquarians, babycakes. It's our time. Every age lasts two thousand years, so it's all about us for the next two millennia. The solar eclipse of August '99 signaled the end of the Age of Pisces, during which we saw the rise of spirituality and religions, even Christianity. But now it's over, the fanatics are dying off—the evil ones too—the ones murdering and treating the better gender horribly. They're going extinct along with the dictators—primitives going the way of the past—like the Cro-Magnons ousted the Neanderthals; they're finished, they know it, it's why they hit the towers, it's why ISIS came into being, a last, desperate fail Mary—"

"Billy, this is depressing me so—"

"But it's going to be great. This new age upon us is a golden age of unity. And peace. Only thirty years away—" He started singing and not half-badly.

> " *'When the moon is in the seventh house,*
> *And Jupiter aligns with Mars,*
> *Then peace will guide the planet,*
> *And love will steer the stars,*
> *This is the dawning of the Age of Aquarius,*
> *Age of Aquarius!*
> *Aquarius!*
> *A-quar-i-us!'* "

Finishing off the chorus, he launched the pop quiz. "Who sang it? Come on, what group?"

"Beelly—"

"The Fifth Dimension—you know that!"

"Enough," she said despondently. Her lids were overflowing and water trailed down her face on both sides.

With an eye on the highway ribboning ahead, he'd give it one more try. It was his way: relaxed, but sensitized overkill.

"Halloween is coming, what do you want to be?"

She was stripped and disturbed enough to have a raw response, about to say "free." She knew not to let controversial, much less incendiary thoughts slip from her mouth when menstruating, however, especially with Billy. Her dour truthfulness could spark the fragile hold he had on his temper, a temper forever laying at the ready, on a slow burn, on a trickle charge for chaos and disaster.

"Let's go," she pleaded while spearing a hand into her suede, multi-colored Flower Power bag. She drew pills and downed them.

"Period letdown?"

She ignored him. "You've got this worked out, right?"

"We drive by night, we play by day—"

"Can he hear us?"

"No, it's soundproof with the partition closed."

Knowing that she would not be heard, she would speak candidly. She waited for her breathing to calm itself. She took another deep breath. "Don't get upset with what I have to say …"

"Upset? Me? Baby, I'm just so thrilled you're here with me—"

"—but I'm going to say it again. Promise you won't get upset?"

"Promise—"

"Please, hear me now—*do it.*"

"Do it?"

"For us, for you, for me. Do it. *Now.*"

"Frenchy—" His head began to teeter in peaceful disagreement.

"The longer you wait the more difficult it will be—"

"You don't think I'll go through with it?"

"I mean to *get away with* it—"

"It's all going to plan—"

She felt weak. She didn't have strength for an argument. Only compromise. "I'll help you," she boosted.

"You will? You mean I have your blessing?"

"No." She bowed her head, not thrilled with the concession. "You have my permission. As your sister, lover, family member, whatever you think I am to you, I advise you to do it. And I pray I'm saying the right thing. If he did what you say he did then I hope God sees it the same way. I pray He does."

Billy was struck by her words. He wrapped her with his free arm. "So will you?"

"Where do you think he'd like to expire?"

She hesitated, hopeful he'd act now on her advice. "I don't know."

"I mean, we have choices. Lots."

Her forehead surrendered to smooth, her expression brightening. "Where there's the least traffic," she counseled with renewed vigor.

"Don't worry about traffic, he won't be missed for another day. He's supposed to be on a business trip. By then we'll be on the rez and no one'll find us there—"

"How do you know he's on business?"

"I've only had seven years to prepare for this, snookums—"

It had been seven years since Billy's previous offense when he was tried and convicted of abducting Alexander Clemmons, holding him hostage for several days. He had served five years in prison for the crime in the Arizona State Penitentiary in Flagstaff.

"Specifically—"

"I know his secretary."

"You do? *Une femme?*"

"Baby, I'm all about preparation."

Though not one for gratuitous adventures of the flesh, Billy could seduce any woman and Frenchy wondered then if he'd slept with this person. She would not bring it up; she was strangely numb to it, on her period no less. A jealous type, she could cause a scene, but not now. She didn't care and she didn't know why.

"Now, where you think he wants to go? Doesn't matter to me, but might to him."

"Billy—" she appealed, fearful her advice was not being heeded.

"I can grant him that, right? I figure he's a Thirty-Six—"

"Just do it! Now!" she beseeched. "Don't wait! Don't risk it!"

"Beyond that I'd be very surprised—"

"Wait—I thought you were going to do it!"

"He's no Forty-Eight … Clemmons was a Forty-Eight. But he had more intestinal fortitude than ol' Rollie here. Rollie's kind of a puss—"

"Billy!"

Her point-blank pleas were ignored. "Yeah, Thirty-Six sounds right, he'll be fat and ready about mid-afternoon tomorrow. He took a napper on that Tucson flight and had fair recharge, so …"

"I thought you had this worked out!"

"I do—but the human body's capacity to withstand sleep deprivation torture, their coping index, is tricky to assess and it's particular to a person. Like DNA. I do know he'll suffer relentless streams of fear through the night, then he'll go ill running chills with no appetite either and with no intake, his will to live will fade—appropriately. He'll be a basted Butterball begging us to stick the fork in. He'll pass out and then, lights-out."

To dramatize the fatal event and the doomed man's demise, he crooned, *"Farewell and adieu to you fair Spanish ladies, farewell and adieu young ladies of Spain …"* The performance doubled for more gaming, of course. "Come on, Frenchy, play! Robert Shaw in *Jaws*—Captain Quint!"

But she would not engage now and reacting to that, he pressed the green button to the intricate dashboard panel.

"No!" she shouted in protest. "I told you! I don't want to talk to him! *Merde!*"

Frenchy shot low in her seat as the glass divider separating the cab from the rear motored down. Billy located Roland in his rearview, the prisoner framing him wide-eyed and expectant.

"Rollie, giving you an option: where you want to be buried? Any ideas?"

The captive's face tightened and he began to grunt indecipherably, his voice muffled by the thick wad of tape. Billy spoke over him.

"Guess the desert somewhere, very natural and all, you'll be part of the whole worm trip, returning to the earth in a mucus trail, the eternal living cycle. Could be worse, right?"

The man's eyes blazed with terror.

"So—Arizona?"

The man nodded exaggeratedly, but Billy had already redirected his gaze to the road and was still unable to make sense of the groans.

"No?" he intuited wrongly. "How about New Mex? Some great terrain over there, get you a butte, maybe some cliff dwellings—"

The suggestions elicited more of a throaty protest from the captive, but Frenchy had already sent the partition sliding up and Billy was now unable to hear the man.

"Okie-dokie, New Mex it is—"

Frenchy punched him hard in the arm. "I told you! No contact!"

"What's wrong with New Mex? Our former home—"

"And get rid of that stupid cowboy accent! Talk regular!"

"Frenchy you're just so *fin de siècle*—"

"That shows how much you know about me!" she blasted, furious. She'd had enough and had regained some strength. "I'm a hippy and I'm waiting for hippy times again. This world sucks! And you're part of it!"

It tickled him. He was poised to launch, *Everyone wants to be a hippy when they're young,* but decided against it. In his mind she was too biologically fragile now.

"And I don't mean that in a silly way," she added. "I'm talking about a better world, in which people are kind, think about love, and compassion! Not death and 'my religion is better than yours'—"

"It's gonna be hippy times again, Frenchy. That's what the Age of Aquarius is about—it's what I'm trying to tell you."

"Stop your teasing! I can't handle it right now!" She was about to cry again. "And talk normal!"

The incorrigible little boy couldn't resist disobeying the teacher's command. "But I'm feelin' kinna Confederate," he whispered.

"Yeah, well, *arrête!*"

"It's flowing truthfully off my nervous system."

"It's getting truthfully *on* my nervous system!"

"As you wish," he termed politely erudite, only to finish off with— *"Punkin' Puss!"*—so deliberately hillbilly, producing a sorcerer's mix of language, instinct, and psychology that few would attempt under the circumstances.

"Beelly!"

"Come on, you be Punkin' Puss and I'll be Mush Mouse—"

She slugged him again and missed and he let out a whoop. His silliness was so relentless, it was actually neutralizing her failing mood.

"No? How about a game of *roche, papier,* and *ciseaux*—?"

She tried, but could not help holding back the grin and they began a best-of-seven World Series of rock, paper, scissors. In French.

"Stop with the rock! They don't beat paper!"

"If they smash scissors, they smash paper! *Roche* encore!"

"No—"

"Boom! Boom! Boom!"

"Beeellly! *Arrête!* " But now she was chuckling, the game cheering her considerably. They both loved to game and she was now his playdate again.

"Wanna hear some Stevie?"

"*Pourquoi pas?* " Rocker and *chanteuse* Stevie Nicks was Frenchy's idol and creative muse.

"After I get a shortwave report—"

An every half-hour ritual, he spun the dial, scanning. The instrument received police communications from the Four Corner states.

The prisoner in the back was now sweating profusely, foaming cotton at the mouth, drowning in panic. It was happening again; his simple wish to perish and be buried next to his boy was being cruelly denied in total disregard, if not mockery, of his hopes. He was on his way to the Land of Enchantment with a certifiable psychopath and his toy French sidekick. In an uncharacteristic fit he suddenly began to kick at the seats, tearing apart the red velour until the stitching separated and wads of padding became exposed.

After the display he grew still and silent and that was when he became terrified. Not the nighttime brand of fear Billy had predicted for him; it was a terror the man hadn't known existed. His heart was pounding deeply and painfully as though he could have a coronary at any moment. And the thought of that and its implications on his mission only made his condition worse. There was a chill to his bones and shaken to the core he began to heave and dry vomit. He was more frightened than he'd ever been his entire life.

11

Instead of heading north from the Roosevelt Dam to Show Low, the Stretch slid back down Route 88 to Globe picking up the 70 into New Mexico. The sophisticated communications and radar indicated no foreseeable threats; no accidents, patrol cars dispatched, or pointed chatter on radio. They zoomed with a fury to the sounds of the Bella Donna, Frenchy playing "Nightbird," also known as "One-Winged Dove," eleven times consecutively. They feasted on spears of dried mangos and bananas, chewy to the molars like licorice.

After snacking, Frenchy took a nap while Billy attached an earpiece to listen to the shortwave more attentively. As was often the case, he was torn; part of him, the adrenaline-thriving, ADHD-fueled, risk-taking—and thereby narcissistic—ego aspects were dying to hear of his criminal deeds on the airwaves. The wiser perfectionist and survivalist part of him were relieved Roland Polsonby had not yet been considered missing.

Carving it southwest across the border into New Mex, he avoided Interstate 10 and took the back roads he knew well. He picked up the 90 at Lordsburg and followed it through the Gila Forest into Silver Springs, the legendary town spawning Billy the Kid, and where the Kid performed his first bank heist.

"What time is it?" Frenchy posed groggily.

"Ten-clock-3-0. We'll be there by midnight—"

Surging onward into the Gila Wilderness, the Stretch ascended the rugged terrain, Billy pulling off onto dirt track in the thick forest. They snuck up on a herd of elk dozing in the misty blackness, the sudden spray of headlights scattering them anxiously into the wood.

The car came to a stop beneath a dense evergreen canopy, four hours after the prisoner's muted pleas. The voyage had taken longer than predicted, the back roads winding extensively and not directly through the vast Gila, but Billy had been careful.

The rear door spread and Roland located two figures painted in silver by a healthy moon. The captor was wearing a backpack and flashlight. Frenchy had a waist pack and was purposely angling herself away from him.

It was time for introductions, Billy determined. "Roland, this is Frenchy," he initiated, his breath tracers shooting forth. The temperature had cooled as they'd left the desert and ascended the next geological zone, the Mogollan Rim, a pinyon pine-forested region higher in altitude. The going was steep and difficult to hike.

Roland greeted her with a nod, but she would not acknowledge him.

"Frenchy—" Billy clutched her hand to position her closer.

"—*Ola*—" was blurted dismissively from her mouth.

"Now wasn't that easy?"

"Shut up, Beelly."

The captor unlatched the wire loop holding the prisoner, then stripped away the tape from his lips. "Let's go—"

Roland shifted forward, rising up and out of the car.

"Quick recap, Rollie—death rules apply," the captor issued. But as he locked the car, something abhorrent stopped him in his tracks.

The torn seat upholstery.

Roland vaulted forward suddenly, crashing to the dirt his face scraping along the earth. Billy sprung after him to resume his assault, horse-kicking him repeatedly.

At first Frenchy didn't move. Then she couldn't take it anymore. He was not executing him; he was just beating him.

"Beelly!"

The enraged captor administered more smacks and kicks to the man's ribs, a full display of his slow-burning but ferocious temper.

"You'll—" and she was going to add, "kill him," but found it too confounding to verbalize.

"Bet your ass I will!" he picked up anyway. "*Motherfucker!* Would I come in to your home and tear up your *objets d'arts*???" Bending low, he screamed in the man's ear. "That piece of shit architorture you pasted up on the hill with the Ikea couches? An eyesore monument to a plastic, monogrammed, Gucci-loafered, tasteless, faithless, fucked up existence you and your kind call a *life!*"

"Billy, enough!"

His head snapped back. "Enough out of *you!* One minute you want to factor him, the next you're worried about him getting a fat lip!"

Roland cast her a look and she eyed him fully a first time in the silvery light, but quickly averted her beam.

"Just don't be cruel," she sent back feebly, the emotion rising in her. She covered her face with her hands.

Billy kicked the dirt hard, a dummy substitute for his uppity captive. "Did you see what he did to my car? Did you?" She shook. "Well, take a goddam look!" He gripped her by the arm, yanking her and she shuffled over and inspected the car's interior. She covered her mouth that had dropped open.

The prisoner lay there coughing and panting still, fresh blood trickling from his mouth. "I'm very sorry," he said.

"Shut the fuck up!"

As Billy stammered off beneath a gangly juniper, Frenchy stepped away from the car and retreated to the moon shadows. The captor was soon heard chanting Supai verse, delicately so, while Roland lay flat to the earth panting still. Upon returning, Billy appeared placid even refreshed, his face devoid of tense expression as if nothing had happened. Flashlight in hand, he proceeded to march toward a break in the wood. After a pause, Frenchy fell in behind.

"No, me first. Then him. Then you," he commanded. "If he makes a move cap him!" He eagle eyed the prisoner. "Frog's a damned good shot, and me? The backgammon cube did not grant me my name—"

Aligned in formation, it was past midnight when they began their ascent through the dense forest. Billy knew the way, of course, and he even pointed out carvings in pinyon barks that were natural markers.

It wasn't long before he sparked conversation.

"Ever go hiking?" No one spoke up. "I'm asking you, Rollie—"

The direct questioning caught him by surprise. "Oh … Yes—"

"Where?"

"New Hampshire."

"Camp—? What was the name?"

"Uh, Camp Dewitt."

"Didn't like it, did you?"

"No," he said. "I didn't."

"Read it in that upstart Florida mag. *Fashion Spectrum*? So nineties. He said something hysterical in the interview, Frenchy—"

Again, Billy's capacity to shift temperaments on a dime amazed him. As he listened further, his fascination turned to awe.

"When he was ten he wrote his mom an 'I hate camp' letter. He said, *'The kids are all pussies, the tennis courts are dug up, and I don't think they even have a scuba program. But I'm reading* The Exorcist, *I really like it a lot.'* Then he said to the interviewer, *'That's when my Mom knew she had a special kid on her hands,'* " and Billy cracked a hearty laugh, which produced a sharp, natural reverberation in the darkness.

The extended sounds spooked Frenchy. "What was that?"

"The echo—cliff walls are right above ..."

Refreshed with oxygenated blood and revitalized, the prisoner's thoughts fired and the writer in him suddenly found metaphor in the natural setting, his past echoing all around him. The interpretive thought caught him by surprise, as that part of his brain seemed to have shut down a while back. More impressive to the captive, Billy had not quoted him accurately, but *exactly*, as in word for word. He'd either memorized his letter or had photographic recall. The man's capacity for detail seemed limitless.

"Hysterical, eh, Frenchy? I mean, how's a mother to please a kid with Jack Kramer tennis racquets, Polo shirts, Chocolate Cows, and WASPy club burgers when he's already grooving to real *Exorcist* horror? Kid was twist, what's a poor mother to do?"

"I read it," she tossed deadpan. "It's a good book."

"Well," he mused, "couple of literati we have here—"

"I read *Rosemary's Baby* too," she added.

Roland had read it too, but would not offer up this added bit of personal information, to further any commonality between them. He could tell she despised him.

"Lemme ask you, Rollie—what became of that kid?"

The man unfurled it bluntly without hesitation.

"Faded away."

The remark was the most personal comment he'd made in ages and in saying it, he'd surprised himself again.

Recognizing the gravitas of the confession, Billy, for once, was left with nothing to say. He was used to lesser responses prompting his insightful follow-ups, but the prisoner's declaration was so honest and succinct, to overburden it would be overkill. Billy imagined a misstep of the sort to be sinful, like spray-painting Picasso's *Guernica*.

The exchange was a silencer and the group marched on in darkness without another peep. Billy stuck to the twisting trail only he could follow, alighting the flashlight every twenty paces to ensure the proper line which also conserved batteries.

Roland floated along surprised he wasn't more fatigued, enjoying what seemed a second wind. His feet had begun to blister in his loafers and thin socks. He'd dressed to say good-bye not to hike, but it actually felt good to walk with freshly replenished blood and rejuvenated limbs.

"For you history buffs: Geronimo lived here," Billy issued.

"Where?" the captive sent back spontaneously.

The quick response made Billy eyeball him singularly and he slowed his step and came to a halt. He rested eyes on the man and addressed him smoothly in between breaths as a field trip guide would an inquisitive student, choosing his words purposefully, careful not to overstate. "He was raised on the Upper Gila," he began, "and when the army was after him, his band hid out up here. From these cliffs he crossed over the border into Mexico. When the government took control of the New Mex territories in 1846, Apache bands struck out from camps in these mountains, and along the Continental Divide—"

Frenchy adored this side to him, the man at peace, his demons neutralized temporarily. The rare calm gave way to what she considered the real Billy, passionate for life, the mysteries it held, and the people he cared for.

"The more pressure the government put on the Apaches, the more dangerous they became. They resented the white encroachment and hit and ran and raided as a means of survival. And to defend their way of life. When pursued, they vanished up here into the knots of hidden canyons and high plateaus known today as the Gila Wilderness.

"For a decade, Geronimo was the most notorious and feared of them all; he had a small band of warriors, specialists in guerilla warfare. But time ran out, they were outnumbered, and they made a last dash to the Sierra Madres in Mexico. But General Miles persevered and rounded them up eventually and shipped them to Florida, then Alabama, then and Fort Sill in Oklahoma where Geronimo died in 1909. You like history, Roland?"

The man noted Billy's name for him had been changed back to the more formal, perhaps a gesture of respect.

"I was a history major in college."

"I thought you were a literature major—"

"I doubled."

The captor eyed him steadily under twists of blue moonlight slashing through breaks in the pines. He nodded and not disdainfully; it was more contemplative. Then he resumed with the march, pleased to have what seemed his very own band of followers like the legendary Indian hero.

The three soon turned up a steep pitch, climbing hand over hand. The air was thin and crisp and a cool blanket lay over an enormous landscape they could feel, but not see. As they scaled the rock mountain to a new elevation, an expansive geological theater was revealed, offering a sweeping vista. The faint glow of Silver Springs could be seen fifty miles away.

"Time, Frenchy?" Billy called out, ahead of the others.

"Two-thirty."

"First light is in two hours."

"Where are we now?"

As Billy stopped suddenly, the pair caught up from behind.

"When rainwater seeps through cracks in a mountain's reef, it can slowly dissolve its limestone, as oil and gas deposits below leak hydrogen sulfide gas upwards. When the hydrogen sulfide meets the rainwater a highly corrosive sulfuric acid forms, eating through huge amounts of limestone rock, creating vast chambers," he said pausing. "Like this one. Chilly-willies, we're here—"

Dipping past a towering wall of limestone, the captor disappeared and only his flashlight could be seen through the break in the rock. The two were left alone a moment for a thickly tense interval.

"You go—" she forced nervously, "—*man*," she added, the only generic label she could think of.

Nodding, he slipped inside first and they found themselves dwarfed in a marvelous space, an enormous cavern with no end in sight.

"Welcome to *Caverna Magica*," Billy greeted.

There were jagged rock formations spearing down, delicate stone draperies, natural sculptures, underground chambers, and rows of hanging stalactites and rising stalagmites—a veritable Middle Earth spectacular.

The captor followed a natural walkway leading to the cavern's obscured recesses and Roland could feel heavy moisture settling on his skin. The sounds of a flow could be heard. He paced quickly to follow the flashlight's glow alighting the shiny walls and ceilings, a natural seepage from an unknown source running steadily down them.

"Natural spring," Billy identified, his voice echoing.

After trekking within the space another ten minutes Billy suddenly laid down his pack and sparked a lighter. As he lit a pair of small candles a fantastic limestone apartment came into view that even seemed to have been lived in. At one end, a semi-circle of tree stumps was arranged before a pile of half-burnt logs and ashes. The rock wall behind was blackened from fires and Roland located silver light streaming through the apertures in the ceiling.

"The Mogollon settled in here eight hundred years ago," the silence was broken with, Billy sending a light beam up a sidewall exposing a series of petroglyphs, handprints, and shamanistic figures. "Autographs of the ancients."

"Beelly, it's incredible—"

"Yes," he said, still moved himself. "Please, have a seat, Roland," he offered like a gracious host, the captive perching on a rock stump. "Here—" Billy extended some dried mango spears.

The prisoner took a piece and began to chew. He took in an exhausted Frenchy slumped to a cavern wall in the glow of candlelight. Her eyes were closed, her head cocked to a tapered stalagmite.

At the same time Billy studied his captive, to gauge his condition and elicit any sign of weakness or crack in constitution. Rather than failing, the man seemed invigorated, sporting a healthy glow. He appeared noticeably better than he had at the airport indicating he still had reserve.

"I know what it's like," the captor posed starkly into the quiet.

"Sir?"

"To be held against your will."

The prisoner remained silent then.

"Frenchy?" She ignored Billy's beckoning, totally wiped out.

The flickering light caught Billy's eye and he became entranced. He stared at the dancing flame, his pupils contracting only fractionally.

"There's a story passed down from class to class at a reform school in Las Cruces," he said. "Telshor claimed to be an orphanage, a place of 'higher learning' for children with no parents, but the disinterested and heartless shipped off their kids too. The school had curious methods; electroshock therapy, lockdowns, paddles, and physical abuse were a way of life there and some kids never survived. Interns took advantage in that way of course. Eventually, the school was shut down when a boy was killed from too many shock treatments."

The prisoner, of course, wondered why Billy was telling him this.

"Telshor was like jail only worse—the kids hadn't committed any crimes except having been born. It was every student's dream to break out; it was on everyone's mind every single day. There had been many failed attempts. What gave them hope in this way was the story of Dennis Roy—"

Unbeknownst to the others, Frenchy's eyes unsealed then and she framed Billy first and his exploding black pupils. She absorbed the prisoner as well, a man who seemed a peaceful person, gentle even, not your "average killer," which was said often of killers. He was perplexing to her and she could not help wondering what had driven him to do such an awful thing.

"Dennis had a lengthy record of insubordination and was seen as a disruptive influence, especially on the young ones, so he was cut off from the rest. He wasn't the only one, but he was considered the most subversive and thereby dangerous and by fourteen, he was in Private Block, the school's solitary confinement. For six years, he was held in isolation, eating alone, walking alone, unless a guard or intern wanted his fix. He nearly slit the throat of one and conditions got worse for him. Some said he'd never be permitted to leave. Many thought he was dead already. Most kids were released in their mid-teens, eighteen at the latest—but Dennis Roy never was. He was never freed. And he was already twenty years old.

"When the school was closed down, stories came out. The Headmaster and other school officials were put on trial. One doctor even testified he was given the order to perform a 'procedure' on Dennis Roy's brain: a lobotomy. At the time, a kid overheard guards discussing it and they got word to him.

"So in the middle of the night, using a fork he'd hidden away, Dennis removed screws to the barred window and climbed out, jumping forty feet, breaking his leg in the fall. He limped off, leaving a blood trail that a sudden rain washed away. Instead of heading east to the Organ Mountains as others had done in failed escapes, Dennis went west across the Chihuahuan desert scrublands, over a hundred miles of scorching desert sands and rocklands, until he reached the Black Mountains of the Gila. No one had ever even dared it let alone survive to speak of it later—

"Except Dennis Roy—" Frenchy interjected suddenly, her carriage now pitched forward. For the first time, she glared undeterred at "Man," speaking directly to him as she'd taken over the story and curiously so.

"It was June. Already a hundred-three degrees. The boy walked twenty-five miles. In day and night. He drank from a bottle of rain water taking small sips. The second day, another fifteen miles. On the third day, he got dizzy sick. On the fourth day, he had no water and had to drink his own pee. The fifth day, the vulture birds circled over, waiting for a chance. He was crawling. He heard voices. His vision tricked him. On the sixth day, he fell and said a prayer for the dying man. He thought he had died. But a cool wind of mystery came to the desert in the night. He reached the mountains of rock and climbed with the energy given to him by the Great Spirit. As he was looking for a spring, anything, he came to this cavern. He knelt before the walls and licked them until his tongue was bleeding. He drank from these walls. And these walls brought him back to life."

A sudden draft of warm wind swept through the space.

The captive sat there, cuffed in that deep rock chamber and he could not help feeling a certain respect for this fractured, psychopathic man. And it came from him like that, from his heart. "Pleasure to meet you, Dennis Roy—"

Billy was angled off and didn't acknowledge it.

"They give the name to orphans who are not identified. Or claimed. Like John Doe for dead people. Billy kept it—"

"The effect is a slow thickening of the blood as it turns to sap," the captor picked up. "The pain extends to the nerves in your teeth, everywhere it hurts, but it's the blood thickening you feel most. Your organs beat to the edge of your skin and your chest feels like it is going to pop, your heart ready to leap out. You press your chest to keep it tucked in its cage; it's working overtime as the blood turns thick like peanut butter, the biological equivalent of dirty motor oil having lubed an engine too long. You're ready for it to stop at any time. Then of course you want it to stop."

Silence fell again over the increasingly intimate space.

The captor shot up suddenly, his impetuous movements the most alarming, a sign anything could happen. Roland wasn't sure why he'd been told the remarkable tale other than Billy needed to tell it, as if he needed him to know what he'd been through. But why?

"Watch our boy; I'm going to listen in—"

Billy unstuck a burning candle and repositioned it down at the opposite end of the cavern, the departed flame dimming the others into a deep opaque shadow. He unpacked the portable shortwave and began flipping through trucker channels, mimicking their accents. He chose Channel 68, the Arizona Highway Patrol, and lay down to listen in on headset.

The prisoner surmised that Frenchy had helped recount Billy's escape to demonstrate her empathy for this man. She was likely communicating support while presenting the psychological portrait, to show how this unique and unforgettable person had come into being. He was fiery, unpredictable, magnetic, and dazzling—and tortured. He was a victim it would appear, having survived years of the most terrible forms of abuse. In contributing this way Frenchy was offering the prisoner a fuller understanding of Billy's personal profile, and that seemed to mean something to her, though Roland did not know what. Her motives baffled him as much or more than Billy's.

As she laid cards for solitaire, a game she often played on computer at Versailles West, she could feel his scrutiny even though the prisoner rarely looked at her. Though lacking formal education, the young woman possessed the wisdom of a street animal, acutely sensitive to energies repellant and attractive, her emotional intelligence also keen and well developed.

The cave was silent except for the intermittent shrills of bats in echo and the low drone of Billy's radio. The prisoner's mind drifted off to the relentless shortwave hum.

In that oxygenated, sensitized state, Roland conjured sediments of forgotten memories. He hadn't any desire to drift back in time, but felt less burdened. The grueling hike had revived him and the strange and fantastical events had altered his mindset somewhat. No longer did he find meditations heavy and debilitating, his wife coming to mind as well, and he contemplated what she'd think if she knew what had happened and what she would do. The last time he saw Adele was at the Biltmore awards gala and he recalled that final encounter in detail.

He'd been staring into the depths of the Paradise Pool, bringing to mind images of summers' passed on the white sand beaches of eastern

Long Island, only to redirect suddenly and move on when Tom Stafford sidled up, on a wander to the lavatory.

"Everything okay?" the man posed perfunctorily, immediately fearing the phrasing inappropriate.

"Quite."

"I'm sure you know Irving Berlin wrote 'White Christmas' right here by the pool." Tom had quick-tossed the follow-up to his personal query, to realign the faux pas if misconstrued as probing, Roland could tell.

In pondering the exchange now a sudden chill of shame came over the prisoner for the way he'd consistently made people feel uneasy all those years. Billy's radio continued to buzz like an insect as Roland drifted back into memory scape.

"Coming back inside?" the man asked.

"You go ahead," he'd said. "I'll be in."

Tom then nodded, patted him fraternally on the shoulder, and continued on his way as Roland veered toward the main bar. Once inside, he heard a gruff, raspy voice calling out: "Evening, Roland."

He turned and spotted Sheriff Harlan Graves holding a brandy snifter, looking uncharacteristically dapper in his formal set. Graves was old guard Phoenix, the most senior officer on the city's police force. Born in the city, he started as a cop in his teens. He volunteered for the war in Vietnam and did two tours and was decorated for valor. After the service he rejoined the local force. Graves had been a contemporary of Adele's maverick father, Frank Griffiths. Though the Sheriff was considerably younger than Griffiths, they'd been cohorts and colleagues. In essence, Graves had been around a long time and had seen Phoenix grow as few had. He could have retired sooner, but always claimed the city had been "too good to him" and he wanted to give back as long as he could. Roland had seen the man often in recent years. A decorated officer and prominent citizen, he was an indispensable guest on the city's gala circuit.

"Hello, Sheriff—" He remembered the two of them shaking hands.

"Congratulate your wife for me will you?" the Sheriff asked him, his amicable West Texas twang, nearly musical.

"I will."

"Calling it quits this year."

He'd nodded absently, but the Sheriff took the liberty of inviting his own follow-up on a nearly involuntary social reflex. "Yep, fifty years."

"Quite a contribution."

"Town's been good to me, ever since it was called one," he jested. "Gonna have a party. Hope you and your wife can attend."

Roland remembered not only thanking him then for the invitation, but when Graves repeated his sacred credo, the prisoner was mindful also of its unintended accuracy. There'd been a corrupt element in Phoenix's early days. The city experienced a sudden industrial growth and economic expansion and Adele's father Frank Griffiths had been a major part of it, Harlan Graves too. Rumors persisted Graves had turned his back on the city's shady business dealings—for a price. There were more unsettling stories about him concerning women. Roland had noted the irony to the man's claim tapping on the knowledge he had. He considered the man's fifty years of service which brought to mind his own contributions and that inspired a precipitous dropping of the meditation.

When Roland returned to the table he remembered a couple joining them: new friends Parker and Barbara Prescott. Adele had offhandedly mentioned a vacancy earlier in a private discussion. It was a surprise to everyone including Adele the Prescotts showed up.

After dinner was served, the awards were presented along with some long-winded speeches. Adele was a gracious recipient and when she took to the podium she spoke eloquently but succinctly and received a generous ovation. She thanked a healthy roster, but had neglected to mention Roland, an honest mistake in her consciousness, and she did apologize when she returned to the table.

Roland recalled observing the evening's theater in a watchful but detached way, like a social anthropologist. What had been happening at the podium was a mere sideshow to what was going on in the room. Adele had her cycle of suitors and he was acquainted with most of them. At a large function, there was usually a minimum of three players in the circuitry representing the past, the present, and future. There was the jilted and depressed one whose time in the sun was up as in Dale Widger. The present dalliance was represented by Parker Prescott and Roland knew she'd been carrying on with him for some time. Then there was the one she had her eye on—the catch of the day—and it seemed the young architect was being quickly groomed for the position. He knew Adele as well as a man could know a woman and which qualities pleased her in a man. Elocution and sense of humor were important, but mostly it was about one's stature; a celebrated sort who would make her look better, who would reflect well upon her and give her a boost in the eyes of the public.

Her philandering had begun four years prior, a year after the death of their child. He hadn't been jealous; those emotions had passed on long ago. He became merely a witness to the passion play, an audience to players' performances from an ensemble cast and highlighted by the respective and petty individual dramas.

Roland's last glimpse of his wife that night he remembered came as he bid the table farewell while citing his business trip in the morning as reasoning for the sudden departure. He'd stepped up beside her while she was enraptured with Slaughter still as the boy wonder discussed Gaudí and Puig, pandering to her perfunctory knowledge of modernist Spanish architecture.

"You know a group proposed a design of Antonio Gaudí's from 1908 for the Trade Center site in New York, now the Freedom Tower," the young man had tossed.

"Good night," Roland had interjected and pecked her on the cheek. "And congratulations."

"Thank you," she'd said rising up. Her movement also prompted the architect to stand. "I'm staying for a dance," she'd added politely.

Nodding, he passed before the young man who seemed light-headed, his guard ebbing if not crumbling. "Good night, Brandon."

"Cheers," the young architect piped with a clumsy grin.

That was the last time he had seen Adele and the memory brought to mind another reminiscence from that final soirée, one that surprised him when he arrived home.

It had been after midnight when he passed through the gates of Luna Plata. As he advanced up the driveway he could see the lights still on in the caretaker's house inhabited by Gonzalo and his wife, the beautiful and exceptional Fernanda.

He immediately went to his bedroom, closed the door, and placed the small carry-on on the bed and packed a change of casual clothes. He'd decided on a dark suit and hung that on a closet door. He inspected the plane ticket to confirm the nine AM flight. He folded the contract with Dignitas in thirds around the ticket and stuffed them inside his inner jacket pocket.

At that moment there was a knock on the door that surprised him. He was certain Adele had not made it home yet. Without opening it he inquired with a, "—yes?"

"Mr. Polsonby? It's Fernanda—"

"*You are married?*" the soft, accented voice initiated.

Roland immediately snapped from his private reverie and angled over in the low-lit space. Frenchy wasn't facing him, but she'd directed the question at him, having pierced the enduring silence.

He was stunned. Her gesture seemed some sort of gift and he did not understand why he felt that way. He cleared his parched throat though out of respect. "Yes."

The eyes of the young woman remained leveled on her cards. "Do you have children?"

He shook. "No."

Children had been on her mind during the hike after they'd spent the afternoon with Genesis. "Why not?"

Pent up emotions were triggered in him then and seeped forward, the strain of his botched attempts to reunite with his son, the stress and violence of the day, the sobering reminiscence, and the girl's loaded query all bringing him to the tipping point. A lone tear slid down his face and carried forward to his chin, but it went undetected in the low light. "Didn't work out," he pushed thickly.

"How long have you been married?"

"Fourteen years."

"A long time."

"Is it?"

She raised her chin up and took in his face, tinted in the misty amber glow. She noticed it was different about his face, which now appeared delicate, fractured, and quite beautiful, the way only failing light can paint. "To me, yes. Fourteen years is a lot. Do you love her?"

He hesitated again. "Yes."

Her tone drifted into skepticism. "I see."

"It doesn't seem like enough."

"Enough for what?"

"To be respectable. You know, you hear stories of fifty-year marriages."

"*Mais oui*, 'stories.'" She hesitated and once she spoke again he understood why. "You don't really love her, do you?"

Though he was taken by her intimate curiosity, he was more impressed with her acute sense. Either that or Billy somehow knew more of their marriage and had informed her. Clearly he could not underestimate his captor.

"Not in that way; that was a while ago."

"Why?"

"People change. Then, of course, they don't."

"You mean you got tired of her—"

As Roland shook, Billy blurted from his end. "She was no good, Roland!"

His suspicion was confirmed. Billy had uncovered the gossip.

"She was not faithful to you?"

He eyed her pointedly and thought to say, "Is this amusing for you?" He held back. "Yes."

"No!" Billy blasted, overriding him.

"Billy!" Frenchy sounded irritated.

"In the beginning, yes. Then she lived a different life. Guess after a while it didn't matter."

"Take notes, Frenchy. This is great for the 'Diaries'—"

"*Arrête!*"

"Frenchy is handling the archives," he bellowed, undaunted. "Doing the *fin de siècle* before The Fall of the TTs-Warhol thing, you know, who was banging who in what closet at Studio 54, pitching, catching, Quaaludes, eighties-but-greaties. The devil's in the details and Frenchy records everything; the pages are like scales to a reptile's skin representing the passage of time, demarcating the evolution of human 'progress,' mankind/man-not-so-kind, the meaningless race forward to nowhere and back—the futility—chronicling the downward spiral of human existence as we spread across the globe like cancer choking off all that's good in our wake. It's called 'The Dolce Vita Diaries,' *c'est vrai ma petite?*"

Billy was notably upbeat and Frenchy discerned he must have learned the crime hadn't hit the airwaves and the police were not yet giving chase. So he had time to kill and he loved to kill time, his favorite pastime. But what others considered killing time was Billy's life. She remembered bumper stickers he'd stuck everywhere boasting, "Every Day is *Cirque de Soleil!*"

"Ol' Rollie here is excellent subject matter. He used to write dolce vita fiction until he retired ... but we've got him here in the flesh! Our own D-List celebrity tell-all, working title, *The Chronicles of Polsonby*. Or, *Roland Polsonby: the Final Days*. Or how about, *To Die in Black Tie?* Love titles. Anyhoo, the 'Diaries' will sell better than the 'Bugger Me, Elmo' doll, just like Andy's did—"

Frenchy held off until Billy's verbal lawn mowing ran its course.

"So," she continued, "you didn't give her attention and she went with other men. What were you doing? Fucking other women, of course ..."

He was made aware now she knew nothing. "No."

" 'No' is right! May I speak, Rollie?"

"And if he says 'no?' *Merde!* "

The captive was astounded by their sudden change in demeanor. They were treating him with respect like a new friend, even fawning over him, which was seemingly a positive development. He was also aware the dynamics could reverse at any moment.

"It told a tale of men beside themselves," the man launched, adopting once again a tone of literary oratory. "Altering behavior patterns, changing schedules, embracing the daylight hours like never before, all to dream up their finest seductions. Energy spent which would make millionaires of the poor and billionaires of millionaires if channeled properly to give the illusion of the most intrigue along with the most potent and precise verbals delivered—metered poetry might help—a best foot forward, to shave away the rest of the pack and move within range of the private spaces in the night, with half-truths or deceptions, sorcery even, whatever it took to take it to the next step and touch if for only one glorious pass. If the Going Gods of the Day shined on them brightly enough, maybe forcefully enough to possess it for a weekend or—forever—because she had it all, unlike others they'd met in a lifetime."

"The wife?" Frenchy posed which didn't warrant a response.

"Most indicative of its potency was the way it crushed the herd, her own gender; women, semi-confident, always semi-confident, forever on guard and fearful of what was out there, clinging to auras created in small towns with strings of baby successes generated, giving way to beliefs they possessed it, the sought after gifts mental and physical, subconsciously aware she was out there framing their fragile egos in her crosshairs, lurking, a daunting persona inspiring the severest trepidation, better trained and equipped, bettering taste and besting diction, no matter in sapphires or strings, silhouettes or YSL, she was out there, the one who could devastate them and the Manolos they strutted in on, thieving their aura, making off on a dime with the heart of the man they'd wagered their future, their weekend, their brief chat, on; and in so doing producing all the 'good' stuff, the best in feminine wiles, the envy, the claws, the feline ferocity, the spite, the mendacity and sweet revenge, that a face, figure, intelligence quotient and social genius packaged like that and delivered to their doorstep, could conjure. Adele Griffiths-Polsonby could inspire those desperate sentiments in a woman."

The prisoner's head hung low, but didn't move an inch.

"She had the physicals, adorning herself to her advantage with whatever designer she wanted, her ashen-blonde hair shaped in a dazzling retro-beehive by a hired house call squadron, projecting an astonishingly youthful appearance for a woman almost forty-one, for a woman of any age—gal had bank, too—yet she'd been gifted in other ways, separating her from the similarly advantaged pack, the biting wit, the tactful understatement, the effervescent, but refined *joie de vivre* …

"But as the harmonics of life dictate, along with a physical and social genius, privilege and good fortune, came the shadowy aspects, the personal misgivings, mysterious and hidden, perhaps, or even buried, reeking psychological havoc, and the losses, it's about the losses too, which eat and consume the brittle mind space. Ravishing? Yes, but in a fragile state trace imperfections outweigh copious gifts and besides, nobody remembers what a beautiful and gifted woman used to look like, except a beautiful and gifted woman; the latest perceptions never come close, never live up to former days. Beautiful gifted women are not objective, beautiful gifted women who drink are worse—they act on it."

Roland was shocked. Like the informal, but literary dissertation Billy had given on Roland's character earlier, the accuracy in Billy's profile and spot-on appraisal of his wife was staggering. He was so much more than smart or savvy as it required so much more to understand Adele's complexities.

As the prisoner continued to ponder and marvel in silence, the captor popped up like a jack-in-the-box and removed the earpieces. Fearful of the burst, Roland angled sharply up too.

"Are you finished?"

"Yeah, we all are—it's first light."

"But Beelly—" She was eyeballing him suggestively.

Though the comments were arresting, the time spent in the cave had not been unpleasant. Roland was heartened having communicated with Frenchy. Their talk had left the impression of a conversation perhaps cut short. Something pleasing to them both had been initiated and left dangling even—maybe.

"Where are we going?"

"Pueblo Bonito."

"The dwellings? The tourists will be there—"

"Not the ones we're going to—"

"How do you mean?"

"Can't get to 'em, no one can. 'Cept an Apache." Billy groaned as he arched into a stretch. "Anybody feelin' fecal?"

"Billy," she droned, resistant.

"Rather I say 'bowelitis'? Okay, anybody suffering some bowelitis? Roland?" He shook. "You can talk fecal, can't you? Natural body function. Some people say don't trust a man who doesn't drink; I don't trust a man who can't wax fecal—"

"Billy, you're boring."

"—waved off." He readdressed Roland.

"Some of us like sharing it, especially colonics. 'Cause when you get on the subject of colonics everybody cheers up, you can really brighten a room. You get the right group around a fire or in the bleachers of some sandlot park and jump-start a little colonics repartee with a nice fecal-friendly highlight of your own and if one of your colleagues has had a recent good movement or hemorrhoidal flash-flare, or a thrombost, or good God, an endoscope? or colonoscopy? *Damn!* Some of the best chatter you'll find. Can go on for hours! Little smiles dancing around the circle. Why? Because you're all talkin' *shit!* Real shit! Purest conversation you ever had, 'cause who would lie about it? It's a total relief! All them secret thoughts they've had hunched over a bowl and now they can unleash 'em? Hell. Everyone gets real polite, no one talks out of turn, fecal folk are polite folk, chiming in with tales of recent bowel wars, regrettable movements, embarrassing ones too, wet winds and ED—that's explosive diarrhea, Rollie Boy—and o' course what they've banged off the porcelain lately ..."

Frenchy groaned deeply.

"The whole scatological lexicon takes over—'stinky curl's, a 'brown slinky,' 'Baby Ruth's, 'floaters'—you'll hear that. When I went in for a full piping—"

"Stop! I've heard about your damned colonoscopy stories a hundred times!"

"Well, Roland hasn't. It's not all about you, little Miss Self-Absorbed—"

"*Me* self-absorbed?"

"Miss I've-Heard-It-Before. Don't deny, don't deprive. Damn, *am I wrong?*" The query was directed at Roland. "See? He wants to hear ... What they do is give you these saline solutions to drink the night before, you can't eat solids all day, so later on when those solutions hit you—bam! You gotta move. You do it twice until there's nothing left, until you're shittin' clear Poland Spring. It's a damned waterfall and a mite refreshing, I might add ...

"Next morn' you go in and them nice nitrous ladies knock you out—kaboom! And you get piped while you sleep. And it's done; you don't feel a thing. You wake up an hour later in the RR totally buffaloed ...

"If that ain't enough of a treat, you may luck out and get a real character from some offbeat place—can really make a recovery room. One poor bastard botched the solution instructions and was still half-impacted so he had to come back to do it all over again. It's all in the preparation. Like life. I go twice annually now just for the flush and a 'roid peek—gotta be on polyp watch, don't want no Egg McPolyp, that's Ronnie Reagan-butt for a newcomer like you Roland—"

"Enough, Beelly."

He pressed on disregarding her. "Perhaps you'll share a memorable colonic experience, RP? Don't be selfish now, like the but-back-to-me froglein here ..."

"I am not being selfish, it's disgusting!"

"I reckon you are ..."

"We said no more cowboy talk!"

"Pardon the interruption; this is authentic folk hero fat. Feeling very Bob Zimmerman today, that's Bob Dylan to you, RP. Poetry ought to be caustic and ribald—very sharp."

He shuffled over and squared before the prisoner, his eyes wide and aglow.

"You see—my art is *me*. That's my canvas of expression. In the now, in the present, whatever I do. That's my art, *capisci?*"

Roland smiled vaguely and nodded appreciatively, though unaware he was doing either.

"You remember Marcel Duchamp's Ready-Made art? This is Billy Six's Whatever-I-Do art and I'm in my Ivory Period. Should be the crowning jewel of my career. Frenchy—I implore you to take notes!"

Billy tugged on the pack straps and jaunted off back through the deep cavern, helping himself to a two-fingered taste of wall seepage. Roland followed, but spied Frenchy rearranging her waist-pack and he glimpsed it for the first time. She did in fact have one—a gun.

12

The pink and tangerine sweep of dawn was rising and the lush, colorful ravine could be seen below, half-painted in sunlight and the green deciduous trees at the bottom had begun to yellow. As the weather stayed summer warm deep into October, the Mogollan Plateau was the last place to exhibit resplendent fall foliage.

They'd been hiking on their ascent about an hour, climbing hand over hand. Roland was beginning to show fatigue, his feet cracking and blistering, his eyes bloodshot.

"Time, Frenchy?"

"Five-thirty."

"You're almost a Twenty-Four, Rollie. Not quite, but nearly." It seemed to uplift the captor and he broke into Bob Zimmerman's "I Shall Be Free No. 10," the significance of the song's title not lost on him.

> *"Now I was shadow boxing earlier in the day,*
> *Figured I was ready for Cassius Clay,*
> *I said, "Fee, Fi, Fo, Fum!*
> *Cassius Clay, here I come!"…*

"Beelly! Look!"

Frenchy pointed to the mesa at the other side of the canyon gulch. Below the cliff and under the overhang were the remains of an ancient village, brick and mud walls, and circular rooms of the kivas.

"Thar she blows—Pueblo Blanco. It's Mogollan, a thousand years new."

Roland slowed. Frenchy now winded, head hanging, came from behind and bumped him. "Sorry," she mumbled awkwardly, "Man."

"My fault," he returned, having noted the spare significance of the exchange, the second time she'd called him that. Now he had a name. He'd been personalized by her.

"No rubbernecking!" Billy cried out and it was remarkable how all sensory and all knowing he was, even out of sight. The captive knew then he could never escape. Billy was too adept, ubiquitous, keenly instinctual, and intelligent.

"Stop there, Roland!" it was commanded out loud. "Put your right foot on the sandstone step that's carved out for you—see it?"

He stepped up. "Got it—"

"Then the next one, then the next. Keep following, they'll appear before you like magic. Can you make it out? The stairwell?"

"I do now … Wow!"

After ascending the "invisible stairs" for half an hour while face to face with the rock wall, Roland twisted partially back and surveyed behind. His heart nearly jumped from his chest at the sheer drop-off several thousand feet to a forested valley below. He was scaling a vast wall of rock with no ropes, nothing.

Billy constantly hollered out directions to them. "Take that line, hold it flat, and use your hands to balance!"

"*Merde!*" Roland heard from behind. "I hate thees part—"

To the naked eye it seemed absolutely impossible and the perilousness hit the prisoner deep in his gut, fearing seriously now he could fall off, not that he would lose his life—that he would never get his wish. He would end up rotting in a mountain gully picked apart by coyotes and buzzards; or lay unidentified in some New Mexico morgue if found; or, if he was fortunate enough to be identified, sent back to Arizona with no one apprised as to what to do with the body. Keeping his plan secret until the end, he hadn't included any instructions in his will. He thought now that this omission was a terrific blunder. He'd be sentenced away from his son for all eternity.

The prisoner figured correctly he could not depend on these deviants to carry along the message. In his estimation, Billy and Frenchy would soon be fugitives from justice if they were not already.

In a rush of epiphanic clarity, he knew what he had to do—to make certain, however his captor decided to end his life, he'd be delivered back to *Escalera al Cielo*. That was all that mattered.

He thought to write notes and place one on him with a spare in his rectum in order to be found in an autopsy in case the first was not. The digestive track aspects struck him in passing also how Billy would appreciate the notion.

"Just take a leetle step at a time—" He heard behind him.

He craned back and detected a faint spark of concern in the young woman's eyes. She looked away, as if snatching the tone of her comment immediately, though it was noteworthy.

"You can do eet," she added, her head angled away. "I deed …"

"You did?"

She nodded resolutely.

His face grimed and dusty, Roland was perspiring heavily. He closed his eyes and conjured the image of his boy and locked it in his mind as he negotiated the vast wall, careful not to view the abyss again, scaling steadily, grasping rock spires his only defense from a death undiscovered. He inched his feet across the smallest crack of a ledge for ten feet or so.

As the captive rounded the last edge, Billy was positioned before an extraordinary cliff dwelling inset into the rock mountain face. The construction had walls of mortar and wood beams, truly ancient, and a natural archway and recess into the pink sandstone.

Roland had made it.

His captor began clapping. "Congratulations, Rollie. Look—"

Only now would the prisoner view the treacherous drop-off and a spare but prideful grin grew on his face.

The sun had inched its way above the mesa, causing the valley of trees to glow gloriously with multicolored fall leaves, an exquisite blast from nature.

Frenchy then emerged from the curved rock, panting. "Beelly? Are you crazy? You could have gotten me killed!"

"She's an excellent climber," Billy whispered aside.

"I hear you talking! … *Woof,*" she gasped. When she raised up she saw Roland mouthing it silently. "Thank you." The young woman jerked away, purposely communicating nothing in return.

Billy started beneath the archway and the two followed. The passage led into the dwelling, a damp, musty smell of earth and antiquity hovering, and on the floor were real artifacts, pottery chips, and even an ancient sandal.

"Raiders haven't made it here; few people have—"

Roland studied the well-preserved interior. "How could that be?"

"The few who know its location are too old," Billy explained. "And they won't tell anyone outside the tribe. It's a shrine to their past, maybe the only one left. They know that too."

"What about the government agencies and the parks people?"

"Can't see it from the other side—it's hidden from helicopters. The last bend conceals it and head-on you can't see Geronimo's Stairs."

Roland twisted sharply at Billy.

"Yes'm, Geronimo's hideout. Had the ol' boy taken up here instead they never would have found him. All he had to do was stay put—"

Roland crouched to examine the artifacts, genuinely awestruck.

"You know why I big-upped you?"

"Because I made it …"

" 'Cause you're the third Caucasian to make it." He pointed to Frenchy. "She's the second."

"How did you find out about it?"

"By accident. I was living up here for months after I escaped and I was trying to bag a mountain goat. I'd been surviving on roots and berries and I was starved—"

Roland noticed Billy had broken back into a western type of drawl different from the one he'd spoken in before.

"Chased that so'm'bitch up them stairs. I was so hungry and determined to get him that I kept on climbing—"

"How do you know no one else did the same?"

"Artifacts woulda never lasted; they'd be in some attic somewhere in Albuquerque or auctioned off or with any luck, a museum. That sandal there is said to be from one of Geronimo's wives."

"How do you know?"

"Curious, ain't he?" he put to Frenchy. "The Supais told me when I became a member. They needed permission and got it only because I'd described the hideout—"

"What about Frenchy?"

"You can tell family or someone on their deathbed."

"Guess that covers me," he quipped. The chilling remark, a first of its kind from him, forced a glance between Billy and Frenchy.

"Yes, it does," Billy said eventually and he paced beneath the arch. "You were either gonna slide off, or, well, I didn't think you'd make it."

"Yes, you did."

Billy hesitated on a reaction, but finally let go of a smirk. "Maybe."

After such a vigorous ordeal the prisoner was flush-faced and appeared boosted somewhat, emboldened even.

"Frenchy!" Billy called out suddenly, the echo bouncing off the surrounding mountain walls. " '*I'll wash your clothes and I'll take care of you when you're hurt, but I won't watch you die. I'll miss that if you don't mind.*' "

"Katharine Ross in *Butch Cassidy and the Sundance Kid!*" she sent back, picking right up on it.

"Give the furry stuffed marmite to the little lady!" he cheered. "With the pointy free-rangers and no brassiere, over there!"

She was belly laughing now, releasing fully, and to see her expressing herself joyfully was a pleasure for the prisoner to witness. Since the outset Frenchy had appeared despondent in his presence, but no longer. She looked incredibly beautiful in the thin misty morning tangerine light. He could not help but enjoy the interplay, games, quotations, and skits spontaneously introduced into conversation. The two seemed sponges for pop culture trivia and used the material for their own private stage. As he caught himself the smile faded and he settled in the dwelling's foyer gazing into the hazy void.

"You're officially a Twenty-Four now," Billy pronounced. "Think we should have a drink to that. Roland?"

A water bottle had been drawn from the pack and Billy was extending it, but it seemed the man didn't hear him. Frenchy took a swig instead and Billy nearly downed the rest.

"Beelly—"

"There's more. Finish her off, Roland—"

But he declined, much to their surprise.

"You know," the man began thoughtfully, "I admire you, Billy …"

The captor was paused by the personal comment, Frenchy more so.

"Your vitality, your passion—for living, I mean."

"Goodness sakes—"

"No, it's marvelous. Remarkable." The prisoner hesitated, his eyes clearly sparkling though. "Fantastic, really. I had it once. Not like that, yours is unique, but I had some—for me, I think. And lost it."

A smooth calmness had come over him, a serene quality. He seemed in no hurry.

"My secretary has a boyfriend," he resumed. "I've been hearing about him for a while. His name is Oliver. He sounds very similar to you, Billy. In character, I mean—"

Frenchy fastened on Billy.

"And my secretary—Margaret—is in love with this Oliver, very much so. She never told me, but I could tell—"

"Who knew?" Billy spat, blatantly sarcastic.

"She did volunteer something to me about their relationship once; that he never slept with her. He wouldn't, but that was not of my affair."

The captor stood stiffly erect, staring without comment. All the while Frenchy's eyes didn't leave Billy's face.

"Anyway, Margaret was the only person who knew of my travel plans. And when of course I was returning to Phoenix yesterday. In considering it further I began to think that maybe this Oliver was actually you, Billy ..."

"Baseless conjecture!" he blasted.

"Perhaps. Margaret is reasonably efficient and the information she had was accurate, but—incomplete."

Billy rose and sauntered away to the edge of the cliff.

"You know why I went to Tucson, Billy?"

"Your latest cafe society movements, post office tell-alls, restaurant booth hops, maneuvers and motives don't interest me ..."

"Do you know, Frenchy?" he followed up.

Her face turned away, her head shaking slightly.

"It was not a 'business trip,' as Margaret had been informed. It wasn't pleasure either—"

She was mindful of what Billy told her. "Then why did you go?"

The man paused briefly. "To end my life ..."

He looked up then at both of them solemnly.

"I went to Tucson to end my life."

Billy kicked a stone into the vast void. It took seconds to hear the impact echo from below. The prisoner took his time.

"But plans were interrupted—twice. First, a miscommunication. A second time by you, Billy. I was headed to Oregon when you picked me up—"

The cackling call of a buzzard could be heard emanating from an adjacent rock wall.

"Even if this is true," the captor charged. "What are you trying to say? You didn't murder my parents? You're a changed man? Enough so you wanted to kill yourself?"

"I'm just letting you know—"

"Should we feel sorry for you now? Should we cry?"

"—That—" he continued undeterred, "I'm prepared to die ..."

Frenchy put hands to her face.

"I'm ready, Billy. To die ... now."

Billy spun back to face his prisoner. "You're ready?"

"I've been ready a long time, yes, but—"

"To die?"

"You were right, I was in shock—and I couldn't go this way …"

"Which way is that?"

"By violence, by a gun," he said. "I feel differently now. I'm prepared for that—even that."

"You want me to shoot you? Here?"

"Somewhere my body can be physically recovered, but yes."

"Now?"

"I think it's time."

Frenchy was astounded. "You really don't want to live?"

Billy swiveled as the prisoner shook, the terror of the abduction released from him, and they could see his dead-souled and haunted expression. "I only ask you make sure I'm found by the authorities."

The unbelievable exchange prompted an enduring silence.

Finally, Frenchy angled up at him. "That's eet?"

"I'll prepare a note to describe what to do with my body. Please leave the note and do not tamper with it. That's my only request."

"And the cadaver?" Billy fired, as if to expose a hitch in the man's proposal. "What do you want them to do with that?"

"From the beginning you've been honest with me, I suspect. And I'll be honest with you, no matter what you think about the past. I want to be buried next to my child in our family plot in Phoenix."

"So you did have a child?"

Billy filled her in and as he did she now saw the pain in the man.

A secondhand recounting hadn't happened in a while, reminding Roland how much worse it was to hear it stated by someone else.

"Let me get thees right—" she posed. "You were going to commeet suicide?"

"Assisted suicide."

Billy lowered his head and faded out to the cliff's edge then back again.

"*Mais pourquoi?* Why didn't you just to do eet yourself?"

" 'Cause he didn't have the guts," Billy snapped.

Roland's reasons for not doing it himself had little to do with cowardice. In his mind the chosen method was the last vestige of integrity to which he'd held fast, for his boy as well. But he wouldn't articulate that to them now.

She gasped sharply. "Ooh la la. *Suicide assisté?* "

Billy was equally astonished. He stood there motionless as though he'd been hit with a stun gun. He was all about research, preparation, strategy, and all the necessary details and this revelation placed him in unfamiliar territory—unprepared—and he was forced to consider it.

"Either that or he's a liar in addition to being a murdering bastard," he scoffed at last. "Help-me suicide. I'm so sure. To strum a few chords on my heartstrings? How about insult me a little more?"

"You think I'm not telling you the truth?"

"You wouldn't be so dumb. You're telling me you want out because of your dead kid, but you say nothing about my dead parents. No remorse, nothing. Not even an apology!"

"I'm sorry for what happened, I truly am with all my heart—"

"Here it comes! Go ahead, finish it. Come on, '*But*—' … come on Polsonby," he goaded, impersonating him, reproducing the captive's patrician voice, "… *'but I didn't kill your parents.'* Come on, you can do it, your million-dollar line, give it to me!"

The prisoner hadn't wanted it to go this way.

"I suppose you weren't even in the state of Arizona when my parents were murdered, right?"

The man would not answer him, not now.

"So let me ask you again—on the night of October 22, 1995, were you or were you not in the state of Arizona?"

Billy's face contorted, his temper ready to flare. The prisoner feared this—riling the unpredictable man. He could get death without the requested burial. He better answer. "Yes," the man uttered. "I was."

"And were you or were you not checked into Kino Community Hospital in Tucson at four AM, the morning of October 23rd?"

His head bowing, he nodded. "I believe I was."

"With blood all over you—"

"Yes."

"Four hours after the murder?"

"I guess."

"You guess?" he repeated threateningly.

"Yes."

"But that doesn't mean he—" Frenchy inserted.

"Shut up! There's more too, isn't there?" He squared up and kicked the prisoner savagely. "*Isn't there?*"

Roland expected the worst now. He prayed silently.

Yet as striking, his captor hesitated. "Yeah, he knows," he said, steadying himself. "Knows damn well where he was and why—"

If Roland had planned to issue a flat denial, he would no longer do so. Billy had sucked it from him. Any credibility it might have had had been diffused, if in fact, he *was* innocent. It could only get his captor agitated, perhaps desperately so. Certainly a confession—even a false one—would yield the same; it would set him off, the confirmation. Roland was trapped; he could neither confess nor deny. So he sat there and remained very still and repeated his prayers.

"While we're on the subject, how does it feel losing a family member? Not *beaucoup* grins, is it?"

Billy stopped short and pivoted back into him.

"Damn, all that time in the car and that's all you could come up with? Well I'll tell you right now I'm in no mood, I've prepared too long, it's my party and you're not going to ruin it with any eleventh-hour requests, beggings, reprieves, or stays of execution, anything of the sort—"

"Not a stay of execution, the *order* of ex—"

"My party!" Billy slammed. " ... You dig?"

The prisoner didn't say anything more.

"I'm talking to you Rollie! *You dig???* "

He nodded.

The three were silent and neutralized to each other in the middle of the wilderness at the crack of dawn.

Roland angled up morosely and caught Frenchy taking him in in a vaguely soft, perhaps sympathetic way. If he had an ally—not for his perceived innocence, but for his pending execution—it was his best chance and he would have to take it. "So then, will you?"

Billy was ignoring him, but—not nearly.

"Do it?" he pressed. "Perhaps when we get back to the car ..."

The captor angled him a devastating look.

"You can shoot me, put my body in the trunk and drop me on the side of the road ..."

"Hell I will!"

"Or by a lake somewhere where you can't be seen—"

"I said no!" Billy's pupils were hotly black now.

"Or leave me by the car so you don't get the trunk dirty—"

"Beelly—"

"No way in hell!"

"I don't care if you don't get caught—I'll write a suicide note and it'll be corroborated by my trip to Tucson. I have all the paperwork." He was pleading now. "In the car you asked me, you gave me a choice—"

"I was horsing around!"

"You want to get it over with, Billy—just like me. It'll be easier to get away with if you do it now, won't it?"

"He's right, Beelly—"

"Enough!" Billy shouted. "Enough …"

"What's wrong with—" she tried again.

"I said no! Abso-fucking-lutely not!"

"Why not?"

"WHY NOT???" he roared. "Why the hell should this creep, this murdering scum who's been living the sweet life for years, black tie balls, monograms, Stubbs & Wootten, rainbow golf tees, callus-free, get to pick and choose *anything* let alone his time of death? Is that justice for my shotgun-blasted parents? Did anyone give them a last request? He didn't give them a goddam thing! At least I'm giving him food and water! No-sir—*no fucking way!*"

Frenchy led Billy aside by the arm.

"*Billy*—" she urged. "For your sake, for ours—*please!*"

"I will not!"

"Do it now and get it over with!"

"I can't!"

"You must! And let's get on with our lives … So what if he wants to die!"

"I won't!"

She shook her head and it was all rising up in her now, the bile of their fractured lives representing the mounted frustrations of their copious misadventures and failures.

"Why not?" He ignored her. "Because it's not going the way you thought? Because it's not your big design?"

"No—"

"Because it's about your *ego*???"

"It's not about ego!"

"It's always about ego with men, stupid foolish men! Damn you!"

"That's not it!"

"Egos make people stupid! You said it yourself! You should be smart and do this now while you have the chance, when they don't know he's missing!"

"This is not about *convenience!*" he shrieked. "I could have factored him back in Phoenix if this was about convenience—"

"Then what is it about?"

"Justice!"

"Yes, Billy, your perfect justice. Your perfect justice will have him killed. But it will get you killed too!"

He charged away from her.

"And maybe me too! You ever think of that? Huh? *Merde!*"

Closing his eyes, he blocked her out and mouthed something inaudible, appearing to calm himself. After a minute he broke from his silence.

"Frenchy?" His voice was now freshly controlled. "Not another word about it, *d'ac*'?"

"Yeah, *d'ac.*'" She was seething. "I hate it when you do this!!!"

Still ignoring her, he knelt, said a prayer, and meditated. It gave way to an oddly melodic chant in layered Supai verse.

As this was taking place before him, the prisoner was glaring out into the void. Freshly devastated, he could only ponder the worst.

It was minutes later before Billy rose up. "Let's go—"

"Where?"

"White Sands."

"Beelly—"

"I said, 'Let's go!'" The shout reverberated chillingly through the canyon walls and back and the abductor wheeled around sharply.

"If you are sincere about wanting to die, Polsonby, I'll let you in on a secret—if you fall, jump, or even think of trying to off yourself before it's time, meaning my time, I promise you this: you won't be buried within the Four Corner states of your lonely little boy! And you can take that promise to your nearest drive-thru teller …"

Billy pushed himself onward and quickly scaled down the sandstone ledge that led to the secret cave dwellings and aggressively entertained the most dangerous part of the climb that was perhaps even more difficult on descent. He did it fearlessly and effortlessly, a man so possessed he was immune to the danger all the while anxiously ranting aloud.

"The nerve," he blustered while marching, "trying to pull a game-changer on me ... Perhaps we should bury him in Pére La Chaise in Paris. Next to Molière. And Balzac. And Yves Montand. And the daughter of Jean-Louis Trintignant murdered by her twist boyfriend. And Sandy Bernhard. And the girlie grazers—Gerty Stein and Alice B. Toklas. You still have juice with the Paris cemetery voting boards, Frenchy? Slot him right next to Chopin. Ask Rollie if that would be okay, will you? And when the groupies smoke a fatty on Jim Morrison's grave, they'll see old RDP two stones down and the hippy overflow will make sure he gets some fat backpacker-ass appreciation. And when the soft boys kiss Oscar Wilde's fruits-free-in-flight monument they'll pee they'll be so thrilled, the golden flow rolling right on past R. D. Polsonby, killer of my parents, but a man so incredibly underappreciated, misinterpreted, and misunderstood who merely wanted an honorable burial after his crimes. Sure, let's get him a plot in the designer cemetery, Pére La Chaise, they even have bouncers and velvet ropes, we'll get Rollie on The List, it's the only way to honor a fellow of such stature, integrity, and cultural achievement—"

Disturbed by the sardonic outburst, Roland uttered another simple prayer as he shimmied down the steep facade. He moved steadily now with fewer hesitations and no stops, but still cautiously, almost as if he'd done it many times before. No, he would not fall now—not now.

13

They call it "Little Mexico," a square-mile hamlet eight miles south of downtown Phoenix founded at the turn of the century by the Yaqui Indians. The town is nearly all Hispanic now, with its own school and two-towered cathedral, Our Lady of Guadalupe Church. It even has its own mayor, though he wasn't the law there.

Sheriff Harlan Graves curved a lazy turn down *Avenida del Yaqui* and that meant something to the locals. A self-designated rooftop scout yelled "Capítan!" and it was all that needed to be said.

The Sheriff heard the alarm call, but he didn't give his prowl car any additional; he coasted a steady ten miles an hour over the speed bumps. Pulses tap-danced, cell phones fired, and the small community buzzed and not because it was welcomed news. Sheriff Graves was the most feared man in Phoenix to men and women of color as he held the personal destinies of many in the community next to a ballpoint in his breast pocket. Necks craned, window blinds were spread on the jitter, and elderly *signoras* secretly peered from behind handheld fans as the prowler passed. Villagers preferred the ghetto birds even, the Phoenix Police helicopters, to this solitary car driven by this dreaded man. When El Capítan came to town, nothing ever good came of it. It could mean a shakedown with an uncle or cousin or wife hauled away and sent back across the border, perhaps never to be seen again. There was talk of even more untoward things happening as well. Parents were terrified of El Capítan.

The car drifted past the fruit stands, the grade school, and the run of *carnecerias* that sold the "bomb-ass" meat. Graves eyed the soap suds frothing out of the neglected fountain and gave a quick glimpse to the three auto shops crammed together. You could almost hear a collective sigh as the car passed out of town.

The vehicle glided south on *Calle Van Nawi* past Dead Body Park and continued to the outskirts where housing conditions grew more slum-like. The car followed beneath the twists of power lines, past raunchy trailer parks and dilapidated homes in the brightest rust and orange colors. Though a community rich in tradition it was no secret Guadalupe had the lowest per capita income in the city.

The Sheriff's vehicle took a purposeful pause where a pair of tennis shoes were hanging from the power lines, the ghetto's latest advertising campaign—the sign where to buy the drugs, the yeyo and the hooch. There was not a stir inside the shanty beneath except a skittish gecko scooting around the cracked facade. Local pot dealers called him "Yellow Eyes" because of the searing golden-yellow color that blazed menacingly when he removed his eyewear and when he did, they knew the shit was going to hit the fan.

The squad car eased on having issued its tacit warning. Yellow Eyes wanted the pushers to know they weren't fooling him, but he wasn't coming for them today. And he wasn't coming for the pottery or the leather goods or anything at the *mercado*—he was coming for something else.

An errant collie with a bad hip gimped across the road in front of the car. Yellow Eyes offered an unlikely grin. "Hey boy."

The wayward pooch reminded him of Freddy paying him a biscuit visit from next door on McGoffin Street in his old neighborhood in El Paso. El Capítan was a border town boy at heart and he could envision the ridge right then from Murchison Park. That was the angle he remembered the Sierra Madres and the sunsets over them and little Maria Mendoza and her perky breasts. Life had never gotten measurably better than that.

"Hey Capítan! Give me the Diablo!" the Mexican-American boy hollered from home plate, wagging the bat high, eyes wide and expectant. But no matter how many times he threw it, they couldn't touch his heater. El Capítan got his name from the Mexican kids across the border in Cuidad Juarez. The most feared pitcher in West Texas, he had a fastball they called the "Diablo" which could hit a hundred miles an hour, striking out thousands in those sandlot days. El Paso East High had been twice state champions with the Capítan on the mound, their run coming to an end when young Harlan threw his arm out playing a pick-up game in San Elizario. He needed surgery, the damage extensive, and dreams of a professional baseball career were dashed.

Graves pulled up to a dusty, run-down intersection bordering scattered domiciles. He veered right driving past five vacated slum houses and came upon the last *casa*. There was no grass, just brown dirt surrounding the structure, a Virgin Mary shrine on the porch with plastic deer and year-round Christmas lights dangling from the roof.

Outside, a wide portly woman was collecting tiny socks from the clothesline, her baby boy sitting beside her licking a milk carton. A pretty fifteen-year old girl fed goats in the backyard. When the mother spotted the car, her face tightened and her heart sank. She immediately called out to the girl who ran quickly inside. Then she gathered the infant.

The Sheriff cut the engine and sat there a moment. He soon heard a disturbance and crying, a commotion that did not faze or surprise him.

A small, wiry Mexican in his mid-forties came out the front door, his face long, shoulders slumping. Yellow Eyes was already out of his car to greet him. "*Buenos días,* Julio—"

The man didn't say anything; it would not be wise and his eyes did their best to hold on to the burn within.

After casual "pleasantries" including talk of the drought, Graves served it up direct. "Where's my girl?"

"She gone …"

"Where?"

"Mexico City."

Graves tossed a look of concern at him. "Now why would she go and do a thing like that?"

"She have family there."

"Julio, *amigo*," the man tethered as he kicked the dirt. "We had an understanding …"

"I could not help it—she not my daughter."

"But she's family. I mean you're talking three degrees of separation here."

Julio did not understand the racist crack, but felt intimidated enough to respond. "She daughter of my cousin."

Yellow Eyes took the sunglasses from his face, that brutal face which folded severely into the meanest crags. The man had witnessed gruesome death and administered as much in his tours in Vietnam, his years on the police force merely adding to the memories. Those goldens knew death as well as any man's could, boosting naturally intimidating glares with threat and imperilment and making his grill a blunt-force weapon.

"Tell me, Julio. That how family treats family? You're in a heap load o' trouble and we have an agreement. You telling me now you can't honor our agreement?"

She peered out cautiously through a side window, her black hair cascading down, bangs crossing over one eye. Graves angled up, catching the pretty one gazing out curiously. When she saw him ogling over, she ducked out of sight.

"I can work for you—"

"Oh?"

"Your *casa*, fix your car—"

"Pedro already fixes my car ..."

"—get you the coca men, the dealers, just tell me. Capítan, tell me, and I do it—"

The terrified Mexican's heart slammed through his chest as the big man reflected on it. "Introduce me—"

"Introduce? *En serio?* To who?"

"The little one ..."

"Who?"

Graves chinned a pointer at the house.

The man's eyes froze, his frame shaking so much so words could not come to his mouth. It was his worst fear, worse than going to jail or even being killed. He'd thought of this day as long as he had known this despicable man praying it would never come to this. He pondered his gun in the goat shed. He trembled in place as a tempest mounted inside, a tempest he knew he had to endure if he wanted his family to survive intact; to survive physically, anyway.

"What's her name?"

"No—"

"*Amigo* ... that ain't too neighborly."

The man was shuddering through it, the worst moment of his life, resisting pressure on his intestines and rectum, clamping his legs together to not drop a load in his pants. "*Por favor*, she only twelve ..."

"Been twelve goin' on three years. Make her fifteen now, Julio."

Julio Ramirez hated the way this man spoke at him, like a child, like he was his father. He had never despised a man so much.

"I said, 'What grade is she in?' "

Julio felt the perspiration drip from his chin onto the dirt.

"If you don't tell me I'm gonna have to look at the papers. You have the papers, don't you?"

He could not lie again. Still he hesitated as long as possible.

"N-n-ine grade," he stuttered. His frame stopped buzzing. His life force had been released and he went limp. His head dropped and hung low, as if hanging on a nail and a tear fell from his eye and hit the dirt in a dusty puff beside the drops of sweat. He prayed silently.

After more commotion inside the Sheriff watched the young girl he'd been inquiring about emerge from the back of the house with a pizza box and disappear in the goat shed only to reappear moments later.

Just then Graves got a whiff of excrement that he chalked up to one of the yard animals producing a fresh movement. But its source was not an animal.

"Tell me her name—"

Julio twisted back and when he saw his daughter slip in the house holding the box he broke fully and wept.

"C'mon Julio, you and the fam got lots to look forward to. Good ol' American Dream ain't so bad, way I see it."

The man didn't say anything, whimpering silently.

"You don't want to cross me now, do ya?"

His bowed head offered a slight shake. "T-T-Tania," the man whined helplessly.

"Just want to meet her, Julio, that's all."

The man reversed unevenly, fading inside the house. There was screaming and a scuffle and slapping sounds, then—silence.

A short while later, the screen door spread and the girl stepped from behind it wearing the new jeans with the fancy stitching her father made her put on. She remained on the porch a while. When she started forward, she advanced slowly but evenly toward the man by the car.

"No taco gene there," Graves muttered, his goldens giving her the infected up and down. He was referring to the young teen's hourglass curves, a trait men like him considered often absent in Mexican women.

She had thin tight lips and the points of freshly formed, upturned breasts spiking through her T-shirt. Crying and wailing could be heard inside while the girl, expressionless, floated steadily toward him. He noticed a fresh red welt to her cheek.

"Hello there, Tania," said Yellow Eyes.

She peeped out from falling bangs protected only by her silence.

"*Yo soy un amigo*—of your daddy's."

"I know who you are—" she returned without hesitation in a mature tone that was forthright, but not insolent. She knew not to be.

His mouth curved sparely and he extended a hand for her to shake. After a pause, she raised hers and let him clasp it. He felt the lightness and softness in her hands and he finished off his grin.

"You like *raspados?*" He was referring to the local high-heat treat, chunks of fruit mixed with shaved ice and syrup, also known as a *Mexican slushie.* "Pineapple-chile's my favorite—"

He waited on her response. Eventually, she nodded.

"Say we go get us one—"

The girl didn't turn around or twist back, not even once. She was strong enough not to and she knew it would kill her mother.

She only spoke in the car and it came in the form of a request. "I want to stop at the Church. I told my mama I would." There she would say a prayer of course for her family.

"Sure," the man said. "Later." He then complimented her spoken English and gave generous praise and credit to the local school which he claimed he helped fund.

They did not stop for a Mexican slushie either, the car rolling off on the dirt track away from town and further south through the industrial section of the city.

"Don't worry, where we're going they'll leave the light on for us," the Sheriff cracked, though she did not understand the remark.

The man took her to a cheap motel in Chandler not far from the one Billy Sixkiller had stayed two nights before. He instructed her to bathe and shampoo and then he moved her change of clothes from the bathroom to the bedroom. When she stepped out of the bathroom in a coarse motel-issue hand towel that was too small to cover her, he ravaged her. His decrepit and leathery sun splotched hands chewed on her soft olive skin and thickly invaded every feature to her freshly blossomed lithe body. He then did everything a man can do to a woman and he showed her everything a woman could do for a man; and more.

"You like your *raspado?*" he posed from above and waited on her nod. He got it.

Presiding over her like that while laying witness to the destruction of sweet dreams of youth and an innocence held under lock and key until now, he found his special ecstasy again and felt himself to be, however fleetingly, a master of the universe. Poised on the precipice of immortality he shuddered and his eyes slowly coasted back in his skull. The feel, the taste, the implication—to him there was nothing more rejuvenating and life enhancing than the consumption of young unspoilt meat. This was his nectar, his elixir, the greatest gift of the Gods. Yellow Eyes was the most depraved of men.

He instructed her to swallow what was in her mouth and held her head in place until she did.

Then he downed another little blue pill.

When she was poised on her abdomen with pillows doubled beneath her stomach raising her backside in the air in the most feared, compromising, and taboo position, the Sheriff asked her what she had been concealing in the pizza box. When she didn't answer, he administered it rough, penetrating deeper and without pause and he kept it going on and on and on, drawing blood from her backside along with his stinging spankings until she yelped and shrieked, all the while threatening—her family would be wiped out if she ever attempted anything foolish.

Then they did it all over again. Everything. Twice. It was her first time—for everything. And it would not be their last.

Around nightfall he would drop her at the nearest intersection and give her face a final study. She had not shed a tear; she would not for Yellow Eyes, nor would she let him see her limp. She would cry only into a pillow through the night so her mother couldn't hear her and for several nights; then never again. Tania was a strong one.

Before leaving the motel, he would offer to take her to Church as requested. She did not answer, but shook a hanging head—the shame would be too much. He would not have taken her in any case as he'd received a call from a concerned woman, an old family friend, claiming her husband hadn't returned from a business trip and was long overdue. Had he not gotten the call, he wouldn't have given the girl from Guadalupe a ride home anyway. After all, the intersection he left her was only a couple miles from the bus stop.

14

The Dolce Vita Diaries III

We are taking back roads, I don't know which direction we're going. Billy has changed course three times. He is not talking now, but I feel his mind racing. I think he's so shocked about you-know-who it's upsetting him and his plans.

I'm more scared now than before. Could Billy have gotten things wrong again?

The ride is so bumpy. It is hard to write. We are listening to Native American flute music. Carlos Nakai. Soothing, but Billy is in a terrible mood. He spoke of going to the Trinity Site at Alamogordo, known for "WMD," where the first atomic bomb was tested. "When human civilization went on the decline, forever," he often says. The Site is a disappointment, he said too. The heat of the explosion caused the desert sand to melt, forming a green glass called Trinitite. The rest was bulldozed away. It's just desert. I don't want to go, it's too depressing. It's better if he doesn't see it, it will make him feel sad too.

My English never seems to get better no matter how much I write.

Billy is slowing down again. Merde …

"Everything okay?" she asked.

"Peachy."

I never like it when he says "peachy." He's getting out. I will try to relax. He must have gone to the bathroom …

"So where are we going?"

"Back to Arizona."

"I thought you wanted to go to the—"

" 'What-Have-I-Done?' Dunes? Not today, next time."

It's what Mr. Oppenheimer said, the man from the bomb project. "What have I done?" he said after the big mushroom climbed the sky. I'm happy he changed his mind. He sounds better.

Billy's moods changed quickly and without warning. He seemed to have come to a decision and whatever he'd decided he appeared at peace with it.

The two had always been happiest when they took to the road in the vast southwest, traveling to offbeat towns, hiking through ruins, chasing down environmental art structures, exhibits, and odd local festivals. Billy considered road education irreplaceable, not to be found in books or online. He referred to both himself and Frenchy as "Road Scholars."

"He's weird …" Frenchy initiated, taking pains to be delicate. "But I have to ask, if he wants to die and is afraid to do it, could he really have what it takes to be a killer? A cold-blooded killer?"

Billy lit two cigarettes and gave one to her. "I have the facts—"

The notion he'd been caught unaware of the prisoner's trip to Tucson was, of course, unsettling to her. Perhaps there was more he got wrong; a thought that was even more terrifying to her.

"Wouldn't put you through it otherwise. I love you."

She noticed a layer of mist collect on his eyes and intuited his raw and sensitive, perhaps fragile state. "I love you too, Billy."

"I would never let anything happen to you."

"I know—"

The fact is he had thought long on this and wanted her to understand fully, so much so the emotion had crept up on him.

"I've been studying him for years. Nothing indicates he still possesses any force of life; his heartbeats, but he's dead. I could off him in two seconds, but that's not what I want. I want to see his guts pour out his throat like a Bacon portrait, you know?"

"You gave me the Francis Bacon CD-ROM for my nineteenth birthday," she corroborated.

"Remember the Bacon we saw at the restaurant Morton's in L.A.?"

"The twisted body? Yes …"

"That's what I want—the raw him—like a piece of meat, from inside out, as we all are, the most violent, arresting version. It's not about ego, I couldn't be that boring. I hope."

"So what is it?"

"It's about obsession; as we are anthropomorphic beings trapped in the human condition and caged within our skins—I want to see this man fully pulsating, alive and vital, coming through his skin. Not a caricature, not an illustration, a real portrait of the man, the killer of my parents. Like the fascination I have with highway crackups, buying back issues of *Paris Match* for the real gore; but it's not the gore, it's the truth surging through the carcass, like the morgue shots of the Hussein brothers, the JFK watermelon shot, the Chechnyan war photos, to see the rawness of human behavior, even the *New York Post* reportage— the twisted souls paying for and begging for boldface ink. The clawing, desperate, wannabe energies, the whole gamut of disturbed and demented *homoerectus* behavior—like the man who cross-dressed, cut off his neighbor's head, then palmed cashews over drinks at a swank hotel."

"These are awful people, Billy—"

"Awful? Yes. Haunting? No doubt. But invigorating to see? *Absolutely*. Like an excellent car accident, a chic emergency; and it's the rawness, the uncut aspects that are so exhilarating. We're all just pounds of flesh and whether you go now or fifty years from now it's the same, a nanosecond on Earth's time clock, whether your head is chopped off or you jump from Tower 1 or you take a bullet at the time of sleep or millions of parasites infest your carcass so you go down in slumber at age ninety-nine which is what dying of old age is, the infestation of parasites—"

"—you've told me."

"And this guy is not interesting to me, not right now."

"As a human being or art project?"

"Neither. I couldn't do this as a straight abduction. Or even as an assassination. I could have paid someone to do that."

"Then what is this about? The revenge is not enough?"

"I need the other dimension; this guy's already dead. Without the rawness, the realness, the blood and the pulsations—I have nothing. There's no portrait; nothing which will remain fossilized in memory which is what all the great portraits do, the ones so vital and violent to the senses they're unforgettable. I'm not talking some Jackson Pollock paint thrown on the wall or Matisse cut-outs, or shapes and colors—I'm talking about an image with order, like Rembrandt's self-portrait or Jack Kennedy on the slab at Parkland Memorial, eyes wide open after his autopsy. True off the senses, unforgettable, and unmerciful to memory.

"What we have back there is not even a still life. It's far worse—it's dead life, it's flatline, it's cliché, it's unoriginal, it's a sack of potatoes. I'm not a grocer, I don't want a bag of spuds; I want *him*, a surging, oozing him, pulsating, breathing, defecating—vital. So when the hand strikes Zero-Clock and his time comes and the mail gets delivered, the bullet going in, the brains blasting out the other side, a glorious spray of jumbled genetic codes, a DNA pizza, of a figure so unconscious then so incredibly alive, that picture, that mental image will remain with me. *Forever*. The motherfucker owes me that much—"

She'd heard permutations of his interpretive portraiture philosophies before.

"That's a portrait—*that's* what I'm looking for."

"But Billy, is this justice?"

"That is justice. For me. My payback; don't I deserve my payback? The way I want it? On my terms?"

"Okay, *je comprends*." She would not challenge him now.

"Doesn't matter where the idea came from. And I will not adhere to a plan just because I came up with it—so it's autographed like a baseball. It's what my nervous system requires to get rid of it; to get rid of the shit, to get past it, to get some peace. Don't you want me to have peace?"

He wiped his face quickly, the water having filled his lids.

It was the word he'd used—*peace*. The thought of Billy at long last getting some peace weakened her and she twisted out her ciggy and settled her head on his shoulder, wiping her own topaz blues dry.

He placed her Road Scholar hat on her head, an orange fluorescent crusher. Too consumed with present fears, she didn't even notice he'd done it.

"Billy?"

"My little Mistral?"

"How will you do it? To make the portrait more interesting, to get him more alive—"

"Sleep deprivation for starters," he said. "May not work, but it's my only chance. You taking this down in the 'Diaries?' "

His tone indicated he was smiling and she nodded into his chest.

I see method to his madness. It's a form of art to him. He's satisfying that part at the same time he gets his revenge. If it was anyone else I would think they were full of it. But Billy is an artist and he loves to make beauty—more than anything! He may be deceiving himself on purpose, to let himself believe it's art, because it's not beautiful and he must know it—it's ugly. And cruel. Like a cat torturing a mouse, playing before a kill. Billy loves the portrait of the wild cat too, the stalker, the predator; the victim also. Not for horror, for the beauty. His visual mind works like this. But Man is not a cat. Maybe a mouse? I am not sure what he is. I wonder what his power animals are …

No!!! I don't want to think about him personally …

For all Billy's craziness he can be so loving and caring. I love him, I can not help it, he is a part of me. He wants me to reach my dreams. Many men do not want that for their women, their girlfriends, or wives. It is why I put up with the rest because I know his portrait. The Francis Bacon one with the guts coming out. Even though I tease him about being a pig, I know he wants the best for me, to realize my potential as a human being. He is very spiritual. He says prayers for my family—people he doesn't know. He prays for people who have been bad to him. It makes tears come to my eyes. He's driving quietly now with a little boy smile on his face. That is when I know he is happy. He is such a little boy!

I tried to talk him out of going back to Arizona. He committed the crime there and the police will be after him. I want him to take another route, but he is sure no one is on the trail. He's sure Man's secretary has not called him in missing yet and his family would rely on her word. By the time they think something is wrong we'll be in a place police don't go. I know what he means. The rez.

I don't think he's lying to me, but he knows it worries me and makes my stomach hurt. Oh no! We are pulling off the back road and heading into the woods now. I don't know why ...

15

Still afternoon, the sun was blazing from high up and blinding eyes of the creatures below. The Ivory Stretch was scorching its own path through dusty trails crossing back into Arizona. Billy slashed through the Apache National and the San Carlos Rez to satisfy Frenchy, certain he could have attacked it directly by returning the way they'd come. Nobody knew it, but he was still taking them right back from where they'd come from.

I am back now, three hours later!!! We hiked to a natural hot springs. There were lots of them in the Gila because of the "subterranean geology." Billy said I should read "The Subterraneans." It's by Keriwack. He was in good spirits and we hiked past old mining ruins to the Gila River, then walked upstream to a canyon and we saw the steam rising up from the earth. I was about to jump in the water, but Billy told me there was an amoeba bug living in the hot springs that is fatal to humans! But there is a million in one chance to get it. After ten minutes of being scared I went in. I took all my clothes off. It was warm and soothing. We did "Boris and Svetlana" also, the Russian mobster fat cat and his Ukrainian gold digger wife. "Dahlink"-this, "Vare is Goochi?"-that.

Man stayed beneath a tree. I think I saw him laugh. That's what I call him. "Man." I wish he would disappear and it would just be the two of us again.

Billy gave Man an orange road hat too. It is hunting season and we didn't want to get mistaken for deer or animals—and shot!

When I got out of the springs I saw Man look at me naked, but I didn't care. He turned his head away out of respect. I don't think he was trying to see me, but I hopped out as he was looking. Billy made him get in the spring. That was the reason we went there. To get clean. I think he did it for his car more than anything.

Man looks well for no sleep. I want to cross these lines out because I don't want to talk about him—but he does exist. I don't want to be phony that way. To deceive and hide truths from myself. And though I don't approve of it I am still here. It's hypocritical the other way. But I am not happy with myself. We are not making beauty. Definitely not.

I washed my underwear in the springs. Billy gave a thumb's up when I looped them over the antenna to dry. MEN!

We are back in the car now and Billy has put that fight on so Man can watch it. That same fight Billy always watches. He has seen it 363 times! Fifteen times in one day! I asked him why. He said, "Everything you need to know about life" is in it.

I feel stronger. Probably because my period is over.

Billy sent the glass partition down and the Sensurround system was blasting. The sounds of the overly excited crowd inspired him and he sat high in his seat. "The bell ring yet?"

"About to—"

The drag in the prisoner's eyes seemed to have disappeared. The soothing waters of the hot springs had smoothed them, the dark circles gone. He'd been pasty white a day before, but was now sunburned, his pallor bright, his skin tight with a glow. The man looked refreshed.

"You never saw it?"

"I remember it, I read about it."

"Who Izenberg? Dick Young? Kram in *SI*? Bastard. The *Times*?"

"Maybe on TV."

"Cosell on *Wide World*?"

"I don't remember."

"How could you forget? October 1, 1975, Cayzon City, six miles outside of Manila, ten AM—unforgettable!"

Frenchy had been sleeping deeply several hours dreaming of the white lions and the Easter egg-colored Victorian homes. She snarled at the opened partition. "What are you doing?" she spat grumpily.

"He's never seen it, can you believe it?" Frenchy knew Billy took a huge thrill in being the one to introduce the fight to someone so she didn't say anything further and Billy angled back. "You have that pad of paper?"

He did. He'd secretly drafted two copies already of a testament detailing what were to be his precise burial arrangements in the hopes at least one copy would be discovered by the authorities. He folded them small, buttoning one in his back pocket; the other was to be rolled in his rectum.

"You're gonna judge the fight, take notes each round," Billy spoke loudly over the broadcast. "That's Flip Wilson the comedian talking … Ken Norton's in the booth, Marcos and Imelda are ringside. Guess which fighter Imelda had a crush on?"

"Would have to be Ali."

"Sure as hell wasn't Smokin' Joe!" he teased. "Good old Imelda, the gal with an 'edifice complex'—"

Roland was struck then—the captor could be a vicious gossip too.

"She was always spending money on building. And the shoes. Duchamp could have done wonders with her shoes. Ready-Made Imeldas ..."

"She's a beautiful woman."

"Course you think so Rollie, you're a beauty junkie—like all Libran writers. Faulkner, Fitzgerald, Eliot, Wilde, O'Neill, Miller, Wolfe, Greene, Kafka, Capote, Rimbaud. Even Nietzsche and Gandhi. Lest we forget John Lennon."

The assessment was true. Throughout Roland's life he'd been consumed with aesthetics and not just faces, but beautiful words, music, paintings, places, the finer things. Billy was right. He had been a "beauty junkie" like the famous Libran writers. *And Polsonby*, he thought, adding himself to the list in silent derision. "I had my days."

"No shit ... What did you think of the frogette?"

Caught off guard, the man met Billy's intense glare in the rearview.

"Gal's at peak estrogen," the captor added. " 'Cause it's the estrogen that produces feminine beauty. Those perfect tots? Bee-bit lips? Cantaloupe behind? Less estrogen, the more cosmetics're needed. Makeup 'makes up' for a loss of femininity." He paused. "I saw your lamps burning down on her; gave her the high-beams you did. Body charts its own course, don't it?"

Roland felt embarrassed. He had thought about it; he'd replayed the scintillating vision several times in his mind as they hiked back from the hot springs and again later in the car. He'd seen Frenchy fully and he absorbed it as only a man could. In the backseat they had come on of their own accord, thoughts of that nature and the bodily responses he hadn't experienced in a long time. His biology could not turn its back on it. There was more. The penetrating visual provoked an additional reminiscence—the second part of that last soirée when he returned home from the awards gala. There'd been a knock on his door that startled him as he was certain Adele had not yet made it home. "Yes?"

"Mr. Polsonby? It's Fernanda."

"Everything's okay," he told her. "I took down the bed myself already."

"Mr. Polsonby?" Hearing the frailty in her voice, there was little he could do. He spread the door and she was standing there looking troubled. "I-I-I'm sorry to disturb you."

He had not wanted this; no emotional outpourings—not then.

Physically, she was an exquisitely feminine, natural earth beauty; a glorious mix of Cherokee, Chocktaw, and Spanish. Her fine cheekbones were sculpted high and she had a tiny straight nose complementing the elegantly drawn face and thin soft lips. Her hair was long and shiny black and she braided it or let it fall freely. Thin dark eyebrows and eyelashes gave the appearance of paint, no makeup needed. Her skin was a deep red and smooth and her figure curved sharply and often, her ample chest rarely tended to by undergarments. She could have been paid handsomely to endorse products she never used if she'd had the yearning.

Billy had conjured the prisoner's memory speaking of femininity and superior estrogen levels as Fernanda was similar to Frenchy in that way.

That night, Fernanda was wearing sheer white linen, drawstring pants, and no underclothing. Her perfect breasts fell in a savagely natural hang, perked, hard-candy nipples peering through, and the curves of her beautiful body were backlit from hallway sconces—a vision one could remember a lifetime. Yet he knew she was so much more than a physical beauty.

She was poised there, swaying tenuously and he could see the fear in her clairvoyant eyes and it mercilessly came to him the day they'd first met and he'd had that interior vision of her, one they'd shared mutually as windows to each others' souls. He was captivated by her wonderful essence encased in the exquisite packaging, she was beauty and soul and enlightened spirit and he knew that, but he could not appreciate it any longer; he could not feel her now or anyone.

She eased in steps closer until her full, pointed breasts made a soft landing at his chest and she wrapped him; yet he remained still and unmoved. Her tears flowed freely as his arms would not come to life around her. Pulling back, he took in the almond eyes made fragile, a loving expression made vulnerable. He spoke hoarsely.

"I'm taking a private car to the airport. I'll leave mine in the garage. There's a briefcase in the trunk and I want you to take it. Hide it. I want you and your husband to have the chance to live your dreams."

Then he handed her the keys to the car.

Her tear-streamed face showed the devastation. He eyed her as compassionately as he could, hoping her life would hold every blessing and happiness and he prayed for it silently as she stood there.

"Go to Gonzalo. He is a good man."

She probed the depths of his eyes one last time and he sensed she knew now; she would never see him again. The woman turned quickly and ran so he would not see her break down.

A few hours later, he was on his way to the airport.

Though Billy was responsible in part, the image of a totally nude Frenchy brought to mind Fernanda's embrace, the sweet one, the loving one, which had been an offering of her to him.

As he sat alone in the dark in back his imagination, underutilized and rusty, took over. He indulged in the fantasy awarding a second chance at her as he'd been secured, but not cuffed. When he reached climax, something he hadn't enjoyed in years, he heaved and gasped. Lying nearly prostrate, he was shocked by it, that he had the desire and capacity for it, that it could even happen.

In this layered and loaded way he'd frozen when Billy brought up the notion of a stark naked Frenchy at the springs.

He was reclined to the seat back now, his ankles still wire-locked to the door. The roar of a boisterous crowd to a dazzling, widescreen High-Def image redirected him, and then the bell went off.

"There they go!"

"Shall I pause it?"

"Hell no, you're ringside!"

"Beelly!" Frenchy snapped, awoken again. *"Arrête!"*

Picking up the Dylan song he'd crowed earlier, *"Fee, Fi, Fo, Fum, Cassius Clay here I come! Knock his block off Joe!"*

The round ended with the bell. "So, what do you have—?"

" 'Ali hits him with fast shots,' " Roland read from his notes. " 'All to Frazier's head. Hard for Frazier to get to him. Ali is so fast. At one point it looked like Frazier was in trouble—' "

"So who took the round?"

"Ali."

"No brainer—Frazier always dropped the first round."

The next round he reported: " 'Ali keeps hitting Frazier in the head. Frazier tries to move in, but takes three or four punches before he can get one in. Ali plays with him. Holds him away. Commentator says he has six-and-a-half inch advantage in reach …' "

"The round?"

"Ali, I have to say."

Billy nodded neutrally.

Then, the third round; " 'Ali keeps Frazier away with his jab. Then goes to the ropes. Lets Joe hit him. Commentator says it's what Ali did to George Foreman. Ali taunts Joe to come back. He does. Ali breaks loose with a flurry. Sensational shots.' "

"Round goes to Ali too," Roland added, unprompted.

"Joe's a slow starter," Billy returned, nearly defensive.

The car came to a sudden, screeching halt in a desolate expanse of barrel cactus and choked vegetation. The quick stop woke Frenchy.

"Baby, you gotta take over—"

"I'm not driving!"

Billy tossed his sunglasses to the dashboard. " 'Kay, but I gotta watch this—"

He sprung out and piled in the rear door. Frenchy craned back, disoriented and grumpy. *"Merde!"* She closed the partition.

On an uninhabited stretch of dirt track crosscutting the San Carlos rez in the middle of nowhere, the Ivory Stretch was on pause. The car was docked to the shoulder, a washed-up novelist on a death march and an uncommonly configured psychopath gathered now like fraternity brothers to spectate a vintage prizefight, Billy the elder and Roland the pledge.

"Come on, ref!" Billy jeered. "He's holding Joe!"

Joe Frazier had begun to "smoke" in the fourth round and Billy rooted him on vociferously. Roland noted, " 'Ali spending time on the ropes, Frazier closing and connecting with precise shots between Ali's gloves as he rope-a-dopes—' "

"You're picking up the terminology—"

"Frazier seems to have found his stride—"

"Who takes the round?"

"Frazier."

"The rope-a-dope was the death of Foreman—not so Joe!"

"I have to credit the commentator—"

"Joe loves the ropes, he pounds the body, wears a guy down. He's too short to fight in the middle of the ring where Ali's at his best.

Because he can jab, jab, jab, then move away. But Ali didn't have the legs any more, not like in his twenties."

In the fifth, the captor cheered wildly whenever Frazier landed one.

As Roland scored it: " 'The crowd getting behind Frazier. Ali coasting, getting hit, Frazier looks revitalized, ducking, weaving, and scoring. Ali has slowed down.' Frazier's round again."

"Not bad—" Billy noted, impressed by the prisoner's quick and accurate grasp.

In the sixth, Frazier connected with thunderous left hooks thrown ten seconds apart, clearly stunning Ali, Billy going berserk.

" 'Ali looks tired, Frazier keeps coming, cutting off the ring, throwing huge left hooks—six in all. Big round for Frazier—' "

"Fight's even now, wouldn't you say?"

"I would. Billy?"

"Yes?"

"I'll take you up on that soft drink—"

"You bet ..." Billy drew one from the ice well. "Sprite?"

"Is there a Coke?"

"Sorry," he said, denying him flatly. "Water or Sprite—you'll have to earn your caffeine."

The prisoner considered this development encouraging. A caffeinated drink could boost him if he tired.

At the end of the seventh he reported, " 'Ali moving again, picking his spots, Frazier connects with good right hand, left hook, Ali good uppercut.' I give it to Ali."

"I had it even; you've got 4-3, Ali. Isn't Joe a thing of beauty?"

"He's in excellent condition, Norton said."

In round eight Roland noted, " 'Ali against the ropes getting hit, stages a rally, flurries, Joe returns a hook, Joe comes on strong.' "

"Who do you pick?" Billy asked anxiously.

"Even."

"Even?" he protested. "Come on, Rollie!"

"No?"

"If that's the way you saw it, that's the way you saw it," he spat disappointedly. "I see the fight 4-4; you see it 4-3-1, Ali."

Roland wondered now if he should slant his voting. The ninth boasted little action as both fighters were catching their breath and coasting.

" 'Ali danced briefly, Frazier maneuvers him back to the ropes. They hang on to each other. Ali losing his legs.' "

Billy was awaiting his verdict with an electrified expression.

"I give the round to Frazier—because he was the aggressor."

"Good man! You'll make a ref yet—"

For the tenth, Roland read again from the notepad: " 'Ali against the ropes again, he's tired. His corner yelling at him.' "

"You heard that!"

" 'Even exchanges, but Joe more aggressive. Ali's legs buckling as he goes back to corner—round to Frazier.' "

"Yee-ha!" Billy howled and vaulting up, he slammed his head on the roof. "Isn't he awesome?"

"So tough; he just keeps coming—"

Roland determined then it was his toughness the captor was referring to in calling him a "thing of beauty."

"You got Frazier 5-4-1, right? Come on Smokin' Joe!"

The action changed again in the eleventh. Ali came out dancing, perhaps miraculously. " 'Ali flurries, Joe comes back, Ali flurries again. Unbelievable comeback.' "

Billy withdrew over the course of the stunning round and became sullen. His excitement faded, he'd been on the edge of his seat, but was now slumping back. He grabbed a beer, snapped it open, and took a draw.

"Who won it?" he posed dejectedly. He was now a different Billy.

Roland hesitated. "I had to give it to Ali—"

Billy threw back the rest of the beer can and nodded.

In the twelfth, both fighters looked tired, but Ali teed off on Joe. His left eye was swelling and Ali spotted it and attacked it.

" 'Joe looks slower, Ali moves to the middle of the ring, scores.' " Roland lifted up from the pad. Billy was not even looking at the screen. "'They go to the ropes, Ali throws more,'" he said, almost apologetically.

"So you've got it—?" he asked curtly, impatience brewing in him.

"What?"

"The score!" he snapped.

He didn't want to call the round, but feared deceiving him.

"6-5-1, Ali. You know, we don't have to watch it—"

Billy flared a look and redirected to the screen.

Ali was magnificent in the thirteenth, dancing and scoring at will. Where he summoned the energy is the stuff of boxing mythology. He hammered Joe with flurries; the kidney and rib shots Joe administered, the huge right hooks in the middle rounds Ali had endured. Joe needed the knock out.

Roland showed restraint. The task of delivering unwelcomed news was harrowing. " 'Ali moving well, dancing—' " he began.

The upset registered on Billy's face. "Hurry up!"

" 'Ali knocks his mouthpiece out. Joe exhausted. Ali flurries.' "

"And?"

"Round to Ali. Score is 7-5-1, Ali." He knew to add the score.

In the fourteenth, Frazier's left eye was nearly shut and his cheek was cut. He stood, planted there like a punching bag, taking a barrage.

" 'Ali hitting with combinations, Joe not able to fire back, both exhausted, Ali summoning energy, flurried shots to Frazier's head—' "

"Enough already!"

"Ali up 8-5-1."

"Enough I said! It's over!"

"What?"

"The fight's over! Eddie Futch stopped it!"

"Who is Eddie Futch?" Onscreen, Roland saw the ref calling the fight, arms crossing over his head.

"Frazier's trainer!" The object of Billy's temper had been diverted which was a blessing. The prisoner now had his exit strategy.

"That's not right. What did Joe say?"

"Joe wanted to fight! He could have still knocked him out!"

"How unfair! That's terrible!"

"Worst corner decision ever made! Joe was not going to get hurt." He mimicked Futch, belittling his infamous quote, *'Sit down, son. It's all over. But no one will ever forget what you did here today ...'* How about you made *everyone* forget by not letting Joe finish, fuckface! You altered history! *Moron.* Joe never forgave him, Futch was a bum ..."

The two were no longer adversaries and the prisoner was relieved.

The man opened the door and charged out, slamming it, the only time Roland witnessed a careless maneuver of the sort.

Billy carved the vehicle back onto the track, leaving a sizable cloud to hover until the car stopped suddenly again. Roland became fearful; Billy's temper had been on the boiler. Should he have called Frazier the victor? Did Billy think Joe had a second chance? Or did he want a second opinion? Roland feared the worst.

He heard Billy get out without cutting the engine and then the rear door was spread. "You judged it well," his captor acknowledged, head held away, as if difficult to admit. "And earned yourself a Coke. Help yourself ..."

He closed the door again, this time gently, and then took to the road maneuvering the Stretch smoothly with no surge.

Roland sat there, dumbstruck; he couldn't fathom getting worked up over a prizefight, never a favored sport, certainly not one from over thirty years ago, its outcome known, its every twist and turn revealed, an event with no surprises. To have that kind of ebullience and energy for an expired drama was incomprehensible. Yet Billy's passionate nature reminded him of basic flaws in his own character, ones that had caused him trouble. Having never possessed that kind of fire, Roland couldn't help but respect it in another, a figure so magnificently sensitized, who burned so. He'd sworn off introspection, but had to acknowledge this lapse, feeling remorse and envy, emotions he hadn't experienced in a long time. Curiously, these sentiments weren't debilitating either—this or the erotic fantasy. The prisoner was receiving again, albeit barely, but was no longer fearing it.

He ached as he leaned forward and opened the beverage well, empty except for the single Coke. He popped it and took small sips. Pain throbbed throughout his body, brought on by the raw stiffness of unused muscles. Remembering his athletic days, he knew ice was required during the first twenty-four hours and to administer heat was illadvised. So far, he'd been on two challenging hikes and the hot waters had surely served to make him swell more and increase the pain and soreness. He wondered if his captor had orchestrated this purposely, to intensify Roland's physical discomfort—a likely possibility.

Oddly, he felt for Billy. He wished Joe had won the fight instead.

16

As Billy Six explained it, a crevice had formed eons ago when the Earth's crust was cooling, allowing water to flow into the molten interior, producing an incredible burst of steam. The awesome pressure forced the molten mass to surge up from the hot mantle through the crevice, creating a monstrous mass of volcanic material that rose thousands of feet in the air. When the mass cooled, it hardened into a range of peaks—the Superstition Mountains—its towering facade in front.

Roland knew of the Superstitions from his freeway travels and from outdoorsy club members who discussed their hikes. More significantly, locating the range before him meant that after all their meandering, the Stretch was only thirty miles from Phoenix now—an encouraging sign.

In the mid-afternoon the Stretch pulled off the Apache Trail. The October sun had weakened measurably, the temperature pleasant. When Frenchy awoke from her nap and surveyed familiar territory a quarrel ensued. They were only five miles from Whispering Palms, the retirement community she'd been holed up in for two years. She was even more upset at the unnecessary risk they seemed to be taking.

Yet Billy perceived any risk was worthwhile; the prisoner's unwavering hopes of a reunion burial were an insurance policy against his attempting the foolish. The abductor never let the man off the hook psychologically, instilling the fear that he was capable of brutal violence at any time. Unpredictable, with streaks of mean and cruelty, he kept the prisoner off-balance and in check, with fatal and drastic consequences implied and pending.

If ever a man was perfectly suited to perform an abduction of the sort it was Billy Six. He relished the plan's design and was its architect. In his mind the drama was unfolding with the grandeur of a Picasso canvas in the developing stages; or the first acts of a Shakespearean play, spiked with the fantastical realism of García Márquez. The plan was continuing to blossom like a flower in spring. He had his man; the revenge had been teed up and the ball clubbed deep down the fairway, his payback in play. But now the plot held a bonus element that had not existed prior—the challenge to resuscitate a man, a living dead man and bring him back to life. In artistic terms, Roland's desire and ready willingness to die had been a gorgeous happy accident that provided a new welcomed test to make the undertaking infinitely more obstacled, sweet, and gratifying and how its architect cherished the gaming aspects. In this way, the drama was taking on a life of its own, reinventing itself, and the realism was getting increasingly magical by the hour. The perpetrator perceived it this way. Unquestionably Billy was narcissistic and could easily become seduced by grandiosity and glory. He did consider himself an artist and envisioned life events and his participation in them, in symbolic, expressionistic terms. What was freshly inspiring now was, his mission had become organic; his revenge plot was a living and breathing organism—it was alive. And thriving. And he had brought it to life. At this point, Billy the mastermind as well as the artist, couldn't be more delighted at the prospects for his mission's outcome or end product—the final work of art.

Billy stashed the car before the two would disappear into the landscape carefully concealing it beneath a sandstone ledge surrounded by thick ocotillo and cougarclaw: a spot he called "The Garage." The Garage was situated deep in the canyon well beyond the busy Peralta Trailhead and he left his car there whenever he camped in the Superstitions for spiritual retreats, sweat lodges, or sleepovers.

Frenchy had been content to stay in the car to watch more courtroom television and read *Soiled Doves*, the latest volume on subject matter close to her heart. The book chronicled the checkered lives of seemingly well-intentioned women in the 1800s that headed west and turned to prostitution to survive. The psychological makeup of these fallen women fascinated her. As compelling she had reasons for that.

From the legends of the Pimas and Apaches to stories recounted by the Spanish settlers and white prospectors, including the famed Lost Dutchman's Gold Mine, the history of the Superstitions was well documented. Each year another tragic death seemed to take place, only adding to the mountain range's sinister mystique. Such lore and intrigue made the range popular with hikers, but by October, tourist flow was minimal and the uncharted routes posed little risk of day-trippers.

Billy had been coming to the Superstitions for years and knew every twist and turn of the terrain. For their excursion he chose an off-trail loop through the Peralta Canyon where they pursued a small creek and rock-hopped it, charging forth at a quick clip. The captor was conscious of the time, constantly referring to his watch. He seemed in a hurry.

Roland had taken a turn for the worse physically, the lack of sleep catching up. He was sore, excruciatingly so, his legs raw, his feet flamed from rows of crushed blisters. Yet Billy pressured the pace, maneuvering through the gauntlet of prickly catclaw with ripe determination as Roland became increasingly lightheaded.

"When do you sleep?" he posed between labored pants.

"One to three hours per; can go a night without, too."

"Why didn't you sleep last night?"

"Too excited—we had a guest—or have you forgotten?"

As the prisoner dragged on he was reminded of his New York City days when he attacked Midtown with fleet-footed strides. His pace had slowed in Phoenix and he hadn't called on that Manhattan step in years. Billy was marching more swiftly than that.

As they rounded a bend, Billy spotted a small cairn, a pile of stacked rocks left to mark the trail and he suddenly launched into it in an accent close to affected eastern prep school.

"Tell you a diversionary tale to keep your mind off the physicals. Jacob von Walzer was his name, the famous 'Dutchman.' A German immigrant really from Wurttemberg, Walz, as he became known, was a lieutenant in the Prussian army and educated at Heidelberg as a mining engineer. He migrated to the States in 1850, inspired by the gold strike discovery in '49 at Sutter's Mill in California. He was a tall man with an imposing carriage and was a crack shot with a .44. He prospected first in Sutter's Creek, but ended up in Arizona working for a few mining companies. First in Prescott, then Wickenburg. Some say he 'high-graded,' meaning he stole gold ore from the mines he worked. Though he was never caught, he was relieved of his position.

"Walz fell in love with a beautiful seventeen-year old Apache girl named Ken-tee which translated to 'sunshine' in the native tongue. Was rumored she helped him spirit away the stolen ore. When he lost his job, they left the area and moved into an Indian community in Mesa about thirteen miles from these mountains, settling down and living in a hogan."

As Roland trudged on his thoughts became more erratic and the image of Fernanda returned, beautiful exceptional Fernanda, coming to him in the night and embracing him, free-breasted, so warm against him, a reverie spurred by the mention of Walz's 'Ken-tee.' Hearing her songs and lyrics, envisioning her singing in the outdoor shower, Roland was entertaining surges of delirium.

"You want a snip-toed boot in the ass? Pay attention—"

The hurting man mauled a response in something approaching English.

Billy knew something of the resignation of the human spirit, having embraced philosophies taught to him by the wise Elders of the Havasupais. Human beings who stopped asking questions of the ancient ones, of Mother Earth, of Creation, of all living things—meaning they'd forsaken curiosity—were on the Road to the Living Dead. Billy was certain if he could get Roland curious, to ask questions again, he could break through and turn him around—that was his plan.

His strategy was to throw life in the captive man's face: intense life, exploding life, perhaps violent life. Again, in artistic terms, he conceived it now as a canvas in the Pollock tradition, tossing the Earth's colors at a dead soul like paint to a blank wall. Only moments ago, he was unsure as to what direction the canvas would take, but the vision he held was now clear and had come to him spontaneously in the doing. Each choice he made was a color; each step was a brushstroke. Artistic direction and approaches always came to Billy in the moment in images of the sort, the creative processes of favorite writers and artists always at the forefront of his mind. He referred constantly to the masters and applied their techniques to his existence as though he was following in their steps. Reflections of the sort made him feel he was on the path of becoming a true master himself.

In midstep Billy caught himself smiling. He realized he had two canvases going, two portraits side by side as if it was a diptych; resuscitating Roland was one, the revenge plot the other. The thought of this living diptych made him tingle with anticipation. The artist in him now was not only proud, exuberant.

"The Apaches," he resumed, his breathing effortless, "had settlements throughout this wilderness and they knew where the Mexican Peralta mine was located. But the Indians did not covet the gold, considering it a gift to their Thunder God and the lesser gods residing in the Superstitions. The voices of these gods was the thunder rolling out of the spires atop the mountains during storms and the Apaches defended the sanctity of the Thunder God's home. This ground was considered sacred and it made passage for outsiders extremely dangerous.

"In addition, it was forbidden for the Indians to divulge the location of the mine to anyone outside of the tribe, and certainly not to any white man whom they felt worshipped money and material wealth."

Roland listened, hoping to hear more of the Indian bride, if nothing else.

"Not long after Walz and Ken-tee moved to Mesa, they disappeared for a while returning weeks later at the Wells Fargo office in Phoenix with two burros packed with gold concentrate. From there, they shipped it to the U.S. Mint in San Francisco. In return, they were sent a check for nine thousand dollars.

"Because of this windfall, it was rumored Walz the 'Dutchman' had found gold in the Superstitions; word of the strike spread quickly. The tribe also learned of it, convinced Ken-tee had revealed the secret to her lover. So the angered Apaches raided the hogan where the two were living and seized her. She was rescued on horseback by a hunting party but not before Apache braves had cut out her tongue. She bled to death in Walz's arms. Devastated, Walz returned to the mine only once more, but after his camp was attacked again by the tribe, he avoided it for another ten years."

As Billy continued to recount the tale, the two descended into a thick ravine negotiating a series of switchbacks. Though Roland's legs felt like cement, he pushed to stay close, to hear Billy's every word. The story was compelling and he was able to temporarily forget the daunting challenge and physical strain. At a break in the delivery Roland urgently posed, "So what happened to Walz?"

The captor was silently delighted his prisoner was enraptured, acting like a child listening anxiously to a bedtime story.

"Walz became a recluse. But he was famous. A true celebrity. Newspapers referred to him as the 'Old Dutchman,' a man who'd discovered a veritable gold mine so rich in high-grade ore he could go to it any time he wished, but ignored it because of personal tragedy. The news was electrifying, exciting the imagination of millions worldwide—the legend grew. People came from all over to see him as well as those wanting to learn the mine's whereabouts. His every move was watched; a tent colony of gold-seekers sprung up along his street while his house became a fortress to keep them away. Many tried to befriend him and gain his confidence; others hoped to track him to it. What insured his survival was Walz himself—because if anything happened to him the mine would likely never be found again.

"Walz was also an excellent marksman and always carried a rifle on the rare occasions he was in public. He wouldn't go out or socialize. Famous writers sought him out, Twain, Beecher Stowe, Thomas Hardy, Whitman, Melville. They all tried to interview him, but he wouldn't talk. He got huge offers for partnerships; others offered protection. But he stayed a loner."

Roland's condition continued to improve. He was no longer delirious or dreamy. His strides were fluid. Though breathing hard he wasn't gasping. He'd found a second wind.

"Walz never went back for the gold?"

"He did. After years of giving money to charities and buying shoes for underprivileged kids called 'Negroes' at the time, he returned to the mine, on foot. With his two burros, Fortuna and Senator, he'd walk a normal pace and people followed him; but as you see, the Superstitions are a natural labyrinth with deep canyons, defiles, and washes of volcanic rock covered in spiny cacti. When darkness fell, the Dutchman would lead his burros into the maze of deep washes thick with this impenetrable growth. Anyone who came near was shot at. It's said he killed a few who crept too close—"

"Wasn't he charged with the killings?"

"There was no ballistics back then. And it was too dark for witnesses. It was a wild time; killings were an everyday occurrence and often ignored and the Apaches were easily blamed, as well."

"How did Walz get the gold with all these people tracking him?"

"He put mufflers and pads on his burros to silence them. When it seemed safe he would descend into the mine and the crowd following wouldn't see him again until he was on his way back to Phoenix. Vouchers of mint records show he made $250,000 between 1879 and 1885."

They were bushwhacking now. They'd been going for an hour and a half and Billy checked his watch—it was nearing four-clock. He led Roland out of the dense uncharted route and they advanced on a long narrow clearing.

Angling up, Roland was stunned; they were situated beneath a monstrous rock formation made of smooth black basalt rising majestically from the plateau hundreds of feet in the air. At the formation's base were sheer cliffs and crevices choked with prickly pear and ocotillo. The blind approach from the other side had shielded them.

"Mexicans named it the Finger of God—"

Roland kept gazing up, marveling at the towering formation.

"Walz lived into his eighties," the captor said, concluding his tale. "After the Great Flood washed away his home in 1891, he died at the home of Julia Thomas, a black woman to whom he had given shoes when she was a child. But before he died, he whispered to her, 'the mine can be found on the spot on which the shadow of the tip of Weaver's Needle rests at exactly four-clock.'"

Billy raised his watch. "See the time?" The face read precisely four.

"That's Weaver's Needle!" Roland deciphered, pointing up at the rock tower. "So the mine's right here, where this shadow is—"

Billy turned him a partial grin. "Right where you're standing, Rollie."

The prisoner's feet were angled across the enormous gray edge cast by the structure. Roland marveled at the notion. The ever-prepared and precise Billy Six had timed their trek perfectly.

"That's what's written, but no one's ever found it; it's why they call it the Lost Dutchman's Mine."

The prisoner's mouth turned up at the corners; he was awestruck.

"But if you get into the technical aspects, the shadow is longer in winter than summer, causing the tip to move. Baffled countless thousands for years."

Roland surveyed the long line of shadow and craning up again, he took in Weaver's Needle and its apex.

"So," he concluded, "we're on a treasure hunt."

Billy grinned him one, self-satisfied. "Feel like digging?"

"No!" he bellowed, gasping. There was a bright flush to his cheeks though and he seemed thrilled, the sprawling grin manifesting it.

A curve grew on the captor's face, more vague and less giddy, however. He handed off the bottle and Roland took a measured drink, there was little left. "Have some more—"

The prisoner heard a series of raven location calls and was reminded of the wilderness enveloping them. He feared them losing their way with no water, and never being found. He shook his head.

"Don't worry, I know where to get more. Finish it off—"

The man hesitated still.

"Come on, live a little." The captor spread one wider, cognizant of his choice of words and the prisoner took a last swig.

Billy checked the receding sun as well as the chromatic index, the height of the bands of orange light on the opposing canyon wall, and determined it with assurance. "There's just enough light."

Roland spoke suddenly, intoning a note of warning. "Billy—"

The perceived change in voice twisted Billy around.

The rustling emanated from the shaded leaves at the edge of the clearing. A six-footer, thick and fluorescent lime green, it moved nearly undetectably, blending with the layers of neatleaf hackberry and scrub oak. The creature slithered on an angle away from them.

Billy's grill slashed severely across. He immediately secured a sturdy stick and drew a pocketknife and quickly sliced a deadly sharp point to it. A feral look to his eye, he advanced on the steadily moving snake, his crude weapon raised. He crept slowly, closing in.

"You really going to do that?"

As the words rolled off the prisoner's tongue, Billy brought the spear down hard, piercing the creature inches below the head. He lifted the stick, the snake stuck to it, its tongue darting out spastically. "Don't usually mind these puppies—"

The captor then broke naturally into his Alabaman vernacular. Roland noted the change and it was again, curious.

"But thissy here's a green Mohave—deadly sucker—and deadly's fine, but this one, musta been his cousin, killed Frenchy's dog Popsi. Had a chance to kill that one too. See that jaw … *some* bite radius—"

The split tongue was still squirting. "He's alive—"

"Precisely, 'cause I ain't done."

With stick in hand and the flailing snake pinned to it, Billy moved across the clearing to the upslope of the plateau at the base of the towering Weaver's Needle and squared before a tall saguaro. He drew the spear back as if to cast a rod and reel and suddenly whipped it forward. The creature flew through the air, the length of it smacking the big cactus broadside, holding fast to the trunk as if crucified. The sharp spines and needles from the cactus protruded through its abdomen.

"Call that 'death by saguaro' in Sonoran slang—kid you not."

The snake was tacked helplessly to the cactus and the prisoner stood there transfixed, thoroughly dumbstruck by the demonstration.

"Mohaves never been good to me, scorpions neither. Only thing I'm sorry about is the varmints—owls, hawks and coyotes are gonna feast on it instead of us. Course, *los apilotes* too. Let's go—"

On the other side of the mountain, Frenchy was awaiting darkness to relocate the car. She decided on a late afternoon stroll and ascended a hard-packed trail that rose to a sandstone plateau. A self-taught dancer, she practiced some ballet spins in her new butterfly dress testing the garment's twirlability. She never allowed anyone to see her dance; it was her secret passion and she protected it from judgment.

Under the golden hour sun with a lone screech owl as her witness, she performed a choreographed "Degas for the Desert" routine of spins, vaults, and pirouettes. Her twirls revealed an orange thong and the perfectly rounded and rolled buns of a Latin Quarter *danseuse*. The butterflies of her dress seemed to soar and fly with her.

The graceful display of near-perfect landings was interrupted by several blunt primal snorts and she spotted a wild pig in the brush along with another smaller in size and two piglets. Eyeing her carefully while chewing a sycamore root, the large javelina remained there undaunted, its two intimidating fangs protruding off its snout.

Frenchy became terrified. She'd heard wild desert pigs could charge and she braced herself, but suddenly the family scurried off in a flash, the little ones hoofing after, a rumbling, thunderous departure.

The young woman was shuddering, her heart thumping from the encounter. At the same time she was exhilarated from the glorious sighting in the wild. When she regained her composure, she attempted another vault and flew across the plateau, leaping to even greater heights. With this second wind of inspiration she carried on with her private performance until the sun faded.

She didn't walk back to the car either—she ran.

17

High up on a cliff's ledge, the Sonoran black vulture landed smoothly and regurgitated the carrion for anxious chicks awaiting a feeding. There was not nearly enough to go around, so the mother took flight again, leaving siblings fighting for scraps. Lacking a sense of smell and dependent on her sight, the shiny bird surveyed the parched landscape, soaring on the rising air currents without a single flap of the wings. Her hunting ground was an open stretch of desert and prey had few options for cover.

The large bird hadn't found a target yet, but focused on something nearly as important: two winged scavengers circling below. The featherless red heads indicated turkey vultures and with their keen sense of smell, the black vulture knew to follow. A third turkey vulture appeared and they soared on thermals together, circling and waiting on a prize.

What had aroused the olfactory senses of the turkey vultures was a carcass stuck in a patch of blond sand, larger than a javelina's, perhaps a mountain lion's or bighorn's. Though it lay inert, predator commotion nearby held the birds at bay.

"Tell you what," the captor proposed in whisper. "I'll ask you a question, and you ask me one—"

The sun had fallen below the cliff and its refracted light streamed from behind making the colorful desert palette increasingly vivid. The men lay on their backs eyeballing the sky and wispy clouds streaking across.

Circling lower, the vultures managed glimpses of not one, but two carcasses, perhaps a horse and bull or two horses.

"Or vice versa … pretend you're at camp—"

"I hated camp, remember? Don't want to play dead anymore?"

"Shhhh, whisper … We're still dead. Birds don't know—"

"Can I close my eyes? To deflect the light?"

"Not going to sleep on me, are you?"

"If I did, would you bury me according to my wishes?"

Billy was struck by Roland's newfound directness that was surprising, even impressive. "Maybe. Then again, maybe not."

"Just shielding my eyes—"

The captor drew sunglasses from his pocket and spread them across the prisoner's face. "It's safer—"

"Yeah …"

"Make you another deal: I won't ask you anything about your personal life, but you can ask me about mine …"

"You really want to play this game?"

"Really, really. And I'll answer first." Nothing could excite Billy more than a game or contest.

"You already made a concession; I'll answer first."

"But don't ask me if I'm a homo—"

"What?"

"I mean, don't get the wrong idea … two guys laying beside each other, alone, in the desert, eyeing a powder blue sky, me with my tight Italian testicle-splitters, you with your soft-boy callous-free hands. I mean there's no turd-burgling going on here—"

"Turd-burgling?" Roland belched, bursting from his gut.

"Wha—? You never heard that?"

The prisoner was throwing forth and couldn't stop.

"Just letting you know I'm not a fart knocker—"

Roland was still gasping in between guffaws, barely able to blurt, "You mean, turd-burglar!"

"Shhhh! You'll scare 'em off—"

He was trying to control his merriment, but failing and he split apart again, roaring openly.

"*Roland*—" Billy pleaded. "Oh God, now I do sound like one, the nagging fag. *Rooolaaaand,*" he mimicked with melting eyes and a lispy crossover whine. "Don't you put the 'boy' in flam*boy*ant—"

Roland was howling still. "The nagging turd-burglar!"

"How 'bout desert butte butt pirate," he furthered.

"Butt pirate? *Stop!!!*" The man fought for air, trying in vain to collect himself.

Roland's demonstrated hilarity and show of fun even made Billy break a grin and laugh. He waited for the prisoner to calm down. And when he did:

"Actually, I *am* gay," he proclaimed afresh, playfully inspired.

Roland's infected grin grew; he was delightfully anticipating more folly. "… Oh—?"

"But I'm gay with honor."

"With honor?" the captive squealed.

"Yes," he stated proudly. "I enjoy a healthy gay lifestyle, but I do it honorably—"

The pause was momentary before chest-crack blasts erupted from both. The more the captor reloaded and rephrased the more the prisoner twisted in hysterics.

"No more narcissistic Versace glam couture or outlandish restroom pirating; no more feather boas and pink tights with yellow lightning-bolt crotches. I say enough of the interchangeable holiday cock-pouch pants with ghosts and pumpkins, Santas, Peter Rabbits, and Union Jacks—swords and diapers too—I mean, a full stop to all the drama! Just a simple Brooks Brothers blazer, white shirt, and loafers; you know, two mature, erotically-correct men going home together, done with taste, integrity, and—"

"Honor!" they both exploded.

The confusing din persisted below and the birds soared higher, fading off to the eastern part of the canyon, the ruckus overpowering them.

"So here's my question, finally. Do you have the Europenis?"

"The Euro—?" He couldn't finish the concept was beyond too much.

"You know, the flappy one with the hoodie. In all my research I could never tell if you were topped or not; you have that kind of Old World Anglo-German name, Roland Droheim Polsonby, so I thought you might have the frocked Belgian bell-end, but—"

The prisoner rolled over punching the sand, beside himself.

"All right, listen up," Billy redirected. "My question for real—okay?"

Roland braced his ribs, still aching from having laughed so hard and he attempted composure as tears streamed down his face. " 'Kay—"

"You wrote both your books in first person. Why?"

He had anticipated an uncomfortable interrogation and the question came as a relief, but less so due to the recent levity. Billy's query was asked often of him and Roland the author had a prepared answer.

"First person was the easiest for me. I could get into the guts of character the way an actor does. But instead of embodying him physically and finding a behavioral language, I'd look for the voice. My books were always about the voice, much more so than the narratives. The plots were thin."

He paused to analyze his rehearsed words as if hearing them for the first time and he suddenly felt embarrassed and wasn't sure why.

"Why didn't you try third person? It's so much more refined and literary, don't you think? And poetic, if you have the word mastery."

"Did you read my books?"

"Numerous times."

"What did you think?"

"You captured something, but it was restrained. I'd like to see what you could do with a deeper arsenal of words and language, incorporating all you know in your writing, not just dolce vita America. Granted, those were the times, but it's a different time now; the Towers have fallen, the world's on fire, fanatical executions abound, tech has taken over, certainly there's to be a reassessment. I'd like to see where a man with your keen eye and social sense and instinct would be now—in literary terms."

He picked up on Billy's change in tenses and weighed what it meant, if anything at all.

"But of course that will never happen," the captor followed up and the remark earned the well-deserved silence it got.

A single question was difficult for the prisoner. Billy was intriguing in so many ways and it inspired many questions including his near schizophrenic changing of accents. Roland couldn't help but enjoy his company; he liked Billy Sixkiller, astonishingly so. The man had abducted him bound and cuffed him, beat him, and vowed to splatter his brains as soon as he tired—and worse. He threatened to alter his final resting place with tragic consequences for eternity. After all that, the prisoner still liked him and was flooded with curiosities about him.

"Well?" Billy was naturally impatient.

"I'm thinking …"

"Not having a senior moment, are you?"

"Okay, a personal question: why don't you marry Frenchy?"

"She never asked me."

"That's all?"

"I follow Indian custom on that passed down over thousands of years."

He spoke now like a true tribal member, in small phrases, five to seven words. His delivery was calm, even-toned, and less Billy-manic.

"A woman asks a man to marry her; it's an insult for him to refuse. He must marry her or it brings shame upon the woman's clan. He's disrespected her and that brings shame upon the man and his own clan. After all our time together Frenchy never did ask me—"

"Do you want her to?"

"Not if it is not her wish; it wouldn't be right for either of us. We don't divorce. A woman stays true to her man forever, even though he may take another wife. I would not do that to Frenchy if we were together." Then he added it with a smile. "She'd scratch my eyeballs out."

"Well, she's French …"

"So she'd do it with a smile …"

"*Then* tell her husband …"

"And lover." They both found the humor in it and laughed.

The prisoner was getting drowsy and relaxed a first time. He was content to lie there quietly as his shoulders nestled in the warm sand and the heat soothingly spread through his body.

"See there?"

Roland's eyes snapped open.

"Introducing the sanitation department for the Sonoran," he stated sarcastically. "*Los apilotes—*"

Directly overhead, the turkey vultures were circling again exposing seven-foot wingspans and two-toned underwings. The odd black one, the mother to the chicks, was soaring a bit higher, but still tagging along.

"They eat all the desert garbage."

"Ugly suckers, aren't they?"

"No feathers on their heads, that's why. No brains in their head for that matter."

"Why do you say that?"

Billy broke in half as he said it. "To be chasing down a couple of turd-burglars like us!" Roland was tossed into hysterics again. " 'Fess up, Roland, you've had a turd burgled, haven't you?"

"Not lately!"

"You sure?"

"I think I would have remembered!"

"Come on; 'once is cool, twice is queer'—"

"Guess I'm cool!"

"Guess I'm queer!!!"

They were uproarious.

"You know those buzzards urinate on themselves to stay cool?"

"No way!"

"I swear!" They broke uncontrollably again. "Called evaporative cooling—see their white feet? That's from all the dried pee—"

"It can't be true!"

"If it's hot out and they're perspiring they'll—"

"Just pee on themselves!" Roland finished, rolling once more.

"That's right! They'll pee on their feet and the pee evaporates and cools the body—"

"They must smell real good—"

"Danderoo—" The hysterics would not let up.

"So, these are your favorite pastimes? Turd-burgling," Roland could barely finish articulating, "and watching ugly birds pee on themselves!"

"To stay cool!"

"To be cool!"

"They think they're so cool!" they wailed simultaneously.

"Some life you lead!"

"Just another colon cowboy—"

"Colon cowboy??? *No!!! … Way!!! … Aaah-haaah!!!*"

The scavengers thought better of getting any closer and drifted on as the two were tacked to the desert floor yukking it up, tossing back and forth on their sides like hyena pups, parodying themselves and others, repeating nonsense and manufacturing more until the sun faded completely and the creepy silhouettes of fallen cottonwoods emerged against the glowing Sonoran night sky.

Circling still, the black vulture mother suddenly spotted and targeted an unprotected finch egg and swooped through the tall tree, snaring it and making a quick feast of the yolk. The sky thief pumped its wings on the rise all the way to the canyon's crest where her offspring awaited—and not quietly.

18

They left Needle Canyon as light was failing and hiked past the lava cliffs to meet up with the Dutchman's Trail. They had run out of water. Roland was now getting faint, forcing them to resort to a "Superstition Slurpee." Billy kicked over a stumpy barrel cactus and tore it open. He showed the captive how to eat the pulp that, though tasting awful, contained nutrient-rich nectar to keep them going.

An hour later, they reached Charlebois Spring that still harbored pools of fresh water. They both lay down and drank freely from it. "Good old Charleyboy," Billy gasped, coining the local handle for the spring named after the French miner who'd discovered it. Frenchy had taken "Charlebois" for her last name and not by coincidence.

Roland's submerged head suddenly jerked up. "What was that?"

"You hallucinating again?"

"I saw something in the water—"

With the remaining purple-gray light, Billy performed another remarkable stunt that rivaled the rest. He lay flat next to the pool's edge and with legs spread, slipped his hands beneath the surface probing the depths. After a short wait, he suddenly spear-pawed something and trapped it and pinned it to the rocky rim. When Billy drew it out with two hands the prisoner could only admire the prize in amazement: a fat eighteen-inch trout.

"Will you look at that …"

"When the seasonal runoffs die down or the Canyon Lake recedes, they get left behind. How many you want?"

"Ten!" Roland was famished.

The captor proceeded to fish out seven jumbos.

As night fell and the high moon draped the desert floor in silver, Billy sat hunched on a slab of basalt and pulled out his hunting knife to gut the fish.

"Tell you what, gather some dry kindling—you'll find it all over. I'll clean these bad boys—"

The prisoner was being offered a modicum of freedom that surprised him.

"I'm not worried," Billy produced instinctively. "You'd never make it back alive even if you found your way—which you could not. You'd be dead by noon tomorrow, bones picked clean by two-clock; another stand-up skelly ready for shipment to an eighth grade bio class in Des

Moines where you could stand around for the rest of eternity, the punks in the back row fanning farts at you on an annual basis.

"And suicide, you know what that does for you. So have a stroll, take that creosote vapor in your pipes and while you're at it, fetch me some dry planks—"

The prisoner was sore all over, his feet aching. He didn't venture far and returned five minutes later with a pile of wood. Billy tossed him the matches and he made a nice stack and lit it, the flame rising heartily.

Clouds rolled in, blocking the moon rays and the silver coating disappeared. The flames danced against the still blackness and the two were poised before the fire gobbling up the fresh trout which fell apart easily in their hands. Billy consumed four and offered Roland his last, a purposefully symbolic gesture.

"They call it Sonoran black ink. What the Dutchman gave the gold-seekers to ponder while he dipped into his hidden treasure."

"Visibility: impossible."

"Unless you were right behind him and he wouldn't let you get that close." Billy checked his watch. "How you feel?"

There was color to Roland's face, as healthy a pallor as he'd had in years. "Don't think I could sleep if I wanted to."

Billy broke one across curiously, his teeth glistening in the orange light.

"Supposed to meet Frenchy at First Water Trailhead at eleven-clock. We're two hours away and it's almost ten. Put out the fire—"

As he started off, the prisoner didn't get up or move. "Billy …"

"We don't have time; talk the talk while we hike—"

"Wait—" The man was burning on something; it was intoned in his voice. Surprisingly the captor spun back around.

"I get it, Billy …"

"Huh?"

"I see what you're trying to do …"

"Not trying to do anything," he shot back impatiently.

"You're making a valiant effort, in fact …"

"Effort?"

"What you are accomplishing, actually."

The prisoner deliberated dropping the discourse altogether. Capitulation had always been a part of his makeup, especially in these years when he cared less about things.

"Bringing me back—"

"Back where?"

"To life," he said. "These fantastical things we've been doing, the water caves, the cliff dwellings, Geronimo's Stairs—"

"How would that bring you back?"

"To show me antiquity, putting me in touch with the lives of the ancients, giving me a sense of the history of the world, nature, that's so much older and wiser and more significant—"

The captor didn't issue a follow-up; he was listening now.

"The treasure hunt—depicting the dreams of men, awesome mysteries and legends which captivate our imaginations—it's been well-designed by you. Either that or it's just coincidence, but I've witnessed your attention to detail and chance is something you don't rely on."

Still planted there, he let the prisoner speak.

"The Thrilla in Manila fight; two human beings in a test of wills exhibiting incredible courage and strength—"

"*Boring!* I could have showed you *Rocky* for that."

"Grueling physical activity, the hikes, the hot springs, all to get my blood flowing, get me moving, breathing, to feel the aches and pains, to feel my body and my biology again …"

"You finished?"

"Today was the finest day I've had—maybe ever. Immersing me, surrounding me with the Earth's elements, bringing me back to it once again, though I've never experienced it so intensely."

"And this 'design' is for what purpose?"

"You're a man of ideals—integrity—you want it pure."

"I want what pure?"

"Your revenge."

Billy's eyes narrowed. "What do you know about integrity?"

"That may well be true. I haven't done much in my life that has answered the call to it. But I do recognize it, even more than before. I feel very—"

"Very what—?"

He paused then cast his beam on Billy directly. "Alive."

"Alive?"

"Thoughts and emotions I haven't felt for years are passing through me, like they did when," he searched, "I was a kid …"

"Let's go, Roland," the captor cut him off. He swiveled around and started toward the blackness once more.

"No—wait!"

Without turning, the man slowed and stopped again.

The prisoner spoke patiently choosing his words cautiously. "The justice wasn't meaningful before. Killing me—"

He struggled now to express it. He knew not to be reckless; one slip up, one error in syntax and it could be all over and he could set off the powder keg. It wasn't a question of being right. He was certain of his proclamation. The issue was whether Billy wanted to hear it verbalized, or could hear it. Roland's mouth parted twice, closing each time.

He decided to feed it, one spoonful at a time.

"Because I'd lost my will. And didn't care. I wanted to die. Already. There wasn't any justice. In that. For you …"

His captor twisted back around sharply to face him.

"For you," Roland qualified, "or for them …"

Water had begun to well in Billy's eyes and his chin trembled. He couldn't prevent it either as he glared coldly at the prisoner.

"How could there be? Your parents were in the prime of their lives."

The captor's head slumped to hide his emotions. Without looking up he muttered, "You're not dead because you haven't passed out yet. That's all. End of story." He wiped his face.

"I'm sorry, Billy," he furthered, perhaps perilously. "Sorry what happened to them."

The man stood still there, motionless, frighteningly so. A moment later the chin lifted, the hot black eyes, deeply set, blazing forth.

"This a confession or a denial? My boredom is getting painful …"

"Neither—"

"You trying to tell me you didn't do it?"

"I'm trying to tell you that—it's done."

"Done? What is done?"

"The revenge. You've accomplished it; you've done what you set out to do. I feel the blood in my veins, the kick in my legs. You brought me back, Billy. To the land of the living."

The captor shook his head slowly.

Roland rose up and converged in a step. "Look at my cheeks—do I look hollow? Look at my eyes, there's life in them! Look!"

The captor continued to shake, the tempo increasing.

"You did it. You've gotten what you were after. You brought me back to life! I'm alive!"

"Stop!" He fired, turning away.

"And I'm ready now!"

"No!"

"I've had a blast, the treasure hunt, the stupid birds—" He paused, to interrupt himself. "The *laughter*—do you know how long it's been since I laughed? Since I was able to?" Even more determined now he pressed. "To get to a point where I *could laugh???*"

Billy was drawn to him detecting the water flowing to the man's eyes.

"I understand the goodness of life, the value and preciousness of it, and of living things—it's come back—in one day with you! I had the best day I've had in thirty years!"

"Damn you!" Billy shrieked. He charged him and grabbed him by the shirt collar, tossing him to the ground. "This isn't for your sandbox pleasure, dammit! It's not fucking summer camp!"

The prisoner's lip was split open and bleeding and he angled up, panting.

"I didn't do it for you, asshole! I did it for me! *ME!*"

He'd set him off; exactly what Roland feared doing.

"Sure you're alive. I see it. How could I not? Alive enough to know without the indifference, the depression, the resignation, and the surrender, that—you want to die ..."

He calmed himself and drew in a deep lungful. His eyes were leveled on the man as he lowered his tone. "... I don't want that ..."

"Then what is it you want?"

"I want you more than alive!" he called out. "I want you so alive you want to *LIVE!!!*"

Roland's mouth hung there, agape, widening still.

Billy quickly stepped up and fronted him. "Do you want to live?"

If he said 'yes' he'd be lying and the captor would know. He would not attempt it, yet he had to answer.

"Tell me!" he roared. *"DO YOU WANT TO LIVE?"*

The prisoner returned it weakly with eyes watering, a defeated look. His head shook as if performing it all by itself—the truth.

Wheeling back around, the captor wound up and kicked the pool of water like he would a soccer ball splashing the fire and dousing it. He marched onward and disappeared into the blackness flashing a penlight intermittently to glimpse the tricky jagged terrain ahead.

The silence endured a while then was broken by, "I'm alive, dammit!" The captor heard the cry from behind and then again.

"I'M ALIVE! "

The primal call echoed hauntingly off the walls of the invisible pitch-black canyon. The creatures of the night heard it, the predators as well, and the prey waiting fearfully on desert standby for the day heard it too. Even Billy paused slightly in his step to the pure and vital release—the most beautiful sound he'd heard in years.

"When you crave the cup of life again," he snickered. "That's when I'll kill you, Mr. Polsonby. With bells on."

He resumed on his march.

"Cheers, varmints. To my justice—"

19

The Dolce Vita Diaries IV

I had a wonderful afternoon by myself. But when I return to this car, my stomach cramps up. It is hurting in knots.

To see the family of pigs was terrifying! They have a reputation to be nasty. I think that is if you threaten them. The animal book calls it a Boar and the animal represents Confrontation. If you pick the card or see it in the wild its medicine is to confront anything (or anyone) you've been avoiding. You must confront it!

I am afraid to follow this advice even though it is what I have been thinking. I fear what will happen.

I haven't taken my card today, I am scared to. Maybe Billy is right. These cards are playing with my mind and mixing me up. Or maybe the cards are telling me the truth! And everyone else is fucked up. I don't know!!! I have never had any real religion or philosophy to guide me. Only a man with stubborn viewpoints! Maybe I have found my religion now—the animals! But I know not to depend on any one thing too much. That's the teaching of my life so far. It's how you get deceived. And hurt.

I am in a car with a man who has kidnapped another. That is not right. But I know Billy better than anyone I have ever known. He is my family and I want to be there for him. So I am confused. I am praying not to be confused. Please help me! Whether it is God, or the Great Spirit, or the animals, please help me! I BEG YOU! Help show me the way!

I will go to the back seat and read.

I'm back and I just saw the news! It was about Man! They showed his picture. They said he was seen getting into a CAR! I'm so frightened now! It's eleven-thirty and where are they???

Billy WHERE ARE YOU??? His phone must be off. Or it doesn't work in these mountains! Merde!!!

Man is a famous writer. They showed a photo of his wife. Very beautiful. It mentioned their son who died. He drowned on a boat. The photo of Man was not good. He is more handsome when you see him. So what?

I wonder what happened. The death of the child must have torn them apart. She probably could not take it. She looks like she thinks she is hot shit though. Those types are insecure. I could see it in her face. It was too good a photo. I don't want to sound like a bitch, but she probably had a thousand taken. To get one! I would like to do her cards! If he wasn't a murderer I would think he was too good for her.

He used to give me the creeps. He doesn't anymore. He was a gentleman when he saw me with no clothes on. I was surprised. I am really worried now.

I hate being alone in this car. Billy told me all the stories. Like the Mexican who found gold, but was killed before he could tell anyone! And the one who burned to death in his own campfire. Another's head was taken off in a gulch! It's so dark out! Merde!!!

Billy, WHERE ARE YOU???

Frenchy had seen a CNN clip earlier that featured "El Capítan," Sheriff Harlan Graves, addressing reporters from a podium at Sky Harbor Airport in Phoenix. The Sheriff, an old friend and associate of Adele Griffiths-Polsonby's father and to the family still, maintained that everything humanly possible was being done to locate Adele's husband, the missing man.

20

It had survived the day in America's most treacherous desert and another day conquered was a blessing bestowed by the Creator. The eight legs carrying the burdened carriage worked harder to maneuver as the creature had feasted on a beetle exoskeleton. It was in no hurry either to escape the thicket of Devil's Claw. The coyotes, the night owls, the diamondbacks, and their nasty-fanged cousins were all on the lookout. Darkness was the time of the night predators.

The tarantula resumed a cautious path beneath a curious foreign structure that shielded it from wind, its twin feelers grazing a smooth unfamiliar surface with a bitter alien smell not of the desert. Unsure of direction, it scaled the rubber surface and disappeared into the hub, ascending straight up the chrome shock absorber casing and wandering across the sticky axle. The arachnid climbed patiently another steel vertical only to get lost in more blackness, feeling its way through an inner maze of irregularly shaped custom mechanicals—the specially designed entrails of the Ivory Stretch.

Billy and Roland reached the car after midnight and hadn't spoken since the discussion at dinner. The captive was placed in back, ankles secured once more to the wire lock attached to the door.

Frenchy was waiting impatiently up front and when she heard Billy finish off with the prisoner she vaulted out. "He was on TV—*Man!!!*"

Billy was steering a pee into the brush. "What'd they say?"

"That he's missing!"

"Let's go—" he barked dismissively, giving the news no weight. She could tell instantly he was in a foul mood and not necessarily because of the news report.

He hopped quickly in, flicked on the shortwave, and turned over the motor. The car shot back out to the Trail, Route 88 headed north.

"Where *were* you? I tried calling—"

"Told you never to do that—ever!" he sent back, miffed. "They can intercept. I turned mine off because I knew you'd forget."

The Road Scholars were floating in different energies now, no longer unified in the same way. She could feel the discord and it scared her. "I'm sorry."

"At least you're predictable."

She was feisty by nature and normally would have contested it, her astute reply ready in French. Translated, *"How the hell should I know how to handle phone techniques with kidnappers?"* But something more troubling was eating away at her. "Beelly, I have to ask you ..."

She shouldn't waste his time, not now, he thought. "What?"

"It's about the cards—"

"Frenchy, I'm in no mood."

"Just wait; you know them right?"

"By heart," he said tightly with a snap. "Like everything. If it was written I memorized it; if it was said I recorded it. I had nothing to do 24-7-365 for ten years living large in a six-by-eight at Telshor, then again at Arizona State. Not the university—Penitentiary, remember?"

Tempted again, she prepared a provocative cousin, "you never let anyone forget"—but restrained herself. "Can I ask you about one?"

"Make it quick; I want to scan the shortwave pickups."

"Spider—"

"Spider," he grumbled dismissively. "Cripes, it's Romper Room all over again. The Spider is the weaver, he weaves the web, create, create, create is his message."

"Is that all?"

"You have the book, read it."

"I have read it—"

"I mean you have all day to do this shit—"

"I want to hear your interpretation—"

He released an enduring, hassled one, before explaining. "If you're getting too caught up in life's web, Spider teaches you to stay aware so you don't ignore other opportunities that are out there ..."

"And Reverse Spider?"

"Wait, did you pull this card today?"

"Yes."

"Was it right side up, or reverse?"

"Eet slipped out of my hand when I took it from the deck. Eet landed between the two, so—"

He twisted at her, incredulous. "You can't even pick a card from a deck without fucking it up!"

"Beelly!"

"You're a disaster!"

"Why are you saying this?"

"You have all day to read, surf the Internet, learn things, learn memes even, get a job, apply yourself, whatever, and all you do is paint your nails, read *Paris Match*, French *Elle*, go to 'Astrology-Zone' on the Web, listen to 'StarTalkers Radio,' post photos on *Insta* of a dead poodle to get more likes—"

"It's not a poodle, it's a *Bichon Frisé* and it's my pet dog!"

"—it's been dead for twenty years!"

"Fourteen!"

"—scribble in your little notebook to describe it all, in essence, what you haven't done or accomplished—*and*—pick your daily animal card! That is, if it doesn't slip out of your goddam hand!"

"Ees not a little notebook! It's a *journal!*"

"That's your day!"

"My days are beautiful! Filled with beautiful thoughts!"

"Whatever—"

"Whatever to you!" she fired. "To make like it's nothing because everything you do is so genius and great, right? *Mon cule!!!*"

"It *is* nothing! You're a NARP!"

"You're a *NARP!!!*" she sent right back.

"Fuck you!"

"Fuck you too! You make fun of my life; look at yours and what you're making of it! *Ta guele!*"

"What about mine?" he blasted on.

Burning in her deeply still, she let it pass, but a switch had been turned on and things were not the same, not any more; the wiring, the circuitry, the emotional grid were different now.

"Everything is in the cards, it's all there …"

"That just shows how lost you are …"

"I am not lost!"

"It's bullshit! You hear me? *Bullshit!!!* The tribe doesn't even use those cards, Frenchy—the tribe!"

"They grew up with it; they have it in them already! By instinct! They know the animals!"

"What do you know about the tribe? I'm the member, not you!"

She would not correct him and reveal his true status in the tribe as "honorary" member. She bit her tongue again, but the battle atmosphere remained.

"Everything they say is true, I can feel it …"

"And what is that, pray tell?"

"That I need to change my life. I saw wild pigs today—the Boar. Its medicine is to confront the obstacles standing in your way—"

"And what obstacle is that?"

"—To not be scared, to not worry, to listen to the lessons of the Great Spirit ..."

"Me?" he overrode. "I'm the obstacle?"

"—To follow me and guide me on my path to enlightenment!"

"I said, 'me?' "

"—That I am giving away my power and it's time to take it back for me! I am a butterfly, Beelly! A *papillon!* "

"ME?" he shouted.

"Yes, *YOU!* " she hollered back.

He was temporarily stunned which gave him pause. "If you're such the fuckin' butterfly, why don't you ever fly?"

"Because you have pinned my wings!"

"—Or fly away? No one's stopping you!"

"Maybe I will!"

Billy fell silent, which was nearly frightening in itself. His unpredictability loomed dangerously.

But it was burning and boiling in her like lava—volcanic—and she had to let it go. It was different now.

"Reverse Spider; I picked it today. That means someone close to you has caught you in a web, in their web, keeping you tied up, treating you badly, criticizing you, and making you feel bad about yourself—"

Billy howled exaggeratedly with laughter.

"What is so funny?"

"You! You can't even read the book right! Reverse Spider means that *you*—you're the one treating your mate poorly, getting him entangled in your crap and caught up in your shit, not the other way around—"

"No! It's you!"

"Which means me wasting my time with an overly-dependent, non-producing, non-contributing, unskilled *liability*, hanging me up, setting me back, a total D.O.R. in every way—that's *drain on resources*—dangling desperately from the other end of a cigarette butt from sun up to sun down!"

"You're the drain on my resources!" she screamed. His words hurt her and tears inched down her face. She was crushed. "Read it, fucker!"

"I did!" he shouted back to a beat of silence. "Butterfly—" he spat derisively.

"Stop making fun of me!"

"Guess what, Little Miss Lost World? I saw a snake today; the Snake is Transmutation and its medicine is to shed one's skin, to get rid of old habits. Only I saw it slithering away from me which is reverse; and contrary Snake is a message to release an outer skin of present identity as in I should no longer be the considerate, enabling, thoughtful Billy who has to be Mommy, Daddy, Brother, Sister, Teacher, and Psychiatrist to an absolutely underdeveloped, un-evolved, unformed, immature, and bratty child!"

Then she saw it.

"Yaaaaaaaaah!!!" she shrilled at the top of her lungs.

"What???"

"Look!"

Making its way to the roof of the front cab right above them, the tarantula paused patiently, upside down, on a brief rest.

"Where?"

"Up there!" She was pointing directly above.

With one eye on the road, and the other scanning the car's interior, his look wild-eyed and devastating, a paw was raised, cocked at the ready.

"Don't hurt it!"

He located it and in his sights finally he swatted the tarantula knocking it away and the creature disappeared into the darkness.

Frenchy craned around, searching. "Now where is it?"

"I knocked it out the window."

"You did not!"

"Did so!"

"You killed it!"

"Did not!"

"Yes, you did! It was giving me medicine and you killed it!"

"I did not kill it dammit!"

"You did! It was the Reverse Spider! Right in your face! And you couldn't take it—"

"It wasn't reverse! It wasn't a spider! It's a *tarantula!*"

"Don't do that!" she cried out.

"Do what?"

"Manipulate me! I got the Coyote card on Friday! The master Trickster! And the Contrary Salmon on Thursday. Meaning I'm being a follower!"

"Frenchy!"

"Yah-huh, and the tarantula was upside down and a tarantula *IS* a spider and you killed it because it was *PROVING YOU WRONG!*" She flurried. There was no stopping her.

"Was not!"

"And your stupid ego couldn't take it and you killed it!"

"*I DID NOT KILL IT!*"

"You did! You did! You did!"

"Stop it, Frenchy!" he warned, a tone weighted with implied ominous consequence.

The drama was too much for her and she cried hysterically. Reverse Spider had appeared, there was no denying it, along with all the other pointed messages accumulated recently. The edict was written in stone and she'd made up her mind. "It's what all the animals are telling me!"

"I don't want to hear that shit!"

"—The Boar and now the Spider!"

"Shut up! You hear me?" He was set off beyond repair; the only thing inhibiting him was the fact that they were going at highway speed.

"I hear the animals! And the *ANIMALS HAVE SPOKEN!*"

As she continued with her fit of hysteria, he swerved sharply and the car screamed to a stop. He vaulted out and as she gleaned his expression through the windshield, that expression—the fire eye—she shuffled desperately to lock and seal herself in; but he'd spread the door already. He yanked her out of the passenger side and threw her to the ground in the side glow of the headlights. As she swung and flailed at him, he flipped her over on her stomach, ripped up the back of her butterfly dress, tore down her thong panties, and exposed her fanny with the "Billy 4ever" heart tat inscribed on her right cheek. Then he spanked her, hard, repeatedly, with an open palm. She squirmed to free herself, her crown shaking wildly, but he held her firm. The young woman was apoplectic and she shrieked and cried into the dirt as his hand came down again and again.

He did it until his hand throbbed, until her backside was on fire.

"Say uncle—"

But she would not surrender, not this time. *"NEVER!"*

In a sudden final surge, she scratched, bit, and grappled violently to liberate herself. He fought her off and countered, pinning her with his knee in the middle of her back. Then, spreading apart her cheeks, he stuck a thick finger deeply into her anus. She yelped and screamed and bucked like a wild animal swiping her paws to slice him—so he inserted another finger. When she did not desist, he added a third, then a fourth, until she slowed finally and stopped resisting altogether. Her body went limp and very still as she whimpered. She had been neutralized. When she became totally quiet, the humiliation was complete. He waited a while, still, before withdrawing the violation.

Frenchy laid there stomach-down, her cheek dug into the dirt, saliva rivering from her mouth. She never detested a man more in her life and this was the final break. She knew things between them would never be the same again.

Billy threw open the rear door, leaped inside, and drew out Frenchy's suitcase from the storage compartment beneath the long banquette. He tossed it outside on the ground and splayed it open never looking Roland's way once. He snatched jeans and a T-shirt and closed the car door.

He threw the articles atop her as she remained stomach-down. He ordered her to put the clothes on and get in the car or he'd leave her.

After more silent tears and a struggle, Frenchy rose up and wriggled her sore backside into the tight curve-cut pants. She gimped to the car and opened the passenger door, withdrawing her book, cards, and notepad from the front seat as he watched. Then she shut the door, collected her suitcase off the ground, and sauntered off into the blackness in the opposite direction towing her bag.

He spun the Stretch on a quick U-turn and drove up beside her.

"Get in—"

Her handicapped gait didn't slow or pause.

"I said, 'Get in' …"

Again, there was no response.

"I'm not going to tell you again—"

She surmised it would mean more violence; he could humiliate like no other and she would not put herself through it. She hated him now.

The car steadied to a stop, but she pivoted directly back and opened the rear cabin door, loaded her suitcase, and got in.

Mulling it a moment from the driver's seat, Billy paused, then reclaimed his focus. "*Oof-mah*," he said. He got out and paced back opening the rear door. He saw the prisoner was wide-eyed, no doubt alert. He'd obviously heard everything if not the small talk. Frenchy had settled deep into the banquette at the other end close to the partition, a good distance from the door and captive.

"What are you doing?" Billy inquired.

"What does it look like?"

He didn't care to take on the stalemate or bother with it now. Billy extended the handgun without hesitation and she took it.

"You know what to do if he acts up, don't you, Butterfly?"

"Yes, I do." She raised the piece and let the barrel hover momentarily then drift Billy's way, leaving it hanging there a moment. "And what about you?"

Planted there for her, he unleashed the devil-may-care smile, taunting her, and they glared each other down until she lowered the barrel and angled her head away.

"Don't fly away now, Butterfly," he added with a snide grin.

Billy Six started the car and swung another U-turn and the Ivory Stretch shot off into the night, negotiating the significant twists, rises, and falls of the Apache Trail. The driver checked his watch; it was twelve-clock and some "teenies."

"Shit."

He stepped on it from then on.

21

At a Mustang service station the car was slotted at the far pump that blocked the notable chassis from the cash register-riding night clerk. Billy went inside and bought supplies ordering Big Stang coffees while pocketing sugars.

Frenchy sat there in the back, her hair cascading haphazardly across her downcast swimming pool blues. Roland checked on her with brief glances aware she was still very upset. Her face was covered in dirty brown tear paths from the road dust. The psychological impact of the intense confrontation had struck her deeply, he could tell.

She glowered at the carpet still burning and never acknowledged the man she called "Man." They hadn't spoken a word since she'd seated herself in back two hours before. She gripped her books tightly instead, the only way to steady trembling fingers.

The rear door swung open suddenly and Billy was standing there.

"Congratulations, Roland," he said gaily, "you're officially a Thirty-Six. And that deserves a shout out." He leaned in and extended the bag to Frenchy. "There's milk and sugar too—"

The prisoner thanked him in earnest and Billy closed the door. Moments later, the car sprung forward.

Boosting up in the seat, Frenchy pitched forward to hand the cup to him and he saw her wince as the maneuver pained her.

"Thank you," he said. "Quite a cup."

She'd already retreated to the far end and didn't speak, gazing emptily out the window at the unrelenting darkness.

"Miss?" he posed gently.

She angled part way toward him then faded back to an ignoring posture.

"I can't reach the bag. Could you pass the milk?"

"*Oui, pardon*—" she said. She slid forward again, grimacing as she handed him the bag. "There's sugar too, if you want …"

Her face scrunched like an accordion as she repositioned herself, reflecting openly and demonstratively the overwhelming discomfort.

"Are you okay?"

"Except when I sit down."

Roland left it alone and took in a long draw. The coffee tasted exceptional. He'd never appreciated a cup so much.

They rode in silence. Roland noticed their bodies were jerking in synchronized harmony as they encountered equally the bumps of the road. The slight movements were the only things they had in common, he thought.

"There was a farmer I remember once," he initiated without worry if she cared to listen or not. "In a town called Mataro, a small village on the coast of Spain. The farmer grew spices mostly; parsley, basil, mint, and tarragon. And as I was walking through his field the sprinkler went on and I got all wet," he said. "I was backpacking through Europe my first time. I was twenty-one—"

He noticed her head had turned in to fasten on him as she sipped her coffee. He was very surprised but silently grateful she was, if not showing an interest in what he had to say, at least being polite.

"But the man came out and I didn't know if he was going to yell at me for trespassing or not. His name was José Maria. I'll never forget that day, the sunshine clean and strong and bright yellow. And the spice farm overlooking the sea. Strange because it was only five minutes from the city, but being there you felt you'd stepped back in time hundreds of years. The man couldn't speak English, but he invited me for breakfast in his tool hut in the fields, the farmhouse was located further up the hillside. He gathered eggs from the chickens and he cooked me a *frittata*, a Spanish omelet with potatoes and onions—"

She recognized the Spanish and nodded.

"The farmer communicated with hand gestures and I knew a little Spanish. He told me his wife had died—just the very day before. But when they carried her body away, he didn't know what to do. So he went back into the fields and cut stems for the distributor …

"He was happy I came for breakfast, however, and invited me to stay the night. I stayed three days helping him with chores. And with the funeral. I said my goodbyes before the service and he thanked me, filling my pockets with parsley. He understood I had to go. I'll always remember that spice farm on the sea. And the man whose wife had just died the day before."

The prisoner unknowingly shifted in his seat. His imagination was adrift, but inspired still. "He's probably gone now."

"With her," she said suddenly and the remark snapped him from his reverie. He was startled somewhat, pleasantly so, that she'd not only engaged, but given of herself.

Frenchy angled back out the window and the silence took over again. She fidgeted with the plastic coffee top and held her books without eyeing him.

"You don't look bad for no sleep," she said eventually.

Again he was taken by surprise. "I'm past the point of feeling it."

"Are you in pain?"

"My feet."

"Why did you tell me that *histoire?* Because of the funeral?"

He did understand the implications of what she was saying. "Funny—that wasn't it—it was just something I hadn't thought of in a long time. I don't know what brought it on. It's been happening … lately …"

"Well, a lot's been happening to you."

He nodded in agreement.

Frenchy connected with her confidence then and noted how it surfaced whenever Billy was not around. She understood the world again and if not her place in it at least she had some personal grounding. She could pass on her knowledge and advice, viewpoints that could be appreciated by others. She possessed a distinct level of awareness and she knew it. Around Billy though she was always muted and confused, as if walking in a fog, her confidence nowhere to be found. He had this neutralizing if not diminishing effect on her.

She was wounded and ripe now though, scratched raw enough to be blunt. "Do you still want to die?"

The question gave the captive man pause. "Yes."

She would not curb her inclinations now. "I wanted to die once. When I was eleven."

He yearned to know why, but he would not ask her; the commonality was intriguing in that macabre way.

"It was either run away or die. I chose to run away."

"I would imagine you made the right decision."

"*Ne sait pas*—maybe there's a better place."

His eyes fell to the book she was clutching. "What are you holding?"

"My journal."

"Really? I always played with the idea of keeping a journal."

"Too late now." Immediately, she wished she hadn't said it.

"Yes, too late." He drew a sip from the cup. "May I ask you something?"

"I know—"

"You do?"

Deliberate, not minced, was her way now. She'd been reticent and held in check by a man and her cocoon of youth; and perhaps her own resistance to growing up. She perceived it so starkly and clearly now and she would speak up.

"You want me to help you, to make sure you are buried properly. Next to your boy—"

"No, actually—"

"That wasn't it? I'm sorry then."

"I did wonder if you could help me in that way, but—"

"Yes," she cut him off. "I will help you."

He was paused as a cascade of relief rushed through him. He'd prayed for something of the sort and the offering had come unexpectedly. "Thank you," he said and collected himself, emotions rising in him. The single tear blazed a fragile trail down his cheek. She couldn't miss it.

"You were going to ask me something—"

He nodded and cleared his throat. "I see you're in pain. What's the matter?"

"I fell on my *derrière*—that bone, you know? The one that steecks out."

She hadn't divulged the whole truth, he was sure.

"The coccyx," he identified for her anyway.

Sensing he'd intuited there was more to the story, she elaborated.

"We don't fight a lot; not like that. Sometimes he's like my father and thinks I need discipline. I didn't have a life at home and it's been a lot of learning a hard way. I'm a kid of the street—"

Tickled by the French phrases and grammar uniquely imposed on English, he was further heartened she was freely communicating with him.

"I'm sorry; may I ask you another question?"

"Because I couldn't stand it any longer," she correctly supplied for him. He was going to ask her why she ran away. "I was very young when my mother died. I remember her, but not well. I didn't know my father, so I came to live with my aunt. She was not married—she liked women," she said and then dropped the subject abruptly.

"Is she the reason you left?" The query received a nod. "Why America?"

"My great-great-grandmother came from Colorado. I thought I could like it so I studied it. Just from the pictures it looked very familiar, like home to me."

"How did you, well, leave your aunt?"

"You mean escape?" She chuckled thinly. "Like you, I have a connection to Spain. I made my aunt take me there so I could get a passport. Then I saved money to buy a ticket to America, the cheapest ticket I could find. To Miami. I made up a false permission notice of a legal guardian and they let me on the plane. On the flight I read a book about the Southwest and I saw the pictures of the animals and the sunset colors, the sky colors, the earth colors, you know? Eet was so pretty I had to go there first. So I sang songs at the train stations to save up for my next ticket, a train to Phoenix. So on this very long ride one night a man began to follow me and I could tell he was going to hurt me—in that way—so I hid in the bathroom and got out in the middle of the night in Albuquerque. Then I was caught running out on a bill for a sandwich at a diner and the owner chased me and threatened to take me to the police saying they would deport me unless I deed things to him, of course. So I deed, in his car. Then he took my passport and brought me to hees house. There I was in a worse situation than I had been in France. Instead of a lesbian, eet was a creep. So many creeps out there," she trailed off disgustedly.

"After a couple of weeks of searching I found my passport and I ran away from that house and that's when I was caught by a policeman. I begged him not to send me back. So I did things again. He placed me in an orphanage and I was sent to the reform school where I met Billy." She hesitated, her expression turning defiant. "I still haven't made it to Colorado, but I weell. Soon." Reflecting still, she raised her chin up. "So many creeps."

He mulled her confession with all its distasteful and abhorrent accompanying imagery and he was struck deeply by it.

Their brief quiet was shattered by the techno music put to full blast in front, rattling the partition. Frenchy knuckled the divider once and the volume came down—barely so.

Alone in the front seat, Billy Six was kicking it; it was after midnight, he was dee-jaying, spinning his Ibiza-styled Fuck-Me-I'm-Famous house grooves and dance mixes by German rave DJ Paul van Dyk. He was sucking on a cig all the while monitoring State Police and Highway Patrol shortwave feeds in different ears. For most this sensory riot would induce a cerebral hemorrhage, but not Billy. With the comforting sounds and surveillance technology he embraced the action all at once, singling out instruments from the trance grooves and riding them. Rock and roll couldn't provide that complexity; it was more a wash of sound and why he couldn't stand it "after eleven," an assertion he'd made to Roland. A creature of the night, one of his totem animals the Owl, he was most sensorial, alert, and vigilant when darkness fell. After midnight Billy Six was at his best.

"Man?" There was no response and she shifted in her seat to angle herself at him. He was immersed, envisioning her as an underage sex slave violated repeatedly by despicable men, but she could not know that.

"I'm sorry, yes?"

"Can you put on number two hundred twelve? That thumping makes me *totalment folle*—"

His puzzled look galvanized her.

"Don't worry, I'll do it." She maneuvered close and settled unevenly beside him and began to fiddle with the instrument panel. "Lucky there are two stereos. Normally it's the other way around."

"How do you mean?"

"Young people like the noise, all zee pounding, bumping, and banging. I like what older people like, the melodies, the slow jazz—"

Those compromising acts continued to be delivered to him, haunting him as he took in her pretty form before him.

"Billy is older than me," she qualified. "He's thirty-three …"

The delicate bouquet rose from her skin and he could smell her now, a special perfume personal to her, a flower's fragrance, sweet and feminine, and he absorbed the aroma instantly and liked it. He was delighted to have her so close, poised before him, and he inspected the snug jeans defining her feminine form. Her clothes clung to her body like a Snap-on glove and it seemed a perfect rendition of her with nothing on. He remembered the hot springs and seeing her that way a second time he was embarrassed enough to avert his eyes—again.

She repositioned herself as her selection began, smooth jazz with piano. The artist had an extraordinary voice, almost angelic.

"Sounds like a woman doesn't eet?" she tossed to him.

"It is a woman—"

"A man," she assured him. "Chet Baker. *Je lui adore* …"

No matter how many times he'd heard a French woman utter a romantic phrase, it still sounded sensual, supremely so.

"West Coast jazz; he played trumpet, you can hear it. They say he killed himself jumping out a window, but really he fell off a balcony. He was wasted on heroin. Have you ever done drugs?"

The question seized him. "We all did. Tried them, anyway."

"It's okay to try," she avowed, soon realizing the error. "They can be good for the mind, to expand it … if you can handle it …"

"I tried coke … Back in the eighties. It was around a lot."

"Makes me nervous … Billy hates it. He doesn't need it," she said with another spare laugh.

"I would guess not." Immediately he wondered if he should have said it. "I took LSD once—"

"You deed?"

"I had a bad trip. Was too powerful. That was a long time ago. I never tried it again."

"Don't worry, I won't tell him—"

His brow pinched in as the subject switch crossed him up.

"—That I will help you."

Whatever the reason, the prisoner had prayed for it in his crude Sunday school dropout way and it seemed his prayer had been answered—he had an ally. She'd bonded with him ever so slightly due in large part to her recent rift with Billy that had no doubt left her raw and open, accessible even. He was privately overjoyed.

"Thank you."

Though his eyes were sagging, they held a spark. More than "receiving" the prisoner was buzzing in a state of persistent reflection and he gave further thought to Frenchy and what she was doing with Billy—still. The man was exceptional in many ways, but unpredictable; brittle as well as brutal—unquestionably a psychopath. She appeared to be codependent, but not unbalanced and capable of much more. She seemed the stronger one in the end.

Yet the meditation tasted of bitter pomegranate, sour to the nerve, the type of judgmental thinking he'd been guilty of for years. People were drawn together for the oddest reasons and he knew that. For these two, difficult pasts and troubled interiors could make for a perfect match. He'd wasted a good portion of his life casting judgment, agreeing with judgments, making snap judgments, passing judgment and it gave him chills, his forearm hair standing on end.

She saw him differently now; his hair unkempt with an oily sheen and his legs crossed in a way which seemed vulnerable even feminine. There was a gentle quality to him and she'd discovered it. He was not threatening at all which surprised her too. "May I ask *you* a question?"

"Please—"

"No, never mind," she recanted.

"Go ahead, really …"

Something else came to her, causing her to vacillate. The question she had in mind could betray Billy and she would not do that so she circumvented any disloyalty by addressing the issue from another angle. "I know I asked you before and wasn't very nice—"

He intuited the rest. "What happened, you mean?" His tone dropped to low and solemn. "She never really recovered after the death of our boy … And neither did I. But I don't like to think about it, or talk—"

"*Je comprends*. But maybe you should. I mean, before, well—"

His expression froze. He was stymied by her directness that was like a new toy to her. The newfound boldness was delighting her, but she needed to introduce it carefully and exercise caution.

"I'm sorry, it is not my place—"

He didn't retreat and cut her off. "He drowned in a storm in the Adriatic. My wife blamed me for it. And she had every right to—"

"Why?"

"I couldn't find him. I tried, but I couldn't. Was my fault." He wrestled with it. "She never forgave me. And I couldn't forgive myself; which made it worse. She went around hurting me, until—" and he stared off, deflated, a revived spirit seeming to release from his body.

"Until what?"

"—Until it didn't hurt anymore."

The silence was left intact; a show of respect.

"Maybe it's selfish to not speak of him. Because he did live. He *was* here. Maybe I should acknowledge that, with my time left on this planet."

"On your Earth Walk, the Indians say."

"And what do the Indians make of death?"

"It's a part of the life cycle; you are here to be vitamins for the soil, which makes the future soil. I know I don't speak well—"

He found her easy to talk to after all and a lightness returned to his frame. He was lifted and escorted back from the dungeon of his memories.

She sipped again from her cup and clutched her books protectively. In the stack were the medicine cards. Holding on to the cards and thereby the animals depicted in them, she was drawing strength from them. The cards had taken on a bold significance, her belief in them furthered by the arachnid sighting and the ensuing chaos and violence. As the animals protected her, she was guarding the stack, though the prisoner couldn't know that until the cards slipped from her grasp accidentally. And he inquired.

Frenchy gathered the cards and rose up again now with an indiscernible smile, the first he'd witnessed, a sudden flicker of spirit. He broke freely himself because of her generous offering and the mutual shows sent a surge of positive feeling through him. He hoped for that offering again now that he'd seen it once. Though he was unaware of it consciously, he would now pursue that smile.

"Animal medicine cards," she said. "I can read you yours—"

He remembered the lovely Fernanda then and her cards, the tarots he'd never asked about and it shamed him. "I'd be honored."

Frenchy lowered herself gingerly and settled herself on her knees opposite him, her mood clearly uplifted. She began to describe the basics of animal medicine as deepening one's connection to the Great Mystery including healing the body and mind and spirit and walking on the Earth Mother in harmony with the universe.

She read from the *Medicine Cards* text by Carson and Sams:

"When you call upon the power of an animal you are asking to be in complete harmony with the strength of that creature's essence. The lessons you learn from your brothers and sisters in the animal world reflect the lessons each spirit needs to learn on the Good Red Road, the harmonious path of one's Earth Walk, and honoring every living thing as its teacher along the way—"

As it was explained to him, he possessed nine totem animals that represented the medicine he carried on his Earth Walk. The animals mirrored and emulated his traits and abilities and they were always there and a part of him no matter how underdeveloped or ignored. Two of these animals guided him on either side at all times, possibly appearing in his dreams for years.

He instantly recalled the nightmare from the airplane and mentioned it.

"Nightmares are signals of inner conflict to warn you or let you know you may be on a different path; maybe a wrong path."

She shuffled the deck and required him to pick seven cards. The first pick from the deck was the Turkey.

"Turkey?" he asked in a droll, leading way. "Is *that* what I am?"

His silliness produced a laugh and he experienced her smile again, the one he unknowingly pursued and it prompted another positive surge. "You speak of the Great Spirit, my Earth Walk, and the Great Mystery all to inform me I'm a turkey? *I could have told you that!!!*"

Her laughter was uninhibited, a girlish release, borne of a brand of humor on which she'd been raised, free of any twist, sarcasm, or jaded absurdity deriving from alternative influences later, which had been Billy's programming predominantly. The free expression was pleasant for Roland to witness as it revealed this natural and wholesome side of her.

At the same time, he hadn't uttered a funny remark in ages and this young woman's uproarious response embarrassed him, though he didn't want it to end.

"No, it's good!" she defended through the gaiety. "Turkey is the Gift animal; it means you're being given some kind of gift …"

A second turn yielded the Jaguar.

"Jaguar holds the spirit of Integrity," she said, surprised somewhat. The cards were not yet falling the way she'd anticipated.

Leaning forth, he selected and held up the Antelope.

"Antelope is the spirit of Action, it means taking action in one's life. As a totem card it implies you are a person of action …"

The prisoner appeared confused, but receptive.

"Whether you are doing it or not is another thing, but eet's what you were placed on this earth to do. It's part of your destiny …"

The dealer was not prepared for what was to come next as the prisoner chose the Butterfly card. She hesitated and skipped a breath; it was a powerful, nearly overwhelming selection. She was held momentarily speechless and sunk to her haunches, staying low to avoid eye contact. The cards were so precious to her now, her faith in them had redoubled, and she suppressed her reaction as best she could.

She stuttered through the revelation. "The Butterfly indicates Transformation …"

The prisoner even noticed a shift in her demeanor as she became stiff and withdrawn, awkward even, as if her "Life Force," Billy's oft-repeated phrase, had been altered. A force was there still, a potent one, but it was ignorant of the inspired interaction they'd shared minutes before.

A fifth selection produced the Whale card.

"The Whale is the Record Keeper, concerned with history and finding the origins. And being true to them …"

Though it made perfect sense to her, the man a writer, she seemed to detach and retreat further after the next card was drawn—the Bat.

"The Bat signifies Rebirth," she said, her voice quavering. "There's to be a death of something. Like old habits." She was hurrying, preferring his reading to be over. "Last one—"

The prisoner eyed her steadily as she continued to avert his gaze. He raised the Eagle from the stack.

"Ooh-la-la," she gasped, unable to restrain herself.

"What?"

Instead of responding, she restacked the pile expeditiously.

"Did you see the snake today also? With Billy?" He told her he had. "Was it coming toward you?"

"No, going away—"

Tabulating the influences, she pretended outwardly not to be affected.

"Does that mean something?"

"Animals coming to you in the wild also communicate medicine just like the cards—"

"What do the cards I chose mean?"

"They're very—" she began to utter, 'strong,' but her voice couldn't carry it. "I'm not sure, it's a lot to take in … I'm just learning. I'll leave you the book, you can decide."

"Frenchy?"

"Too much responsibility," she overrode, her voice cracking with emotion. She rose from her knees, favoring her sore backside. She didn't want to talk and moved abruptly to the far end again.

"Didn't you say there were two more?"

Tears streamed down her face in the dark, the outpour coming on a while and she didn't want him to see it. "I'm sorry, these days have been long." She wiped her face and collected herself, then tapped the partition again which motored down. The pulsating house beats assaulted them both as Billy was craning back, expectant.

"Can you stop a second?"

"Off the hook up here, we're on a good clip—what's the matter?"

"I-I-I have to pee—" she stuttered.

The car came to a stop and she squirmed stiffly past the prisoner, her hair falling across her face. "Bye," she whispered barely audible. A timid smile may have appeared, but he couldn't be sure.

"Goodbye," he pushed gently anyway. "And thank you." But she was already gone.

The young woman traipsed to the shoulder and squatted as if to urinate, but she had something else in mind. She drew the deck of cards instead. She swore she wouldn't pick one that day; they'd been causing too much stress. But it was past midnight and a new day and she couldn't resist. The cards were nearly an addiction now, an obsession, and she was no less confused. She knew not to be so influenced by any one thing, but in her insecure state and not knowing who or what to turn to, any help was welcome.

Her selection yielded the Frog card upside down, the Contrary Frog. The Frog's medicine was Cleansing, but in reverse it was an admonishment, another indicator someone may be leading her astray, warning her of pursuing a dark path if she didn't cleanse and purify. She prayed until Billy pressed her to get a move on.

22

By two-clock-thirty in the morning, the Ivory Stretch had left the Sonoran high desert again penetrating the elevated pine-forested Mogollan Rim, shooting northwest across the state. Billy chose Forest Road 300 to Lake Mary Road to Flagstaff, back roads parallel to the popular I-17. In "Flag," the Stretch headed west to Seligman, a celebrated stop on legendary Route 66, Main Street, USA, chronicled in Kerouac's *On the Road*. There he made a pitstop slotting the car in a row of brightly colored vintage Cadillacs and limousines to "blendify" it. He stepped in to a favorite watering hole, the Black Cat Lounge, and threw back a pair of scotch and sodas.

MSNBC reported missing person Roland Polsonby, last seen on a flight to Phoenix, had been planning to undergo an assisted suicide in Oregon and may have gotten into a chauffeur-driven car at the airport, the Physician-Assisted Death outfit in Portland providing the information. With few credible witnesses and no sightings of the vehicle, it seemed as though the man had vanished into thin air.

In essence, Oliver Martinez had canceled the town car his "girlfriend" Margaret had arranged for her boss, showing up instead as Billy Six. Margaret hadn't heard from her quirky friend for the precise time, but had no reason to connect him. On Billy's shortwave intercept, he heard Sheriff Harlan Graves offering the possibility Polsonby committed suicide himself while another cop suggested he may be "a floater," having drowned, and they were checking lakes and rivers.

The spare reports were encouraging, the lack of information proving positive, and Billy continued his evasive maneuvers driving by night and utilizing back roads, being extremely cautious. He had to; after all, it wasn't a nondescript, subcompact he was driving.

Frenchy had returned to the front, but the emotional anguish prevented her from sleeping. She'd feared it earlier, but now she was convinced—Billy had taken the wrong man. *Again.* She'd fled the company of the prisoner because she was going to break down; the proof in the cards that offered her a unique window into his deeper character. Killing was not in his make up. The protective totem animals surrounding him would not permit any acts of the sort. Her resolve was further supported by her own poignant interaction with the prisoner. She'd absorbed his peaceful, frail quality and knew he could not be the same man who murdered a sleeping couple with a shotgun. He was not capable of that type of violence.

When the Stretch veered from Route 66 and hit Old Indian Highway 18 north, access route to the Havasupai Nation, a badger shot out of the blackness and crossed the road and Billy broke hard to elude it. He was grateful Frenchy had been asleep—certainly if he'd injured the animal, but also to sidestep another riotous creature card debate. He checked his watch; it was three-clock-forty and he slid down the partition to inspect the captive who was now totally alert and intently reading. Billy waved and Roland returned it.

The prisoner had been awake for thirty-nine hours and was experiencing that energized state of sleep deprivation boosted by the Coca-Cola and coffee. He was studying the animal text that described the special medicine of each creature in detail. He was especially taken by the Eagle card, his last chosen, as the Eagle's medicine reminded those on their Walks of Life to take heart and gather courage as "the universe presented opportunities to soar above the mundane." If one was walking in the shadows of former realities Eagle brought "illumination, reminding one of the freedom of the skies, and giving permission to pursue the joy one's heart desires."

Rousting Frenchy, Billy let her drive the final dash to get his requisite hour-plus of restful meditation. At nearly five, the Stretch reached the Hualapai Hilltop, the gateway to Havasu Canyon, an offshoot canyon to one of the natural wonders of the world, the Grand Canyon. The parking lot was nearly empty as late fall temperatures had slowed the tourist trade. Hilo, the tribal clan member who maintained the stables, was there with a packhorse train awaiting them as Billy stashed the Stretch in the horse barn.

No longer concerned with the police, Billy's main worry was keeping Roland in check. He didn't want members of the tribe to learn of the situation, even though they would understand he had cause— but they would not condone it. They'd had experience with fugitives; Supai village was located at the bottom of Havasu Canyon, a perfect haven for hiding out and the rez was private property and state police rarely visited. The tribe had an agreement with the government over aerial rights and helicopters and airplanes were forbidden to enter the Nation's airspace without permission. The only bodies to police the tribe were their own Tribal Council and the Bureau of Indian Affairs, though they were by no means a constant presence.

Since the 1850s, outlaws and fugitives had been seeking refuge in Havasu Canyon. The tribe did not encourage it, but they were a spiritual people who had endured their own suffering at the hands of "white justice." What was once a tribal territory of millions of acres was reduced to a parcel of five hundred by then President Teddy Roosevelt. A dignified people, the Havasupais respected privacy, especially that of a brother and didn't ask questions.

Billy had been coming to Supai for fifteen years, even living on the rez after he escaped from the school in New Mexico. He'd come to the tribe disoriented and troubled. As it was part of their religion, the Havasupais assumed he'd come to them for a reason. So they took him in to fortify his broken spirit, not to the point where he'd be on-balance or healed, but better able to cope with the laws of white men.

Billy Six could never be cured of his demons; too much punishment had been inflicted upon him and the damage was severe. But the Havasupais, the People of the Blue Green Water, had saved his life. The water cave in New Mexico's *Caverna Magica* brought him back physically, but the tribe revived him spiritually introducing him to the Great Spirit and returning to him his Life Force. For these reasons, Billy enjoyed a profound connection with the peoples of the Great Nations, with nature, and the Earth Mother. The tribe had bestowed on him the ultimate honor by designating him a blood brother, an honorary member of the Clan. The scar on his palm and tribal shield tattoo on his back were proof of that enduring bond.

In the car Billy freed the captive's legs and informed him where they were headed, underscoring the supreme honor it was to be introduced to the members of the Clan and Tribal Elders. There would be no cuffs or ropes; he'd be treated as a friend in need of spiritual guidance—not as a prisoner. But Roland was threatened again with the tomb of an unknown soldier if he made trouble. His captor claimed that Clan Members would not assist him; they were Billy's brothers and would never betray him. An unlikely escape into the wild would not succeed neither as it would render him defenseless, helpless, and desperate as in the Superstitions, unable to survive—even if he could get away.

Roland listened carefully. He was sleep-deprived, but still buzzing. Sleep for him was an impossibility. His predicament with its imminent threat weighed on him constantly and kept him on edge. Sleep was not an issue.

In the thin yellow mist of first light the three descended the Hilltop rim on horseback. A pack mule lugged Frenchy's suitcase and other supplies. They followed switchbacks down the chute of Cataract Canyon, a steep drop of a thousand feet, and descended into massive wall formations of Coconino sandstone representing hundreds of millions of years of geological evolution. A mile ahead, the red sandstone walls of Hualapai Canyon rose higher as the trail descended to a deeply carved single lane, the canyon walls narrowing. As the walls pinched in only a blue strip of sky could be seen and the voices of the desert sparrow, the Arizona jay, and other morning calls could be heard.

An hour into the trail Billy raised a hand to slow the horses. "Hear that?" From some canyon crevice a pour of liquid notes flowed.

"That's a rock wren," Roland suddenly identified.

Billy swung around on his horse. "You're a birder?"

"See? You don't know everything about me; five hundred-twelve on my list."

"Damn, ol' Rollie there's a birder," he tossed to Frenchy, who remained silent. "You're close—it's a canyon wren."

"Really." Roland was the impressed one now. "Rarer than the rock, make that five hundred-thirteen."

Billy nodded but he was still focused on the reluctant one.

"Frenchy, you're going to have to give me a compliment," Billy quipped, a familiar jest now representing reversed sarcasm and ironic overkill. "And since you know I enjoy talking about myself, I'd like you to loop random biographical questions sent my way every forty-five minutes or so, okie? But—back to me," he hammed on.

Sunglasses hiding her face, she would not interact, as she had not spoken to him those last hours in the car either.

"Just one big happy family. Bowelitis, anyone?" Roland shook. "No wonder we're peachy. Nothin' like ridin' on a clean set of pipes."

Havasu Canyon was located in Arizona's third geological zone, the Colorado Plateau, and the lower they descended, the more profuse and lush the vegetation became. Redbud trees sprouted blossoms and lone cottonwoods showed verdant leaf. "Water table is nearer to the surface now," Billy called out. "S'why we're seeing more green."

Billy reached low to pick a white Sacred Datuna stem. He rode beside Frenchy and handed it to her, a gratuitous overture of dubious effect.

The red Supai sandstone walls towered over thousands of feet above. The horses were well acquainted with the oft-traveled trek and hastened the pace suggesting they were approaching the jaunt's culmination, Havasu Canyon.

Frenchy still hadn't uttered a word except for required nods and gestures. She hadn't reacted to the prisoner either; it was as if they'd never spoken before, like the first day all over again. Unquestionably she was experiencing discomfort in the saddle.

Her detachment was disappointing to the prisoner, yet there was still much to take in and his head twisted around as he eyed the awesome geological treasures enveloping them. He hadn't been on a horse in many years and was enjoying the ride immensely. His mount had been a wild mustang caught on the mesa above and broken in by the tribe.

Roland petted its mane and whispered to it. His overnight study of animal medicine yielded Horse to be the Power animal—that power was wisdom—and the gateways to wisdom were through empathy, compassion, and sharing lessons learned on one's Earth Walk. The man was stripped and sensitized, experiencing new life, fresh spheres and planes of existence he'd never considered before.

The canyon had its own special music that increased in its intensity, natural harmonies that had excited adventurers for centuries and the unmistakable sound of rushing water grew stronger. The canyon floor was green and lush reflective of its water source. "Hear that?"

The prisoner's face was charged with anticipation.

A half-mile further, Billy suddenly dismounted beneath the shade of an elm and stepped down a small bank where it flowed before him, the amazing crystal-clear, blue-green water of Havasu Creek. Roland marveled at the postcard-colored water, the gorgeous hues of Caribbean oceans.

"Have a drink—"

Roland and Frenchy got off their horses and they all knelt before the stream, cupping mouthfuls. The purest water from deep earth tasted sweet and clean.

"That's why I didn't offer you the bottle before …"

Frenchy took repeated helpings.

"Waiting for that compliment," Billy prodded, relentless.

"*Sweet wonderful you*," she returned invoking a Stevie lyric, flatly sarcastic.

Billy twisted over at the prisoner. "I'll take it." He raised a hand for a high five and Roland lifted his tentatively and not because he was lacking in strength. The captor slapped it.

They rode onward to a steady rise and were greeted with signs of thriving canyon life. Broad-snouted canyon dogs trailed them, mutt litters of several rogue pit bull rapists. Accustomed to sloppy backpackers, the stocky hounds were stalking them for food scraps while random horses roamed and charged freely past.

Another half-mile up, the canyon walls widened and Supai village lay before them, an expanse of farm fields, horse pens, gardens, and the dilapidated A-frame homes of the Havasupais. The town itself resembled an old Indian trading post from a century earlier with two general stores, a restaurant, and post office featuring the only mule-train postal delivery service in the country.

As they drifted up the main street, a wide dirt drag beneath tall shady cottonwoods, Billy checked his watch; it was seven-clock.

He dismounted again and disappeared into the local store, emerging with three coffees and three bananas. They had breakfast at a table outside as the sun inched its way above the canyon walls, birds singing intermittently. A Caucasian family arrived from a campsite and gathered at a table nearby. Billy threw on his eye shields and suddenly turned away.

Still the tour guide, however, he pointed out the King and Queen rock formation on the cliff above. "Havasupai legend states when the royals fall off the ledge it will signify the end of the world …"

An Indian in a white cowboy hat, erect carriage, swept up on horseback sighting Billy. He was about to shout his name, but the captor purposely beat him to it.

"*Gum-ya*, Taylor! What up?" Billy greeted him. "Meet my friend, Gerritt."

"Ho, Gerritt!" the Indian gushed warmly. Roland was aghast, his face turning to stone.

"Woof!" Frenchy objected harshly.

"And you remember Frenchy from Mante-La-Jolie?"

She huffed again. "So boring."

"That's France, yes? *Gum-ya.*" The Indian did not get off his horse. "They been expecting you at the sweat. You know where the new lodge is right? Just above Navajo Falls—"

"Staying out of trouble, T?"

"Mostly … B.I.A. been around some."

That meant something to Billy and his spine stiffened, but he showed an easy smile and a nod. "We know what that means, right?"

They belched the significance of the acronym simultaneously, "Bossing Indians Around!" with follow up laughter.

"There's a Pima shaman visiting from down south," Taylor announced.

"A shaman?" Frenchy interjected suddenly, her interest piqued.

"Oldie but goodie. Name's Grace. She's a healer too." He nodded, tapped his brim, gave a tug of the reins, and his animal trotted onward.

Though depleted, the captive was reeling shocked his son's name had been offered up. Billy perceived his spirit had taken a hit.

"It's an ancient Indian custom to take on the name of your dead child in a period of mourning—"

"But the tribe doesn't know he died," Frenchy protested.

"—*I* know he died."

"—And he died years ago."

"Excuse me, Frenchy—" He then redirected to the prisoner. "To keep the memory alive. So when someone addresses you that way it's an acknowledgment not only of the death of your loved one, but that your loved one lives still within you. It's a proper offer of condolence, a show of the complete respect."

Frenchy shook as she got up and sauntered over to her horse. She caressed it and spoke to it before retrieving her journal from the saddlebags.

Roland remained shaken. Billy's explanation was bizarre and offered little comfort. Frenchy returned to the table settling across from Billy with a pen in hand and she began to record an entry.

A white man with silver-streaked hair came over from the other table, a glowing, cheery expression. He'd been eyeballing them several minutes and the all-sensory Billy had spied it.

"Excuse me gentlemen, miss—you just arriving?"

"Yes."

"Where you from?" He seemed to possess gladness, a happy radiance.

"California," Billy piped casually.

"First time in Supai?"

"No," he returned bluntly. "Where you from?"

"Well, we're from Alabama—"

"I'm from Natchez." Another fib.

"Oh really? We're from Mobile. Dog-gone that's funny. Say, we're giving a concert here tonight, we'd love for y'all to come by …"

"Who is we?"

"We're with the Alabama Mission for the Latter Day Saints. That's us camped over there and we sure would love it if you could make it on over tonight? 'Bout seven-thirty?" The man gleamed one brighter than before while nodding away and he faded off to rejoin his family.

"Highlighters," Billy identified.

"What's a Highlighter?" Frenchy asked.

"An obsessed soldier of the Owen Josephson faith, otherwise referred to as a Jesus freak—"

"Doesn't mean they're freaks, Beelly. They may just have faith."

"Sorry my little *mocha religeuse*, but when they ambush you at seven-clock before you've put creamer in your coffee? That's freaky."

"It was an invitation to a concert."

"Try fire-and-brimstone preachment and change platter—with music."

"Your friend Taylor spoke of the sweat lodge and a healer. Does that make him a freak also?"

Frenchy had heard Billy's catechisms and viewpoints for years, many of which she'd found troubling. Where she would not articulate a position before, she would now; it was different for her.

"So why do you call them Highlighters?" Roland posed.

"They glow like they've been highlighted with a fluorescent marker. Can see it in their face and expression, all lit up like a Christmas tree."

"Because they're happy and comfortable with their faith and beliefs and it makes them feel confident and good about themselves ..."

"Did someone hire you to be my personal contrarian?"

"Just showing the hypocrisy."

Billy couldn't help himself. "You pick your card today?" he jibed.

"Yes, I did. It was an Asshole and its message is to be a jerk and a preech." Even Roland had to smile.

"Little Mistral," he cracked condescendingly. "Don't be bitter. You just have to understand you're not public company girlfriend material; you're a private company girlfriend and yes, you've supported me through the down times in boring RV parks for the elderly, but when Sixkiller Quadruped Transportation Management goes public on the big board of the NYSE, you will be compensated for your time and contribution of life-enhancing youth and beauty with a healthy stipend—"

"Blah, blah, blah—"

"*And*," he hammered on, "as part of your severance package, I will introduce you to a new up-and-coming private company whiz kid so you can help him through the painful process of sweating office rents and delays and false promises of IPOs, stock and warrant offerings—because—now you have experience as a launching-pad girlfriend and all those arm-candy dues you've paid won't go to waste. You're a proletariat girlfriend, utilitarian, and among the best. How's your butty-butt?"

"*You'll* never see it again," she spat back. She was already penning at a ferocious pace, undeterred.

"Ooooh," he played as if outgunned. "Too bad because you were thisclose to seducing me back on the trail." His thumb and forefinger were pinching to demonstrate the thinnest fraction.

Flying across the table, on delay from the previous exchange, it came hard, as loaded and mighty as she could muster, a devastating flat hand wallop to Billy's cheek erupting in a thunderous *FWAP!*—a sound likely heard at the North Rim of the Canyon. For the first time Roland witnessed Billy appearing shocked, and, speechless came with it. He also feared the consequences.

Yet what was equally astonishing, Billy did absolutely nothing as if he knew he deserved it and was taking his punishment; even more probable, he was avoiding a public display. Roland downed his coffee.

"Know why you got that?" Billy asked Roland as if nothing happened. " 'Cause you're a Forty-Eight." He raised his cup and the captive paused before lifting his to be tapped. "Big ups to you." He then extended a red bandanna to him, handing it to him then wrapped his brow with an identical one. "Cowboys keep 'em," he said. "Say we get over to Shit Canyon—"

Frenchy would now state her plans. "I'm going to stay."

"What for?"

"I want to visit the shaman … I'll meet you later at the Falls." Billy eyed her carefully. "I have my horse," she punctuated resolutely.

The man mounted his horse and nodded somewhat reluctantly and as the two moved down the main street, Frenchy assaulted her journal once again.

It was in her voice, the way she attacked the pages and the way she'd stood up to Billy. There was an assuredness, Roland determined, a new force in her at once fresh and courageous and he was impressed by it and admired her for it. She seemed emboldened.

And in some incremental way he felt himself getting stronger too.

Billy was nasty and méchant to Man, he says Indians call other members by the name of the dead one while they mourn them. I must question this.

I was mad at Billy for abusing me, but that is not why I hit him. I hit him because of Man, because of his insensitivity. Even if it is Indian custom, Man is not Indian and doesn't understand. I could see it hurt him.

I have named Man now, it means I have made him personal and that is dangerous. To be personal. I should not have done his cards; I feel I know too much about him. And I don't know if he will die or not and I don't wish to treat him like a familiar person. I was weak when I told him of myself, it was a mistake. He must be just Man, just a no name, with nothing personal between us. I will call him that because I must refer to him as something.

No, I don't. I don't have to call him anything. Man is dangerous for me. It is too risky. For me, Man cannot exist (!) …

23

On horseback the men faded past the old school, the church, a Quonset hut chapel, the medical clinic, and the council building—and that was town. "That's all she wrote on Supai," Billy affirmed.

Ahead on the expansive plain they could see clusters of modest homes with grassless yards and dirt-pack animal pens surrounded by small private farm fields. The fields produced corn, beans, and squash, staples Native American dry-farming clans have been raising for thousands of years.

The prisoner noticed the fork in the road before them.

"Tourists go right, we go left," the captor declared.

They'd be taking the "off-limits" route, a dirt track that wound through the town's private section. The road meandered past the personal residences and farms of the tribe and it was an honor to be awarded this access. It meant acceptance and Billy had been granted it.

To the side of the road the captor slowed to a tree and picked its fruit, handing off a section to Roland. "Figs," he identified.

They picked freely from more rows of peach, nectarine, and apricot trees aligning the road and ate as they rode. They crossed a bridge of thick planks and Roland was reintroduced to Havasu Creek. The water surged beneath with the color and clarity of an estate swimming pool.

As they rode down the private road that followed the Creek, a big Indian on a tractor motored loudly past them in a diesel cloud. He offered a short nod to Billy while ignoring Roland's gaze.

"That's Happy Jack, resident hard-ass."

Further along, Billy pointed out a series of travertine dams formed in the Creek with quiet pools above. Fresh watercress floated atop with waving mimulus flowers. Each dam resembled its own health spa to cleanse in and they dismounted to taste the cress. The prisoner chose his own.

"Never seen anything like it, Billy."

"You ain't seen nothin' yet—"

He'd gone two days without sleep, but Roland wasn't tired or disoriented. He rode along taking in the high walls of sandstone, mesmerized by the dramatic scenery. The ominous sound grew louder as the walls narrowed and he perched high in the saddle, anxious. Further along the canyon narrowed on the storybook crystal creek and chills shot up his spine. He could hear the boom and thunderous roar.

The trail dropped and he looked right to catch a glimpse of a true marvel of nature. From a hundred feet up water surged through a travertine notch in the cliff's edge plunging the full distance into a wide magnificent aqua blue-green lake below generously feeding other falls and travertine dams and natural Jacuzzi-like tubs before dropping again spectacularly to another even higher, noisier cascade. Havasu Falls had the look of paradise.

"A snapshot from heaven," Billy termed it.

The prisoner observed in awe as the captor steadied his horse beside him. "See that mass of green moss halfway down? That's the Big Green Monster; when the sun hits it at high noon the monster comes out—"

"Is it swimmable?"

"Only for thousands of years."

They moved at a quicker clip as the trail spiraled down and a short set of switchbacks brought them to a deserted clearing at the base of the Falls. Tall cottonwoods hung a shady canopy over the banks. The breezes from the Falls carried thin mists from the torrent to their skin. There was no one in sight and they had paradise all to themselves.

The horses were hitched to trees and they jumped in the wide pool fed by the booming fall. The two dove, popped up, gasped in laughter and carried on like preschoolers attempting to swim at the surge while getting repelled by fierce currents caused by its enormous thrust. They dove deep and crawled by hand along the travertine floor, to get close to the point of impact. Resurfacing, they were deluged and the violent surge pushed them back forcefully toward the bank.

Billy pointed out a natural riptide that swirled behind the cascade against the cliff wall. They rode the current sweeping the perimeter behind the fall as residual sprays assaulted their faces. On mossy rocks at the base of the cliff wall they scaled high to a ledge and launched into the heavenly pool. Several inartful dives and plunges later, they retired to the frothing spa-like pools that terraced down from the main lake. Some pools offered natural hot spring jets with smaller waterfalls rushing into them from pools above. Billy disappeared at one point, but he resurfaced momentarily. He demonstrated the maneuver and diving deep they popped up in a breathable space behind a baby fall.

"How are your feet?"

"Torn up."

"Keep still," Billy advised, pausing. "Feel that?"

"It tickles—"

"Those are baby trout—"

"What?" He jerked his knees up.

"They nibble on your toes. Gets rid of the dead skin and cleans your feet. Just call it a spa day ..."

The setting was all too fantastical to the prisoner. They were zippered inside a waterfall as baby fish gave them an impromptu natural pedicure—awesome.

*   *   *

The rising sun warmed them as they dried themselves on the open bank at the end of the main lake. There were no trees, only uninterrupted sky. "Tired?"

"Made me a little weary," the captive man said. "I haven't been swimming in a while ... Feels good though. Do they serve piña coladas too?"

"You should get out of the sun—"

Roland was paused by the sobering suggestion. He fastened on Billy who angled sharply away. Was he trying to help him endure? To stave off sleep? To postpone the inevitability of his threat and fate? The prisoner couldn't be sure. Billy was an ever-evolving enigma, unpredictability his forte. Either way, Roland considered it a positive given his mission.

Impossibly, they both heard a flutter of a voice that emanated from behind startling them.

"Hello—"

Standing opposite them and knee deep in the aqua waters was a girl barely twenty wearing a skimpy white bikini. She'd appeared out of nowhere and was an arresting vision with thin lips, a gorgeous face, a slender, but perfect figure, and drenched honey-blonde hair below her shoulders. Her small, perky breasts were outspoken enough to peer through her top. Grinning away she was sending a palm gracefully over the surface of the water while studying its rippling effect.

"Hello," Billy returned with an appreciative smile, quickly eyeballing the prisoner to note the mysterious showing. "Where did you come from?" he asked easily, instantly sensing a level of interpersonal comfort.

"The fall," she volleyed deadpanned.

Roland chuckled at the flatness of her response and his laughter was contagious enough to get Billy. The two of them passed it back to her and she giggled.

"The fall?"

"I was behind it. I saw you there, I was up higher—"

"Nah-nanny-nah-nah," Billy chimed for adolescent braggadocio's sake and they all found that funny as well.

"Yeah, I was higher than you! I still am!" she laughed playfully, but not a child's release, her own unique expression.

"You still are—" Billy concurred pointedly.

She twisted a look at him, not sure what he meant, but it pleased her in some way. The remaining silence seemed pregnant with significance, a moment brimming with newness, perhaps promise, goodness, and more mystery. The pause needed to breathe before being played or tested: an immaculate life offering. The two of them felt it forcefully. All of this happened in an instant.

"Where are you from?" Roland posed politely enough, speaking a first time. But to the others absorbed by the prevailing energies he'd disturbed a moment.

"Where am I from?" she sent right back. "Who cares?"

Billy cracked up and she was delighted by his reaction, though her response had been well intentioned and not ridiculing.

"That's right, Roland," Billy followed up trying to collect himself. "Who the hell cares?"

"We're right here right now and it's beautiful!" she said, eyeing her new ally. "Let's get on to something more interesting than that!"

Yet her assessment was so true, so on the money, and Roland had to acknowledge it. His pre-emptive, shallow blurt wasn't nearly a crime; but in this natural setting it merited him the embarrassment of committing perhaps a social faux pas, of being cliché if not uncool.

He'd experienced the awkwardness, but not in a long while as in when he was a kid before he'd figured some things out.

At the same time, Roland's remark was nothing at all, no social misstep, no faux pas whatsoever. Other levelheaded minds would not have reacted this way, but these two were Billy Six and a young traveler who appeared to be a kindred spirit and similarly configured. As for the prisoner, there was newness about him—he was receiving, absorbing, remembering, and learning things, and he could understand alternative and special ways of thinking again.

Billy was still busting a gut and Roland broke up as well, which served as his own personal pathos.

The young woman was almost too much to be believed. She'd appeared out of nowhere, beautiful, nearly naked, at eight in the morning, from behind a waterfall. Her eyes were wide and bright and she splashed water into the air, watching the waters fall, the reflections, the visual patterns, and examining the rainbow prisms of droplets. "Why don't you guys come in? It's so wonderful!" She giggled too and splashed some more. "What's so great about that bank anyway? It's just a *bank!*"

Both looked to each other and soon did what males usually do when an inspiring and attractive girl invites them to do something— accept. They joined her and soon after the three swam toward the potent blast.

"This is so incredible!" she hollered against the falling torrent. "You see the rainbow???" she shrilled.

Intrigued, Roland hoped to find out more about her, but was gun-shy. He appraised her as not his type; she was too cool. He'd been cool once, too, but never as cool as the effortlessly cool people. More of a studied-cool type, he could mimic it, give appearance of it, but cool never came naturally. Cool people didn't try, they just were.

He remembered girls like her, usually the hippy types and pot smokers who made him feel inadequate in his coolness, or lack thereof; probably a major reason he found them sexy and wanted to have relations with them. More than that, he liked how these girls carried themselves as they appeared unconcerned with things like homework or team practice or cheerleading. They could just go to the park and get high with guys who looked like Billy, though Billy was no average stoner. A honey-to-the-ladies type, Billy could get any girl, yet he didn't take advantage; the captive had learned of that restraint from Margaret. Handsome, intelligent, articulate, and funny, Billy could smooth, seduce, or mind-fuck a woman into sleeping with him within minutes if he wanted to. But he didn't; conquest and matters of the flesh were not a priority and in a world of male mashers and marauders and sexting and sexgrams it was rare to see. Roland admired the man's composure and reluctance and emotional integrity when it came to women.

There was nothing average about Billy—he was uniquely magnetic and operated in his own realm. The opposite sex was not the only gender Billy could affect or control either and his powers of attraction and seduction weren't only sexual. He could have a cult following or even a full movement, religious or otherwise if he wanted, if he cared to manipulate the situation, any situation.

The prisoner had been attractive to women throughout his life while projecting a softer profile. Women found him honest, open, not intimidating, and easy to talk to and he had a talent for getting them to confide in him. They could get close, even affectionate with him, without fear of sending the wrong message and would often fall all the way captivated by his serene, unthreatening, and decent character. Made comfortable in close proximity to him, they saw no reason why their relations shouldn't go further and get more intimate. He inspired the passive aggressive romantic reflex in the opposite sex.

Billy Sixkiller was different—with danger on his side, he could excite and scare girls like an amusement park ride. He was a stick-your-finger-in-the-light-socket type, an adrenaline shot, an instant rush, a dangerous thrill, and a challenge. He did not fall easily and the combination of the fear and excitement he posed as well as the hard-to-get constitution qualified as pure kitty litter to the ladies.

Entertaining these sentiments was pleasing to Roland. The giddy musings brought to mind high school; reflections and feelings he'd hadn't remembered or enjoyed since and it made him guffaw spontaneously aloud.

"Stop having such a good time with yourself!" Billy called out.

The captor had pursued the girl to the middle, to the most perilous and thrilling place, the thunderous point of impact—no surprises there. They dove, popped up, frolicked, and roared with glee.

Joyfully thwarted by the force, they treaded water close to each other and spoke in softer tones, almost privately. They were very handsome together, a painting of form, figure, coloring, and type which blended harmoniously and the prisoner perceived it immediately. Renoir, Manet, Pissarro and other impressionists came to mind from the prisoner's museum tour days in Paris and how the grand masters would have had a field day with these two in this setting as subject matter.

Roland returned alone to the sunny bank and reclined as the two waded to shallower depths where they could stand and talk. They both shot quick looks at him. "I don't know," was Billy's reply to her.

"Roland, Britt wants to know—" She clutched him to prevent him from divulging while inadvertently clamping his arm to her breast and keeping it there.

The captive's meditation was playing itself out, the effortless way a Billy could attain a comfort index, a degree of physical intimacy in no time with a woman, her name secured as well.

"She wants to know if you've ever done mushrooms—"

She slugged him albeit barely so for the indiscretion.

"I've heard a lot about them, but never tried them."

"Would you like to?" she took over.

Here she was; the girl he could never get, the stoner, the party girl, was asking him to party. He reassessed quickly again; maybe she wasn't that girl. She was just having a pleasant time in a gorgeous idyllic setting. The prisoner reprimanded himself for the judgment.

Yet what should he do? He'd almost always turned down their pipes and joints before. He'd listen intently to their fractured, stoned banter hoping something still might happen with the one he liked until the inevitable impasse, a final blow to any potential union. Nothing ever did happen either; they were on different wavelengths and his crush was not reciprocated he'd conclude. In pondering it now he realized the stoner girls likely misinterpreted him. Because he didn't partake in the party favors and would just sit there quietly, young impressionable minds under the influence would perceive his reticence as a judgment, and a rejection, not of the marijuana, but of *them*; when that had never been the case. He actually liked being around these types. He admired them for their daring and acting freely and expressing themselves; the reasons he sought them out as companions in the first place. He found their adventurousness sexy. With the pretty stoners it would seem it had always been a colossal misunderstanding. The prisoner wondered then how many other misunderstandings his life had procured and cultivated that had been processed erroneously and logged in inaccurately in his mental database as supposed "truths"—when they'd never been anything of the sort.

The meditation reminded him that he hadn't always been the judgmental monster he now appraised himself to be; in earlier years he'd had an open mind of sorts. Only later in life did judgmental thinking take over and belief systems harden—as, it would seem, *he* had hardened.

"Is that silence a *yes?*" he heard the girl say.

Roland's latest wave of uncharacteristic introspection was broken. As he watched the two fast friends scurry up the bank, he was mindful of the fact that they weren't talking marijuana; mushrooms were a hallucinogen and he'd had his negative experience with LSD years ago. Admittedly, LSD was a more potent chemical and drug, but trying it still had sent him to a hospital overnight. Yet he knew magic mushrooms were organic and not synthetic.

"That silence is a, *why not?*"

Billy and Britt both cheered; they had another conspirator. She dashed over to her pile of belongings hidden behind a cottonwood stump and teased a Baggie from her shoe. Billy wandered over and she sprinkled his hand and he immediately shoved the stems and caps in his mouth, swallowing them.

He returned to the prisoner and handed him a generous dose.

"Down them quick in one haul …"

"They taste like shit," Britt warned.

Roland tasted one first before downing the rest. "They're not that bad. Just dry."

The girl jumped into a smaller travertine pool and splashed around and Billy joined her. They were very cozy together and soon found themselves in a lovers' embrace. He was about to smooch her when suddenly she announced—she had to leave.

"Leave? What do you mean?"

"I have to go," she said. "Don't worry, I'll see you again …"

"When?" Billy was astounded.

"Later." She hugged him again. "I'd kiss you, but I'm too high."

"Kiss me now," he whispered and it was interesting for the prisoner to hear him articulate it, an overtly sexual directive.

Her captivated eyes lingered on him and she paused briefly with that infectious smile. She considered the request, contemplated it, and everything beautiful there was to do with him and more until—she snapped from it.

"Besides, I don't want to ruin it."

"Ruin what?"

"When I kiss you for real—"

Withdrawing from his clutches, she stepped back and left him standing there, mouth agape, too astonished to speak. She vaulted from the pool and gathered her little pile and ran up the embankment to the first switchback, waving periodically. She blew them final fairy kisses; then she was gone.

Billy remained standing there mystified, bedazzled, dumbstruck even. "What *was* that?"

"I don't know where to begin …"

"Damn! I mean, did you see that?"

"I did."

"Who was that girl?" His expression was aglow with wonder. "My God, she was like," he dug for a description. "—*Magic!*"

"I think so … But you'll see her again."

"No," he said, hesitating until the disappointment became absolute. "I'll never see her again …"

"How do you know?"

"I know."

"But how?"

"Life. She provideth; she taketh away …"

"If you don't pursueth, yes …"

Billy looked sharply at Roland and smiled vaguely, ignoring what the captive said. He plopped down next to him. "How do you feel?"

The prisoner lay there puzzled, but he knew what Billy was asking him. "I don't feel anything yet."

"You should be getting an energy boost very soon …"

Having ingested the hallucinogen Roland appreciated Billy was knowledgeable; his experience made the prisoner less uncomfortable. The dark humor didn't escape him—he was poised to end his life, yet was taking solace he'd be tripping with someone experienced in the use of magic mushrooms. A man who wanted to kill him, no less!

"You ever launched any kind of hallucinatory substances?"

Out of the blue, the question prompted a sudden jolt of paranoia and Roland paused on an answer. He had just told Frenchy about taking LSD and thought she might have informed Billy. But he remembered also Billy had uncovered the Tucson hospital records from 1995 when Roland had been admitted there for the drug overdose. Was it a trick question? Was his captor trying to catch him in a lie? But Billy had already divulged his knowledge of Tucson and how could he think he would forget so quickly? He would also remember telling Frenchy. Therefore, Roland would know he couldn't lie. A trap of the sort seemed amateurish, hollow, and way beneath Billy. Though a trap was unlikely, the prisoner was nevertheless put on guard.

Billy seemed cheery and upbeat, but was so unpredictable Roland knew to craft his words carefully and most of all not to lie.

"You know what I've done," he said. "Tried acid …"

"Didn't like it, did you?"

He hesitated again. "No."

"This buzz isn't as heavy," his captor diverted and Roland was relieved.

"What's it like?" he posed, pushing the new segue in conversation.

" 'Shrooms are about—truth—it's all I can say."

The prisoner eyed him warily. "Like a truth serum?"

"Don't worry. I promise you're going to like it." He said it with a brotherly smile. "Just go with the flow. And don't give in to negative thoughts. Just let them go like passing breezes. And whatever you do don't panic. If you do just call for a lifeline—"

"A what?"

"*Me* … I'll set you straight."

At that moment, Roland was certain Billy hadn't been trying to set any traps for him and that his paranoid meditation had been nonsensical.

"You seem more worried about me having a sour drug experience than about my life which is going to end." He was shocked he'd said it, but he could feel his mood was shifting. First the sudden spike of paranoia, now his attempt at dark humor. His mindset was being altered.

"I am!" Billy howled. "Hell, I could kill you, but I don't want to be responsible for a bad trip; that would be uncool—*very* uncool!"

They both were spontaneously catalyzed to laugh.

"Besides, you'd never forgive me," he teased to more laughter. "Wait, these can't have kicked in already; takes forty-five minutes and that's on an empty stomach. Could they be that strong?"

Roland shrugged, about to giggle for no reason and all it needed was the faintest spark. "I feel it."

"Do you?"

"Something … Like tingles in my hands."

"That's a sign, good … Proof too …"

"Of what?"

"That you really are alive …"

Roland play-acted like a mad scientist's lab-manufactured monster. "*I'M A-LII-IVE!*"

"Where did she get these? They're amazing—"

Roland delivered it in her brand of deadpan. "Who cares?"

That was it—they howled for minutes on end repeating "Who cares?"

Billy was pleasantly surprised. The prisoner had a sense of humor he was unaware of, encased somewhere in his cerebral cortex and it was now unlocked. He jested to himself: "gonna be fun to party with this guy!"

" Who *was* that girl?"

Roland picked up on it. "*Butch Cassidy and the Sundance Kid*!"

"Exactly!"

"But they said, 'Who are those guys?', but the girl—"

"Overkill, I get it. Don't bore me—"

"Sorry—"

"How do you know we play that game?"

"You tried it on me when we first met—"

"Oh yeah." Billy was now thoroughly buzzed.

"And I heard you when I was in the trunk of the car."

"You can hear in the trunk—??? No way!"

"Comes right through the air ducts."

Billy was astonished, dramatically so. "Damn …"

"But not in the backseat—"

"I worked on that car for ten years! You can hear what's going on up front from the trunk? *Shit!*" Then again, "Really?"

The prisoner instantly felt for him; his piece of mechanical art had revealed a flaw and he was the one who'd broken the news.

"What a loser," Billy piped. He knew not to obsess however. Mushrooms heightened emotions and the intensity could produce a negative spiral.

"Should have stuck to golf carts," the captive quipped and it was all that was needed to prompt more howling.

"My true passion! EZ Boys and Yamahas! Can you believe it? People phone me and actually say, '*Is this Sixkiller Quadruped Transportation Management Group?*' They have no idea it's a total joke name and I have to answer them seriously, '*Why yes, sir, IT IS!*'"

From then on, any snippets of dialogue led to something more uproarious. They were on the mushroom train and it was rolling furiously down the tracks, open-aired, the winds of intense sensory and mind activity surging, blowing back their follicles.

"I have to go to the bathroom—"

"Uh-oh," the captor identified. "The mushroom shits."

"Is there such a thing?"

"I wouldn't kid you. I'd shoot you, but I wouldn't kid you!"

"I asked you to shoot me," Roland said, impressing even himself.

"I don't like being asked—" They both cracked out loud.

"Mighty white of you—"

"I am Caucasian … Just go up there to Shit Canyon."

"What?"

"To bounce your curly. Shit Canyon. Told you about it before. Don't forget the rag."

"I thought you were joking—"

"No, it's where the tribe takes shits."

"Guess I should feel honored!" More laughter.

"You should, good shitting company—"

"What rag?" Roland now processed.

"You're on fungus delay, love it! That red rag I gave you—"

"That's what it's for? Does it make me a real cowboy?"

"After you take that dump, absolutely-maybe—"

Roland grabbed the rag and paced toward the trail only to spin back. "Where is it?" He seemed disoriented. "I mean exactly."

"Don't get paranoid—"

"No, I won't." He was already tweaking, of course.

"Take the path up and when you get to the top, look for the cave. It's black from all the fires."

"Fires? To keep you warm while shitting?"

"No! To burn the shit!"

The man started on up. "I forgot how much you like talking shit!" Uncontrollable giggles were sparked as he went. "Will they take my shit? I mean, I have some pretty good shit!"

"Then they'll take it! Don't let anyone ever tell you you don't have good shit. Be turd-secure!" The comment yielded more guffaws.

Roland located the captor from above and hollered, *"Who was that girl?"* Billy belched.

The prisoner disappeared and returned minutes later, but to both it seemed like hours. Billy wasn't concerned; he knew Roland would be too paranoid to venture off as a result of the psilocybin's influence. Rather than confronting the wilds, he'd stick with the devil he did know, perhaps with perfectly panicked meditations like, "Where the hell is Billy??? I gotta find him!" Roland was Billy's own private toy now, in Duchamp's terms, his Ready-Made Playdate.

At the same time, Billy became captivated and dangerously so by the creepy-crawler show at his feet—a battalion of red ants. Indigenous to the canyons, they were hustling about looking for food, transporting sand, busy little mothers. He observed them, fully absorbed and fascinated as they all scurried and hurried to "nowhere, somewhere, *their where*," he fashioned. "*My where, your where, our where, his where ...*" He loved inventing language and this neologism meant to wherever a person or group wished to go: "their where." He got it. No one else would, but *who cared?* He was fucked up.

As the prisoner jogged back down the trail to the Havasu Falls' base, he felt the language of his muscles and listened to the strange phenomenon of breathing, all inspired by that freshly skewed angle his altered mindset was providing. When he arrived at the embankment, he saw his captor up close and panicked. "Billy! What are you doing?"

The man was planted there with armies of red ants crawling all over his arms, neck, and face.

"Quick! You getting bitten?"

"Now and then," he said, letting loose a goofy grin.

Roland collared him and dragged him down the bank and into the water. He dunked him under until Billy surfaced, gasping.

"Thought you were making a run, RP."

"No, you didn't. But I thought you were going to be the Grateful Dead skeleton; the skull with shades and that bandanna."

"Smoking a cigarette—"

"Picked clean by the Red Army."

"That's funny." Billy's bemused grin remained in place.

His pupils fully dilated, Roland's eyes darted to and fro as he picked up again on the enhanced and sharply defined scenery. "All visual poetry …"

"There you go. Pops, doesn't it?"

The prisoner hollered out suddenly. "I see it!"

"What?"

"The Big Green Monster!"

Painted into form by direct sunlight, its moss shining brilliantly, the imposing ghoulish figure now hulked over them.

"Looks like a giant green Cousin Itt!"

"From the Addams Family, you're right!"

They both retreated back to the embankment to take a front row seat for the electrifying visuals. "What's in these, Billy?"

"Psilocybin. Sensitizes the rods in your eyes and everything appears clearer, more colorful and dramatic … Objects can move too—"

"This is crazy—"

"Good crazy?"

They looked at each other a moment and simultaneously sparked, they blurted in unison, *"Who was that girl???"* The line became a recurring one and oft-repeated, producing instant hilarity—*theirline.*

"I had one of those today with Taylor."

"Guess it's one of those days," Roland ribbed to more laughter.

"But where was she from?"

"I don't know—for all the grief I took asking her and at the expense of being cool the least she could have done was told me!"

"Glad I stayed cool—"

"Yeah, I was the sacrificial jerk—"

"You still looked cool." He paused. *"NOT!"* Howls.

"Yeah, well, you were cool all right—so cool you're here and she's not!" he teased, both breaking out again.

"Yeah, calm, cool, collected and—"

"*ALONE!*" they both jumped on.

"Billy," Roland clearly teed up for them. "*WHO WAS THAT GIRL???*"

The banter went on and on, inspired, sometimes brilliant, at times ridiculous, from novel and obtuse angles. They were operating on a fantastical fascination high, enhanced in no small part by one of nature's more intoxicating locales; turquoise waters made visually more dramatic as sunshine poured over them reflecting a prism's colors. The setting was breathtaking; the shiny green moss to the rocks, the towering red canyon walls, the potent booming roar of Havasu Falls and hawks soaring hungrily overhead. At once humbling and awe-inspiring, this unfathomable sensorial ride in paradise, an experiential odyssey, was as unlikely, coincidental, and totally spontaneous as could be imagined.

Roland was specially affected. He saw the earth before him like never before as a wholly living and breathing organism, surging, gusting, frothing, flowing, rivering, thundering, and rupturing. For the first time, he understood the Native American term, the Earth Mother, often mentioned by Billy, for everything came from her and was nourished by her. She was her own living being who needed to be honored, cherished, and protected. He thought of human beings, him included, who were largely consumers, using the Earth, depleting her, poisoning her, and robbing from her. Just then he realized he was giving in to negative thinking and he remembered Billy's warnings and he let the pejorative thoughts pass.

The captive man recoiled on the sunny bank content to be a voyeur. The manic Billy, however, was not comfortable when held stationary. He was animated and high-energy by nature and the dose of hallucinogens had given him a further boost. He paced along the ledge with the Falls crashing behind.

Roland scrutinized everything in view; sparkles in the water, trees rippling in the wind, birds hopping about, even Billy's face had motion though it didn't. The hallucinatory aspects did not scare him. He was witnessing life through an enhanced smart window that not only featured a visual clarity, but a physiological, psychological, and philosophical one as well. He was seeing himself as alive, vital, and biologically correct. He was a pulsating molecule to the Earth Mother, a part of it all, connected to its mystery that now seemed less mysterious. He was a creature of the Earth like the animals, feeling in better step with the universe. The teachings of animal medicine crashed at once into comprehension and resonated fiercely with him. His captor was another thriving molecule, another Earth creature, a part of its sum, part of its mystery, and right then in that very moment the man's interior surged forth to him as visible as his exterior.

Every aspect of Billy Six's being and profile the prisoner was envisioning a first time fully and comprehensively and in their totalities, the man's life and his past. Roland saw his captor as a pure person, a compassionate person, a good person, given a very bad deal and it was so perfectly rendered, so perfectly made clear—and he consumed it. He felt for this Dennis Roy, abundantly so. The epiphanous meditation came to him then; he'd do anything to help Billy out of this mess and in that moment, in that very moment, he considered making it his mission.

That was, of course, if he survived. *If.* His own situation was difficult to contemplate in this transformed state as it was beyond intense. *What was he doing, anyway? How did it come to this? How could he be turning his back on life? On this supreme gift? With all its beauty and wonder and natural splendor? To give all that up and go where???* Questions of the sort bombarded him and he fought them off, but he couldn't entirely. The probing meditations made him more paranoid which brought on sadness—the beginnings of a "downward spiral" Billy had mentioned.

The revelations kept coming, though, blowing his mind and prompting new questions that were destroying his finely tuned thought-over theses years in the making in addition to his final decision—and he tried to downplay them, erase them, and move past them as quickly as possible. Now he needed a "lifeline" and looked up suddenly and posed it feebly. "Billy—?"

Billy snapped up suddenly, admiring the network of veins to a fallen leaf. "Don't!" he fired.

"What?"

"Don't think about it!"

"This is powerful stuff—"

"Just go with the flow, okay?"

After a moment, Roland found his smile, nearly comforted. "Okay." The axiom was all he needed to pull him out of the black hole. "So tell me, what's on your mind …"

"You really want to know?"

"*Absolument*—" Why French came to him he did not know.

His question was left hanging, however, and it gave rise to a spectacle he would never forget. Billy started in with a pitch, an inspired rant really, born deeply of his core and like the roaring Havasu Falls behind it came charging forth in an unending torrent— unforgettably so.

"Damn, I love this feeling, if I could I would feel like this all day long because this is me normally, this is the way I feel or the way I want to feel, whichever, because you know what it is?"

"What?"

"*Truth*—the rest stripped away, and it's the rawness that's so exhilarating and I love that, don't you?"

"—Uh, yeah—" The sensations were so very new to him. "—I think."

"But when you're in the city you can't do this, I mean you can, but not like this with cliff mosses and tide pools and cascades and Magical Waterfall Fairies emerging from behind them, instead you get bludgeoned by the techtropolis, the Info Age tech machine, up the download staircase, with all the selfie-centric social media feeding frenzies, *Insta, Facebook, Snapchat, WhatsApp,* and the rest of the But-Back-to-Me narcissistic IV feeders, drips, and mainlines, lest we forget the gossip—*TMZ, Perez Hilton, Gawker,* et al, the puff-piecy 'Page Six' press-release runoffs, all blasting the latest Kardashian Big-Ass news, Victoria's not-so-secret-rather-in-your-face Secrets, @badgirlriri scandalanigans, JLo, JLaw, Kanye making love to himself, Trump still trumpeting his trumpet, the hot-off-the-Internet iCloud privacy raids exposing the latest fellatio and flying facial cum snaps and tapes, I mean, can you believe this stuff is thrust in our faces, this unending ridiculous overly personal and private even porno barrage and for what???—that is to say in our big overstuffed melon of a world with too many people and dwindling resources, the rats in a cage manifesto just charges on and there is no room for taste anymore like all the prepubescent, androgynous and heroin chic twelve-year-old models, *in parentheses* (who-look-like-boys-and-I-wonder-why-velvet-mafia?) *end parentheses*, all cherry-picked from economically depressed equatorial and eastern Euro countries featured in all the advertorials trying to fake sexually adult poses, I mean what the hell happened to normal of-age beauties?, where are all the Sophia Lorens, Rita Hayworths, Ava Gardners, Grace Kellys, and Audrey Hepburns? because they're out there somewhere like when you go to the mall, so where are they? I have taste, I know what mature classic beauty is and I'm going to follow your site or *Insta* feed or buy your magazine so *COME ON* give me the real deal, give classic beauty back to its people, you know? because we're dying here, we're down to one or two sexy va-va-voom over-21 superbeauties, not little kindergartners or frail, unformed knock-kneed girls who need to be changed and burped or even worse, the TV Botox impostor trashionistas; I'm talking real beauties who actually look like women, who truly have the capacity to make us feel better about ourselves, about being a part of the human race, about being caught in this lowly circumstance of the human condition on this desperate little chunk of rock three from a sun a billion miles from nowhere! so get with it, let some morsels of taste win out *puuulllleeeeze!*—I mean what about our Who Cares? Waterfall Fairy who would sizzle like a flea on a griddle on the cover of *Vogue*, I'd buy it a hundred times over wouldn't you, Rollie?—a girl so exquisite, gorgeous, and natural, but of course she's likely left to some mediocre little life somewhere because no one wants her to sneak away from beneath that rock in that homogenized suburban palooka life either with that look, that great perspective and aura, that generosity of spirit with sensibilities in proper alignment, dancing along with little dreams she must be hugging, holding onto, and hiding, fearfully clinging to, because you know that girl is ESP-great and she'll never make it to the cover of *Harper's Bizarre* or 'Page Six' boldface heroinehood because there will be a confederacy of total jackasses and backwoods pervs, lunatics, fanatics, and old world cavemen telling her she doesn't have it as they use her, our Who Cares? Cover Girl, wringing the last bit of beautiful youth out of her like a wet towel until she's had six kids, her face is folding in half, tots are down to her ankles, a *Deliverance* daze anyone?—some destiny, huh, Roland? but we can't have her, the girl next door, *noooo-sir*, because let's face it, she's a one in a million rarity, I mean, girls like that—the girl next door—doesn't even exist anymore, and if she does she's nearly extinct, because what used to be the girl next door is now in your living or on your techy hand toy sending tit-grams or spread-eagled gam-grams to the masses, I mean how did our Waterfall Fairy even survive the trappings of her generation? the freshly-hatched flock of me, me, me MEllennials, the sweet darlings raised on the nipples of *Instagram*, educated by witty memes, learning self-worth and self-esteem through hearts and 'likes' while getting Instafed life's goals and dreams from the hot-tubbing wars of Gigi Hadid and Kendall Jenner and they think, 'Ahah, that's what I want' and 'that's where I want to be' and they mistake their *Insta* profiles for real accomplishment and everyone's scandalous posts for real protein and keep feeding on it and can't get enough of the sensorial overloaded barrage until the I-want-it-too fame and celebrity bug hits at 13 in a time frame of 'it's my time' and I-want-it-now and they're already ready for their close-ups and stardom before a first min wage job, with Internship???/pay my dues-what dues???-fuck off attitudes, the 'it's all about me,' in the now, but 'back to me' MEllennials, and you can't blame them entirely, they're only error-prone human fuck-ups too and it's all the generations' previous faults, it's all ours' fault because we brought them into this I-Age tech nightmare we've created as we've failed at offering a healthier setup or guiding them in healthier directions, but was that even possible??? it's all been happening so fast on a time clock we never experienced because we created a monster we were never prepared for or equipped to handle, this TECHTROPOLIS!, and it's any town-every town, and we constructed it too well without safeguards or safety nets and it's a runaway train, it's the last thing you do before bed, it's body-snatching you as soon as you wake up, it's on your bedside table, at your desk, in your pocket, on your wrist, in your ear, in the living room, seizing you again as you leave the front stoop, and where young teens of yesteryear were contemplating a first cigarette the over stimulated, over assaulted, under accomplished, inexperienced, and ill-equipped MEllennials will do anything to join the twisted fray whether it requires dealing black market Adderall for the boys or becoming amateur porn stars for the girls, just to get known, just to pole vault out of their unknown, unheralded, 'mediocre' boondocky addresses and get to the celebrity playgrounds and promised lands Insta-advertised and more destinies programmed while keeping their egos, dreams and fantasies afloat with more growing numbers of hearts and 'likes' from corrupted brethren all appreciating their contaminated maneuvers with the-more-scandalous-the-more-'likes' mentalities, the-more-skin-the-more-hearts philosophies AND SO in this perverted, depraved, overly processed, corrupt, tasteless techy world, maybe it's better our more evolved pre-Millennial Waterfall Fairy stay away from the metropoles like New York, Miami, Vegas, and LA where she'll run into everything plastic, artificial, overproduced and overdone and fall into the dark traps, the black holes, the Malice in Wonderland, dropping down into a netherworld of dastardly deviants, misanthropic woman polluters and pariahs of the most pathological natures, the real scum *de la* scum, and she'll end up so far away from that waterfall fairy spirit, she'll be used, abused, humped, dumped, revered, smeared, coked up, Xanaxed down, Molly-launched, tranquilizer-crashed, and, was she even real, Roland??? Damn, that was magical!!!—*now where was I?*"

"She was in trouble," he reminded him, "I know that!"

"—*Damn right*, she is," he resumed, "dragged down, knocked up, street corner idolized, back barn sodomized, aborted ad infinitum, if she's unlucky getting a private *Insta* invitation to some twisted Arab movie producer's house in Cannes to be Cannes-ed goods, or in the Valley for a glorious defecation dance or a Hollywood-Hills-one-two or some hedge-funder's Manhattan palace with an indoor swimming pool and Harvard-educated, uber-polite civilities and whisperings replete with, 'Pardon, do you mind if I come in your face?'-methodologies, leaving her with an ass that stings for a week or days, *AND SO*, on a purely aesthetic and artistic, even quality of life level, what does she have to look forward to in the big cities? she may be better off staying with Billy Bobbie Ray in the sticks to receive his little daily perversions in a log cabin bangathon/slash/small town degradation scenario, instead of the bigger metro horror and so what? even if you say she's not so galactically beautiful which *SHE IS*, but the fact is, no one is!, *NOBODY* is!, it's like why the fuck are we even talking about beauty or beauties or supermodels??? or even 'Where am I from? Who cares!' because it doesn't matter a good goddam *HOW BEAUTIFUL ANYBODY IS!* or *where the fuck they come from!!!—right???*"

"Right!"

"But as long as we're rutted into the competitions thing programmed into us by the *Instagram*ming of our lives, '*TMZ*'-ing of our lives, the 'Real Housewives'-ing of our lives, the *Sports Illustrated* bathing suit-issue-ing of our lives, the Image-Before-Substance-ing of our lives, the thuggification of music, clothes, and language to a point where 'where oh where has our little English grammar gone?', the Two Dimensions Beats Three, a photo beats a thousand words, and is Internetted globally in seconds, making it a seemingly authentic image and statement of some supposed truth which is really horseshit, more manipulation, and no wonder America has such an image problem because we transmit all this trash *VIRALLY*, we dream it, think it, package it, and home-deliver it for coin, and the world follows our bad lead like sheep, and people don't like it, it *is* viral because it's a virus! they are germs, they are ingenious soul-eating bacteria, really spectacular diseases, platforming all the horror, all the ugliness, and we're not the only ones, and all that computer and digital ingenuity and all those requisite Internet windows have backfired in so many ways, it's given Dark Lords a new life, ISIS, al-Qaeda and cyber-rapists included, *WHAT I'M SAYING IS*, let's push something positive, we have beauty, we can make beauty, let's deliver beauty to the doorstop instead, send the true aesthetic, let taste win out, something a little original, let's try and raise the level, a touch of Gauguin, a touch of Toulouse-Lautrec, a dash of Botticelli, or even a Basquiat-scrawl of it, or tortured Bacon-contortion of it; I don't mean in an art-snobbery way, but let's go in that direction, let's study the masters because they're right there at our fingertips, and learn and grow and evolve and then put out enhanced culturally-significant product, but instead we get tastelessly over-packaged crap, spoon-fed the latest nauseous exploits of seemingly cosmopolitan Action Figures boldfaced in our dailies and flatscreens, and *THIS IS THE PROBLEM!*, as the media does this to us, they target us, they fill our heads with this shit, dumbing it down, dumbing us down, bringing it to the lowest common denominator, taking the lowest forms of behavior and ramming it down our throats, and of course we watch, we mimic, we're only hugely flawed homo erecti, what else can we do? but I know I didn't decide to create news cycle herohoods for murderers, corrupt politicians, and rapists or put Prince's, or Michael Jackson's, or Anna Nicole's morgue wars, sabbaticals, and death marches in my living room for months—*YOU DID! MR. MEDIA-IMPEDIA FATCAT*, and they create this endless, non-stop cyclical news cyclones and hurricanes—*CYCLANES*, appealing to the most crass instincts and brutal impulses, superswirling whirlpools of flash, crash, trash, and burn, manufacturing audiences, creating false needs, hungers, and thirsts, because remember, everyone got along fine without this shit in the 40s and 50s before the Media Mighties and tech took over, and it hits you like a hockey stick to the head, snatches your ever-diminishing attention span, so that you're knocked off stride, off your path of potential life-enhancing pursuits and you end up going on a tirade about people you don't even know and they might be nice, way-cool, respectable people, but you are overloaded with the shit, with their shit, with their hypocrisies, which we all have, but we're not thrusting it in *their* faces!, but you know too much, or not enough, but you know it's true, that it causes stress anxiety and you just want to break free from it but you can't so you continue to take it on the chin because you can't ignore it in the tech-heavy I-Age or you're *OUT OF IT* and irrelevant—what the fuck is *relevance* anyway? I'll take that cliff and falls any day—and there're too many new outrageous tales in the Cyclane with too many twisted twists and hooks, too many freaks, serial killers, and deviant sons of bitches, the newest Scott Petersons, Lacy Petersons, Stacy Petersons, Amber Freys, James Freyes, plagiarists, liars, sociopaths, psychopaths, and crooks, the latest OJs, tsunamis, Katrinas, Ritas, too much excellent horror, *REAL PHANTASMAGORIA* happening on a daily basis— that we just have to see it like the towers falling or Paris getting shot up or a really good car accident, I mean how can you turn your head away?—*no way!!!* and as we reach for more popcorn we realize there is no going back to simpler times, to *Walden*, or 'love thy neighbor,' or 'if you don't have anything nice to say...', women are on the run, men are on the run, transgenders are on the run, religions are colliding, the Middle East war was a backyard brawl over a scrap of desert sand and we made it World War III with apocalyptic, nationless assassins with end game the destruction of earth and beheadings for garnish and we're wondering how the hell did that happen? how have thirteen administrations come in and out of Washington spanning sixty years without getting illegitimately-uprooted, legitimate peoples a homeland?

"And *VOILA!!!* that's how Ugly American vulgarians even have a whisper of a chance at the Presidency or why a pumping iron Gropinator can become the Governator and why people voted him in because everyone else has been so inept they figure *why not?*, maybe he can get the job done, he did it on-screen or on his reality TV show, he solved problems in our fantasy world, why not in reality? Or the, *he made money before he lost money so he can run the country* leap of faith, because what is reality anyway? it's all blending with unreality and becoming: 'all you previous politicians, groups, administrations—*you're fired!!!* ', just like the TV show, it's all the *same!* and THEN CONSIDER how we're left with just a long weekend at Havasu Falls or an afternoon at the Bronx Zoo or some grim petting farm or the Seaquarium sanitarium to ponder it all OR in our little cyber-cafe terminal somewhere to parasite off of some desperate *Instagram*mer's follow-me beggings, creeping off pathetically posed selfies or regrettable narcissistic exploits, or some Facebook friend of a friend's weekend woodsy shots commemorating nature that at best flash-reminds us that somewhere perhaps nature does exist still and we give it eight seconds of thought over a creature comforting franchise guru'd designer soy skim vanilla decaf latte espresso with extra up-the-*derrière* foam, but that's all because we just *have to* read that meaningless meme or IM, e-mail/empty-mail, the next pervy sexting smooch or tit-gram or freshly-shaved cock portrait, the latest Twitter-twit tweet, God forbid we get back to our little self-important life somewhere, crammed into that tiny niche of the removed world we've been living and take care of our other programmed creature needs, shitloads of uploads and downloads and Netflixings to prolong the fantasies, iPodding/Padding into oblivion, iPhoning off into isolation, Xboxes and PlayStations to momentarily tune out the Cyclanes, corruption, and rot, but enhancing the separation and detachment, Hi-Def to give the alienation a spit-spot shine, millions upon millions of techno-pilgrims worshipping that flatscreen, the plastic partition from nature and keeping us on track solidly for a destiny in FLASHDRIVES, SELFIES, CONDOMS, PLASTIC SURGERY, AND GOSSIP, sorry Donald, sorry Kanye, sorry Kim, and all you Housewives and all the press-starved, Press-Desperates, silly tabloid superheroes, but you happen to be in the wrong time of history where you have too much exposure for what you have to offer or say and you press on people's nerves and it's not your fault entirely even though you've been paying ghost texters and publicists up the wazoo for all that I'm Better Than You pub, it's a disaster of epidemic proportions because very few people have enough talent or courage or guts to take all the exposure lavished on them in the modern age as humans have never been that interesting, certainly not to warrant a 24/7 fixation, especially when the subject is with hollow portfolio, falsely propped up there to start with BUT, *THERE THEY ARE!*, all the Boldface Superheroes and Press-Desperates you've been conned into watching and awaiting you on your phone or at your local newsstand and you *CAN'T NOT* become a Kanye-hater, or a Paris-ite or a Kardashianista, you can only take the ride on this one big phantasmagoric flight into who knows where?, celebreality TV oblivion, and it seems better than anyone else had it before us because we get all this information at our disposal, but does it do us any good? and should it be disposed of? because we are imperfect beings and supremely flawed and error-prone and can we take it? the answer is obviously *NO!* and are we closer to that canyon cliff or pine tree perch or gushing waterfall or snowcapped mountaintop? and the answer is *NO WAY!*, we're much further away from nature than ever before because our idiotic *HUMAN* nature has taken us further away!—how you doing, brother?"

"Great," Roland shot back, in step with him and not missing a beat. "Listening, absorbing, going with the flow ..."

"Am I boring you?"

"*Mesmerizing* me. Plainly speaking, I'm in awe ..."

Indeed the prisoner had a sense for his captor's cerebral capacities, but never the scale. In the same way Picasso, a master of abstraction and cubism, could sketch a horse perfectly, Billy, though oft-tossing high-minded concepts and ideas in a disjointed, scattered, and chaotic way, was equipped with an absolutely grounded perspective—in Roland's estimation. The man had a profoundly thorough understanding of how the world indeed worked, his core philosophies and instincts right on. Not just dazzle and show, glam and glitter, shock and awe; this spontaneous outpouring at the Falls demonstrated the man's acute sensibilities and high-leveled awareness. Even if you disagreed with him you could not say he was out of touch. The organics seemed to provide Billy the focus to articulate his viewpoints, stripping away the sensory bombardment he suffered from sober, leaving him with only the essential truths to deliberate as he saw them.

Roland's mind was similarly sparked and enhanced. He was digging and dredging as well, pulling things randomly from the dusty, disregarded shelves of his cortex; so much so Billy didn't catch on at first. "It's indescribable, yet you put it in words—"

"Say what?"

"Succinct and yet long-winded!"

"You heard that?" Billy was briefly stymied.

"Exhausting to hear, yet I want more!"

"In the car?"

"Sergio! … The Sleazy Euro Fashionista Designer Suit at 70% Off Salesman on Madison Avenue! I love him!"

The boys were howling again. "And—"

"Yes! The Desperately Wealthy and Excessively Bored Eurotrash Romance!"

"On their way to Starbucks!" Now they were gutted.

Roland collected himself and spoke genuinely. "Your stream of consciousness verbals are … neo-Whitmanesque. Like primordial poetry. Coming from the core of the Earth. Keep going. *Please*—"

"The Baron of Blah-Blah!"

"How are you so well-informed?"

"Misinformed? Had a lot of time to read, dog. But do you agree with anything I'm saying?"

"You're on the money from where I sit. Course I have no chair …"

"Well, just look out there … Isn't it insane how beautiful this avalanche of nature piled before us is? *That* is on the money! Nature is always on the money and that brings me to the *NATURE OF IT ALL*, human nature destroying real nature, though we've practically already devastated it, including the blue-toed ferret, the little spotted owl out in its lonely patch of bush, the missing bees, the ice caps, the disappearing polar bears, even though national parks are covered with plastic wrappers, discarded bottles, and trash from a million beeping suburbanites, even though there are a few rabbits and deer, and occasionally you get raccoons in your garbage, and a robin red breast for your birdfeeder, nature has been essentially relegated to the absolute *BLEACHERS OF EXISTENCE*, animals have been shoved into the cheap seats, the bleeders, of our little theater of life, and I think you can say we've essentially destroyed nature! and can anyone in their right mind with sensibilities in proper alignment, could they possibly blame that gorgeous evolutionary wonder of a white tiger all the way from the wilds of Siberia reduced to a Las Vegas resident and pitiful attraction in the Big Show in the desert, could anyone blame him for taking little Roy Horn, of the famed Siegfried And-team, one of the superheroic Domesticated-Domesticator Duo, hauling him off the stage in his mouth after years of domesticating and whipping and caging his brethren in the interest of 'helping the population of tigers grow'??? when they just happened to have had a huger than huge, bigger than big, whips-for-grins animal degradation act on the Vegas Strip as a side show to all their grueling, *painstakingly-fought* 'environmental efforts,' stretched plastic surgery faces, the fifty-million-dollar house they just happened to buy with the proceeds from this *EXHAUSTING* environmental push, but if you visited their pathetic little zoo right there at the Mirage Hotel, could you imagine anything more unnatural?, if you had a cartoon of Tony the Tiger telling his family, 'No, I live at the Mirage,' could it get any worse? could you dream up a more severe humiliation for such an incredible beast as the white tiger, next to the hookers, hairy chests, gold chains, the frothing pimps, the scaly capped-teeth con men, the hordes of little hotel masturbators all perved up and tucked away in their little rooms, flocking through the lobby daily?"

Roland was again spellbound, taken less by the words, but the man's compassion and humanity that came through them. He didn't necessarily see eye to eye on everything; it was Billy's passion for life and living that was so remarkable.

"*AND THEREBY, LEST WE FORGET*, who do we owe an apology to? come on Roland, who is the real victim here?"

"… Uh …"

"Give you a hint—the real Mother, the Mother of all Mothers …"

"Mother Nature!"

"*TA DA!!!* " he blasted. "We must extend our apologies which are really condolences to Mother Nature for our incessant kicks in her crotch, our negligent matricide, our unending earthly fuck-ups and we welcome her much-needed flare-ups, to give us hope, to keep nature alive and barely thriving with sparely a pulse, and these destructive fires and hurricanes are a violent reminder and exception, a welcomed sight for sore eyes, even though one was recently called Hurricane Fabian— I mean could it get any worse?—give the damned hurricane a real name, like a Zach or Boris or Gregor, give him some balls, give him his due!, I mean a force with a hundred-and-fifty mile an hour winds and thirty-foot waves with total coastal devastation on his mind deserves more than some gender-perplexed, fashion-victimed, insulting, teenybopper idol-coined, sexually-confused cad in gold pants, like a Fabian, I mean *COME ON!*, and *YET STILL*, insults and crotch-kicks to our great Mother aside, she did flex her muscle and kick back in southern Asia and no one enjoys the death and destruction and children drowning and losing parents and parents losing kids, *BUT* you'd have to say the appearance of those goddam tsunamis was reassuring, to let us know we haven't yet totally destroyed nature, a reminder she is still older and wiser and more honest and powerful than egocentric 'all-knowing' Man, so proud and cocky and self-satisfied because we have a 'soul' and the 'power of reason,' a college education, and religions which tell us we're created in the image of God—a white God and his son—and that we're 'not animals,' all the blistering propaganda and self-aggrandizement we've ingeniously concocted over the centuries, but the fact of the matter is *WE ARE ANIMALS!*, the most primitive and dangerous of all the animals, living in our own private denial-dream world, just go phone, pad, or armchair flatscreen for ten seconds for a dose, and so, *THEREFORE*, from the perspective of Our Earth Mother, we've gotten what was coming to us! And I think we can look forward to some more seismic sensations, some really good hurricanes and tidal surges which are inspiring each year and, because of overdevelopment, there's no place for the water to go and annual flooding can be anticipated, thank heavens, and if you ever wanted to see a slap to the face of human arrogance witness the devastation of Katrina and Rita, the dear girls, man thinking he's one-upped nature once again and *WHAP!* the Great Mother paying us back with a globally-warmed body slam for all our negligence, disregard, and waste, and yet, *EVEN STILL, AS WE SPEAK*, houses on the eastern coastal areas, the Carolinas, the Outer Banks, the Hamptons are being built!, areas which have been flooded every year for the last fifty years, flawed encroachment concepts so illogical you can't even get insurance policies on them, these architortural messes, every year more absurdly arrogant constructions, tasteless and tacky Sopranos houses, shrines to human narcissism and the I'm-better-than-you sweepstakes, flying in the face of nature, attempts to play keep away from nature and then getting devastated, destroyed, and flooded out, but that is the mindset!,

the unstoppable I-want-my-view!-mentalities, to bulldoze nature again
and again, rebuild, remake, re-plasticize, remodel, what used to be a
nice strip of open land, flooding, re-flooding, a haven for the
waterfowl destroyed forever, and let's not forget the timberlands being
cut away more every year, more greedy populations pressuring
politicians into tailoring laws to allow more cut-offs, more culling of
forests so, even though we've lost rural America, Norman Borlaug,
father of the Green Revolution and Nobel Prize winner puts it in the
late 1940s, as the negative turning point from which we began seriously
losing the honesty and integrity of rural America, morphing not
magically, but tragically into a plastic, suburban, logo-manic, Wal-Mart-
this, Starbucks-that, corporations on HGH, one town/every town,
identical franchise melanomas feasting on the population at every
street corner, sucking our blood, tumors designed in blueprint—even
though nature is on its way out, on the run, even though you may have
a good run in Central Park under the shade of a few trees clinging
desperately to the asphalt, their roots a series of stubbed toes on Park
Drive South, even though nature is relegated to the properties people
don't want except for the one or two national parks Teddy Roosevelt
managed to hang on to, now covered in signs and fairly aggressive
garbage-eating bears, so programmed to the anti-natural tourist flow
they've acquired a taste for Cool Ranch Doritos chips and will eat their
way into your car if you leave the window open, even though nature is
JUST ABOUT DEAD!, we have managed to *ADAPT* to the damage
we've caused as if everyday was a May morning, as if things were
getting 'better,' as if 'progress' was a real word, as if things were
natural, we use this word 'natural' all the time, well let me tell you it's
HUMAN NATURE and not nature at all, the ultimate oxymoron next
to 'mankind,' man-not-so-kind and that tiger munching on little Roy's
Horn had the last word on that, and Teddy Roosevelt's hunter pal
Philip Perceval said this about wildlife, 'Once human settlement starts
to spread, wildlife just disappears,' and it goes to show you we are so
far *WORSE* than animals, we're a cancer, getting rid of help in the
areas where we are, cutting, chopping, consuming, and eating up any
authenticity we find, like Pac-Man; spreading, metastasizing, getting
claustrophobically spread, gouging and contaminating the habitat and
there's no end to it, our thoughtlessly overpopulated, overly pressured,
overdone, revolting relationship with our environment, and it leads to

AIDS, perversion, masochism, sadism, religious wars, and more disease and it's without end and when human beings have spread to the point where enough's enough, where's it going to go? Certainly not in the direction of 'hey, let's settle down and have kids!,' but you sure as hell can bet on one thing double-downed, we'll continue to adapt to all the damage we've caused! You may have had enough, Roland—"

"Talk—" he protested.

"Nevertheless, the age is simultaneously phantasmagoric on a daily basis, the Information/Disinformation Age, all you have to do is check your phone to see it's amazing every day, miraculous advancements, new technologies, but what you have to wonder is *WHY?* and when is it going to even off and what is going to be around in fifty or a hundred years which is a snap of the fingers in evolutionary time, what kind of quality of life? what kind of authenticity? what kind of connectedness to nature are we going to have in a hundred years with the computer world sealing us off into these indoor spaces? long corridors of terminals, gaping at glowing tubes, which, admittedly, bring us anything onscreen with a finger-tap? we can flip it, retouch it, computer-enhance it, Photoshop it, pull anything out of any file in the world, any one of a thousand political speeches, amazing declarations of this or that, everything recorded, everything available, I mean there is more technology in a smartphone than was used to send the Apollo 11 astronauts to the moon—amazing! *BUT*—where is the quality of life going to reside? where is the diversity of nature? where is the common sense of life? where's it going to be?, so, even though a certain progress is not in question you have to look in the direction we're going as a very dangerous trap, it's exhilarating, it's fantastic, it's phantasmagoric, and if somehow we survive it, we could really be proud of ourselves, for the ingenuity or on a more depressing level, the level of adaptation, adapting to the damage we've caused, overlooking our burdensome populations, turning a blind eye to the insane pressure causing the sky-rocketing rise in heart disease, heart attacks, AIDS, cancer because we are a cancer on Earth, and we are causing the cancer, the Big C is going to get bigger, baby. Much bigger—"

The Speakers' Corner-style orator stopped pacing and both he and the captive were still wide-eyed and under the effects. After the mood correction and having sidestepped a downward spiral, Roland was having the time of his life again grinning away like the Cheshire Cat.

"Billy?" he cued.

"My jaw's aching … *What?*"

"Who was that girl?"

"I know; she vanished. That's what's so great about her—"

"The fact that she took off?"

"Precisely—if you want greatness just leave, make yourself scarce. That's how you become a Who Cares? Cover Girl. Hear that all you girls in Bettendorf, Iowa? Just leave! How you feeling?"

"Beyond, but so right here. I could listen all day."

"I'm one of the top ten Could It Get Any Worse? ranters in the country, so don't get me started—"

"*It* started you, you should be the one writing books!"

"I wanted to write one: *Citizen Cancer!* But I do have one more thing to tell you, you with me?"

"With you—"

"You know, I'm so glad we did this, I know you needed to and I'm overjoyed to be the one to do it with you because it's all so breathless to experience, the air, the cliffs, the falls, everything great about the world is right here and as a writer, come on, this is the hidden fruit, the World Series Game 7, the caviar and Cristal of existence, I mean, can it get any better than this? you must have a thousand fresh ideas popping into your head every second because I know you're gifted; you have it all, word choice, biting humor, sense of irony, pulse for the dramatic, crocodile-snappy dialogue, but I'll tell you what you didn't have—*THE TIMES!* —a different epoch in history, not that horseshit, free-riding, shallow, gossip-obsessed, carefree cotton candy DayGlo glam America of the nineties and the millennium, you needed the *NOW*, when real shit, incredibly turbulent shit is happening! There's incomparable surging turmoil, it's World War III, people are getting massacred and it's the dolce vita follies no more like the previous twenty years, I mean this is what made Hemingway great, it's what made all the great ones great, Shakespeare, Tolstoy, Molière, Flaubert, Fitzgerald, García Márquez, Dylan and Lennon, they all had periods of enduring domestic strife and international unrest, wars too, to instantly tap their quills into when the juice of their own lives dried up, and *WHAT I AM SAYING TO YOU IS*, I would love to see you going full-bore literarily, in times of destruction, death, and global chaos, instead of the blah-blah-blah relationship squabbles in Guns 'N Roses' 'Story Behind

The Story' VH1 doc, to expose the true pain of human existence flashing before your eyes every day and then you'll become the new champion of a New Realism, a Post-9/11 Sober Realism, post-millennial stories that depict the sense of brotherhood, compassion, and the love which are essential if there's to be any hope for a future of global unity, as a writer that's where you want to be, and you, with your abilities, you should be writing it, the Book of the Fucking Century! I mean, *GET WITH IT!* the world needs your POV, throw American literature a line! As we watch non-fiction become an OJ 'If I Did It' confessional and fiction hogtied by hollow, clitorally-correct chick-lit, more excuses for a Happy Meal cable series—I ask you—what happened to that authentic American voice? Not good enough for HBO? I say *BULLSHIT!* Blow up the life raft and save the Old Gal before she goes extinct! Stop letting us get embarrassed globally by our genital runoff! We're living in a time when TV cameras follow heirheads, duck hunters, hoarders, swamp rats, dysfunctional housewives, all the trailer park All-Stars, all the ditch-digging deviants, while actors become politicians and religious disciples—and—Dostoevsky, Dickens, Twain, Hemingway, and Salinger could never get published! These are the times! So come on, Roland, to the rescue! Bring the voice back to its people! Toss Yankee lit a little white ring!"

The prisoner reclined, flummoxed. He'd heard his captor's appeal, Billy was challenging him, as if Roland still had a job and a future—a second time he'd done so. On top of that Billy was tripping. Could the captive take stock in what was being communicated? Was he getting psilocybin-inspired "truths"? or the unfiltered hallucinogenic-driven rantings of a sociopath? Or, as he was tripping too, could he be overanalyzing everything and thereby didn't dare trust his instincts?

Meanwhile, Billy was still hopping around like a hyperkinetic stadium rock star, moving stage right, then stage left, his veins popping, head shaking. The man seemed so overwhelmed with incredulity and societal disbelief that he had no alternative but to let it out, the sweat beads leaping from his brow.

"So now I'm looking back and envisioning, there you were trying to write things of significance, but all you could absorb was more primitive Americana, fluff, and silliness and the best material, the material of personal significance you could tap into easiest—you *AVOIDED*—the stuff from your own life, because you had a slice of

your head out of whack because of family, a naturally flawed father and
mother because they all are, because everyone has to find their own
way, no one is perfect at life or parenting, life is always a Work in
Progress—for everyone—and they were reacting to their own stimuli
given the limits of their own stubborn DNA and molecular
configurations and psych programmings and like everyone else they
silently supported the Gene Pool closest to them and you were not
overtly like either of them and so you got caught in between where you
had a mother whose first son was The Temple, the apple of her eye,
and her first-born and the favored one because their baby pictures
matched, then you came through constantly playing second fiddle to
that Big Debut and your parents who were having their own marital
problems reflected in their treatment of you because of the
interpersonal wars they were fighting based upon their own dashed
dreams of partners for life they never got for themselves, and in that
context, you were not the favored one, yet you displayed all the great
attributes of the one who should have been favored and it was obvious
to everyone not involved in the family where the chips really lay, the
fact that You Were The One, you were always the one and they tried
to hold you back and make you feel like you weren't, and you saw it
constantly being played out, this confederacy of jealous jackasses trying
to thwart you, *AND* where I'm going with this is, the reason I showed
you the Ali-Frazier 'Thrilla In Manila' fight to you *WAS NOT* to show
you two tests of wills or human courage which is of course there, *BUT*
to show you who you were—Muhammad Ali—you were always Ali,
more gifted, faster, you were 'float like a butterfly, sting like a bee,' and
they saw it, but made like they didn't and no one wanted what you had
more than your under-producing father who never had the real gifts,
never had it so good, he was riddled with envy deep to the core that
you indeed had it all, *BUT YOU*, soft and sensitive to his feelings and
failings, and to your brother's shortcomings, and to your mother's
needs for denial, you wouldn't rub it in their faces and you had tons of
material if you ever wanted to let loose on them and you didn't, you
wrote around them and kept their desperate private struggles intact
and their miserable subplots unrevealed and all the *Long Day's Journey
Into Night* family rot you endured which is by definition gold to a
writer, so you took on less familiar subject matter that teased and
prodded your intellect instead so you wouldn't have to hurt or expose

anyone and yet you still pulled through and why? *BECAUSE YOU'RE ALI!*, and the reason I showed you that fight was to let you know that yes, like Ali, you're a genetic accident with machinery capable of anything, but to do that I could have showed you Ali-Foreman in Zaire in 1974, which truly showed the greatness of the man, but I didn't show you that, I showed Ali fighting Joe, and not because of Ali either, not to show you yourself, but to show you Joe, and so I ask you, *WHO WAS JOE?* who was the Joe in your life? the guy with the guts but without the 23 and Me chromosomal grid for magic and genius? and the answer is, it was your old man, Zach Polsonby was Joe, he had the heart, the desire, the cross-the-tracks chip, but he didn't have the goods and after enough defeats he got lazy, the kiss of death for dreams, but here's a guy with third place genes, without the advantages, who wasn't your equal, yet he gave it the best shot he could, he fought the good fight and there's something to be said for that, he got you to the dance, he provided a nice enough life for you to showcase your talents, a place to nurture and launch them, and though he didn't do the nurturing he deserves credit for getting you there, and you should not feel resentment, not anymore, not ever, because you must take it from his perspective, from his shoes, from Joe's flat-footed shoes against Ali's elegant tassels, how frustrating it must have been for Joe to know he had been sentenced to second place, that no matter how many big left hooks he threw and threw so hard his feet would come off the ground, that Ali, who had three women in bed the night before, would not go down!, that he would come back even stronger with physically impossible flurries and this is not to say your father had the same heart as Joe because few do, but he was the guy who had less God-given talent, the underdog, the genetically inferior one, the third place guy, the bride's maid on his best day, and you should empathize and have respect for him, he didn't give up, he was a prick, but he didn't quit, he kept up the appearances, the ego, the fire, but next to you, it was tough playing catch-up, swallowing your fumes, and had you been more selfish and power-hungry you would have sailed right past the shit, but you were too nice and cared about his feelings, about his journey even, you were that advanced and evolved and intuitive, you cared about all their feelings and life arcs and journeys and DNA setbacks and all I'm saying is, you should know you were always Ali and you should have always been Ali and you should never have felt guilty about being Ali, which you did and *YOU STILL DO*, and you never should have buckled or considered your efforts a failure when it was time to rescue your boy Gerritt because physically you did what few could humanly do and that still was not enough and you consider it part of your makeup now to lose like that, you've equated yourself with that failure, which is a complete *JUDGEMENTAL MISREAD*, and now you're lost and it's game over and you're wondering what does all this mean? and I'm here to tell you it's okay dammit—you lost your boy, but it was not your doing any more than those Sumatran fathers in Banda Aceh were responsible for the death of their children lost in the tsunamis, *IT WAS NATURE!* and *NATURE'S WAY!*, and Nature, who is so much stronger, older, and wiser than us, she did not want you to find that boy when you dove and searched and it was beyond your control and things like that are beyond everyone's control because no matter how much we pitifully try to interfere with her, to think we can control, outsmart, or manipulate her, Nature controls all, everything, and the sun will prove it one day when it torches the planet once and for all or it explodes and leaves us standing on an ice ball—*BUT*—in the silence of your heart you must know it was the *WILL OF THE GREAT SPIRIT THROUGH THE ARM OF NATURE* that took your boy, it was your boy's time, Nature would have her way on that no matter what you did or didn't do, that is what I have to say to you, Roland Polsonby, on this, the last day of your life—"

The captive was at once immobilized, silent, and stunned. Water had been flowing evenly down his cheeks for minutes, never slowed by a convulsion or heave, just noiseless crystal tears intermittently streaming down. Emblazoned and sparkling with sunlight the tears formed paths demarcated in relief through the red sandstone dusts powdered on his face giving the resemblance of ski slopes.

Appropriately, however, nature's whispers brought him back; he was revived by the delicate chirping calls of a canyon magpie.

"I can't express myself … in words …"

"Don't—just a little postcard from me to you."

"Thank you for sending it."

"The most heartfelt thing I could say? Perhaps."

"But Billy?" He had to tell him. "I'm depressed now."

"Part of the trip; you go up, you come down, don't worry—"

The captor gripped his wrist like a brother and hauled him up from the supine position. "Come on, some hydro therapy'll do you good."

The two scaled down to the lower travertine pools before the steep drop-off. Roland tagged along shakily, stepping gingerly, as if he'd been through his own fifteen-round grueler. They climbed down a thick rim and settled into a swirling natural tub.

"You know," Billy began with an infectious grin, "whenever a buzz of mine went south or I got down and depressed, I always turned on the Discovery Channel and searched for the turtles—"

The prisoner perked up, intrigued. "The turtles?"

"The giant ones, the sea turtles. They're safe animals; they just paddle along slowly, gliding in their own space and time without a worry. So calming to watch. If danger presents itself, they just retract their paddles, pull their head in, and float to the bottom until the danger passes. If you're feeling out of sorts or down or paranoid, the turts can be a lifeline—"

Roland unleashed one. Billy was pulling him out of it.

"Think about it; they spot a great white but don't panic. They know a shark won't try to smash its teeth on a prehistoric hardback. The sea turt just pulls in the paddles, ducks in the shell, retreats to the fortress, closes the castle doors, and floats below like a giant hockey puck. May take a while, they don't have great pick-up, but they get there eventually, settling on the ocean floor, peering out occasionally until the coast is clear—and live to be a hundred. Not a bad life."

"Safe animals," Roland repeated, his mood elevated.

"In their own turtle world. Peaceful meditation, isn't it? Really the way you want to live your life—"

"*Billy*—" he intoned, startled, which prompted the captor to swivel.

A gorgeous butterfly was hovering now, floating in the air above the prisoner, with brilliant, six-inch iridescent blue wings. The wings resembled azure gemstones with oscelli on the reverse sides like bronze eyespots, essential for camouflage—a spectacular showing.

"Stay still," Billy cautioned, "it's a Blue Morpho ..."

"What's wrong with that?"

"Nothing, except he's thousands of miles from home. They're from the tropical rain forests in Costa Rica and South America ..."

"Sounds lucky ..."

"A rain forest butterfly in the desert? More like a *miracle* ..."

The blue butterfly fluttered uncertainly for a half-minute, air-dancing ever closer to Roland, until it silently touched down on his shoulder, holding fast, giving slow, rhythmic, inward folds of its wings. The butterfly seemed comforted and at peace and it remained.

In a jubilant display, Billy extended arms to the sky like phoenix rising while gazing upon the tops of the cliffs and higher, the heavens. "That's what I'm talking about! Truth. Nature. Transformation! Thank you, Great Spirit, thank you!"

Roland was entranced; nothing like this had ever happened to him. He couldn't go swimming—he had a guest—so he meandered along the travertine rim with the wings riding his shoulder. He stepped from the pools and moved on to the warm sun splashed bank beside the fall. He sat there and ruminated, conjuring the man's dazzling diatribe and this bizarre and incredible journey which now seemed so much more than a revenge abduction; right up to a butterfly finding refuge on his shoulder. A creature from another climate zone, no less, it remained with him for minutes on end. The two took pause together, man and butterfly, baking in the sun, his eyes closed to block the rays.

In the lower travertine rims, Billy was enjoying his very own spa, his feet raised to the ledge, eyes sealed as well.

Their tethered horses began to huff and neigh and Roland snapped to attention, identifying the reason for the equine chatter. A mounted horse was descending the switchbacks toward the base camp by the Falls. In the saddle was a stout Indian, perhaps part-Mexican, in a beige cowboy hat and gold badge to his breast. He seemed an official type. The horse changed direction on the last twist of trail and a gun revealed itself at the man's hip.

The man rode past their unsettled horses and approached the bank sighting the captive where he lay. He dismounted, tied his horse to a lofty juniper, and climbed over the travertine rims, advancing.

"Howdy—"

Roland was prompted to stand. He flashed a glance Billy's way, his captor nowhere to be seen. He noticed his own hands were trembling.

"Nice spot you found here—"

"Yes, it is."

"I'm Lewison Marks, Bureau of Indian Affairs. Whacha got there?" The man was pointing to his shoulder.

"Oh that—a butterfly."

"Pet?"

"No, no," he threw nervously. "He just flew there—"

"Aren't you the lucky guy. From around?"

"No, back east."

Eyeing the stern-faced man cautiously, Roland was paranoid; the pores of his forehead prickled from perspiration pressuring to escape. He was suddenly panicked as to what he should do or say. If he hadn't been under the influence, he would know, he thought.

Dammit!

Over the man's shoulder he caught a glimpse of Billy perched on a travertine ledge hidden behind the massive waterfall, the Glock nine-millimeter raised at the ready.

"Tourist?"

He hesitated. "Yeah … Tourist. Anything wrong?"

"Looking for some people. One, possibly two. The Bureau is searching the rez."

"A man?"

"Yes. And perhaps his abductor."

What came crashing to mind was whether the agent knew what the "victim" looked like from a photo or television; perhaps not, judging by his reaction. The wet look made Roland pretty unrecognizable.

"He was kidnapped?"

"May just be missing … Don't have all the information yet. Seen any people in the area? Anyone at all?"

The paranoia surged through him again and Roland was overwhelmed with conflicting thoughts. If he turned on Billy there would be a shootout and the results would likely be bloody and maybe ending the same as if he'd said nothing. Billy could survive and he would have only betrayed him and what would he do with him then? Someone would perhaps be killed too. Yet how could he be betraying someone who'd abducted him? He was still heavily under the psilocybin effects, and was growing increasingly unbraced and skittish.

"Uh," he stuttered, not knowing what to say.

The rhythmic, slow flapping at his shoulder caught his eye, mercifully, and it brought to mind the medicine book. He'd picked the card, the Butterfly, which was one of his protective animals. Had the butterfly flown to him for that reason? Whatever the answer, the thinking grounded him, unbelievably so, and it provided him with his own.

"No sir, no one. I mean I saw some missionary people."

He couldn't believe he'd said it and didn't know why. This was his chance—his big chance—and he was letting it go! Somehow it seemed right, the alternative a certain disaster. Either the BIA agent was going to be dead or Billy was and he didn't want that even though the man had done terrible things to him. Roland saw his captor clearly now, more lucidly than ever. He had a window into his soul and he did not want Billy dead. He wanted neither.

As the agent dug in his pocket, the prisoner twisted another search for Billy. The man held up a black-and-white mug shot of Billy with long black hair gathered in a horsetail like an Indian.

"Name's Dennis Roy … Goes by Billy Sixkiller too, an adopted name. He has a record. Likely he's involved in the missing man's disappearance …"

Roland gave him a befuddled look. "Where did this all take place?"

"Phoenix area, but they believe Roy was heading north."

"Did someone see him up here? In Supai?"

"Had contact with the tribe in the past; State Police thought he might come here to hide out—"

The prisoner nodded innocently. "No, I'm sorry."

"Thanks for your time," the agent said. "If you see him or hear of anyone fitting the description, let us know—here's my card."

He extended it. "Be careful … Man is dangerous and armed. Wacko too." Then Agent Lewison Marks twisted a smile. "Say he's been traveling around in a limousine. A big white one—"

"A white limousine?"

"Takes all kinds, don't it?"

His own smile was his most sincere and blended harmoniously as he was overjoyed the man was taking off. "Sure does."

The man tipped his hat, faded back, and clambered over the travertine pool rims. Unhitching his horse, he remounted the steed and began to negotiate up the switchbacks.

The captor nodded on Roland, commending him.

But in the following instant the agent's animal slowed and swung back around. Billy cursed. The prisoner froze and continued to hold steady.

"Say, Mister! Who does the other mount belong to?"

Roland nervously eyeballed Billy's horse. "My brother—"

The Indian waited on it holding out for more.

"He's up above ..."

"Where?"

"In Shit Canyon."

"Oh, I see," the man laughed, informed of the place.

The prisoner felt a bounce of aplomb. "Can get him if you like ..."

"No, let him do his business in peace. *Adío*."

Roland returned the wave. He glanced over again at Billy whose head was cocked to the wet wall perhaps relieved or disappointed, the prisoner couldn't tell. Reminded, he checked the ball of his shoulder, but it was gone. The Blue Morpho from the jungles of Central America had flown away. He'd hoped to see it off, but whispered, "Bye-bye, butterfly."

The pair waited it out. Eventually, Billy had the prisoner ride up with the horses while he shimmied high up on foot to scout ahead. They met at the split-log bench at the Falls' crest and Billy remounted. They followed on hard-pack higher up the ridge past the Clan's ancient cemetery. He put it to the prisoner then: "Why did you lie?"

Roland suspected it was coming. The rush of paranoia and consequent analysis already had him consider most angles.

" 'Cause the outcome would be the same for you?" Billy pushed.

"No, because the outcome would be different for you," he said. "I don't want you to get into any more trouble than you already are—"

The captor's eyes fell to the passing ground.

"You would have shot him, right?"

"Rather than go back to prison? Hell yes."

"Would you have killed him?"

"When you shoot there is always that distinct possibility," he said. "And the tribe gave me my name for a reason."

They rode in silence along the high ridge that extended halfway up the canyon walls and provided a superb overlook of Havasu Creek. They followed it to the village from high up, hidden from view.

"Doesn't change anything what you did back there—"

Roland was reminded then of the butterfly and wondered where it had gone. He soon realized it mattered less, the setting was all too much paradise and the creature would surely find another splendid location to dance in the air and spread its wings. Good for the butterfly, good for the butterfly, he thought.

It was also a "safe animal," he concluded; his totem animal too and it had served him well.

"I know."

24

The Dolce Vita Diaries V

I have made my decision. I will concern myself with my own business. And that's what I will write about.

I am going to see the shaman woman now. I am so looking forward to it and I will take notes. She is staying in the home of a Havasupai family …

… and now I have come back …

I spoke with Grace. She is a very wise woman. She is from the Pima tribe and she blessed me and handed me an eagle feather. She said animals are our brothers and their medicine is important to us, and that we must listen to them. At the same time, we should not rely on any one thing too much, except for our own instinct. That includes gurus and "false prophets." We know what that is! Billy religion!

She said in Billy I was looking for a young girl's guidance, a father type, seeking his approval, like many girls do, but I've outgrown it. I am a seeker of truth now and I am searching, which is good, searching for answers to the big mysteries, that is why I have been interested in the cards, astrology, hippy times, and other religions. But in the end, I must depend on myself and no one else, no other movements or philosophies because they can be misleading, they can also deceive and hold me back and close me down.

But never to forget the cards and other medicines, let spiritual teachings guide me and my morals and give me faith, but not rule me and my life. I must now rely on myself and this is very important, the most important: I HAVE MY OWN MEDICINE (!!!) to offer others as well as myself. And I must be confident of my medicine. I must practice the "religion of the self" now, she said.

At the same time never lose that curiosity, the desire to search for answers, and to trust, but mostly to trust my instincts and open myself to new things, experiences, and people. I can open myself up by trusting my instincts; I have good ones. I am not a girl, I am a woman and it is a time for opening up.

I spoke to Grace about the long letter my mother wrote to me before she died. I have never spoken of it to anyone including Billy (especially Billy!) I read it to her. After listening to my mother's words, she told me my mother was with me, always. That she heard in her words a tremendous pain my mother felt writing it, but knew it was important for me to know my history, my true history.

The letter claims my great-great-grandmother, Miss Lil, had been a madam in a ladies' house in Ouray in the late 1800s. This letter I have read a thousand times. Thinking I was a descendent of a woman who had made her money giving pleasure to men, Grace felt it was making me feel shame about myself and not confident. But that it should be the opposite—that my great-great-grandmother was a strong woman, that it was only the women of great spirit who went west, as pioneers, the ones who had courage and confidence they could succeed. Some did not though and had to survive the hardest way, but they were the strongest of women. And I should feel pride about my history, it is a beautiful history, she said.

Because it was this strength, a special medicine passed down to me that gave me the power to save myself, to run away, to get away from people who were hurting me. And to be a seeker of truth and to have faith. It helped me follow my destiny including bringing me back here to these beautiful lands.

I am on the right Road now, she said.

When my great-great-grandmother met the Frenchman de Chantilly, a rich man from Paris, he married her and took her from Ouray and they moved to Silverton and lived there before returning to France. The shaman said I was fortunate to have different bloods from different nations, that it added soul and depth to me and my character and made my medicine stronger.

Billy thinks I want to go to Ouray because it's the "Switzerland of America." That has never been the reason. Grace praised me for keeping my past private, saying it would give my medicine strength if I held on to it privately. That my past held power, that my past was power. If I did this courage and confidence would be my reward.

She said my life here on Earth, our Mother, is just beginning. It will open up and blossom like a wildflower when I let go of the old ways of thinking about myself and my past. That it is not a weakness, but a source of strength! To go to it, to ask of it, and its power will be given to me.

It is true, I am feeling stronger, seeing the world through new eyes. I feel I have a force, like the animals, like everyone, I have my OWN SPECIAL MEDICINE. I never felt this way before.

Grace said she saw me as a spiritual being aware of the Great Spirit, and of all faiths, possessing a love of nature and animals, but I am also of this world, searching for its truths, and having practical earthly knowledge which will help me on my Walk of Life.

It is important to be open to new experiences, yes, but also to stay aware and be loyal, to stay close to friends who may need me. To help them, maybe even protect them.

My duty now is to stay close to him. They will be after him, they will try to get him, probably to kill him, and he will need me and it is with my strength he will have strength. It is his hour of needs and I must be there for him.

Grace is a great human being, I hope one day I can be like her. She made beauty with me, the most beauty I have ever felt. I feel it; I feel beautiful now.

It was my favorite day.

I will visit the tattoo man now. He lives behind the chapel.

Frenchy noticed fluidity had crept into her writing that made her feel gratified, even prideful. She was reminded she hadn't yet picked her daily animal card. She would not. Though she respected and cherished the medicine of the animals, and of all living things, she would never pick from the stack again.

25

The sweat lodge was located in a ravine along Havasu Creek on the outskirts of the village hidden from trails to the falls. Just after two, the group assembled, seven members clustered beneath the big, leafy cottonwood. They were perched on milk crates and tree stumps, a fire lazily burning to the side.

The sweats were private bastions in an already closed-knit society. Essentially a men's club, the lodge was a religious and social gathering place where men could converse and relax the way the tribe had been doing for a thousand years. There were no women allowed though they could sweat, but not in the afternoon; it was strictly for men and guests. It was an honor to be invited; not every tribal member was.

"Billy Six!" the large man called out, sprawled in an upended wheelbarrow.

Wil was a member of the Tribal Council and was well respected in the Clan. He was a physical force with hands the size of baseball mitts. His father and grandfather both had been Chiefs of the Havasupais. Wil was delighted to see his old friend descending the hill along with the unfamiliar guest.

Billy saluted him along with the others and he quickly tied the horses to a low swooping branch of the grand tree. Each member came forward individually to offer a brotherly hug and handshake. Roland felt curious eyes were upon him.

"My brothers," Billy addressed them, "I present my friend Gerritt."

Incredulous, Roland froze again momentarily. He was compelled to step forward though and his hand got lost in Wil's grip.

"Hello, Gerritt," the big Indian greeted him warmly.

"Gerritt wants to sweat, don't you?"

"Uh, yes, it would be an honor."

"Billy is our brother. If you are his friend you are a friend to us and you are welcome to join."

Roland met wiry Faron, a tribal Elder, Waylon, Wil's brother, Elder Rushton, Jim "Big Badger" Ellis, and Stephen. The group chatted while awaiting the heating rocks. Happy Jack, an enormously powerful man resembling a Sumo wrestler with a Fu Manchu, took in the proceedings from an oak stump with an ever-watchful eye—an intimidating presence.

The sweat lodge was a dome-shaped hut made of sapling branches, sculpted and cemented in with thick layers of dried red earth, a natural mortar. A heavy burlap flap covered the opening. As a newcomer Roland was required to help prepare the sweat. He was instructed to fetch buckets of water from the Creek flowing sweetly nearby. Next he filled drinking water bottles at a member's home and Billy joined him on the errands. While fulfilling his duties the prisoner had the distinct impression of being scrutinized by the Clan. The more potent effects of the organics had worn off, but the substance was still in their systems, prompting the alertness, sensitized awareness, and clarity of thought with occasional spikes of paranoia.

"You see how they're all staring at me?"

"Of course."

"I feel like I'm being tested …"

"You *are* …"

"—like they don't trust me."

"Well, you're white," he teased. "It's more spiritual than that. They seek out the meaning in things …"

"Like, why me?"

"Like why *you? here?* and *now? today?*—exactly."

Though he'd been introduced to the clan by an honorary member, the intense pressure of being observed wouldn't abate. As Billy explained, in their minds Clan members hoped to understand why this man had been brought before them, why he'd crossed their paths, why their destinies were intertwining and what kind of medicine did his presence signify in their Walks of Life. And thereby what medicine did they have for him as well. Roland had been introduced to the concept of "medicine" in Frenchy's book and was struck by it, that every being held its own unique brand; humans, animals, all of earth's creatures.

"Remember," Billy reminded him, "just go with the flow …"

Roland's final task was to carry by pitchfork the hot rocks smoldering in the fire and place them inside the structure. The coals provided the intense heat necessary for the sweat. While preparing the rocks he overheard his captor informing the men his "guest" was a writer undergoing personal struggles. He didn't elaborate beyond "a sweat would do him good."

"We met someone this morning at the Falls," Billy also recounted, "and she gave us some medicine—mushrooms. So we took them …"

The men all found that funny.

"Got any more?" Rushton posed to more laughter.

"I can't do it like that," Wil countered. "I need a couple of days to prepare for medicine, to be in the right frame of mind."

The prisoner joined the semi-circle after he placed the larger coals inside. He studied the group, strangely drawn to the imposing Happy Jack, sensing the man's obvious skepticism. Jack was not given to quick bonds, amicable words, or gestures. Friendship with him had to be earned, over time, then maybe never at all, especially if you were white. As the truth road along side his paranoia, Roland felt uneasy.

"So what do you think?" Here it was—Happy Jack was suddenly coming directly at him as if he'd read his mind, perhaps perceiving his insecurity. He was now putting Roland to the test.

The prisoner was caught with all eyes on him and an indescribable nervousness swept through him; his face began to prickle with hot blood. He'd already absorbed enough of the nobility of these earth people to know his obligation here was to be truthful. Throwing easy-winded cocktail party chatter, the kind to which he was so accustomed, would be shameful. He couldn't rely on the tiny lies of his life as he had done for many years either and it made him further self-conscious. In this setting, he felt bound to communicate full truths or say nothing. "I'm very thankful," he twisted up, "grateful to be here."

"What books do you write?" Wil asked.

The meditation struck him at once in a focused surge, like an epiphany. The ridiculousness of his past efforts seemed clearly and starkly platformed and more blood rushed to his face. A disassembling if not a full stripping was occurring that was more penetrating than embarrassment. Before these pure people, removed from trappings of the high-tech 21st century or pop culture or even dolce vita society, the milieu and genre in which he'd made a name for himself, all the literary buzz words, rehearsed verbals, canned answers, and smooth-winded performances he'd coasted along on were useless. Yet something significant was going on here he needed to respond to, but was at a loss for words to articulate.

"Dramas, uh, narratives, dramatic ones," he muttered feebly, his face buzzing again with another hot rush of shaming blood. "—That take place in New York, where I'm from—"

The silence remained and the prisoner overanalyzed his words, thinking the worst. He felt himself then to be a void—a house with no beams or planks.

Wil rose up which was a sign to proceed to the lodge for the first round.

Billy tapped him. "Go on, I'm right behind …"

Roland eyed him uncertainly, unmanned. "I feel hollow, like—I don't know—*deconstructed*."

"That's good, open yourself, go with it—"

"Am I really here?"

The captor then squeezed his arm until there was pain as proof he was in the present. The prisoner nodded, appreciating the support. Billy patted his shoulder then like a friend, perhaps even a brother.

"Go with the flow," came from the prisoner's mouth like a mantra.

"Right fuckin' on."

Wil folded back the door flap, careful to keep the high heat. Faron entered first, crawling backwards as was the custom. Roland watched them and replicated the reverse maneuver.

They were plunged into darkness. A tight fit inside, he was beside two big Indians with the pile of heated coals opposite. There was the thick smell of earth to the mud walls and steam rose from the rocks. The cramped space with heated bodies in proximity to the hot rocks had a thermal intensity beyond any sauna and was overwhelming to the prisoner.

Wil began the sermon with a short prayer in Supai, then another in English.

"Great Spirit, we come to you humbly today, to give thanks for all you have given us, beautiful Earth our Mother, the magnificent red walls of Supai, the animals our brothers, Father Sun who makes our crops grow and gives us power and light. The precious flow of water we drink and use for farming and swim with our children. We thank you, Great One …"

Faron sprinkled water on the coals and the heat surged, the lodge reaching a temperature the prisoner had never experienced. The steam seemed to sear the skin. As the mist rose to their faces, Wil launched into a tribal song and Faron broke in and together they produced a beautiful harmony and chorus.

Trying to manage the oppressive heat, Roland felt his flesh burning. He was forced to overcome the temperature mentally with diversionary techniques and he mouthed his own quick prayer that he be able to withstand it. He hoped to honor the tribesmen with a best effort for allowing him entry into their private sanctum. Knees to chin, arms bracing them, he resisted succumbing to the scalding sensations.

"Today we welcome Gerritt, brought to us by Brother Billy. He's been going through tough times; we wish him strength and courage, Great Spirit, to get his Walk back on sure footing and to overcome obstacles and new challenges he will face …"

Rushton later explained to the prisoner that prayers delivered were ceremoniously burned in place by the high heat, deep to the marrow of the bones, to the core of one's soul. The water of life was then administered to the coals, the coals representing the long-deceased ancestors of the tribe and the ancients sent the prayers to the Heavens in the form of the steam rising.

"Blow on it where it is hot," Faron counseled him. "But don't think about it; the more you think about it, the hotter it gets." As Roland blew on his burning parts, Faron added more water. *Hiss!!!*

"This song comes from our ancestors, the Cohoninas, the ancient ones," Wil introduced, "the song about the pain I feel when I see the Earth being polluted and contaminated; lovely Earth Our Mother harmed by those who abuse and exploit her. It hurts us in our hearts and souls because it hurts my Mother, which hurts me."

"Sa-qui-ña! Sa-qui-ña, Sa-qui-ña!"

At the conclusion of the "round," the four staggered from the hut dripping wet; Roland had difficulty standing. Billy led him to the Creek where they collapsed into the crystal blue-green water floating facedown like corpses.

The prisoner spun and surveyed the setting, the canyon, the clear waters, the lodge, and he eyed the Indians he'd just met. He felt blessed with a sort of power, a force he hadn't known that energized him. The jump in the creek seemed a natural baptism and he conceived of it that way.

Roland pulled himself from the creek before Billy. Feeling revitalized and refreshed, he returned to the clearing. He settled on the ground out of respect though a crate was available. Wil extended a joint, which he declined. "Was it hot for you?"

"Yes. Very."

"You did well," he said and Roland was pleased with the compliment. "I have a back problem. Whenever I sweat, the pain goes away, the heat burns it out. And your Road has been difficult?"

"Yes," he offered without pause or any shut down reflex; he surprised himself with his honesty.

"We all go through tough times. Illness. Financial problems. Deaths in the family …"

Wil was pious man of great honor and integrity and he respected individuals and their privacy. Roland was taken even nurtured by the man's noble essence.

Billy drifted up. "Gerritt tell you what happened at the Falls?"

The prisoner noted the name change again and ignored it.

"A butterfly landed on his shoulder … Stayed a while too."

"That's powerful," Wil accorded. "A white dove-tailed deer came right up to me in the forest once and stood with me—but there was no one around to see it!" he said with a laugh. "If you seek it and you are on their wavelength, they will find you."

Roland mulled the wavelength of the butterfly. Had he been seeking it out? Had it come to save him from a violent scene? Or remind him to stay on a path of Transformation, its medicine? Raw, vulnerable, opened to fresh ways of thinking and in the company of these earth people, he was not discounting, judging, or fearing the questions—or the answers.

*   *   *

The sermon was different in the second sweat and Wil inaugurated it.

"We offer prayer today for those having tough times, the world in a troubled place, people fighting over beliefs. We acknowledge one Great Spirit whether Jesus or God or Buddha or Allah and consider each other as brothers sharing Mother Earth, the same Moon in time, all warmed by Father Sun—a team—showing respect and love as one people …"

The coals were splashed and the heat rose. The parlance Billy had invoked periodically over the past two days was then introduced.

"*Oof-mah!*" Faron chanted aloud. "*Oof-mah!*"

"Keeps the evil spirits from entering the lodge," Wil proffered for the prisoner's benefit, " '*Oof-mah*' sends them away—"

Roland gave thought to his captor then who had seemingly followed his instincts and was convinced of his mission. He'd been warding off the evil spirits to purify and sanctify the abduction. The prisoner understood now.

Water was tossed over the stones and wisps of scalding mists filled the space. He interpreted the inevitable sounds as the hissing voices of the ancients as the prayers were carried on the beds of steam rising to the Heavens, the unbearable heat burning the prayers into the bones and soul.

"This song celebrates our Mother," Wil resumed. "Made of all colors, the greens of trees, the blues of oceans, the reds, yellows, and browns of the leaves; the Great One enjoys this variety, and people made of all colors too, taking different Walks, and we rejoice and welcome the colors and embrace the diversity."

Wil and Faron sang in a delicate, interwoven chorus: *"Da Ay ma-ta-ñute!, Da Ay ma-ta-ñute!"*

Water was sent over the coals again, the heat punishing. Roland was burning up in this natural earth sauna.

"Billy—?" Wil was passing him the torch of speak.

"I'm honored to be reunited with my brothers," Billy responded. "I thank the Great One for bringing me back safely. *Hañ-gyu.* I wish health and prosperity for all of you and your families; I pray for Gerritt, also, that your soul be healed, guided on your Earth Walk by the Creator—"

The prisoner realized now his captor had referred to him by his son's name in preparation for the sermons—to purify and purge in a spiritual way the ill feeling and negativity associated with his son's death, to help him cope with and survive it. Roland was profoundly touched by the stunning revelation.

"I pray for your son no longer with us and with the help of the Great Spirit may he hear us; know earthly departed one you're never alone, you're always in your father's thoughts."

All was silent and an expectation hovered. Roland intuited it.

"Gerritt?" Wil asked. "A prayer you'd like to share?"

The ritual was foreign to him and he searched for words. He hadn't said a prayer aloud since Sunday school when he was ten years old.

"I thank you. All. For having me. Allowing me to participate. In your ceremony. I wish you health. And good fortune. And I pray for my boy. Whom I love so much," his voice cracking then, "I'll see you very soon …"

Prayers concluded, water was then administered to the rocks— *HISS!!!*

A fresh burning assault scorched their bodies and Roland spoke up suddenly. "And you, Billy, I pray for you, that you receive, at long last, the justice you seek and the peace which comes with it."

He pictured his own prayer issued from his soul being carried to the heavens and delivered by the ancients. Roland beheld the Great Spirit.

The round was completed and the prisoner delighted in another plunge in the creek. When he retreated to the clearing he perched upon a crate across from Happy Jack as the intense man glowered his way. Wil settled his big frame into the wheelbarrow beside him.

"I understand from Billy's prayer you lost your boy," Wil said.

Roland nodded slightly and Wil placed a big mitt on his shoulder, the identical spot where the butterfly had touched down. Roland had never entertained thoughts of this kind before, but he had been introduced to another dimension and he was now seeking it out. He was seeing the world through fresh eyes as not just a place of chaos and random events; there was a design to it, perhaps a grand design. There was a world beyond science and facts and that seemed to make sense. From this angle the world seemed a better place to him now.

Wil confided to the prisoner he had lost his wife to pancreatic cancer. There were days he couldn't get out of bed, but he knew the Higher Being was urging him to move forward, to give his wife's death—and thereby his life—meaning.

"How long ago did it happen?"

"Six years ago."

Wil conferred with Happy Jack and Stephen in their native Supai.

"You sit this one out," Wil informed him.

Roland fell back to the ground gazing to the sky. He'd experienced paralyzing soreness in his limbs, neck, and shoulders—but not now. The high heat had burned out the severe discomforts. His eyes closed, he was relaxed, but not for sleep; he still could not. His extremities were abuzz as if electrified, alive, and raw. They were the best sensations in memory—like lying in bed as a boy listening to a summer rain pitter-patter on the roof. He was summoning that energy, the energy of youth, and he contemplated the last few days; this shocking, brutal, imaginative, awe-inspiring odyssey and all the places he'd been was like a dream, but he knew it was real. And it was still going.

Through the walls of the sweat lodge he heard the tribal members offering prayers to Billy then singing in that mellifluous layered chorus.

The captor issued in his own prayer, an apology for deceptions he'd orchestrated and lies he'd told. He'd tried at a path of light, but found himself wavering, angry and lost at times and shrouded in darkness. He was aware of his shortcomings, confessing to missteps and admitting mistakes, and he asked his brothers for forgiveness. He claimed accountability and he promised to work on himself daily, vowing still to follow the path of the Great Spirit.

Voices nearby lifted the prisoner from his meditation. He spied over and witnessed a conversation between Wil and Agent Marks. Marks had appeared silently and seemingly out of nowhere. He'd already dismounted and Wil's expression showed concern. The big Indian shrugged—he hadn't seen Billy or anyone else.

Roland sat up, his torso wedged forward. Here it was, his golden opportunity for a peaceful solution with no violence or tragic consequences or negative repercussions. The abductor was contained in the sweat unarmed. Roland could simply identify himself and the operative would collar Billy—there'd be no guns, no blood, and that would be it. The prisoner could return to Phoenix and bid farewell to a former life and carry out his plans for eternity atop the mesa beside his boy—as if nothing had ever happened other than a mild delay.

Roland converged on the agent and waved, receiving a smile of recognition. Wil eyeballed the sudden advance uncertainly. He couldn't know "Gerritt" was in fact the kidnap victim "Polsonby" whom he'd just heard about, but it gave him pause.

Instead, the prisoner veered off approaching his horse and he settled there to deliberate while petting the animal's broad snout.

If he blew the whistle, this would all end. If it did end, what would he do? Beyond being freed of his captor, a helicopter ride with the authorities, and inevitable sit-downs with police, what was waiting for him on the other side? So many things had happened. Would he really end his life as planned? And therefore, what was the choice?

Part of him didn't want the extraordinary sojourn *to end*. He was receptive again, his valves of sensation had been unlocked. He was feeling life through his extremities. He'd discarded former perceptions and discovered new ways of thinking, even spiritual interpretations. Questions invited more questions and there seemed not only a desire to ask them, but to answer them as well. Plunged in the dark for so long, he was basking in the light of a newfound curiosity; though a threat of death hung over his head—perhaps—enhanced by that. Could his captor be feeling similarly compassionate toward him? And if so, could Billy really pull that trigger? If he did and knowing his prisoner's wishes for burial, would he step in the way of that?

He had no definitive answers other than what awaited him if escorted off—nothing; which was more of what he'd wasted away his life on. He did not want to say goodbye to this tortured, twisted, eccentric and brilliant man, gun or no gun, life-threatening or not. Billy had turned his world upside down, maybe around, in only three days and what might happen if he was given a fourth? What was in store on this absolutely "phantasmagoric," as Billy put it, journey? Excited, anxious, yearning to know, Roland was drawn to a healthy anticipation of that future.

Was he concerned the law get their man? For unlawful deeds done? A fresh new window into character and motive had been revealed at the Falls. Billy Six had been wronged by so many on numerous counts and he wanted his revenge—understandably so. In apprehending him the law would not be getting their man, they'd already missed the true murderer of his parents. They'd be locking up an innocent instead— the real victim—maligned and abused for years. The law was not deserving in the prisoner's mind.

Borrowing from the Who Cares? Cover Girl, the issue concerning the man's alleged transgressions was exactly that: *who cared?*

Planted, his heart blasting, his blood surging and pulse raging, the prisoner was alert and on call. As wide-awake as he'd ever been, he caressed the horse affectionately. He eyed the gorgeous creature with its smooth beige coat and sinewy musculature—the Power animal—his book study yielding the reference. As the animal lowered its head to him he felt they were encountering mutually that "wavelength" of which Wil spoke. They were two of their Earth Mother's children harmoniously sharing the same air and sun and love and respect for each other. Roland pecked its soft round jaw with a newfound strength.

He couldn't let the strange odyssey go; he'd play this out even if it meant his destruction. He'd been hooked, hooked on life, as his captor had designed it. The man was genius and there was no denying it. A mind-fuck? The interior journey experienced by Roland at the hands of Billy could not be a deception; it wasn't something to believe or not believe, follow or not follow. Not a con he'd fallen for; rather, it was a sensation and he felt it deeply all the way to the marrow, all the way to his core. Burned and broiled in by the heat of rocks a million years in the making, his soul was now branded with affirmations of life.

The B.I.A. agent mounted his horse and Wil escorted him from the clearing and watched him disappear as he rode off. The big Indian spun and leveled a look on the prisoner, a profound and penetrating one. He shuffled over and wrapped him with his big arms, an acknowledgement of the man's desperate struggle. Roland gave in to the strength of this great man, physical and spiritual, as he embraced him. Emotion surged forward. Receiving the love of a brother felt so damned good and he was overwhelmed.

Roland had opted twice now to remain silent not by accident or mistake, nor had it been in his best interest to do so. It was not; clearly not.

Foregoing freedom and risking his cherished plans, he elected to proceed on this questionable albeit dazzling journey with a known psychopath, at once erratic, reckless, and dangerous—a man who openly professed a desire to execute him. These were remarkable choices the prisoner never would have been able to conceive of, much less make as the Roland Polsonby of old, two days before, two decades before. Ill-advised, perhaps crazy, or maybe one needed a little crazy to be courageous—whichever—a resolve had come to him. A passion had entered his frame, a fire was lit, and these forces were guiding him.

As the third round of sweats came to an end, the men crawled out heavy-footed and slicked with perspiration.

"Gerritt—?" Billy was calling out to him. The captive wheeled to see if Wil heard it. He had. "His real name is Roland," the captor corrected for the group. He was making good on his vows to amend his ways and be truthful. Wil had gleaned it already of course.

Roland trailed Billy toward the creek and gave the Indian an assured look and the pair drifted onward.

"Man from B.I.A. came back … Spoke to Wil …"

"Didn't turn me in—again." Billy shook slightly and broke to a near grin. "Funny thing, life."

"—Roland?" was called out from behind. Wil sauntered up. "You ready?"

The prisoner nodded.

Wil fastened on Billy and they shared a look of complicity; they were brothers at a crossroads. "You're family, Billy Six."

"I know, Wil," he said. "But this is my Walk."

"I reckon so. We will pray. The Great Spirit be with you."

*　*　*

Roland was wedged in the final sweat between the four big Indians and the lodge heated up again to flesh-burning temperatures.

"A special song for our guest," Wil commenced, "a man of courage. And we dedicate it to his son Gerritt and we unite them through these stones of the ancients; we ask you Great One to grant us this reunion, break the separation of spirits and men, father and son, to let them caress each other's faces, connecting their souls still yearning and warm hearts still beating for each other—"

"Oof-mah!" Ruston gasped, chasing off the dark ones. Happy Jack repeated it then Faron and the mud walls resounded with *"Oof-mah"*'s delivered from all sides as Wil introduced, "A song about our Mother, the earth, the prettiest girl you will ever see …"

The four sang to him in layered chorus invoking the ancient ones, the earth, the sky, the moon, and stars. In honor of the Great Spirit they cast the love and Roland saw it—his boy smiling. The tribute was wondrous and replete with the most beautiful sounds he'd ever heard.

The tested man lasted nearly a minute and then broke. Like a building no longer able to hold its weight, he fell apart. The man heaved and cracked in half. He'd tried to suppress the emotions, but could no longer. There had been so much pent-up sadness, grief, guilt, and misery and so many years' worth to hold in. It had been so long.

The chorus called him out through his upset and beseeched him. Their voices and his cries formed a primal and vital harmony and it melded with the hisses—the "voices" of the ancients, ancestors long since passed. The drum beats and thigh slaps of tradition kept them in time silently and the man opened himself. His boy was smiling and the deep hurt which had debilitated, devastated, and effectively destroyed the man rose up from his system, from disturbed recesses where it had been trapped, cemented in by years of torment, depression, and grieving. The medicine of the ancient ones pierced as an arrow the impenetrable layers of trauma that had been smothering him and suffocating his Life Force. Tears and sweat poured from him like the falls, toxic lava released from the volcano of his soul. Rising up from his torso and projected forth, the dolorous poison discharged was swept up with the steam and carried off and away by the spirits of antiquity to the Heavens—forever.

"Tried, I tried!" he bellowed in anguish.

These prideful Earthmen administered their curing chorus profoundly medicinal in its potency and kept it on through his cries.

"I'm sorry, my little boy! But I am right here with you! Take my hand!"

The water of life was sprinkled, vaporized, and steamed on the rocks burning off the last scar tissues of the troubled man as the song filled his ears with compassion and forgiveness, penetrating and cleansing him. From this loving fraternal escort down the road to wellness, he was a man purged, healed, and reborn.

When it was over Happy Jack put his log of an arm around him and drew him close.

The man's body shuddered, his flesh was seared, his chin quivered, and his gut ached from the dry heaves; but it had been burned into his bones—Roland Polsonby belonged once more to the living.

26

The sun was setting on Supai as the easy-listening band composed of members of the Alabama Missionary group finished off a final set. An aggressive sermon followed delivered by an incongruously tiny man on microphone producing a booming voice. His verses bounced eerily off the canyon walls and echoed back. As night fell, the service became more haunting as the oratory exploded from sheer blackness. Parishioners then took turns at the podium describing how they'd discovered their faith.

Frenchy observed the gathering as captor and prisoner hiked down to Mooney Falls for their own spectacle. At Roland's suggestion they experienced the sun's retreat before the majestic two-hundred-foot fall, an idyllic spot for it. The colors of the Grand Canyon at sunset were absolutely resplendent. They didn't speak of the sweat as was the custom. Billy knew what had taken place though; he'd orchestrated it from the outset.

The captor was also aware it was incumbent on them to leave the rez immediately. Wil was a member of the Tribal Council that answered to the B.I.A. and Billy wouldn't put his brothers in a position of harboring a fugitive.

A special helicopter was scheduled to pick them up from the village. The flight was preferred under the cover of darkness as the "night birds" were often used in medical emergencies and the sudden departure wouldn't arouse suspicion.

The three set off for the landing field after joining Frenchy in town. Wil, Rushton, and Happy Jack were there to see them off.

Roland embraced them; he would never forget them. They were, in fact, his brothers now. The bond had been burned into his bones, into all of their bones.

"Hañ-gyu," he thanked them in their native tongue.

"You are welcome always," Wil told him and the invitation served as a parting gift.

Billy wrapped Wil and the others.

"Goodbye, my brother."

"You know better," Wil corrected. "No goodbyes, only hellos."

The three dashed beneath the whirring blades to the awaiting helicopter and they lifted off. The missionaries craned skyward on a stirring pause to the God-fearing fervor blasting from the canyon.

Seven minutes later, they touched down at the Hualapai Hilltop.

Billy had never been fearful of the Arizona police or overly concerned with any law enforcement forces in the Four Corners. He regarded them all as slow and inept, even corrupt, and certainly not in his league. His appraisal was valid and applicable had it not been for that intoxicated hunter taking a late night whiz in the tree line off the Mogollan Rim crosscut. He'd spotted an unfathomable white limousine appearing out of the darkness and swooshing past on its northern surge.

The game had changed—the State Police had identified the perpetrator, his approximate location, and vehicle type. The sagest course thereby was to alter both, but Billy Six took the predicament head on, silently relishing the fresh challenges. He was a gamer after all, and new obstacles posed a greater degree of difficulty and upped the ante. He would have it no other way. The police now had all methods at their disposal to apprehend him, helicopters included. With the ominous ramifications in mind, he needed to get a little bit genius for a while.

Thusly, with danger staring him straight in the face, what would be his course of action? Where would they flee? Where would they find refuge? The three stepped into the horse barn where the Stretch had been stashed, piled in the car, and went precisely—nowhere. At eight-thirty, they reached the Hilltop and in three hours, Roland would be a Sixty. To celebrate the captor popped bottles of champagne and launched a Clint Eastwood Film Festival, a mini-movie-marathon right in the car. Billy screened his "Top Three": *The Good, the Bad, and the Ugly, The Outlaw Josey Wales*, and his favorite, *High Plains Drifter*—an appropriate blistering tale of revenge. He passed out Tiparillos as well, the trademark thin cigars Clint smoked in the flicks. He flamed the long brown rolls and the captor and his French sidekick called out word-for-word snippets of dialogue, like the hatted midget who asks, *"What did you say your name was?"*

"I didn't—" was the shameless drifter's memorable reply.

Roland was mindful of the *Josey Wales* title, a now-familiar addition to his recent Walk. His awareness ripened, sensibilities expanded, he was no longer caught off-guard by the "coincidence"; rather, he was enlivened, emboldened, and inspired by the synchronistic connections. What he'd previously dismissed as meaningless and random he now knew was further proof how in the dark he'd been concerning seemingly inexplicable life forces.

Physically, he was exhausted, but there was a special radiance to his face. The prisoner was cherishing his sleep-deprived state as if he'd taken over another pod, another mind and body. The sensation was akin to driving a new car and giving it a full test ride. Yet this was no foreign pod, it was him, within him, and it always had been. He'd just never called upon it and what it had to offer until now, he determined.

As the three of them sat smoking the thin brown rolls, puffing a cloud's worth in the limo's interior and barking out macho Clint lines, Roland couldn't help but guffaw to himself at this scene that seemed out of a crazed fraternity house movie.

Toward the end of the cinema marathon, however, Billy became preoccupied, staring off with intense, consumed looks. Cognizant of the task at hand, he only had a sip of champagne and it pleased Roland to see him taking the situation seriously. Like Frenchy, he was scared for him.

Just before midnight, the captor took to the wheel with a final detour in mind for Roland. There was only one drivable route leading all the way to the Colorado River; Diamond Creek Road on the Hualapai rez in nearby Peach Springs. Billy took to the dirt track with all windows motored down to stage dramatically the performance, the roar and rage of one of the world's most extraordinary marvels of nature.

In the black of night illuminated by clouded-over silver strips of moon rays, they got out and stood in silence absorbing the majesty of the mighty and ferocious Colorado as it surged and flourished past. Except for the intermittent ribbits from chatty bank frogs representing millions of years of evolutionary amphibian music, nothing was said and nothing needed to be.

After the lengthy pause Roland thanked Billy for the drive-by detour while his legs were being bound. They were abductor and captive again and Roland didn't mind at all.

Billy joined his companion already seated in front and they shot off into the darkness.

"Don't you think we should change to another car?" Frenchy suggested. "They know what to look for …"

"Yes, they do—"

"We're easy to spot—"

"Not where I'm going, Frenchy. Not where I'm going." He squashed out the last Tiparillo. "How about some Chuck?"

The proposed selection was a favorite, the soundtrack to *A Charlie Brown Christmas* performed by the Vince Guaraldi Trio. Holidays had always been a somber and difficult time for the two orphans and Billy played it throughout the year to remind them—to acknowledge and celebrate their union as a family duo. After all the turmoil, sleepless nights, and grueling days of the abduction, he fancied it a welcomed treat.

"I want to sleep," she returned bluntly instead. She had the distinct impression he was trying to win back her favor.

Day Four

27

Instead of taking Indian Highway 18 back to Peach, Billy had enough reserve in the tank to attack service roads. He worked it easterly along the Canyon's Southern Rim through the Kaibab National to Desert View. This way they stayed on the Havasupai and Navajo territories. He'd be harder to find on the reservations and could refuel without watchful eyes. He knew the landscape better than the Statesters, right down to the dirt tracks that supported the back roads.

The distance was only twenty-five miles as the crow flies, but the way Billy drove it, carving the circuitous route like a surgeon, it took two hours.

Frenchy caught a nap only awoken when Billy stopped to fuel. As her faculties returned she wondered why he'd never asked about the shaman. He'd become strangely awkward since their violent quarrel, his poise before her slipping. Though not overjoyed in his presence she was increasingly vigilant and sensitive to his feelings and knew to be after her meeting with the insightful medicine woman.

Billy bought a round of coffee and a *People Magazine* for Roland in jest, but seemingly apropos to his rant on celebrity boldface journalism.

As he settled into the driver's seat Frenchy announced, "I'm going to stay in back if you don't mind. So I can stretch out."

Billy was paused momentarily. " 'Kay—keep watch on our boy …"

She nodded. They were cordial again though something had happened. He seemed neutralized—respectful, not pressuring. Their relationship had arrived at a new plateau, a new station. In her mind they'd become equals and that fortified her even more.

In back, the prisoner was flipping through pages as she ducked past him. The partition was closed. Billy had not bothered to open it.

"Hi," she intoned amicably.

He angled up. "Hello. Sleep some?"

"Do I look it? I had a crazy dream."

He was heartened she'd returned and her effervescent personal greeting was welcome. He'd missed her smile over the course of the long day and the pleasant connection foundered in each other's company on which she'd closed the curtain. Perfectly radiant now, she glowed before him—as beautiful a woman as he'd ever seen.

Frenchy perceived the different orientation in his eye and flush to his complexion. He was tanned and healthful; "Man" looked a new man, perhaps a changed man. Her confidence had grown and her instinct no longer clouded and compromised was guiding her and accurately so. She felt empowered.

Her dream had been the recurring one with the white lions and Victorian houses and she recounted it to him in detail—except the part he'd appeared in. As he sat there peacefully with a smoothness to his voice and a non-threatening energy, it was easy to avail herself of him as she'd imagined it happening in hazy half-sleep. Unrestricted and unrestrained, she hoped to learn more about this mysterious man and why he'd crossed her path. She wondered what his medicine was and if the medicine she had to offer was appropriate for him. Because she knew now for sure she had her very own special medicine to bestow.

She'd ruminated over it two days now and needed to ask. She introduced it gently, but with a new candor and vigor. "Tell me what happened—"

He eyed her questioningly, but not entirely uncertain and strangely hopeful.

"—*s'il te plaît* …"

He knew unequivocally now noting that though her request was the most personal and potentially debilitating that anyone could ask of him, it was somehow in an odd way pleasing to him as if his subconscious desired her to know and was driving him to open up.

More silvery light streamed in the space from a plentiful moon having nearly broken through the clouds that shrouded it. Roland lay down the magazine and leaned forward to reposition his ankles that were bound at a cross. A bone in his temple adjusted and his jaw flexed, but didn't tighten. Clearing his throat, he fastened on her directly and offered up cleanly and succinctly the details of the tragedy without pause.

"We'd chartered a sailboat that summer in Venice. It was very late, the middle of the night. We were two miles offshore. A huge storm had risen up suddenly, unexpectedly, a force nine gale. My captain and I couldn't strike the sails fast enough, the heavy winds filled them, the force tipped the boat over. My wife was asleep at the time and luckily was tossed clear of falling debris and she was able to hold onto the mast. The seas were very rough; it was pitch black out. The captain was flung over to the side and received a blow to the head, but he managed to swim to safety. I'd been on deck trying to take down the sails when I saw we were in desperate trouble and I went below and took Gerritt out of his bed. I tried to get the life preserver on him and that's when we went over: while I was still holding him in my arms. We plunged underwater and another wave hit and the force pinned my arms back and I lost hold. I dove under to search for him … three hundred times I went down; I should have drowned. I didn't care, of course; I had to find him. Eventually I did, but it was too late. That's how I lost him, Gerritt. My boy—"

He took a last swig of coffee and spun the cup in his hands. "I've never told anyone before—"

"I'm very sorry, Roland."

She'd addressed him by his name for the first time. He was touched and thankful for the gesture.

"May I show you something?"

"Please."

Sliding her suitcase from beneath the seat, she spread the bag open and dug beneath layers of clothes. A fancy garment bag was at the bottom of the pile. She unzipped the bag and drew the article out, unveiling it, really. The long dress was slender and fancy, wedding white, with frills and bows and ruffles at the edges, its arms sheer, to be worn off-shoulder and down the arm. Though an antique, it looked astonishingly modern, an authentic, of-the-period, courtesan's dress.

"Belonged to my great-great-grandmother. She wore it in the 1860s. Her name was Lil."

"In Paris?"

"Colorado. Creede, Colorado, originally. Then Ouray."

"So you are American—"

Her smile was coy, not the one he was unknowingly pursuing, but it was magnetic in its own way.

"Partly; on that side I come from a line of women of—" she broke off. She too had never told anyone her secret.

"Of?"

"Easy virtue," she articulated through a brittle laugh. She raised the garment. "What do you think of it?"

"Exquisite, really."

"A real-life soiled dove dress. If only it could talk, right?" He laughed and it sparked her to. "I think it's wonderful, *vraiment génial.*"

"I would—" he dared, but did not finish.

"Yes?"

"I would love to see it on you."

She brightened. "Really? I don't know if it fits anymore; all this junk food I've been eating. Sometime, maybe …"

The playful sparkle in her expression bounced to her movements and she edged forward in her seat. "May I tell you something?"

"Of course."

"I don't know men very well. Does it surprise you?"

"Let me think about that … I guess, yes."

"Because I'm French?"

"No. First of all, I'm not really sure how complicated men are. Granted; you've been around very special and unique types."

She was prompted to laugh; they both did.

"At the same time, you seem to have an aura of experience, a knowledge and understanding of people which—"

As he paused to reflect she filled the void. "I've never been with anyone other than Billy; of my own free will, that is—"

"Okay. But you seem to have a distinct worldliness—" He paused, trailing off. "I'm sorry, this is personal and I don't know you—"

"Yes, you do," she said gleaming, that delighted him. "Tell me."

"—Well, it transcends what I would think a young woman with such little experience would. Maybe because of your interesting mix. The French offers cultural depth; the American, a brash, pioneering spirit, perhaps. The combination can be very strong. Rebellious. Courageous. A powerful hybrid. Pretty explosive DNA, I'd say—"

"You're sounding like Billy—"

He processed it as a compliment and nearly said so. "He's rubbing off I guess. We've been spending a lot of time together."

She chuckled again, but didn't pursue the subject further meaning Billy. That struck him though he was encouraged by it.

"I've always been a science person," he added. "Now I know better. But if that is the case—just one partner—I'd say you're lucky …"

"Lucky?"

"Love can be devastating; can take your spirit away and once it's gone," he paused again, sobering somewhat, "it's tough to get back. You don't seem injured in that way."

"Do you still love her?"

"I don't think you stop loving someone; someone you've gone through so much with."

Eyeing him thoughtfully she'd felt his pain for days—the loss, the grief—so much so she could shape it in clay. Seeing it haunted her and chilled her bones. She'd absorbed his sorrow within herself not knowing why it affected her so and wondered how difficult it must have been for him. She'd never tried before; she didn't know what she was doing, but she was unafraid—unafraid to embrace the unknown.

"Why did you gasp when I picked the Butterfly card?"

A vague smile grew upon her face. "Well, according to the book it's one of my totem animals. The world presents us with many influences; I don't think it's wise to rely too much on any one thing." She would leave it at that, having learned it was a process—life—like growing up and finding one's way. "It's a beautiful book. I think it's helped me with my writing."

"Did you choose a card today?"

Fearlessly, the full white comet of a smile smoothed from her.

"Yes, but not one of those. I have my own … The 'Mélodie Card,'" she said proudly. She'd chosen after all—herself. "It teaches the Song of Life. And Love."

She was in unfamiliar territory, but the interaction was how she'd always dreamt of it. This was the way she'd always wished to treat a man, to serenade him.

A faint curve was creeping to his mouth too, breaking through.

"Does Mélodie sing too?"

She nodded to him. "One of my favorite songs, ready?"

Pausing to find the tempo she rocked a single foot, then initiated it softly, her own French version of "The Windows of the World." The song from the sixties was made popular by Dionne Warwick and reflected the civil unrest over the Vietnam War.

"The windows of the world are covered with rain,
Where is the sunshine we once knew?
Everybody knows, where little children play,
They need a sunny day, to grow straight and tall,
Let the sun shine through.

"The windows of the world are covered with rain,
What is the whole world coming to?
Everybody knows, when men cannot be friends,

> *Their quarrel often ends where some have to die,*
> *Let the sun shine through."*

Her voice carried it along with a fragility made more delicate by her accent. When the performance concluded, she laughed in a bashful release.

"Bravo, Mélodie —"

"Brav*a*," she corrected. "Don't take this the wrong way, but I want to, well I want to ask you ... What I mean is—"

"Yes—?"

She was sweetly glowing. "May I sit next to you?"

What he'd yearned for these waking hours had miraculously landed at his doorstep—to be in proximity to her. His hand pressed his hard-beating heart, covering it, so she wouldn't hear it.

She settled beside and though she hadn't communicated extensively with him it was right and as soon as she set down they both felt it. Two energies merged—complementary, harmonious, and seamless—a fit. Fresh, alternative, if not zany meditations from the day were ripe in his mind and he saw them as two vibrant and pulsating molecules of the Earth coming together to form a new element or compound. He chuckled spontaneously; their meeting was so much more than that. She was song, she was Mélodie, she was beauty incarnate—a gift.

In her mind, his pulsations had been coming across vitally for nearly three days. With every passing hour he'd become more revealed, defined, and attractive to her; the "dangerous" aspect she wrote of in her journal. She felt magnetized by him. And toward him. He was her reward. In as many minutes, gift and reward, they were both floating in each other's space and consciousness, on a cloud together.

And yet, though they were instantly experiencing individual revelations amorous in nature, both having been made newly receptive and unlocked to the world with fresh eyes, given fresh hopes, him revived, her fortified—they were still held by the limits of biology and humanness. They both wore the memories of relationships failed, of love's risk and fickle nature, the fear of letting oneself go, of setting sail on the vast ocean of human emotions. At the same time, each was unsure of the other's unspoken adoration and it made them wary of acknowledging it and offering up themselves. So they remained to each other in the rear of that car as two beating hearts—hopeful hearts. But they were both protective, both unable to share or articulate any of this. Yet they bathed and reveled still in the raw good feeling of a potential promise; a terrific consolation. There was time for the rest, perhaps, and the anticipation of that was no less thrilling.

She grinned warmly as she sent eyes over him—the distinct hairline, the dark stubble, the crow's feet at the corners, the water at the base of his eyelids, the kind expression. She had seen the hollow-eyed, tortured version of the man less than a day before. There was now peace in his countenance. She stroked his hair, sweeping it neatly across his forehead.

The young woman had been thieved, robbed of life-enhancing memories of the gender, both genders, in fact. The first ones were disturbed adults; the most recent male loved her passionately, but unrequitedly. She'd fallen madly for him and had dedicated herself completely as only a girl of fifteen could. She'd become a woman in the meantime—Mélodie—only she didn't know it until the last twenty-four hours and she was uncertain still as to how things should happen. She was behaving truthfully off her biology and nervous system; there were no games to be played. Raw desire was imposing its will and she was letting go, doing it the way she wanted, on instinct, her own instinct, the way it would have been if she could have those early years back. Her time to decide how and when and how much, it was her time to choose. She had prayed daily for the opportunity and she was now in control of her own destiny, and thereby, in control enough to let life proceed organically and pass naturally. A love was advancing quickly and she would not interfere or regulate it, hasten it or slow it down. She would let it flow, let it unfold and blossom. And let it become the resplendent flower she thought it might be.

Her hand was magnetized to his thigh and her carriage drew closer, hovering before him. She was drinking him in, her looks returned and slowly, ever so slowly, the space between them narrowed until she felt warm breath at her lips, hearing it rise and fall. Her head steadied close, she grazed his lips with hers and remained there briefly until her chin settled on his shoulder. She wrapped him and squeezed and his arms awoke and rose up and came to life around her.

His cheek slid back along hers, his starved lips seeking hers, the thirsty ones belonging to the smile he'd been pursuing. He found the smile and kissed it gently, giving more of himself and she responded as generously. Her soft chest pressed against him and the memory of seeing her beautifully nude that day at the hot springs crept into his thoughts while kissing her. As if to know what he was thinking she lifted her cotton top giving of herself, her exceptional olive breasts sunned to perfection and she placed each of his hands over them and held them in place until they stuck there by themselves and the brown nipples candied up hard in his grateful palms. He lowered to kiss them, tasting and sucking them as her torso arched and her hair cascaded back. His kisses trailed lower.

Just as quickly, she drew down her shirt, sealing them off. She clutched his head instead and drew it close and pressed it against them.

He adored her smell: a fragrance so very light, delicate and feminine. She smelled like an angel. Her breath was still on his and he could taste her. Eventually he pulled back to look at her as if to confirm that it was all really happening.

She could feel him beneath her; she could tell he wanted her, but it was not going to be like that and not how she wanted it to be. She would not follow anyone else's desires, program, or time clock; she had her own ideas.

It was her time.

And her time had come.

She kissed him and finally eased away from him. She settled back on the banquette watching the night pass outside as her womanly convergence hummed and flourished. They rode in darkness as clouds were again concealing the moonbeams. The evening's fresh turn and weighty personal revelations did not fade; she'd yearned and hoped and uttered prayers for the chance and the desire wouldn't abate as long as they were in each other's presence and the longing intensified.

The Stretch was now in Hopi territory, passing Third Mesa and Kykotsmovi, about to stage the climb to Second Mesa. There'd been no police sightings as hoped though shortwave reports indicated an intensified search in the Flagstaff area. White limousines had been spotted in Sedona and were seen idling outside America West Arena in Phoenix where the city's professional basketball team was playing.

Billy keenly monitored the activity with earphones in place. The partition separating him from the rear cab remained closed.

Roland again seemed plunged solitary into the blackness. He listened to the silence as they rode the occasional bumps of off-road, off-track, but he recognized the charged atmosphere and knew better; until the whisper came from close, "*Je vais vous traiter bien.*" He understood the words—"I'm going to take care of you"—but not what she could have meant by it.

His head slumped to the side and his eyes sealed a moment only to reopen suddenly, startled. The trouser flaps were tugged and pulled apart and he felt a rush of chilled evening air. He didn't look down.

Releasing him cautiously, she clasped it in her hands, her slender, elegant fingers cold to the touch. The sensation aroused him more and her blowing from close added to the coolness. She stroked it with care.

The point of her tongue made contact to the tip's erogenous underside and it resumed a trail down along the shaft before climbing back up. At the same time she cupped them beneath as she tongued a wet line down again, taking one in her mouth, then the other. They were warmed soothingly as the rest cooled. At last he felt his full rising, enveloped by the hot and moist *caverna* of her mouth.

His head melted into the headrest; time was on her side. He writhed in the cool heat and prickles and tingles spiked throughout his overwrought, overtaxed body; from muscles in his shoulders to his arms and thighs all the way down to his immobilized feet.

"Time" was his fleeting thought. It had been such a long time.

For everything.

As the Indians had purged him the young woman was mending him, controlling the act, owning it, awaiting it. She would taste it, draw it, and make his biology mix with hers as both willed her to have that knowledge. His eyes spun back and he cried out sharply giving her the knowledge, his frame bouncing several times. Helplessly, magnificently, he shuddered and shuddered more—like a rag doll.

She remained fast and took of him directly and plentifully which could be perceived as ribbon to her gift. She was giving that part of him to herself as well, imbibing him, which served as her reward. She buzzed with him inside her now having tasted and taken it, connecting their biologies, bringing him back, transporting them both back, to *right here, right now*—to the present. Nothing needed to be articulated any longer. Hopeful hearts were hopeful no longer. She felt completely new. And so did he.

28

The Stretch came to a stop and the driver was heard getting out. The prisoner was lying back scanning the celebrity rag's last page. He'd read it cover to cover, a glaze to his eyes. Fatigue had hit him. Frenchy was conked out the length of the couch. The rear door swung open.

"Hey there," Billy prodded. "Annie Oakley—"

She awoke in panic, startled and gasping.

"Where is it?"

Still disoriented, she craned around the interior. *"What—?"*

"The gun?"

"It's—" She fumbled for her hippy bag and checked beneath the seat. She drew out the semi-automatic handgun and rubbed her eyes with her other hand.

"Fine job on security detail. Good thing Polsonby here is a star of stamina and fortitude. Either that or he snuck a catnap—"

Roland shook in protest with an emerging smile.

"Almost five; made record time … We're here."

"Where are we?" Roland posed.

"Where, Beelly?"

Billy spread the door as wide as it would go. Still dark, the sky held a glowing moon that cast a whitening shimmer over the landscape.

"*Canyon del Muerto*, where else?"

"In Canyon de Chelly??? *J'adore* Canyon de Chelly …" She climbed past Roland, whispering tenderly, *"Bon jour."*

The car had been driven to the floor of the canyon from a special service road available only to the Navajos and known friends. Billy had taken the serpentining track deep into the canyon beyond the horse ranches and farms and past Massacre Cave and Tsaile Lake.

Canyon de Chelly was the jewel of the Navajo nation and *del Muerto* was the legendary canyon that forked off it. For centuries, the tribe summered at the canyon's cooler bottom and returned to their homes atop the mesa for the rest of the year. The fall season meant they were alone. Billy had planned for it; and other things as well.

The night sky was blocked by the spread of overhanging oaks and the Stretch was docked beneath a thick of intertwining branches and leaves which blanketed it from potential aerial surveillance.

Frenchy stood planted there as Billy scanned the silhouettes of thousand-foot sandstone walls. A lone bright-yellow leaf fluttered down and landed upon her shoulder then another prototype of burnt orange. Fall's foliage was in the Technicolor stage; it was that time.

"Ooh-la-la, *regardes*, Billy—" She presented the orange one moonlit silvery blue, tendering it to him.

They marched beyond the car and out of earshot.

"How's he doing?"

She did not respond immediately. "*Pas mal.*"

"Not bad, you say? He suddenly looks worse. How long were you asleep?"

She did not know what it would bring, but she would let him know. She had to. "I kissed him," she said, fearing the worst. His unpredictability knew no bounds.

Billy leveled on her steadily with a curious, indecipherable regard. He wasn't registering shock, jealousy, or even surprise. His head bobbed briefly as he processed the news. He twisted off and delivered it almost clinically, void of emotion or prejudice. "You fuck him?"

She'd survived the perilous part and was relieved. Usually untoward surprise made him lash out. The telltale pulsations of her and Roland's connection must have reached him, she determined. Billy had a sixth sense for these things. "No."

"You sure?"

"I was intimate, but—no. You know I don't lie to you …"

He did know that. "No fucking, Frenchy—you hear me?"

"I did not fuck him—"

"You hear me? *No fucking!*" he snapped, repeating as rule.

He stepped away and contemplated the rising wall. The silver blue blanket of night was giving way and the lift of first light brought up the sandstone reds painting the canyon in early morning purple— breathtaking.

"Fucking ruins everything," he underscored. "*Everything.*"

Pivoting back he ambled up and squared before her. "I need an hour's rest. I want him bound 'til I wake up—"

"Beelly—"

"Don't jump my route! No argument …"

"I won't argue, but I need to ask. I think it's time—"

"Frenchy—"

"It's *time*, Beelly—"

"I'll be the judge of that."

She beseeched him, her head shaking. "Please Billy, let him go!"

In total disregard of her wishes, perhaps because of them, Billy charged over to the car, opened the trunk, and drew out the silver manacles. Then he piled in back and cuffed the prisoner's hands behind him, releasing the wire lock at his feet. He eased him out of the car in silence and Roland noted his captor's uncharacteristically abrupt even reckless demeanor. He acted like a different person to him, decidedly not the sweat lodge brother of only hours before.

Billy marched the prisoner several hundred yards down the riverbed where the water free-flowed into a quiet stream. He positioned him at the base of a thick maple propping him against the trunk, then fastened the wire lock around the tree and looped it through the cuffs.

Roland was seated and planted upright and the trunk's round of bark served as a backrest. "May I ask you what this is for?"

"Wait until sunrise—you'll see. 'Una Naturaleza Muerta' in *Canyon del Muerto*."

"What is the 'still life'?"

"Didn't know you knew Spanish—"

"Me?" he ignored, continuing his line. "Am I the still life?"

Billy unleashed an eerie twister of a grin and responded with his own note of disregard. "The greatest one you ever witnessed …"

The captor eyeballed him rigidly too. Clearly an antagonism had been reborn between them. Roland surmised Frenchy had informed him of their interaction and unwisely so. If she had, however, he found it surprising that Billy hadn't punished them, much less called them out on it. Or maybe he was preparing to as in the soon-to-be still life—*him!*

"You're almost a Seventy-two, so behave yourself. You'll need all the energy you can get—" The tone of admonition was clear and Billy wheeled around and strutted back in the direction of the car.

Birds of sunrise winged through the canyon as their upbeat fluid conversation cheered on the fading darkness and the enfeebled captive was settled there haggard and weary. His head was cocked to the tree and he was thoroughly depleted, his extremities deadened.

Not long after, with thought patterns sketchy and scattered, he located it advancing from the other direction, emanating from the lush row of greenery at the base of the canyon wall—stark white, flowing, and spinning—a graceful apparition unlike he'd ever imagined. He was transfixed by the dazzling show; whether caught in a dream state or conjuring a dream forgotten, he could not know.

Crossing his line, hopping left then traversing back right, the figure catapulted itself over a fallen log; feet nuded, snow-white ruffles and cascading layers pinched high so as not to snag on the terrain. One of Degas's finest was smiling coyly and barely, a smile he'd perhaps pursued and maybe never at all. His delirium was beginning to surge.

The vision spoke of a world gone by, a past forgotten, existing in the minds of a select few ancients or academics or passed down in letters and studied. The oncoming presence in that light, in that dress, at that hour, was worlds away from any *naturaleza muerta*, the still life advertised by Billy—the one he'd readied him for. This forest ballet performance was so immaculate, silent, and unreal and yet it thrived as she flirted, flitted, and twirled right there before him as if he could catch it.

The recital was close, so very close and he wondered if the canyon dancer was real and the sweet breath swept into his lungs, a fragrant wind not his own. The gentle mouth landed softly on his and his torn corpse was given life; fresh warmth stirred his limbs. As he smelled the signature fragrance and tasted her lips, the notes to the song returned to him. She had come back for him and slender elegant hands saved for Sienese noble women of early Renaissance portraiture combed his scalp.

He couldn't move, maneuver, or desist. He was at her mercy, whatever brand she chose.

Delicate kisses caressed his face; it was life, but not the "still" type—perhaps the afterlife with even more to offer.

"A butterfly landed on my shoulder." He hadn't consciously said it; it just rolled from his tongue.

"From the front?"

"Yes."

"Like the one in your lap."

"Are you my medicine?"

"*Mais non, mon petit*—you're *mine* …"

She took him in a last time then rose. Her unkempt honey hair fell past her shoulders and her raised cheekbones elegantly drew in her face from her fleshy swollen lips.

She zippered free and stepped from the cherished antique preserved for four generations; the one she herself had protected for fifteen years and had taken to the road and held in suspense for the right moment and—partner. Alongside her, the dress had outlived the turmoil, the trying childhood, and the darkness. Like the feisty, independent and courageous woman and thinker who first pinned it against her breast and purchased it all those years before, the garment had possessed a will to survive. That woman's great-great-granddaughter, heiress to both dress and indomitable spirit, was carrying the tradition forward and into the future. She'd fought for this day and now it seemed it had been worth the pain, the longing, and the wait, and she would not be denied.

Everything was distant as she believed in the past, but also the death of it. Life, intimate life, was novel to her and in that dress she'd always sensed it could begin again—she felt it—as a woman untouched and never touched, a fresh song, a Mélodie.

New. All over. Again.

Morning light shot over the top of high cliffs and made marvelous the muted colors of the canyon floor. The colors, the Earth Mother's finest, all kinds of colors, were activated, popping out of the grayness blooming all over again like the dancer, sparkling. The canyon was coming to life.

She floated the dress down over a branch and returned to him.

Poised above, her hair was teased by the breeze and tickled her tanned erect-up breasts. Her browned legs were dimpled at the knees and her little tanned feet with a peachy-pearl finish on the toes pressed the bed of psychedelic leaves. Where tiny swimming strings had been, an untanned triangle of white skin framed a shy one shyly shorn in the shape of two tiny diamonds stacked atop each other.

The canyon dancer stepped toward the propped prisoner, her exquisite nudity fronting him. He desperately yearned for hands to wrap her and sink them in to the prominent globes, perfect and round. She hovered above him and her legs drifted apart to stand over him. He was taking in delicate folds floating down, a gardenia in bloom. She settled upon him, the bound one, and her legs parted fully, thighs wedged off his. The knees folded and pearlies braced the earth as the twins hung in a tight dangle scoffing at gravity's pull. Handicapped and cuffed as he was, her teeth gleamed mischievously, lovingly, and her eyes sparkled at his predicament.

Fastened steadily on his eyes, she liberated him and held it aloft. Both hands cupped them and rifled kisses to them tonguing and tasting the droplets of dew. She endorsed it and prepared it, but for a minute as her medicine had not been administered—not yet.

The song rose and he angled off agonizingly to see where the music was headed. He was so alive and electrified and she reversed the choreography, positioning over him. The softly curving buns faced him, double rounds goose-pimpled to the edges and he begged for his hands again to knead and squeeze them deliciously, but no one heard his silent cries. He was made a voyeur to the convergence beneath, the petals moistened and glistening in the sun splash—a pink dawn—and she floated down and the flower spread itself, blossoming better at every fraction of descent. She guided the riser as she fell and it pierced her. The hot contrasted to the canyon's cool and her weight slid over him coming all the way down and she stuffed herself with it completely until it rammed her abdomen.

The *naturaleza viva* flourished as he eyed her broad tapered shoulders and back, her tiny vertebrae aligned and arching. The honey tresses flew and swept his face and she twisted back to plant her meaty lips. Bound in a state of ecstatic torture, he desired to touch her, to dig his chin in her back and cup and squeeze her suspended breasts and brace her there as she straddled him.

He was her captive now, her prisoner and no one else's—it was her show—and she gave to him everything a man could possibly enjoy. Bare heels raised from the ground, calf tendons taut, tanned pearlies lifting her from the foliage floor made white from the pressure, her pear halves spreading—as she rose and fell upon him.

And yet her song was not over; far from it.

She lifted and pivoted and gams crossed over as she repositioned again to face him. She eased and slithered upon him softly, slowly until he filled her again. She wrapped, hugged, and adored him kissing his face, cheeks, and neck; hard candies to his face, presenting him one then the other and he sucked them. She charged and retreated offering everything she had, her bronzed body, trimmed puss—all the warmth and femininity that was hers. Quickly and smoothly she fell, letting him part her wetness as she rocked over him and passed herself to him.

Their bodies' meeting was indeed a transferal. Through her legs, lips, fingers, and warm intimates she delivered her spirit to him, a flow of intangible life force—her Life Force. Perfumed waters dancing off her nape he swallowed in his lungs, letting them pass through him. She came down slow and gently then fast and furiously and arching back, she cried out. Of course, he wanted to do everything to her and she would let him know her in every way, but not now. She would make love to him, but her own way and this was how she wanted it—all to herself. She watched his revived eyes, no longer haunted or hollow, but brightened and made more vital and she kissed him harder for it. She kissed the breath from him and filled his lungs with her own—the winds of her Life Force. She guided herself up and down and gripped his shoulders, bracing herself, using the tree for leverage. When she began to shrill he roared gorgeously into her ear as she whispered, "*Je t'adore*" into his. She was so gratified if not ecstatic to hear him enjoying himself, to hear him crying out and feel him shuddering. He was enjoying her and his moans of ecstasy fueled her cries and she shivered from it all the way to her toes.

Roland and Mélodie made beauty for the very first time.

As their bodies settled harmoniously, she wiped her glowing pool eyes so he would not see the flood. But she would not move and she still felt him firm and deep inside her and her swollen around him. Her chin found the niche between his neck and shoulder as it had grown already a fondness for the spot; a place she could smell him best. Her body was entwined around him with knees high and arms wrapping and it came then from kissed-raw lips, the one she'd sung before, but this time in whisper …

> "*The windows of the world are covered with rain,*
> *There must be something we can do,*
> *Everybody knows, whenever rain appears,*
> *It's really angel tears, how long must they cry?*
> *Let the sun shine through …*"

She drew back. "I'm sorry. After I make beauty, I like to sing. It's a part of me—"

"And if you make beauty—?"

She leaned in and found his now-familiar lips and attached hers to them and they remained there. "It means I love."

She hesitated before speaking again. "I know people run away when they hear that, but you can't …"

"No?"

"You're tied to a tree, so, I'm not afraid of saying it. You will just have to deal with it—tough …"

Water had filled his eyes and he could not wipe them. "Guess I'll have to deal with it," he said, his chin trembling. "Squeeze for me."

She pressed into him tightly and forced a tear to fall and she saw the cascade from his face and she kissed the remaining golden droplets, tasting them salty and swallowing them. She let him know it was okay, wordlessly, and her spirit was sent to him and through him—to every part of him. They'd embraced the unknown that was now known; two butterflies now in flight, having transformed before each other. To their silent flap of wings the sun painted the canyon floor in autumn golds and oranges and yellows and reds and all the colors of Wil's "prettiest girl you'll ever see," as they danced freely in the air.

His eyes rolled in their sockets and back; then again.

When he opened them, the song was gone.

29

The driver's window of the Stretch had been open all night. He always left it open just a touch to keep fresh air and a coolness circulating. His head was sloughed back to the ivory Italian leather custom headrest, a single earphone in place. The captor had one chamber of consciousness attuned to the authorities; the other needed a break.

Sleep was not a possibility; his mind didn't allow it. Short naps were the best he could hope for. He was burning it, burning it hard, not in a Kerouacian "mad ones" way which may have been welcomed, but in a way peculiar to the tech-driven, sensory-saturated I-Age. He was one of its children albeit residing on his own Planet Billy.

It took position on his leg first and inched up, having found its passage in that break in the barely opened window.

Billy's eyes unsealed and he spied it. He'd had his share of run-ins with them and would flick them away, never killing creatures for sport—so their death would not be purposeless and without honor.

This one affected him more.

He spread the car door, cocked an index and finger-punted the creature sending it sprawling to the red earth where it overturned. Then he got serious. He knew secrets about them most did not; the dark ones, secrets most private to any living creature—the Indian secrets.

After the scorpion righted itself and traveled onward, the captor planted a wooden matchstick tip up and directly in its way to obstruct its passage. As the creature rerouted and took another path, it was confronted by another identical blockade—until all passages to freedom had been blocked. The scorpion was stockaded in by a circular fence of tip-high matchsticks. Now its life had met its destiny.

The captor lit one stick and set the ring of sticks afire. The scorpion dug to its core to conjure a reflex formed over millions of years of evolutionary response behavior. As the flames surrounded it, the creature flipped its tail back over its head and attacked itself, stabbing the razor point of its tail into its heart dozens of times ensuring its destruction, until it collapsed to its side. Each matchstick burned to the earth and the funeral pyre was over.

Billy tossed the dead scorpion into the brush and heard the rear door open. Frenchy emerged from it, her hair mussed. She was wearing embroidered jeans and a vibrant, "Versailles Butterfly" glitter tee, one she'd designed. But it was etched on her face and unmistakable—a fresh orientation. She was different, someone else and no longer his.

For him, she'd broken that bond; for her, she'd broken through. She'd mixed with the biology of another, her chemicals altered inside and the transformation beamed with certitude through calmed azure eyes. He saw it instantly and began to seethe, yet not for the perceived act itself surprisingly, not in a jealous way. "I told you, didn't I?"

"Beelly, I—"

"I told you!" he shouted. "How long has he been alone?"

" … half hour. *Peut t'être.*"

He dashed back to the driver's side of the car. He snatched a long-barreled Smith & Wesson six-shooter from under the seat. Frenchy lunged at him, but he tossed her aside. "—Beelly! *No!!!*"

The man sprinted off at full speed. She quickly searched the glove box and found a key, but still needed both.

She chased after him as fast as she could, but was not nearly as fleet of foot and Billy had had a head start.

Roland was still poised upright against the tree, his energy tapped. He was totally wiped out, diminished, and nearing sleep.

"Don't go out on me now, *NOT NOW!* " Billy spouted, charging hard.

The eyes of the prisoner were closing, the last of his power drained from him, threat or no threat. Fatal consequences or not, he could not save himself from slumber as the eyes rolled heavily in their sockets like weighted bowling balls. Unable to glare or gaze, unable to take in anything, no more marvels of nature—nothing—the eyes of Roland Polsonby had had their fill and it was time.

As the man's eyelids fell to half-mast drawing to a close, Billy loomed closer. At the moment they were shutting completely, the barrel was placed there and the hammer found its thread with a *click!*

Frenchy could see it happening. *"NOOOOOOO!!!"*

With that tiny metallic snap the bloodshot whites of his eyeballs revolving back were seized and halted in place. They slowly spun forward again exposing the retinas and the eyelids sprung open slightly.

"I told her, dammit!"

"Billy—" the man mumbled deliriously. "Told her … what?"

"I told her *no fucking!* "

" … sorry … Billy."

"You're *sorry???* Almost got you killed!"

"Were you—? Were you going to do it?"

He took in Roland's frail expression.

"Were you going to shoot me?"

The captor drew out an antique blue bottle from his pocket.

"I 'member that bottle ... iodine." Even the man's smile was fractured.

"Nope." Billy tapped yellow pills into his palm. "Open up—"

"What is it?"

"Open up, dammit!"

Roland eyed him almost trustingly. His jaws separated. "Goodbye."

"No goodbyes, only hellos." Billy shoved two in his mouth. "Lemme see you swallow." He did. "Now lift your tongue ..." Nothing beneath. "Straight caffeine, keep you going ... *Damn you!*"

Unbeknownst to the both, Frenchy silently crept behind the tree and inserted the key in the wire lock that secured Roland to the trunk. Billy heard the lock unsnap and he wheeled back around and saw the lock fall to the ground—releasing the captive.

"What do you think you're doing?"

"It's finished!"

"Gimme that key!"

"It's over, Beelly!" She backed away. "Now his hands! Unlock him!"

She swiveled as he lunged, hurling the tiny key into the brush.

"Fuck, Frenchy!" He grabbed her and she shoved him away with a newfound strength she'd never demonstrated and perhaps never possessed. Her resolve irritated him more and he pounced on her, smacking her repeatedly.

"Billy! Enough!" the prisoner called out.

"Shut the fuck up! Everybody has a plan until they get cracked in the mouth! Iron Mike said it, fuckers!"

The willful young woman stumbled and the incensed captor kept hitting her in the face, punching her in the stomach.

"Stop it, Billy!" Roland hollered again.

But Frenchy sprang up. Ready for more she mounted an attack of her own. She fought him off impressively with fists and kicks.

"You dirty son of a beetch! You're fucking *fou!*" she screamed.

"You're gonna get a taste of it, too!" He had that five-alarm flare in his fire eyes, the ominous ones.

The two crashed and wrestled in the dirt like sandlot hoodlums until Billy popped up and drew the blue glass bottle and smacked it on a rock, raising the jagged end. He broke into twisted verse.

" 'Froggy's looking/For her lunch/She croaks when some comes by/She flicks her tongue/And yum, yum, yum/Catches herself a fly!' " Come and get it, froggy!"

"Don't! Mélodie!"

Billy snapped a look at the prisoner. "Mélodie??? You gotta be shittin' me!"

But she wasn't going to back off, not an inch. She squared before him, totally unafraid of the threat or the outcome.

"What the hell are you doing, Billy?"

"Gonna slash her into strips!"

"Go ahead! I'll still keeck your ass!"

"She's family!"

"She's nothing! And I got no family, thanks to you-know-who!"

"Okay!" he blasted. He would throw it now. He'd considered it before, but now it was the only way. "I confess—I killed them ..."

The captor slashed a vicious one at him, his nostrils flaring.

"I killed them, Billy! I did it!"

He feared the worst and so did Frenchy. Everything he'd tried to avoid with this psychopath and all the repercussions, he wagered it and put it out there on the table; his life, his death and burial plans if it came to that. There was a frozen stillness in the canyon.

"I know you done," the captor said easily, breaking one sickly across. "Still not gonna save her—nice try!"

"She's been there for you since the start! Your supporter all these years! Don't be a jackass!"

"Listen to loverboy—little nookie and he goes all to pieces ..."

She waited, then rushed while his arm was cocked to slash.

Out of nowhere Billy was sent flying forward, bowled over by a charging bull, the prisoner's hands still manacled behind. Billy tumbled end over end and hit his head on a jagged root. He lay there dazed a moment and probed the numbness to his forehead. He found the wound and the blood. His sights shifted.

"Think you're ready for me? Let's see how alive you are—"

He pounced on the man who lay prostrate on the ground and began pounding him. He whacked him in the face, kicked him, and punched him in the head with point-blank blows. Roland was unable to defend himself from an ugly, terrible beating.

"*ENOUGH!*"

The cry was resolute and Billy twisted around. She was standing over him, the six-shooter aimed directly between his eyes.

The broken smile eventually found its mouth. "Your move, Butterfly—"

"Get off him!"

"You go girl—"

"How do you like it?"

"You should know—it's win-win. Death will become me …"

"How brave, beating up a man with no hands!"

"C'mon, do me the favor—"

"You are really a hero, Beelly."

"You mean a 'real hero'? Shucks, Frenchy—"

"Get off him! *NOW!*"

Eyeing her carefully, he rose to his feet ever so slowly.

"Think he's your boyfriend 'cause he fucked you once? Doesn't work that way in the world of hos and hustlers, *Mélodie* —"

"Shut up, Billy!"

"Told you, you dumb cunt—it ruins everything!"

Employing a disinterested, steady calm for tacit misdirection, in a flash he lunged and submarined her tackling her to the ground. He wrestled the gun from her hand and bolted to his feet.

"Don't worry, punks," he spat, catching his breath. "I'm finished here, just wanted my damned gun—"

He started back in the direction of the car. "Good workout," he winded. "And Polsonby—you may be Donnie Juan now but next time use a damned condom. Slut doesn't know any better—"

"Fuck you!" she yelled.

He stopped in his tracks and slowly revolved back around.

"Fuck me?"

"Yeah, fuck you! You're a stupid fool, Beelly!"

"That's what I get after all I've done for you, French fry?"

He shuffled back toward her.

"Yeah, *what?* " she roared. "What have you done for me that wasn't good for yourself first? Tell me that! You helped me, gave me clothes, a place to live—that was years ago! And I waited for you! And since you got out of prison all you've done is stop me from having a life!"

He was still panting. "You having a life, you say?" he asked almost gently, pathologically so. "*We* were going to have a life. That was the plan—"

"Not *my* plan! I will not pay you with my life forever! Not any more!"

" 'Billy 4ever.' 'Member that tat? The one on your pumpkin?"

"I was fifteen!"

"Didn't she show you, loverboy?"

"That was ten years ago!"

"Or maybe you're still in that early euphoric stage where she can't tell you all the men she's bonied, ex-boyfriends' carrot size, the tit-grams and anything-goes Ambien sexfests, and the semi-sincere justifications for all the rampant beer hall sodomy chatter—"

"No, moron—when I sat on his face this morning there was no tattoo! I got it removed in Supai!"

He eyed her thinly; the revelation paused him. "Okay. Fair enough—"

"And I *would have* been with you—"

"Don't look at me, Polsonby. I'm not the vengeful cuckold—"

"—Forever!—"

"—We had no smooch-free pact with strangers—"

"—But you could never stop doing it!"

"What?"

"*THIS! This SHIT!* This inability to let it go! Your stinking past!!! Well I say *fuck the past!* And fuck *your* past!" she hollered and paused to let her lungs reload. The blood cable bisecting her forehead receded momentarily. "And it will kill you! But I won't let it kill *me!* I don't want to be a part of it anymore! *Tu comprends?*"

The sound—a cry from her core and a note of anguish she'd never struck, was from a vocal chord he'd never heard, not even in the brawl. But he heard it now, the cry of a desperate animal, cornered and dangerous; her species' alarm call. Everything sounded different now and it penetrated him profoundly and where he lived, silencing him.

"Fuck the past! Never does anyone any good—*ever!*"

She faded paces back and angled away from the other two, screaming unintelligibly at the top of her lungs. Another primitive release, it was stark and equally piercing and it bounced directly off the canyon walls into infinity.

"But don't you want a life—?" he intoned softly her way.

"Yes, I want a life!"

"Together we have a life … We've always had a life—"

"I want *my own life*, dammit!"

He angled down and kicked the earth, nodding. But he still couldn't let it go. "So that means you two are a couple now?"

"I'm no couple! I'm not anybody's! Yours OR his! I'm *nobody's!* I'm my own person and I'm going to have my own life, no one else's. *Mine.* Of my own, *ON MY OWN!* Do you understand, Billy???"

"Yeah, I understand," he muttered. "Tell loverboy—"

After a beat, Billy glowered at the prisoner.

"Polsonby? You got ten to get your ass in the backseat of that car or I come hunting for you and you'll get to know the true meaning of *Canyon del Muerto*—the reason I came here in the first place …"

He admired the .38 briefly, caressing its barrel then swaggered off.

Frenchy looked down upon the soiled and bloodied man slumped in a pile. "I'm sorry," she said, her face folding with emotion, "that I told him to kill you. I should have listened to myself sooner …"

The *fight* and now *him*—it was too much for her and she broke.

Roland propped himself to try and console her. "Wasn't your fault."

"Yes—it was." Her chin trembled and water drowned her eyes. "And no, *amour*, I don't regret one minute of it …"

She didn't move in his direction; she couldn't. She knew that whatever it was they'd had was no longer possible.

"Are you going your own way now?"

Still sniffling, she shook before answering, her head bowed.

"No. I can't …"

He asked her why.

" … I can't leave him."

Though it was perplexing to him, he understood them for a first time. They were inextricably linked, albeit inexplicably so.

"I'll be there in a few minutes," he assured her.

She twisted back and trudged off against the vibrant leaves of the autumn canyon—a glorious backdrop producing now a striking but gut-wrenching canvas. He conceived of it that way as her shrinking and slumping figure captured in nature's Technicolor embrace seemed a starkly potent portrait of abject loneliness.

As her figure disappeared beyond the bend, Roland struggled to pick himself off the ground, his body a sack of cement. During the violent exchange he'd manufactured adrenaline and had been spiked to alertness. Scanning the ground however he was reminded. He squatted low and with sticky bloodied hands tacked behind he gathered a couple dozen pills from the soil where the bottle had been smashed. He rose on wobbly pegs and slipped the pills carefully in his back pocket then took a slow, heavy-footed pace through the canyon toward the car.

Brilliant morning sun poured over the canyon floor and he could see then the endless rows of deciduous trees in dazzling peak fall hues. Every color imaginable enveloped him and there it was—the *naturaleza muerta* he'd been promised. The captor was right; it was truly splendiferous.

As he hiked, his faculties returned in increments. Soon he came upon the clearing beneath the canopy of tall oaks and cottonwoods.

A warm wind blew over him as he stood there alone. There was no vehicle, no Billy Six, and no Mélodie. They were nowhere to be seen. The Stretch had disappeared and the pair had taken off. He knew it was a final farewell.

A gift had been left on the dusty dirt track in the precise spot where the car had been; a key to the handcuffs along with a twenty dollar bill. The key lay on a piece of paper pinned by a short cairn and a note was scrawled across the page in Billy's handwriting.

> *"We all are conceived in close prison. And then all our life is, but a going out to the place of execution, to death. Nor was there any man seen to sleep in the cart between Newgate and Tyburn—between prison and the place of execution, does any man sleep? But we sleep all the way; from the womb to the grave we are never thoroughly awake."*
> — *JOHN DONNE*

As quickly as it had entered his life three days before, the Ivory Stretch was gone. In his seventy-second hour of captivity, Roland Polsonby had been set free.

30

The Recruit

When the call came in the twin squad cars were docked beside each other beneath an abandoned off-ramp to the Estrella Freeway in west Phoenix. One of the cars blasted the directive on shortwave. The other car was shaking violently.

In parlance chosen by her colleagues Lucia Alvarez was the most coveted "piece of ass" in the Phoenix Police Department. Every cop from traffic to homicide had tried to woo her—unsuccessfully. The daughter of a first-generation Mexican cop, she had high-arching brows, a beautiful face, ample chest and a swollen provocative rear. There was nothing not to like in the eyes of many unless you were on a high-speed chase opposing her talents behind the wheel.

Yet, if Lucia was the Eva Mendes of the Department, Sean O'Brien was the force's Monty Clift. He sported his Ray Ban aviators and wore them well, prompting desk-job gals to swoon, sway, flutter, and flirt when he passed in the halls of West Washington Street.

O'Brien was more than *GQ* fluff, however. One hell of a cop in the making, he'd been a recent standout at the Academy and was a superior marksman with pistol or rifle. He'd only been in three shoot-outs and fired a total of three shots—all self-defense kills. He had a cocksure personality to go with his law enforcement talent and savvy. His father, Hamilton "Bud" O'Brien, had been a decorated officer on the PPD and was a close pal of Sheriff Harlan Graves. They'd been through a lot of street hell together and had turned a profit or two as well. Graves had known Sean since he was born.

When O'Brien got the radio alert El Capítan wanted to meet with him, the young recruit was curious, but not surprised. He was excited, too. Like his father he was an opportunist, perhaps even more ambitious. He just needed to finish off with Lucia in the back of his prowler and she him. She preferred the position chosen at present as it showcased arguably her finest asset.

There's just something about pretty people getting together and everyone knows it—could be said about this union.

"What's he calling for?"

"Dunno—" he gasped through rising grunts.

"Fuck me, Sean!" As an answer he swatted, spanked, palmed, and mitted the *cafe au lait* colored rounds before him. His thick, strong fingers gripped the ample buns like bread dough. "Don't you dare … come … yet!" As she shrieked, he could no longer hold it and reversed himself in time to spill the buttermilk over her backside, slathering it in afterward as she was known to appreciate. Eyes closed, teeth dug into the seat cushion, she didn't crane to watch; she felt it though, silently approving of his methods.

"I gotta go—" he said, catching his breath and he reached into a discarded Taco Bell bag to draw out the wad of napkins and clean up.

"—Go …"

They pecked once and Sean arranged his pants while checking for stains. He spread the car door and nearly fell out on rubber, spastic limbs. "I'll text you—"

"You *better* …"

El Capítan didn't care for meetings at headquarters. He preferred casual sit-downs over black beans, rice, and Spanish coffee at his favorite Latino diners and lunch spots where he received a celebrity's welcome. There were some politicians who thought they ran the city, but it wasn't necessarily the way the Capítan saw it—or acted.

When O'Brien showed up at the Puerto Sagua six minutes late, he appeared somewhat disheveled, protected though by his partially soiled uniform and teardrop shades. But the seated man didn't bat an eye. The Capítan rose up for his former colleague's boy and gave him a full macho embrace.

"How you doin', OB?"

"Not too bad—" Of course the young cop couldn't not flash on "Lieutenant Lucia," as he affectionately called her, perched on all fours minutes before not-so-silently relishing his offering.

"Haven't seen you since that dustup in Gilbert—"

"Yeah …"

"Dulles said right above the nose."

"Didn't want it to go that way, but didn't bother 'bout it too much, either. Lucky shot."

"Lucky shots seem to be your forte. They're callin' you The Kid."

"Ignoramuses. Simple cases of them or me, really."

"How's the woolly-wool treating you?"

"Can't complain."

El Capitán's energy spiked in dialogues with the handsome recruit and his normal game face didn't break menacing; rather, it glowed. He could envision all of life's perks and privileges which would avail themselves of the kid in the years to come, pussy included and most notably. He enjoyed these chats and nourished himself off the boy's youth like a vampire.

"I know you been puttin' it to Alvarez—"

"Wha—?" His attempt to show innocence was unsuccessful and eventually the touchdown grin blasted forth.

"Ain't much goes around here I don't know about."

O'Brien sighed. "My dad told me 'bout your spies."

"Done a lot together your daddy and me. 'Fore we was married even had overlap. Me first, o' course. So what she like?"

"C'mon, Cap'."

"Spinner?"

The squat Pima-Mexican waitress nervously carried two coffees to the table taken by the man she knew as Yellow Eyes. Though they were the same breed of hound separated by forty years, neither cop gave her a second look, not even a once-over.

"You seen that inventory? She'll spin *me*—"

"Some caboose on her, grant you that," Graves undersold with intent and leaned back to fake less interest.

"Lawdy-lawdy—" The recruit couldn't help himself now. Graves was a master at getting folk to gush, from criminals to lawyers to red-light lookers and corralling an ambitious and cocky young cop to talk "puss" or "wool" offered little challenge.

"C'mon, give me somethin' I can take to the hole …"

O'Brien paused a moment and lit one from his pocket. Cops could always smoke at the Puerto Sagua. "She's a facialist …"

"No—"

"—ain't lyin'—"

"Damn … Dog's life you got."

"Don't start—I know you're gettin' some, Cap', somewhere."

As the Capitán let loose a full belly one his *arroz con pollo* was served. O'Brien had decided against ordering after his fast food Gordito belch clouded the table. Graves had waved away the smellies, identified the franchise, and the item, and ribbed him for it.

"Tell ya, Sean, remind me a lot of someone—"

"My dad?"

"No. *Me*. When I was your age." The man shook his head, his grill hardening. "But the 'Nam fucked it all up. Always wonder what would have happened if I hadn't gone overseas." The remark was the most candid he'd utter about himself all month, perhaps all year. "Like I said, Bud and me? Hell, we did a lot."

"I've heard the stories."

"I know you done. Reason I wanted a huddle with you is for that situation we got up north—"

O'Brien nodded. "The abduction—"

"We got JD and I'm on point and I'm puttin' together a TF. We'll be usin' helly-birds, maybe some outta-staters—Collies, New Mexis— 'pendin' on where that nut surfaces …"

"Where is he now?"

"Ain't sure. I'll be seein' the victim later—"

"Heard he turned up …"

"Unharmed. See what I can get outta him. But I want to let you know I'm addin' you to the force—"

O'Brien nodded again with restraint, but was secretly very pleased.

"And I have my reasons for puttin' you down—I'm givin' you a special assignment. I'll tell you more about it when the time is right."

Sufficiently prompted, El Capítan hovered in on the table beaming the searing yellows of a night predator.

"Now I got nearly three thousand cops to choose from for thissy one and I chose you. Why? Sure I know where you come from, but it ain't 'cause you're Bud's kid. When I saw you at States and you overrode Coach in the fourth, calling five keepers in a row—that's the effort I'm lookin' for. Kinna guy who wants the ball when the game's on the line. Don't let me down."

"I won't, Cap'." Truthfully, he'd been expecting something from Sheriff Graves before he stepped down and it would seem, here it was.

"You remember that." The Capítan lowered his voice to a sordid rustle. "And there'll be somethin' in it for you and I'm not just talkin' a career boost. You know, copper salary only go so far—"

El Capítan liked informal settings for this reason. He'd made enemies in the Department and was especially leery of the new breed envious of his position and influence. He was calling it a day and didn't want any eleventh hour scandals to interfere with his smooth transition to private life.

"I do business the old-fashioned way; so did Bud O'Brien."

"I am his kid, Cap'. Think I know a good deal when I come across it."

The men both smiled more than vaguely and shook. As the recruit's hand recoiled, his fingers grazed over a coarse patch to his fly. Investigating, he noticed the dry flakes of indulgence on the navy trousers and adroitly brushed them beneath the table and finished off his coffee. Getting beyond a "copper salary" suited him fine, just fine.

31

He stepped off the bus at the terminal in Phoenix just after four in the afternoon. He hadn't slept; the caffeine pills had made sure of it. There was too much to ponder to sleep anyway. Roland drew the bottle from his pocket and downed another.

Drifters and panhandlers with hungry depot eyes milled around. Seeing the freed prisoner in his condition—the grimy face and tattered clothes—they looked through and past him, disinterested. He could be of no help to them. Roland slipped into a restroom to clean up and washed away the remaining patches of dried blood in his hairline.

He placed his call and Margaret immediately became hysterical, of course. Calming herself she listened to his instructions. Roland asked her to collect him at the Greyhound terminal downtown on East Buckeye and instructed her to bring a clean oxford shirt and the banking card she held for petty cash. He had counseled also not to say anything to anyone. She would deliver him to his meeting from the depot.

Margaret was certainly overjoyed that he was alive and told him so, but she was very upset, still choking back tears.

"Billy Sixkiller is my Oliver!" she blurted.

"I know, Margaret. I'm very sorry."

Roland was promised no special treatment, but no hassle either. He'd comply with the formal visit, but wanted to talk first before giving a statement—his demand. The compromise had been reached. They met in a dank, sticky-floored university bar in Tempe that smelled like stale beer. He arrived early and slid into a booth in back.

The Sheriff dominated a room when he entered it exuding power with that puffed chest, steady stride, and swagger. Roland was struck by the showing, freshly receptive to many things he hadn't previously been. He was familiar with the man's amiable cocktail party demeanor, but would not get it today. As soon as Graves settled before him he could tell the imposing man was on the job and in a no-nonsense mood.

"You're damned lucky," the Sheriff let loose as an introductory teaser to see which way the wind was blowing. Roland didn't bite. He knew to be cautious and was determined to say little.

The Capítan took in the film of sweat on the victim's face, the bloodshot eyes, and gray circles which would have been darker had it not been for the sun. The man appeared bug-eyed. The fact is he'd gone nearly four days with no sleep. The pills were keeping him going, pressing his nerves and giving him that wired look.

"I've seen some beauts, but this takes the cake. Plum-dog crazy."

The Sheriff then proceeded; the questions were fired. Had he been hurt? Why had Dennis Roy, also known as Billy Sixkiller, singled him out? Why was the abductor driving such a high-profile vehicle? Where had they been? And, of course, where were they now?

Graves also inquired as to what the perpetrator had revealed to him of the past before he turned to questions more personal in nature. Did anyone know he was back in Phoenix? Not even his wife?

"And what about Oregon?"

"Oregon has nothing to do with it or my involvement with Billy."

"Wasn't implying it did."

"Sheriff Graves," he said in earnest, "I came to you because you're an old family friend. I don't know anyone else on the force. I thought you could work it so there'd be no media circus."

"I can help, but they'll be out there. It's a national story; you're a well-known New Yorker. And you know what they do back there."

"The quieter the better. I'd appreciate your efforts in that—"

"Granted and gaveled."

"Enough said. So I wish to tell you—" he paused, suddenly becoming tentative, shifting, his pulse beginning to quicken. Then it hit him like a wave again the sound, the booming roar of Havasu Falls, sweeping through him, emboldening him.

"Tell me—?"

"Yes, the truth …"

"Okay, Roland." The large man with the yellow eyes shifted back, the skepticism in his voice undeniable. "What is the truth?"

"I should have placed a call earlier, but the truth is that this is a huge misunderstanding."

"Misunderstanding? Which party is not being understood?"

"Mr. Sixkiller. And me."

"How so?"

"I was not abducted."

"No?"

"I went of my own volition."

"I'm listening, Mr. Polsonby—"

The Sheriff's change to the formal "Mr." did not go unnoticed.

"I haven't been myself lately; that bit about Oregon? All true."

"You were planning to undergo an assisted suicide—"

"But I decided against it largely to Billy's counsel, or however you want to characterize his contribution."

"He talked you out of it?"

"Yes, he did. And I—"

"Yes, Mr. Polsonby?"

"I don't want to press charges."

"No charges," Graves repeated woodenly.

"I got in his car of my own free will and left of my own free will. He wasn't holding me. I could have turned him in any number of times, but there was no reason to. I wasn't kidnapped."

"And why's he still runnin'?"

"He's scared."

Graves took a draw on a coffee mug he hadn't yet touched. "May I ask you a personal question?" He leaned in with a steely gaze and waited on the nod, but jumped it anyway. "Do you enjoy kinky sex?"

"Sir?"

"I mean bondage, S & M, that sort of thing—"

Stunned, but forced to ponder it anyway, the man shook.

"Ever tried it?"

"No, sir."

Graves tore open a sugar packet and poured it into his coffee, falling silent for a half-minute.

"Huh …" The release was guttural and primitive and the law man didn't add to it or take away from it—he let it hang. Roland eyed him expectantly, but no less warily.

"Trying to decide who's crazier. You. Or Billy Sixkiller—"

"I haven't been feeling too great, I know."

"We are concerned with your health. But regardless of your physical and mental wellbeing I'm going to let you in on two things I know. First is, whether you press charges or not the state meaning yours truly with the assistance of the District Attorney—will. This is another incident stacked on a mountain of trouble this boy's stirred up over the years, fifteen to be exact—"

"He was mistreated for years—"

"I know the stories—"

"They're more than stories. A court case in New Mexico. With convictions."

"No denying the wrongdoing happened, but let me finish. A man— no matter how wrong he been done—has got to straighten out over time and become a law abiding citizen. At this point all those 'Yeah, but's don't hold a jug of water with me, the judge, or the laws of this state. His *second* abduction—the boy is going up the river, that's if he's lucky enough to make it out of this manhunt alive. I want you to understand that. Prepare yourself for that. As it would seem you care about the boy—"

"Why wouldn't he make it out alive?"

"He's armed, he's got a long, violent record, he's on the run, and he's a psychopath. Something I left out?"

"What crimes has he really committed?"

"The bipolarity?" he supplied anyway.

"Has he ever hurt anyone?"

"The schizophrenia?"

"Wasn't the last guy he abducted set free?"

Roland was sitting on the edge of his chair and a fire was lit in his eyes. Graves spied his zealousness and let a weighty chunk of air from his chest.

"Polsonby, you're a respected member of the community. Never read your book. Not a reader; my wife was before she passed on. But you've made a name for yourself in a town bigger than this'n. I been around a long time—a time when they didn't give two shits if your Sheriff used good grammar. Hell, I've known your wife and her brother since they were born. We go to the same restaurants, same social functions. But this here is out of my hands ..."

He hesitated. "Can tell you're impressed by the boy. As strange as it sounds you think he's done you right. And maybe it's my age, but I'll be just as daffy and tell you I understand—I reckon he has done you right—you haven't taken your life, you ain't dead. And I'm happy for that, happy to see you've come back around, you and your wife are fine people. But breaking the law is breaking the law and members of the Arizona State Police force are trained to handle individuals who break it, especially armed and dangerous ones, with an emphasis on providing for their own safety first," he finished pointedly.

"I understand, but—" He was cut off.

"Which brings me to the second thing I got knowledge of. For whatever reason you've been lying to me. And I'm not happy about it. I see you ain't been right in your mind, but lying to a cop is also an offense. Good thing I'm conducting this prelim and it's not a statement 'cause some of them rooks've been trained in hard-ass police towns—L.A., Dallas, Atlanta—they're gung ho, got hair triggers 'n take it very personally when someone tries to make a fool of 'em. They'd have no qualms about throwing you in the pen right now—"

"What makes you think I'm lying?"

The man eyeballed him squarely, his Texas jaw jutting, and there was no worry in his look. In a lightning maneuver one would not consider a man of his age able to perform, he tore back the victim's shirt cuff and exposed the scabbed and lacerated wrist.

The victim froze and they faced off eye to eye. The Sheriff then casually unbuttoned the second cuff. The damage to the skin matched the injury on his other wrist.

"Moments ago I asked you about kinky sex practices. You maintained you do not engage in them. Wanna tell me again you took this little joy ride of your own free will?"

Graves leaned back and took another haul of coffee.

Roland remained guiltily silent a moment. Then he told him about Mélodie, that they'd repeatedly engaged in bondage sex.

"Why you lie before?"

"The sensitive nature of it."

The table went silent and a disbelieving Graves let it go—almost. "Quarter-inch gashes? Must really dig your pain—"

"Let me ask you a question, Sheriff. Who was Billy's father?"

"He didn't say nothing to you?" The Sheriff didn't look directly at him. "He was a cop."

"A cop?"

"Right here in Phoenix. In my division. We worked alongside each other. On many occasions."

Roland reacted sharply.

"Losing Jack Randall was a big blow—"

"And Billy knows this?"

"Course he does. It's what I'm telling you. Look—I don't want anything to happen to him. He's not a son to me after all he done, but it's close. There's history there—"

"Why was Randall killed?"

Graves let out a gust of a sigh. Then he paused again before going into it.

"Okay. I'm going to tell you this so you understand. 'Cause I can tell you do care. There's what you read on Google. And there's the truth. Jack had been in the 'Nam. Like me. He got out, took a job with the force, was a good cop, done his job well. But the wounds from the war never healed. He felt betrayed. Like the rest of us. Not by any one person, by the whole damned deal. By Uncle Sam. Back home, we were the ones who 'lost;' didn't matter our buddies were shot to hell— we lost. A war we were never allowed to win. Know how that hurts? After risking your ass for a bunch of hippies? Jack took it hard. A quiet man, a real honest, loyal, fight-for-his-country type. Until he went overseas. Experience broke him; he wasn't the same when he came back … he was damaged. Like a lot of us. When he came back, he was going to get his—his due—from a country that used him. So he started in with the wrong folk … taking payoffs from low-level hoods. Vegas types came next then the horses. Casinos. Ladies. Got in over his head, owed a ton o' money and couldn't pay. Couldn't deliver more favors because they were watching him in house, to nail the big-ups. So he was left hanging out there alone with no protection—and big debts. And the debts done him in. Vegas boys don't play around, not with corrupt cops …"

The Sheriff lifted his mug and almost sipped, but didn't.

"Billy was an only child—parents dead. Diane Randall's sister had passed away and her mother was dying of cancer. So with no relatives he was brought to Telshor."

"Who was behind that?"

"State D.A.. Arizona didn't have a proper foster parent program and no good schools for orphans. Thought of taking him in myself, but couldn't do that to my wife. So he went into the New Mex system—"

"Hardly a system—"

"No one knew that back then. Tell you another thing: I didn't let Billy know who his father really was—on purpose. I didn't want him to think his old man was a corrupt son of a bitch and figured he'd have enough problems, the pitfalls of growing up with no parents. But ol' Billy got crazy on a few folk with threats and such at the state's

Orphan Placement Council, the one that recommended Telshor. They coughed up information not in the public record; that his father had been breakin' the law, got involved with people who had no respect for it, and they murdered him and his wife in cold blood. So for ten years he went crazy trying to find the killer—the one who tore his parents from him, the one who made him an orphan, the one responsible for sending him to a school which abused him for years. Lord yes, he had cause and it drove him nuts. That's if he hadn't gone nuts already."

Roland processed the information for a moment. "And now, Sheriff?"

"How do you mean?"

"You and Randall were colleagues, maybe even friends."

"We were—"

"Don't you want to make sure nothing happens to Billy?"

"I'll do all I can, Polsonby. But this is a two-, maybe three-state effort. How can I protect him from that? And how can I protect him from himself? He ain't pointin' confetti pop guns—"

Roland lowered his head, stymied by the series of revelations. "Any sightings of him?"

"Not since Canyon de Chelly. He disappeared. Boy's good at that. Damned resourceful. But smarts only take you so far and good fortune always runs out," he said putting the hat to his head. "Think I heard that in a movie. But it's the truest thing I can say after fifty years on the force. *Hollywood* …"

"You wouldn't tell me even if you knew anything would you?"

"Would I, or could I? No, I cannot. He's a fugitive from justice."

Graves paused to eye off briefly and as quick and athletic—the move of a zealous recruit—he spun back devastatingly and smothered the tabletop. He honed in tight, thickly, and intimidatingly with those searing golden beams.

"Gonna chalk this one up to personal trauma, Polsonby. *Yours.* From the abduction. That's giving you a reprieve for eighteen hours. But I want a statement first thing tomorrow morning. In my office. Now, you can watch me finish my coffee or I can watch you and that part o' you that needs a swift kick get the hell out of here—"

Roland rose from the table. Only then did Graves let go of that charity gala gleamer the public was accustomed to, the one which exposed selectively repaired teeth, the overly-white caps fronting a line of neglected yellow brothers stained from years of mediocre coffee and tobacco chews. The smile turned twisted. "Hope it's not a recurring problem of yours—"

"Sir?"

"Lying to a police officer." Graves extended his hand and Roland's came to life. They shook and the big man hadn't lost his grip, either. He didn't forget to mention the upcoming retirement party. He and his wife would soon be receiving their invitation.

"You know, my First Lieutenant's kid goes to the local grade school. Guess what the most popular Halloween costume is this year?"

Roland shrugged.

"Billy Sixkiller," he said, a grin sparked by the simple irony. "And guess who's second?"

Roland understood and nodded neutrally which surprised the old Sheriff who'd anticipated a reaction of sorts, if not a curve.

"Funny thing, life," the man repeated.

That caught Roland's ear. "Billy says that—"

"Ya-huh. So, who you gonna be for Halloween?"

He didn't have to think about it. "Myself," he replied flatly.

"Damned good to hear." Graves raised his mug. "Welcome back."

He nodded and left Graves to stay put and do whatever he would do in peace.

Roland never knew Billy's father had been a cop. He'd never asked him directly about his parents when he was in captivity. He couldn't. He was too concerned it would set the fragile man off. And he'd have been right.

32

The Polsonby's sprawling estate, *Calle de la Luna Plata*, had been featured in architectural magazines worldwide and was considered a masterpiece by those who appreciated its ultra-modern design. The main house's construction and sizable guesthouse blended harmoniously with the natural beauty of the desert setting, boasting extensive glass and water and surrounded by a swimming pool moat. The underwater depths of the pool could be viewed from a lower level of the house's interior. The three hundred-sixty degree view welcomed the McDowell Mountains to the north, the Sierra Estrellas to the south, and the Superstitions to the east. Directly south lay the sprawling desert city and its gorgeous nightly sea of lights. *Luna Plata*'s rock garden was designed by environmental sculptor Andy Goldsworthy and light and space artist James Turrell had been enlisted to construct a skyspace observatory.

News of Roland's safe return had hit the airwaves and the vans of television journalists had already motored up to the Polsonby residence.

Gonzalo was the first to see him from the garage as he'd heard the hum of the motorized gate. He greeted his employer with a hug and called for Fernanda who came dashing from the caretaker cottage. She threw herself in his arms in a loving embrace, but modified it appropriately enough for her husband who was standing beside her.

The two followed Roland up the driveway toward the main house.

A gaunt and weary Adele emerged from the front door and she skipped over to him, teary-eyed, and drew him close, clutching him tightly. "I'm so happy you're not hurt," she whispered in his ear.

She held on a while as Roland's arm wrapped her waist. When she was done he stepped back and grinned politely for the wellwishers.

"Thank you, all of you, for your thoughts and prayers," he said. He looked into all of their eyes, Adele's included, and saw people who truly cared for him and he needed to articulate what had been on his mind for days.

"I also want to say I'd like to apologize for my behavior these last months; years, really. None of you did anything to bring on my troubles, of course. They were my troubles, mine alone, and in many ways I feel ashamed by my behavior. It wasn't me, but it is what had become of me. And there is no one else to blame."

Adele clasped his hand and led him forward and they passed through the front door. There he indicated a preference to lie down and rest.

"I can't tell you how happy I am you're home," she said, to which he thanked her.

Roland passed directly to his wing to shower and shave. He changed into fresh clothes and noticed the massive and vibrant arrangement of flowers Fernanda had placed in the window for his return.

He drifted over to the big bed, enormous to him now, and settled on its edge. Falling back fully on his back he found it impossible to turn his mind off, much less sleep, the same state he'd endured on the bus ride. He was wide-awake with eyes glued to the ceiling. His mind was revving, exploding at times, rich in memory recall and vivid detail. He'd lived more in the last days than he had the last twenty years of his life combined and he was acutely aware of it.

The memories of his captors dominated his thoughts: the electrifying, unpredictable Billy who was now likely in mortal danger; and the wondrous Mélodie, of course, who, in such a short interval, under the most extraordinary circumstances, had become his improbable lover and maybe much more than that—in a matter of hours. Perhaps.

Roland was convinced in that place and time that their feelings for each other had been mutual—two butterflies soaring—on the same amorous wavelength. Yet the way their melodious song abruptly ended in that canyon, violently, and dramatically, he had to question their romance's legitimacy, given the instability and changeable nature of love. He could not disregard Mélodie's disturbing past before Billy and the troubled history with him and their profound connection. Still, with the dire situation at hand—a manhunt—would they even survive it? Would she? And would Roland even see her again? He was left with so many questions.

On top of it all, he feared for her life.

Yet his mind, so raw and freshly equipped and attuned, though boosted by stimulants, would not and could not leave him alone.

Had Mélodie been administering her medicine to him as she had intimated? And for what reason? To get him to the next stage of a butterfly transformation? She seemed to discount the significance of the cards in favor of her own medicine, her song of life and love. She even professed her love for him—she'd "made beauty" with him, after all. But was that contention reliable? Was the Mélodie card any more dependable than the cards in the book of animal medicine?

She claimed he was her medicine. Was that in the moment passionate euphoria, hyperbole, and dreamy chatter? Was she just a lonely girl, emotionally and sexually starved, who needed a quick fix? Or just an intimate fix from someone new? Had she been using him physically to break the bond with Billy psychologically for her own self-preservation?

Or was it only about Frenchy and Billy? That they were inextricably linked in an oddly symbiotic way. That they needed each other to survive. Or perhaps their connection was forced. Billy had that power, to keep someone psychologically entangled even encaged. He was a master. At the same time, maybe she held a similar dementia to his, one she couldn't shake after the difficult childhood and orphan teen years, and the damaging sexual abuse. And they were on the same wavelength of dysfunctional codependency and that was the wavelength that truly mattered. Or maybe living with Billy for so long had made her a bit warped, touched, unstable, crazy, or worse. She had never been alone long enough to know independence and get stronger and heal. She may have been petrified at the thought of leaving him.

She was admittedly younger and seemingly inexperienced in the ways of love. Perhaps this all was immaturity speaking; that she'd become intimate with a man and was not used to the waterfall of feelings it conjured. She couldn't handle it part of which was leaving without saying goodbye.

Or was it as Wil had said, a life of "no goodbyes?"

Thusly, what was Mélodie's song in the end after all?

And what of Billy? He'd shared moments with the man he had never shared with any human being. He was tortured, but in many ways, Billy was all too beautiful and a man who'd altered his life. As Roland had been a veritable corpse laying flatline, Billy, with perhaps the help of a greater power, the Great Spirit even, had blown the winds of life back into his lungs and revived him, filling him with a fresh spirit and will to live. He had a new Life Force, it would seem, and his captor had orchestrated it each step of the way by brilliant design with his own brand of genius.

The meditations marched on in Roland's stimulated, buzzing state. He redirected thoughts toward himself also in that space, in the bedroom of his home, even more sobering reflections. With this new Life Force, if indeed that's what it was, what now constituted his life? And who was Roland Polsonby? If he was transforming as a winged creature at which stage was he? The larva still? The cocoon? Certainly he hadn't attained rebirth-butterfly status—or maybe he had. Ruminations surged covering a flurry of personal emotions—love, compassion, hope; the darker strains as well, paranoia, regret, loss, and fear.

With so many questions unanswered he was not at peace; he could not let go. There was no sleep to be had, nor did he have any desire for it. And that was a positive, he discerned, because on top of everything what became clear to him in his bedroom right then—his revelation—he no longer feared confronting these issues or entertaining the emotions and sentiments; the personal ones and those in the larger philosophical contexts. He was no longer practicing the passive reflex. He was galvanized, the way he'd confronted the Sheriff, even trying to help his friend. Because after all was said and done, that's what Billy Six was—his friend; Mélodie too, no matter what had happened between them romantically. Billy had done for him what no one else could. He'd been a goner and he was no longer. The freshly inspired outlook, his ability to see things this way, his rediscovered capacity to open up, emote, feel, and no longer be passive and—to *act* more than anything—was his proof, the *undeniable proof*, that he had been resuscitated and brought back to life with a will and a desire to live. This was the proof he had a new Life Force, one of courage and strength and he was determined to get things right this time. He'd been given a second chance and he would use it as a man of action now—this—the final proof he'd been reborn.

Roland downed another caffeine tablet before going to dinner.

He sat opposite Adele during the meal and answered her litany of questions concerning the abduction politely, but tersely. She understood his reluctance and didn't want to impose any stress.

Yet it was less for him than an unwillingness to share.

A rush of empathy for her came over him. He asked her what she'd been doing and as she recounted the recent Phoenix news as in who'd said what, the fifth line into her encapsulation of the daily calendar since his disappearance she burst into tears.

After dinner Roland perused his mail in addition to a packet of correspondence Margaret had sent from the office. Later, Fernanda served him tea and delivered an envelope handwritten to him. He did not recognize the writing. "Who dropped it off?"

"An African-American boy, maybe twelve. Driven by another older kid. They didn't seem like messengers."

Roland took it, silently struck.

Fernanda hovered there and he was aware of her prolonging posture. He felt her deeply now and more than ever. As she was about to leave, having arrived at the usual impasse, he would not let her go. He would not shut down or block. He would no longer avoid or sidestep, much less close the curtain on life. "I thought of you often when I was away."

Fernanda angled up sharply. "And I thought of you. Too much."

He rose and fronted her, stepping in as close as people who love each other do.

"You are a beautiful spirit, Fernanda. I know you prayed for me and I envisioned you doing it; your face, the way you look at me, everything that is you and it gave me hope. And made me ashamed for having taken so much for granted. Had we met years ago when we were young, you and I, it would have been different—there is beauty in that. Isn't it wonderful, absolutely wonderful, knowing that?"

Her face was streaming and the lids filled and overflowed. She wiped her eyes and they refilled again. He closed on that small wedge of space between them and smashing the impasse, wrapped her in his arms.

"I will always love you," he whispered. He could feel her trembling, her frame shuddering in his grasp. Their lips were so close now, magnetized, and with a will of their own they converged and met wholly, though briefly. The two had needed to taste each other and share that moment and in that very kiss they both felt would never happen in this life they, if not purged, relieved themselves of the greater passions.

Overcome, she spun and quickly stepped back down the corridor.

"Fernanda?"

She slowed and turned back around and he went to her again.

"Have you done my cards?"

She hesitated, caught off guard, as she had never discussed her tarots with him. "They told me you would return."

"Anything else?"

"You were chained to the past. It was holding you back. No," she corrected herself, "—it was killing you …"

She paused and weighed telling him more. "You have made a special alliance with not one person, but two. One needs your help. But there is danger—"

"Thank you."

"May I add my own interpretation?"

"I'd be very appreciative."

"Be careful, please. I couldn't bear to visit you up there on the mesa. Which you know I would—daily."

A frail smile followed and then she hurried off as noiselessly as she'd appeared, as she always appeared.

Fernanda had not divulged everything, falling short of informing him he may have fallen in love; but this was not appropriate nor was it her place. He'd have approved of her decision, she determined.

The oversized envelope was stapled shut. The return business label was emblazoned with "Quadruped Transportation Management Group." He identified the likely messenger to be their Apache Junction friend, Genesis. The short note penned in the boy's grade school block print confirmed it.

"Their in New mex. On terkoys trale. In gost town seril los fer hollaween. Billys favrit town in america! Frenchee sez tell him i lov him.
— GeNEsIS"

" 'The Turquoise Trail,' " Roland deciphered, reading aloud. He was unfamiliar with the term.

He lifted the dust cover from a long-neglected desktop computer and learned the Turquoise Trail was a state road, specifically Route 14; a two-laner meandering from Albuquerque to Santa Fe aptly named for its numerous roadside jewelry outposts. MapQuest yielded no "seril lose," but identified a "Cerrillos," a small hamlet rich in history in the state and now a ghost town. His concerned expression warmed over smoothly as it would seem for the oncoming holiday the pair was on their way to a ghost town—for Halloween. The setup was vintage Billy, he mused.

A sheet fell from the envelope, however. There was no writing, just an image—a faxed copy of the Raccoon medicine card.

Frenchy had apparently communicated with him one final time, after all.

Though he'd scrutinized the book cover to cover, he couldn't remember the Raccoon or its medicinal doctrine. Roland instinctively got into his car and drove to the Borders in Scottsdale. The store didn't carry the title, but he was directed to a New Age boutique nearby which sold crystals, CDs of ambient meditation music, and spiritual and Native American books. He found and purchased the animal medicine text used by Frenchy and he sat in the car, referencing the book.

Raccoon was the Generous Protector; its medicine offered assistance and protection. The Raccoon card also emphasized being circumspect and to look for those who may profit from one's help and strength; in essence, to seek out a friend in need. He was also reminded he'd drawn the card days before.

Roland deemed it a thoughtful gesture of Mélodie's since he'd chosen the card, a reminder of their time together and the formal communication he felt had been missing—a "no goodbyes, only hellos" greeting. A smile grew on his face. The missive was perhaps also an acknowledgement of the difficulty he faced returning home and that he was being protected perhaps from slipping back to his former ways.

While parking the car, however, Fernanda approached him in the driveway. She handed him from the laundry an item found in the pocket of his dirty shirt—the actual Raccoon card from Mélodie's deck. She had obviously placed it there in his shirt. The fax was clearly a follow-up in case he hadn't seen it.

The message wasn't a greeting; it was Mélodie's call for help.

Day Five

33

That night he tossed in the king bed unable to sleep. The pills kept his synapses firing and nerves abuzz, but his jaws were uncomfortably tight and clamping. He struggled with his predicament, if indeed there was one, his eyes tacked to the ceiling. Sleep was not an option. Then he heard the soft pitter-patter advancing down the corridor.

"Hello," she whispered loud enough for him to hear through the door. She was a fabulously gifted woman at the core for so many reasons and he'd always known that. "May I talk to you?"

"Sure."

The door opened silently and she slipped inside, wearing a translucent nightgown. "I'm so glad you're home. I missed you—"

He said nothing.

"May I lie down?" He was flat on his back as she stretched on the bed with her body angled awkwardly toward him.

She floated a soft arm across his chest and gave him a squeeze, caressing his head and pecking his cheek. Her arm extended beneath the covers and reached lower. He placed his hand atop hers holding it in place, not firmly, but so it wouldn't go further.

They were silent to each other; they were used to it. The recent harrowing events could do nothing to change that. Silence had become the easiest thing to do as husband and wife, but he didn't want things as they used to be.

"I'm scared."

He didn't need to ask her why; he already knew and nodded into the darkness. "Don't be. Things will work out."

"You think so?"

"Not necessarily the way we intend them. I'm not sure if they ever do, but they do work out. Eventually. We both know the deepest blessings are sometimes born of the biggest disappointments."

"What happened to us was not a blessing and it was my biggest disappointment."

He hesitated, wondering whether to tell her or not.

"You know I saw him—clearly. And he was smiling."

She was struck by his words, even the way he spoke them. She wouldn't inquire further. She would give it time. A rush of cool air swept across her face. She lay next to a man she no longer knew, everything confusing to her now.

"I'm sorry," he said.

"No, I'm the one—"

"I wasn't much of a partner. I understand things better now—"

"You may find it hard to believe," she whispered. "But I have always loved you. I've never loved anyone else."

Caught prostrate and excommunicated she fell into a disturbed and tangled sleep, the kind of sleep she had almost gotten used to.

Roland remained still as his wife's body jerked and twitched beside him. Eventually, he spread the quilted throw over her and got up. He found his pair of ancient blue jeans still rolled at the bottom drawer of the bureau and pulled them on along with a T-shirt and sweater.

Mosquitoes and cicadas bounced from the headlights of the sedan as it shimmied up there high on the mesa under the bright white light of the moon now coming off full. Just before three in the morning, he took the serpentining dirt track slowly.

Roland slowed the car adjacent to the plot clearing, got out, and paced up to the monument. He spoke to his boy and revealed his joyous heart at having seen his face glowing and smiling when it appeared to him in the sweat lodge. He took it as a sign his son was comforted and not lost. He would see him soon, but needed more time; how much he wasn't sure, but hoped Gerritt would forgive him for his vacillation and confusion.

Then he prayed and respectfully addressed his influence.

"Great Spirit, I come new to you, but humbly and grateful. As you know the great men of the Havasupai Nation took me in and helped to heal me giving me their medicine, a medicine that brought me to You. I pray for them and their families and thank them for the medicine they've given me.

"I'd like to say another prayer for a friend and special son of yours, Billy Sixkiller. He brought medicine to me, as well, making me see the world through different eyes and giving me another chance at life. I believe his heart is pure; he's trying to overcome his Walk's challenges. It is a dangerous time for him. He needs guidance perhaps like never before and I ask the Great Spirit to look out for him."

Roland uttered a prayer for Mélodie too; that she remain safe and secure as she was perhaps also facing great peril. She'd brought her medicine to him and showed him he could experience love again and whether they were destined to be together or not, he thanked her for that.

Lastly, he prayed for his wife. Though flawed and capable of mistakes, like everyone, she deserved a second chance and he asked the Great Spirit to grant her one. For Gonzalo and Fernanda, he hoped one day they'd receive life's greatest gift: a child of their own.

He invoked the Great Spirit to guide them all on their Walks.

Most of all, he was grateful for having been connected with his son, whom he could see clearly now. The fog had lifted, the pain was released, and the once-crippling memories had dissipated allowing him to cherish his boy freely and without worry. He still hoped to be reunited with the boy, but at a time of the Great Spirit's choosing, not his own.

Roland remained on the mesa painted in silver tasting the crisp October air as it passed over his revived lungs. He relished the night sky and the sweep of city lights below, a city with which he now felt at peace. He wondered what his future held under the guidance of the Higher Being. He considered what could be done to help others in need of his *own medicine* which he now understood he unquestionably possessed.

The crackling of a twig underfoot suddenly spun him around and he saw the two yellow dots lasering at him; twin golden beams firing from a wad of creosote brush. In the silvery light blanketing the thick growth he saw the animal's rear and tail angled to him, its head twisted back over the shoulder and he mulled its significance—a contrary medicine card, he could recall. When Coyote the fabled Trickster crossed one's path in reverse, deception was looming. Landing that card meant someone close may be trying to trick or deceive. He kept the spontaneous nocturnal message from the wild in mind.

34

Roland had breakfast before sunrise at the diner next door to the unobtrusive Motel 6 in Scottsdale, the one he was known to frequent. After finishing his coffee he downed another caffeine tablet. He needed to be expedient as well as vigilant until the situation was resolved. There was no time to catch up on the sleep debt he'd incurred.

In Billy-speak he was a "Ninety-Six." He'd been awake for four days going on a fifth and he would postpone that sit-down with Sheriff Graves, reluctant to risk time away from his friend and his predicament. He sensed a ticking time clock as in a limited window to catch up to them.

He'd be in trouble with the law for leaving town, but he'd be in deeper if he made a formal statement and lied. And he would lie about Billy and Mélodie because the truth was not the truth, they were his friends, his best friends. Even more, they were family, his family, and he needed to protect them.

He set off finally at "six-clock." As it was five hundred miles to Albuquerque, he'd be on the road for a good nine hours.

On the lengthy stretch from Phoenix he noticed numerous vegetable stands selling gourds and wreathes. Pumpkin festivals were advertised roadside along with store windows dressed with scary jack-o-lanterns, ghouls and goblins. The displays reminded him it was October 31st, Halloween. In his repartee with Sheriff Graves he'd articulated a desire to "be himself" for the masquerading holiday with no other character ambitions. He cautiously delighted over what his friends would do to celebrate; no doubt something and who or what they would like to be, the inspired performers they were.

Roland hadn't had extensive contact with Mélodie's age group. She was a Millennial, the unsettled Generation 9/11; a group besieged by tech, social media, celebrity obsession, global uncertainty, the Twin Towers falling, ISIS, global warming, more war, and intravenous Internet feeds overselling it all. He perceived these I-Agers as highly advanced, but paralyzed too by their fast-forwardedness. What used to be "offbeat" locales were no longer in the dark by New York or Washington standards. Palookaville no longer existed. Everyone was able to plug in to Planet America, Planet World, and—scroll down. Not necessarily do. Just watch and move on. Mélodie represented that group, he thought. To her credit, though, she seemed a hybrid. He hadn't noticed any obsession with smartphones or constant need to go online. She was spiritual, enjoyed hardcover books, and sought out nature in the wild. The modern world seemed to inspire the hippy reflex in her, perhaps, a longing and nostalgic embrace of a more giving, trusting, and wholesome time and value system.

On the stretch from Holbrook to Gallup, New Mexico, the legendary Route 66 converted to the I-40, Roland surveyed the pristine interior of his gorgeous Mercedes sedan and became suddenly unnerved. He'd never given thought to cars; he was merely programmed to go for top-of-the-line in elegance and luxury. Yet after traveling with a veritable car freak whose vehicle so typified his essence of being, weighing it now he decided the navy sedan no longer reflected his persona. The immaculate vehicle felt uncomfortable and "not him," or not the way he now perceived himself.

In Gallup he pulled into the first dealership that displayed rows of sparkling new cars. He scanned the selection and paused before a metallic gray Toyota Land Cruiser, an older model.

"Baby's pre-owned, but a classic," he heard from behind. A sturdy man with black hair advanced eagerly, his neck wrapped with a silver and turquoise tie clip. "She'll go five hundred thousand miles …"

"Are you Native American?"

"Betcha. Zuni. Born and raised on the rez."

"What about this one in particular …"

"You'll find out when people leave notes on your wiper asking if you'll sell her. Only fifty thousand miles on her."

He wondered if Billy would recommend the model, but he was also drawn to the authentic spark in the eyes of the Indian man. His sincerity seemed genuine.

"I'll take it."

The car would serve him well on his mission, he thought. Rugged and not readily identifiable like a Mercedes, the vehicle also had temporary New Mex plates, a dressed down and offbeat profile.

On Route 66 east he motored proudly in his new Land Cruiser all the way to Albuquerque absorbing the road color of storied highway Americana. He even enjoyed the flat and boring desert stretches. He had yearnings to make stops like a true "Road Scholar," but was pressed to track down his friend. He vowed to return, however. And he would.

35

The Dolce Vita Diaries VI

We're in New Mexico visiting Tinkertown again—one of my favorite places. Billy didn't go inside, but I had a nice time looking at all the miniature characters.

I'm relieved we got rid of the car, Billy's friend Max (from Telshor) took it in the middle of the night in Madrid. He owns a gas station in Golden. He gave us his Volkswagen bus, a real hippymobile from 1979. I love it. It's bright orange with flower stickers on the windows and we're calling it the Flower Power Mobile.

It has drawers and a sink and a bed and we slept in it last night in his friend's backyard. Finally a good night's sleep! Billy of course was up most of the night listening in. He hasn't been saying much. His spirit is low and he is keeping to himself. I know why. It is not because of me or what happened—he misses Roland.

And so do I—a lot!!!

I worry about Roland, I know he is changed, but how long it lasts I cannot know, as he sees his old life again. This could send him into a depression. I pray for him, such a beautiful man!

I hope he received my message … I know Genesis can't spell!

I am not trying to get Roland to come here for me. (although I think I love him unlike I've ever loved anyone … I feel him so deeply inside me, everywhere on me!) But he is the only one who can save Billy. Billy loves him, truly, and it is a love that has many layers.

How?

Roland was a spirit at the door of death knocking on it. I think Billy knew very soon Roland did not commit those crimes so he kept him around to give him his medicine. When Billy heard he didn't want to live anymore that's when he went to work—peeling away the layers of sadness, loss, and guilt—like a sculptor, hacking away, chipping, and carving him new, with no sleep to protect and comfort him and let him slip back, to strip him raw, every day more raw and vulnerable, then— receptive. Then he fed him with nutrients, the "Nutrients of Life," he said— Nature, History, Brotherhood, the Great Spirit—and in doing so, showing the Love. This revived Roland's spirit and brought him back to life.

Knowing Billy as I do, I'm certain he thinks Roland is his work of art—the masterwork he was trying to make all his life. Roland is a masterpiece, HIS MASTERPIECE, not like pottery or a dead rock sculpture, more alive, "vital" as Billy says—a living sculpture—or maybe a painting, the kind that breathes, like a Botticelli, and he sees Roland as a living breathing spirit to who Billy gave the "Four Rs": resuscitated, revived, rejuvenated, and Renaissanced—he "Renaissanced" him and I understand it now.

Here I thought he was being cruel and foolish when all along Billy had been making beauty. What a masterpiece!!!

I think Billy sees the figure of a father in him too. I could tell he wanted Roland's approval though he would deny it. A friend, a father, a brother, he had that with him—he never had that medicine before, from any white man anyway.

And Billy is like a son to Roland, a man who missed being a father, there was a hole in his life for that. In this way they had medicine for each other and seeing them together was génial. For this reason alone it was worth coming.

I pray I have the strength to help Billy and that Roland will come to help.

It was not the making love to Roland which made Billy upset. He was scared it would change things, and set Roland free and he would lose his friend—that is why he fought us. He was mad at us for ruining the beautiful time they were having, the connection he had made with another human being, finally, after all these years. And the beautiful work of art he was creating because I know how Billy thinks. He saw it developing day after day, getting better and better. He thinks what Roland and I did in making our own beauty together, was stopping his creation before it was finished—like taking an ice pick to his Pieta. I still remember him saying, "#*%^-ing ruins everything!"

But in my opinion his work was done and what we, Roland and I did together, was the proof his creation was art! He took a dead man and made him alive—then made him better! Like what Michelangelo did with chunks of marble, making them come to life—better than life!

Yes, Roland is Billy's masterpiece, the masterpiece he had to give away. That's what upsets him. Billy is not jealous, he wants the best for me, it's why he stopped making love to me. He knew it would be taking me in the wrong direction, to remain hopelessly infatuated and dedicated to him. And I would have been. He is not about sex, he supports whatever will make my spirit grow and being with him intimately was stopping my growth. He wants me to transcend what is ugly in the world, that is what Billy Sixkiller is about. He is a wonderful man and beaucoup misunderstood. I pray Billy doesn't die, but if he does, that he doesn't die that way—misunderstood. Because his medicine is beautiful and that should be known.

Tonight is Halloween and Billy says there's a party. Can you imagine? He is wanted in three states and he's going to a Halloween party! Of course for Billy every day is Halloween!!! I love him so!!!

We are in a real life ghost town now, Cerrillos, in our orange pumpkin-colored Flower Power Halloween Car. That's where the party is—Halloween in a ghost town! In the 1880s, Cerrillos had 21 bars and 4 hotels and it was almost named the capital of New Mexico. The Cerrillos Bar is 94 years old, still owned by the same family. You just walk in and there's no one is inside. Eventually they hear someone is downstairs and they come down as if you have taken them away from their favorite TV show and they ask you "what the hell you want???" Not politely! Like you're bothering the heck out of them! And you are! It's fabulous!

I'm worried we could get caught being in public, but Billy says we're safe with the hippies around, because this is "Hippy Land, USA." These are people who still call cops "Pigs" and the hippies are on our side! Yaaaaaaay! Hooray for the Hippies!!!

I know what I'm going to be for Halloween. "Rhiannon." From the song (Stevie sang it of course!) and the song will be my costume.

> "Rhiannon rings like a bell through the night,
> And wouldn't you love to love her?
> Takes to the sky like a bird in flight,
> And who will be her lover?"

If I were a man I would love to hmmm-hmmm Stevie Nicks. And to hear her sing "Rhiannon" in my ear while I did it! Heaven!!!

> "She is the cat in the night,
> And she is the darkness,
> She lives her life like a fine skylark,
> And when the sky is starlit."

That is woman to me—elusive, magical, free, mysterious, unpredictable, unconsciously and consciously sexy, run by the moon, and the stars, happily so.

(not run by men!!!)

I found a beautiful dress at a hippy vintage store in Madrid and Billy bought it for me. It's deep red, it has frills and lace and ruffled layers. I knew it was Rhiannon, 'taken by the wind,' 'taken by the sky,' living her life like a 'bird in flight' … !!!

(let's not forget the 'cat in the night' … !!!)

Billy thought someone recognized him yesterday in a coffee shop, he got one of those looks. I'm afraid the cops will hurt him badly. Because I know him. He will not surrender.

36

The Land Cruiser reached the outskirts of Albuquerque four hours after its departure from Gallup. Roland continued east past the city proper and climbed through a pass in the nearby Sandía Mountains. "Sandía" which translates to watermelon was the name given to these mountains by settlers from Spain for the color the range turned at sunset. He received an exceptional dose as the afternoon sun waned.

Through the mountain pass Roland turned off at Route 14 north, otherwise known as the Turquoise Trail. He passed through hippy refugee hamlet Madrid and stopped for coffee at Java Junction. He marveled at the galleries of offbeat psychedelic arts and crafts. Men had back-sweeping ponytails and the women wore cheesecloth pullovers and sandals.

At eight-clock, the Land Cruiser pulled into Cerrillos, the tiny town nestled between rolling mountains with its five residential streets, all dirt track and clustered off a main drag. A towering cottonwood stood to the side, its leaves bright yellow. The storefronts gave it the appearance of a western town from the movies. There was a wood-shingled hotel, food market, post office, and the Cerrillos Bar that seemed an authentic saloon from the 1800s. Roland slotted before it and beside a vintage orange Volkswagen bus—a true sixties relic—the only other car visible on the entire street.

Coincidentally, and not terribly so in this one-horse town, Billy and Frenchy were enjoying a round of tequila shots inside the bar with Huey Whitecloud and his wife Dottie. Huey was a Rhode Islander who'd adapted handsomely to the ways of the west. His home doubled for a trading post that doubled for a western museum, two rooms filled with antiques not for sale and western junk that was. Sporting a brown horsetail, he was a good-time hippy imbued with a sixties consciousness. He was the town administrator because no one else wanted the job and the position offered him private access to the town's turquoise mines in the hills behind. He'd brought his two guests for a stone harvest that afternoon.

Huey's wife, Dottie Owens, was tending bar, a husky, cheery-faced woman who peered from behind John Lennon frames. She was the granddaughter of Longburt Owens who'd opened the bar in 1920.

"Got company!" Huey called out in a raspy cackle.

"A customer? Dammit all!"

"Frenchy!" Billy called out. She spun back on her bar stool and caught sight of him, screaming out. They dashed out the door.

"Damn—" Huey said. "Must know 'em."

Frenchy flew into Roland's arms. She embraced and kissed him enduringly, separating barely so Billy could give him a big Indian hug.

Inside was heard a deadpan, "Yup."

"Look at you all showered and cleaned up like a baby!"

"Great to see you, Billy—"

The former captor's laugh was infectious and everyone whooped it up. Frenchy let loose her soccer club fan appreciation whistle. She turned to the man she'd longed for and they both saw it, their togetherness trapped and glimmering in each other's eyes. They kissed again.

"We got us a shindig tonight!" Billy announced.

"What are you gonna be?" Frenchy posed eagerly.

"Let him be himself for a change! Then again, maybe not!"

They all split up.

"I do know what I'm going to be," he countered. "The most popular Halloween character in Arizona this year, according to the Arizona Republic—*Billy Sixkiller!*" The reveal unleashed an uproar.

"No shit! Then I'll be *you!*"

"Second most popular!"

"Been the Mad Hatter for sixteen consecutive years, but tonight I will be," and he teased, impersonating him, "—Roland Polsonby."

"What about you, Mélodie?" Roland asked her.

"Rhiannon," she said. "It's a song."

"A beautiful one. A song is perfect." The two seemed to be in that special space again, tingling in each other's proximity.

"Course I said she should be the Who Cares? Cover Girl—"

"Would need a twist though, no?" Roland proposed. "Like that she actually *cares*—"

"The Who Cares? Cover Girl who cares ..." Frenchy processed.

"Doggonit, you're right! The ultimate horror! Obsessed with her looks, desperate to be beautiful to the point of turbo plastics and fix-me TV, the tacky, trashionista, anti-natural, Queen of the Dolce Vita Follies pouring out the spigot!"

"*Woof*, sounds great!" Frenchy spun, sarcastic. "What would I look like? The happy jumping hooker?"

Roland gathered her and smooched her smoothly, a kiss that lasted again.

"Well, if I ain't the odd man out—"

"You're never the odd man out," Roland asserted. "You're the odd man, rather, the very strange man *in*." They others laughed.

"Listen to that sense of humor just crackle. Damn if you ain't been Renaissanced," Billy said in his freshly adopted New Mex twang.

Then both men turned to each other and locked on and lifting it from sensorial memory they delivered it together, *"Turd burglars!!!"*

They buckled like children nearly spiraling to the ground.

Seemingly a sophomoric guy thing, their spontaneous hysteria was more drug-induced and biochemical in nature. Once the psilocybin curtain had been lifted at Havasu Falls and the barrier crossed, they'd arrived at a certain psychological station, a wavelength of philosophical truth and humor sparked now merely by the presence of each other's company and the mix of their energies in proximity.

"Had him bound and gagged and he never said anything—now we can't shut him up!"

The sun dipped below the hill crests that sheltered the turquoise mines leaving a gorgeous and cool purple night sky and Roland recounted his tortuous journey home from Supai for all to hear.

Dottie emerged and held trays aloft; one with tequila shots, the other beer chasers and everyone downed the shots. Roland pondered whether to or not. Other issues weighed on his mind.

"Hey, barkeep," Huey drawled, "what about me?"

"You fella, been overserved!"

"Overserved? I'm the mayor! Next thing she'll have me strung up on that hanging tree!"

They all twisted around and the group took in the old cottonwood, its thick main artery branch suspended right over Main Street.

"Really? That's a hanging tree?" Frenchy gasped, struck by it. *"Dídons ..."*

"Claimed eighteen, she done," Dottie chirped.

Everyone paused, gazes falling silently on the tree and an eerie feeling crept in and hovered—it was Halloween, no less.

"Zat poor tree," Frenchy observed. "All the history and still hanging over the town, the sad form of the arm reaching out, fighting time and the memories, spanning across like a bridge from the past—

like a ghost—forced to do horrible things, none of its own desire, enduring eighteen cries of death, yet it stands still with such pride, purpose, and integrity ... And she's a daily reminder how evil mankind, man-not-so-kind can be ..."

Her poignant words furthered the quiet and they all stood in silence, reflecting.

"Damn if she ain't a poet," Billy issued finally, impressed.

"*Brava*, Mélodie," Roland remarked. "The work on your journal shows." She was pleased to hear it. "Journals are transcriptions to the soul and the content can be called upon whenever needed ..."

"Maybe you should keep one again," she said, the implication not lost on him.

"Think I will."

"I want to trip with *her* ..."

The out-of-the-blue comment caught their attention. They all spun back around and eyed Dottie and burst out laughing in unison.

"Aw hell with you all! Squares!" was her response, which prompted more hilarity.

"I'm so excited!" Frenchy redirected. "Let's get dressed!"

Another round of TQ was poured inside the bar, but Frenchy bowed out to get ready for the evening. Roland stayed on with Billy.

"Huey, you know we're short on trick or treats," Dottie declared, before she joined Frenchy outside to escort her home.

"Aw, come on! I went to Target twice this week."

"We'll go," Billy volunteered. "Roland and me."

As his friend downed the shot, Roland wheeled away to not be observed and spiked another caffeine pill. He'd keep mum on the dangers of running a public errand with Billy Sixkiller—for now.

The two finished their drinks and stumbled out of the bar. On the street Billy took a moment to admire and praise the Land Cruiser, but insisted however on taking his new orange toy. Roland did not protest. They got in and he started it up.

"Hear that tranny? Beetles, Fastbacks, Squarebacks, the VW bus all had that same engine. Sound takes you back, doesn't it?"

"Haven't had this much alcohol in a while—"

"Drive better with a little TQ; the landscape pops. What was it like in Phoenix?"

"Same, really."

"Your wife?"

He switched it up soberly instead. "I spoke with Graves …"

Billy glanced quickly at him. "Yeah, what'd he have to say?"

"Your father was a cop—"

And the man bulldozed right over it. "What he want from you?"

"A statement."

"You give it?"

"No. I came here."

"Why?"

"To help."

"Me? I don't need help—got everything worked out."

"Billy—"

"I'm serious. No one can help me. Can hurt, but not help—"

"Turn yourself in—"

"I'll say it once. No way I'm going back to four walls and a pee-pot, no frickin' way!"

Target was located in a sprawling mall off Route 14 on the way to Santa Fe. Billy docked the bus boldly near the store's entrance.

"Be right back," Roland announced to counter his maneuver.

"I'm comin'." The mutual glares played to a standoff. "You don't get all the fun—it's Halloween!"

The intoxicated pair drifted inside unevenly, assaulted by blinding fluorescent lights and an endless labyrinth of product-filled aisles.

"You have a chance; a well-documented history of mistreatment—"

"A well-documented history of breaking the law—"

"Nothing that can't be challenged in a new trial with a good lawyer, best lawyer money can buy—"

Billy angled over and his friend affirmed the implied offer with a nod.

"A mite assertive you've become. Impressive. Now where's all the damned candy? Says aisle '3.' "

"I'd be a witness."

"Yeah, you—another kidnap victim. Case sounds like a regular slam dunk—"

"Ssssh, Billy listen …"

His former captor suddenly spun into him and cut him short in the middle of the toiletries section. "Don't do this," he played in a threatening tone, "or I'm gonna take you for a squid ink pasta special."

Roland had readied a speech he'd formulated for what seemed like days, but was temporarily stymied by the potent spirits. "… What?"

"Make you a black-toothed ghoul all day …"

"What are you talking about?"

Billy found it so funny he doubled in half.

"I got a friend in Pahonix—that's 'Phoenix' for dumb asses—if he doesn't like someone or can't do business with him, like can't get what he wants, he takes 'em for lunch at a swank Italian restaurant and recommends the squid ink pasta lunch special, his treat. Says it's the best thing on the menu only he can't have it cause of the iodine in the ink that doesn't bother most—and he's buying! And most folk, dirty scavengers they are, they'll take the free lunch …"

"Why does he do that?"

"To fuck 'em up. So the idiot goes around the rest of the day looking like a jackass, smiling at people and they all see his dirty black teeth and them folk run for the hills!"

Roland burst out. "The squid ink pasta special?"

"But it's gotta be lunch—"

"Why?"

" 'Cause then you look like an asshole all day long! Eat it at night, no one sees your scary grill and the black Orc teeth!"

They were uproarious.

Eventually their department store safari yielded the candy section and they stocked up on favorites and drunkenly munched all the way out to the car in the parking lot and on the drive home.

Once they delivered the booty Huey gave Roland a tour of the trading post. There were knick-knacks of all sorts; silver rings, skulls, bear teeth, Indian beads, and assorted oddities, even inventive pipes for smoking whatever.

In the stonecutting workshop Billy offered Roland one of the turquoise nuggets he'd gathered in the mines. "You can make something for the frogette—"

For the next hour, the pair toiled on gemological creations. They cut, sanded, and shaped, crafting pretty stones with Huey's help. They huddled there polishing away all the while sobering somewhat until Huey brought in double shots for each and they were soon delivered back to that inebriated state.

"You gonna take care of her?" Billy slurred. "Or was she just a three-and-out fuck?"

"What do you think?"

"Ain't punting her, eh? That's good … gotta know she's in good hands."

His friend eyed him cautiously at the ominous implication.

"I scare you, Roland?"

"No, Billy." He shook too. "You're an inspiration."

"You know I've told you everything you never wanted to know about yourself … So now you tell me about me."

"Happy to," he said forthrightly. "You have an abundance of words, as much as anyone I've ever known. With an ability to articulate them. If there's something I know a little bit about it's language and you are a master. I've only known you a few days, but I know how much you care, it comes through the words, right through the skin and grabs you. You can be a mean bastard because of your past and your disappointment in the way things are. Human nature. And the sadness follows you like a shadow, but you need sun to make a shadow. You're brilliant, you radiate, and at the core you're warm—you have a lot of sun. I was lucky you came across my Walk. You saved my life, Billy Six. And I'm damned proud to say you're my brother."

The man chuckled there and his eyes misted. "Great Spirit brought you back to us—"

"Perhaps. But I know I came for you."

"Destiny rules."

"And aren't we the better for it—?"

"Listen to you—"

"But destiny's rules can be modified—"

Billy's head snapped up and bobbed with a hazy glaze to his eyes. He eyed the resolute man taken momentarily by his "creation," which allowed for the faintest spark of self-gratification. And that was all. He grinned pridefully. His work was done. "Gal's fantastic … that's where you're lucky."

"She's been put on a proper path. I know you've had difficult times together, but you're responsible in many ways, good ways."

"Young lady is—"

He decided to tease and play with him in a Billy-like way to elevate him from his brooding fatalistic mood. "Don't say 'a keeper,' you can do better—"

"She's way more than that—"

"Tell me Mr. Sensitized and make it good—"

"She's—"

"Damn, I'm dying here, Billy Six," he ribbed. "It's a one-man show, thought you had all the sledgehammer verbiage," he badgered.

" … The Perfect Egg."

Roland skipped a breath and they both stopped talking. Their silence was in homage to the brilliant coining and encapsulation. They eyeballed one another knowingly, gathered their stones, and staggered outside arm in arm.

"The Perfect Egg," Roland repeated eventually, like Billy would.

"Wished you'd said it?"

"You bet; the Perfect Egg. Don't mind if I steal it, do you?"

37

Huey had livestock pens in the backyard and the two wandered over to the llama cage and hand fed oats to the furry animals.

"Kinna stinks—"

An idea came to Billy then. "Wait a second!"

"I know!"

"That's what she should be!"

"For Halloween!"

Together they said, *"THE PERFECT EGG!!!"*

"No, we can't—"

"You're right."

"Perfect never works."

"Too chauvinistic."

"Nothing wrong with that—"

"Second wave of feminism is upon us—"

"No matter. These days with the rise of the pussy, the overly sensitized male, and I say, metro boy, the one mating with his feminine side, as well as the caveman experiencing a streaking decline and approaching endangered species status, 'Save the Caveman' bumper stickers and all that, chauvinistic humor works. Can be funny—"

"True, but the implications are off."

"Because then, you're the Perfect Sperm."

"Hadn't thought of that, but check."

"What are we talking about?"

"I don't know!"

"Tequila physics—"

"We're manufacturing nonsense!"

"Genius, isn't it?"

"Think we throw that term around too easily?"

"Of course we do."

"But do we deserve it?"

Together, *"YES!"*

Billy fumbled through his pockets and removed a couple of shiny sticks of sorts. "Get over here, big boy—"

"What are you holding?"

"Target's got everything, amazing, ain't it?" Roland jerked away. "Stay close, I'm gonna do your eyes—"

"You mean makeup?"

"Hush! Rise of the femmy male—"

Who was Roland to say no at this point? Billy squared before him and gently applied the brush to the man's eyelashes and lined them with dark pencil, nearly a professional effort. As a finisher, he flicked a pinch of glitter and the shiny flecks speckled down over him.

"Nothing more enhancing than a little liner and fairy dust. And then absolutely denying it to anyone who asks—"

"Denying it?"

"It's hysterical, you'll see—"

"Why the glitter?"

"So you leave a sparkle trail wherever you go—good for the spirit, makes everybody surge—"

He quickly administered some to his own face.

"Would appear you've done it before—"

Billy cracked one proudly.

"Hello, boys—"

The soused duo were startled and spun clumsily around. At that point their jaws just fell barely clinging to the skin holding them in place. Standing before them both was a sight to behold—a vision. She looked out of this world and it started with the hair.

Rhiannon's mane had been teased high and windswept back to reflect the "taken by the wind" lyric; her aqua pool eyes gone cat-like with extended mascara lines for supreme "she is like a cat in the dark" prowling. The rest of her face was powdered deeply *Vogue*, the makeup consisting of turquoise, gold, red, and purple eye shadow: the colors of a southwestern sunset. Her long nails were fiery orange-red, her pouty lips were greased deeper red, and she wore scarlet bejeweled pumps with Navajo jasper beads wrapping her neck. The vintage red-ruffled gypsy dress brought it all together and Rhiannon even had a thin gold necklace with tiny bell attached to "ring like a bell in the night." She looked absolutely stunning.

"So I ask you, Roland, 'who will be her lover?' " Billy prodded, incorporating the song's famous line. *"You!"*

"And, wouldn't I 'love to love her'?"

Frenchy had hoped for her imagination-best as she'd never been looking so forward to a night.

"How do I look?" she asked him sweetly, but privately—it mattered of course.

Roland eased into her captivated by the vision. "Artistic, happy, hippy, you're music, you're a song. See? You *are* Rhiannon ..."

Frenchy embraced him and squeezed with everything.

"Hey wait—" She took note of something. "Are you guys wearing makeup?"

"What are you talking about?" Billy blasted.

"Are you out of your mind?" Roland followed suit and they both broke up, their pixelated merriment so virulent she had to burst out, too.

"Sparkles? You guys are fruit men!" she Franglais-ed. The boys were crying with laughter. "Now I know why your nature walks took so long!"

"Don't say it, Roland—"

"No, I won't—"

"Turd burglars!" they bellowed.

"I'm going out with a couple of queens! Beelly, I knew about you, but Roland, you too?"

"They call it the Turquoise Trail, but we know it's—"

"The Hershey Highway!" they squealed together.

At that moment, Frenchy spun around and curved a wary eye at Roland as he tried to calm himself.

"What?" he posed to her glare of disapproval. "I'm not anti-gay. It's just funny."

"Judgment free zone," Billy seconded.

"Did Billy make you speak this way? He can't leave talking of the ass alone!"

"No, I swear. He didn't. My father was old fashioned that way."

"A bigot?"

Roland paused and through the fog of his stupor processed the fact that they were having their first row.

"When I was younger my friends and I turned those prejudices into humor. I haven't heard this kind of talk in years. I've never felt threatened by people's orientations; I've always been tolerant. I was brought up this way."

"Overkill, Roland," Billy contended.

"It's not overkill, Billy!" she snapped, embracing her new strength. "I want to know about my man. I need to."

"I'm sorry," Roland said. "We were just having a little fun."

"I know," she said.

"And I'm so very appreciative you are sensitive to it."

They kissed then and Billy stood there respectfully in silence.

"We're turd-secure, dammit," Billy added finally and Roland broke from her lips and the embrace and fell to the ground, once again in hysterics. Even Frenchy had to laugh.

*   *   *

The men borrowed each other's clothes for their costumes and Frenchy finished off their makeup. She slicked Billy's hair with gel and darkened it with shoe polish while penciling in a hairline that slashed back at the temples like his friend's. Billy borrowed Huey's blue oxford identical to the prisoner's during the abduction and he donned Roland's sunglasses. Dark circles were smudged to his eyes as well. He added an old pair of western handcuffs from the trading post to dangle from a wrist.

Roland's hair was coiffed to match the captor's wildly disheveled nest and Frenchy painted in the silvery widow's peak and sketched in fuller eyebrows. He had the aviators and black jeans, a short-sleeved white button-down along with the black chauffeur's cap and the snip-toed snakeskin boots.

Dottie, meanwhile, lined the driveway with tiny candles placed in brown paper bags to welcome trick-or-treaters who were already stopping by.

Huey extended the pistol to Roland that hushed the group. "How can you be Billy Six without a six-shooter?"

"But it looks real."

"*Is* real. You're in New Mexico!"

No one cared to confront the logic.

Roland quietly handed Frenchy her turquoise heart and was rewarded for it with the softest, most luscious kiss. And he kissed her tiny tear away.

38

The spirited trio took to the ghost town in costume. They spied on trick-or-treaters, witnessed their grab bag fervor, and overheard the children's mischievous strategies. In the shadows they even squared off with an enormous bull on the lam from a nearby pen. The animal was massive silhouetted by moonlight and the Texas horns so arresting they screamed and ran.

The New Mexico night was crisp, clear, and starry and the group settled beneath the unsung hanging tree. After years of spooking people with its frightening and macabre history, Frenchy wanted to honor it. She asked the others to participate in a moment of silence and prayer to a "God of Choice" for a tree she deemed "falsely maligned and abused," like many of Earth's survivor trees.

Billy versed a Supai equivalent. He added, "Will you guys stay up with me tonight?"

"Do we know any other way?"

"Guess not—when we get together, it's one all-nighter after another." He spun around and slipped into the bar for another round.

The couple cozied up at the base of the tree's massive trunk and she lay against him. "Did you speak to him?"

"I tried ... I'm not done."

"When he has his mind made up—"

"It's twice as dangerous," he finished for her.

The young woman before him was another person from the one he'd first met, Roland reflected. In effect she'd grown up before his eyes becoming her own woman. She asked him something, but he was distracted feeling the effects of the wear and tear on his mind and body. *"Comment?"* he posed finally on delay.

"I said there are lots of ways to take action—wait!" she stopped herself. "You speak French?"

"Bien sûr—"

"I didn't know that! *Beelly!* He speaks French!" she called out even though he couldn't hear her.

Down the street they heard Dottie chasing off some machete-wielding goblins too old to be trick-or-treating. The place hushed quiet again and it now seemed empty, ghost town-empty, meaning deserted.

Frenchy drew Roland close and his head rested on her breast. Her chin tucked it beneath and she petted him. "I bet you're wonderful to watch sleep," she whispered.

"I hope you're around to see."

"I will be." As she caressed him her hand grazed something angular and seemingly out of place in his pocket. "*Qu'est ce que c'est?*"

"Sssssh—"

"Show me—"

"Pills. To keep me going …"

"You mean … Have you slept?" She felt his head shake on an angle away. "You haven't slept since I met you? Not once?"

Prompted, he tapped out a pill and downed it as an answer.

"Baby?" she called him a first time.

The sound was too beautiful. He'd overextended his capacities and was appreciably more stripped now, his nerves frazzled. He was also tipsy and water accumulated in his eyes, but he knew to keep going—he had to. "There's time for that."

She bowed lower, her lips pressed to his ear. "I'm so frightened."

He let it pass mercifully for both of them.

"Was it difficult going back?"

"Easier … everything was so clear. I had time with my boy; a good time, for the first time." He collected. "We were brought back together with his help. And yours. Thank you for that."

"Are you back?"

"Would appear so."

"Is that a 'yes?'"

Her words were soothing and he admired her feeling at once proud and fortunate. "You *are* the Perfect Egg …"

"That's the nicest thing I've ever heard."

"He came up with it, I admit," he said. "Begrudgingly," he added and they laughed. "He said it about you."

"Billy said that?" She was perhaps even more touched as Billy had always parceled his praise for her. "That's a lot to live up to …"

She rose with her shoes in one hand and extended her free hand to him. He clasped it and stood up and their chests met.

"I couldn't describe you accurately without feeling I'd stolen from you."

She kissed him. "You just did."

"Where's Billy?"

39

The couple joined Dottie in the bar. When Huey stepped inside, the limes were diced in a hurry, the ZZ Top kicked in, and more tequila shots were poured.

"Can anyone tell me where the word 'hippy' comes from?" the eccentric mayor blasted. "Roland? I'll buy you a drink—"

"Don't know—"

"Give ya a hint. San Francisco."

"Comes from San Francisco! Big hint!"

The door swung open and Billy pushed through grinning away. He'd been monitoring the portable shortwave in the bus. He grabbed Frenchy by the hand and had her join him in a Texas two-step.

Dottie handed Billy a beer. He was hyper and seemed boosted by the reports as it appeared law enforcement had no idea he was in New Mexico.

"Billy boy? Where does the term 'hippy' come from?"

"The opium dens, of course."

"Bingo!"

"But what about heeppee? I want to know!"

"Okay, my little roasted artichoke from Mante-La-Jolie!"

"I am not from Mante! *You* are!" she burst out.

Their relationship had been teetering a while in that indefinable, declassified space and Roland was pleased to see it had found new ground, if not a new identity. They had become loving siblings.

"When addicts smoked pipes in the opium parlors," he expounded, "they'd turn to their sides rolling on their hips. Smoking opium induces vomiting and it positioned them to let fly …"

The door flew open again and banged loudly. The stranger in full Halloween costume was posing as a white-collar criminal, a business suit with play money popping from the seams. A skullcap made him bald.

"Where the hell am I?" he belched obnoxiously. "Other than lost!"

"Who's the ostrich?" Huey assessed, Dottie hushing him.

"What's an ostrich?" Roland whispered.

" 'Asshole' in New Mexicalese. You all gonna stand there? Come on! Get the ostrich a shot!"

The man stepped up to the bar and Dottie slid him one.

"Wow, you girls look *mahvelous!* " he cracked. "Guess I came to the right place, I'm Mike Tuccio—" Frenchy shook his hand. In his thirties he was cocksure with the heightened sensibilities of a frat house social chairman to go with the metro accent. The man had an abrasive, unruly edge.

"New Yorker," Roland placed.

"You got it!" came right back. "Had a few on the plane already, what the hell ..." The guy threw back the shot. "Damn!" he reacted wincing. "Tryin' to get to Santa Fe, party there—"

"Santa Fe's thirty miles up the road—"

"What party?"

"My parents are throwin' it for their friends. Father's retired, bought a place there, supposed to be sweet—"

"What do you do in Nuevo York?" Dottie asked.

"I'm a trader."

"What do you trade?" Billy asked as he stepped in front of Frenchy imposingly to box him out from her while facing off and away.

"You name it—trade you for *her!*" he gibed, laughing at the crack and ignoring the freshly imposed choreography. Leaning past Billy he tossed a lure. "Wanna go to a party? Big house, Jacuzzi—" he said, spearing out a hand again.

"Think you already shook," Billy informed.

"Hey, lighten up, mister big boy pants—"

Frenchy immediately interjected to neutralize any further spike in ill will. "What's your costume?"

The ill-humored crack still hovered perilously and Roland saw the intruder's eyes widen. The out of towner's splashy confidence released in a whistle like a radial pierced by a six-inch nail. The man averted Billy's penetrating glare now and pivoted back while reaching for something to hold—his beer.

"That's mine," Frenchy advised.

"I'm sorry," he said suddenly polite.

"So what's your getup all about?" Dottie pursued.

The man's cocky constitution was all but gone. "Kozlowski."

"Who?"

"Corporate head," Roland supplied to contribute to the relaxing of tensions. "Tyco. But he's so five years ago. Take off the hairless cap and be Madoff ..."

The intruder nodded deferentially. "Him too, yeah—embezzlers— that's who I chose this year." The man appeared skittish now and backtracked, his mind more focused on the door. "So I take Route 14 to Santa Fe?"

"Bingo—"

"Ladies," he said bowing. Then he eyed the men, but not Billy. "See ya, guys." The man slipped out the door as if suddenly in a hurry.

The group engaged in decidedly pointed chatter and replaced "ostrich" with the real term while, outside, the New Yorker charged to his car, got in it, and anxiously finger-pecked away at his iPhone.

"Dammit, Marty!" he fired to a voicemail. "You're not gonna fuckin' believe this! I'm in this redneck shit-kickin' bar standing next to 'Billy the Kid'! The guy on the cover of *The Post!* The one who took the hostage and let him go? He's fuckin' nuts and he *looks* fuckin' nuts! And get this, I think he's with the guy he kidnapped!" he howled. "I'm not makin' this up! And if I brought this guy in? Can you imagine the bump we'd get? Press worth millions! He's right here for the taking! I'm gonna bring in Billy the Fuckin' Kid! Beats watching the Knicks getting slammed at the Garden, tell you that!"

His car door was then whipped wide.

"Not gonna happen," a stern voice avowed.

The guy jerked in fright. A handgun was leveled at him and the perpetrator was wearing the mask of the Iraqi Information Minister—a Halloween cult favorite—the figure who brazenly proclaimed ridiculous Revolutionary Guard daily triumphs as the Coalition rout was on in the war in Iraq.

"Put the phone down—"

As the barrel was aimed steadily at the driver, the masked man rounded the car and opened the passenger door, getting in.

"Hey, I didn't mean nothin', swear—"

"Now, drive—"

The car eased down the access road from Cerrillos and headed north on 14. The ten-minute drive was silent except for when the Wall Streeter whimpered, then broke down into tears, begging for his life.

The masked man left him wondering and the perpetrator felt the punishment fit the crime. "Trick or treat."

The guy was ordered to veer down a dirt track off 14 and he became even more of a basket case. He sniffled like a dog and his hollow urban machismo revealed itself for what it was.

When the car stopped, the masked man removed the key and moved to the driver's side. "Get out." He was given an awl and hammer and was ordered to puncture holes in the metal.

"Put four in it—"

With the gun barrel leveled on him, the man proceeded to bang away at the rear hatch. His shaky hands completed the task while pounding thumbs and knuckles twice. He was then forced to hop in and the hatch was shut down over him.

The perpetrator peeled off the mask and ran back out to the highway as the Land Cruiser slowly coasted past. Frenchy jumped over and Roland took the wheel spinning the car back around.

"Beelly said he was spotted at Target, there are things set up—"

"Dammit. What things?"

"He said on the radio, the police—"

"*Mélodie*—" he barked, the first time she'd heard him raise his voice. "Are there road blocks or not?"

"Yes," she said, taken aback.

He apologized for snarling, but didn't speak the rest of the way. Frenchy wasn't upset. With respect to Roland Polsonby, his leadership was what she'd prayed for.

40

The music was blaring inside the Cerrillos Bar as Billy was now "spinning" vintage southern rock from his own portable device. Roland slipped behind the bar and stuffed away the borrowed mask, sending a nod of collusion to Huey. The others were unaware what had happened.

Tasting a fear he'd hoped to avoid—and it wasn't Billy being out of sorts or having erred pulling a gun on a man—it was the fact he was more attentive to present dangers than the mastermind. How to plot and manipulate to get away with something had never been his areas of expertise. And he knew it and it was deeply troubling.

Billy swarmed and hurled an arm around him. "Where you been, brother? Got something for ya—" He dragged him to the other end of bar where whiskey shots awaited them. They each downed one. Roland was still gripped, his senses on high alert, the trepidation mounting. "Hey, you okay?"

"Yeah, sure, Billy. As long as we get out of here …"

"But we got a festival on the rez—"

"That New Yorker was turning us in. We gotta move—"

Billy threw a scrambled look at him, head bobbing. "Okay, okay."

"Billy—"

"After this round we're gone all right? Bottom's up!"

"Roadblocks, Billy? On the interstates? And local highways?"

"Damn—frog gets intimate and her discretion's shot to hell."

"Yeah, well, don't leave me in the dark. We're in this together."

"Do that shot 'n I'll answer you straight up."

Roland paused then did it only to avoid wasting time.

"*New Mexico* cops," Billy rewarded him. "Now there's a sorry-ass bunch."

"Forces from the Four Corners are after you! Graves told me—"

"Then how come they ain't found me yet? Huh?"

"Look over there—Frenchy—she's family. And me: family."

"—perfect egg," he goofed with a silly grin.

"Right! And let's say maybe you can get beyond this. A house, ranch, family, whatever. Fresh start, Billy."

"Little Billie-willies," he giggled morosely.

"The day is coming when it will be all over, I promise."

"Yes, it will," he sent back vaguely, with hints of gloom.

"Make that day sooner than later—"

"I intend to—"

"Make it now. Whole new beginning …"

Billy guffawed at the stark impossibility. Then his grill twisted and clarity dropped a special instant as if maybe there might be another way. Roland was encouraged, hoping he'd broken through.

"Make you a guarantee here 'n now … No Four Corners cops'll ever take me down—I guarantee it. How's that?"

"Wonderful. And what about her?"

"Mélodie—?" he intoned, half-teasing.

"Can you guarantee her safety?"

"Can leave any time she wants."

"She won't leave you. I won't leave you. We want to help you get out of this—"

"Now that's comedy—a frogerazzo and a dolce vita fiction writer getting me out of this! That prods my funny bone."

"If you won't do it for yourself, do it for her!"

The man beamed one stupidly and Roland grabbed him by the collar aggressively shaking him. "Billy—*think!*"

The black eyes were set afire and the frightening glare was back. He wrestled himself free and shoved Roland slamming him to the wall.

"I will never turn myself in—got it? Fifteen years of my life in those joints, I'll never go back! *GOT IT?*" He shouted.

He waddled off and cursed again, loudly silencing the room.

"I'm going to Colorado as planned! Frenchy, you can walk now and spare yourself my phantasmagoric flight into freedom and destiny …"

He waited on her reaction. She shook her head at the futility.

"All right. Rollie? You can hit the road. No one's stopping you …"

Roland withstood it. He'd surrender—for the moment.

"Good. Now where's the damned music???"

The cheers of a live audience rose up. Billy had selected a cut from a concert recording and cranked it. " '*What song is it you want to hear?*' " the voice bellowed to the crowd. " '*FREEBIRD!*' " The crowd roared, and Billy hollered along with it.

The seventies rock and roll Skynyrd anthem dropped with the piano intro and sadly weeping guitar. Billy's eyes sealed softly as if the music incited a temporary personal spiritual retreat. He snatched another glass, poured one, and raised it.

"Wanna thank you all, this special night. Huey and Dot, best ghost town hosts! My oldest and dearest friend, the 'cat in the dark and she is the darkness,' Mélodie 'Frenchy' dee Charlebois, a gypsy's gypsy, my Little Mistral-gone-blossoming Butterfly—"

Weak cheers resounded. Terrified, Frenchy brushed away a tear.

"And my best friend in the world—RDP—who I put through hell and back, but worth every damned minute of it, wa'n'it, brother?"

"Every damned …" Roland barely lifted his glass.

"Great One be with you—all of you!"

They gathered in song, spewing the ballad atonally while extending arm in arm as Billy went down the line conducting the chorus.

> *"I must be traveling on now,*
> *'Cause there're too many places I've got to see,*
> *But if I stayed here with you girl,*
> *Well things just couldn't be the same,*
> *Cause I'm as free as a bird now,*
> *And this bird you'll never change …"*

As the army of thrashing guitars was unleashed, the group whooped and hollered, danced, and arms interlocked at the elbows spun. Billy, Roland, and Huey arched their backs and pretended to grind the axes where they stood.

> *"Oh won't you fly high? oh free bird, yeah! …"*

Billy vaulted to the bar top and the men joined, then Frenchy, even Dottie, and five across they sawed off some stinging air guitar for six minutes as the song's guitar solo screeched on and on and on and on.

Day Six

41

At four in the morning, the group took flight. Dottie prepared Spanish short coffees made of espresso and warm milk to serve as eye-openers for the coming journey.

"Takes booze in yer gut, mixes it right," she said. "For sleep it puts you out, if you need to rise you'll be wired like a woodpecker, the beauty of the *cortado*—"

After a round of hugs the vehicles took to the road.

The couple drove miles ahead to scout in the Land Cruiser. Billy trailed in the bus. They were in mobile phone contact in case problems arose. The Colorado border was two hundred miles away and the strategy once again was to utilize the back roads across the Indian territories. They headed west in the black of night through the San Felipe and Zia rezes. Billy surged ahead and turned onto dirt track through the Jemez Indian lands which bordered the Santa Fe National Forest. In the remote town of Cuba Roland refueled both vehicles.

They motored north through the Jicarilla Apache rez, quashing inspired attempts by Billy to show them Chaco Culture, the ancient ruins due west in a stretch of wide open and barren landscape.

Cutting through the private territories paid off. Around six, they crossed the border into Colorado on lone gravel track in the lowland rez of the Southern Ute tribe. Continuing north all the way to Hesperus they reached a remote private ranch just before dawn.

The bus was in the lead again and Billy pursued the wandering ranch road past enormous tractor and feed barns. A mousy, wiry man rushed out to greet them grinning from ear to ear. He had missing uppers, a bulbous nose, and a red Agway cap crowning his head.

"Mad Max," Billy muttered under his breath as he braked hard. He dashed out in a hurry and barely acknowledged the expectant man.

"Billy Six!" the cheerful man hollered.

"It be November first."

"Yer *late!*"

"Ten minutes! Big deal!" Billy was already sprinting to the barn.

The man checked his watch. "Twelve!" he corrected. "That means no ... birdie ..." his voice trailed off as he saw Billy couldn't hear him.

Roland emerged from his car and introduced himself to Max.

"*Ungawa*," Max returned, employing Billy-speak of course. "Heard a lot about ya," he prattled. "Read some too—"

"So," the former captive processed, "this detour was planned?"

"Teed up years ago. Bet him he wouldn't make it under par—"

"You mean today? November 1st? This meeting right here was planned years ago?"

"Yump."

"The date never changed?"

"Time never done. Six-clock-thirty. It's six-clock-four-two. *Slowpokes.* And he owes me one!"

"One what?"

"A Kennedy half! Silver! You bet …"

What had seemed a most spontaneous charge, a road trip free of temporal constraints, had been on a time clock and the mastermind had been only minutes off. The unpredictable one had worked it to his specifications—*Billy-time*—and Roland couldn't help but be astounded.

A sudden roar of jubilation erupted from within the gargantuan red barn.

Roland advanced and stepped inside the expansive structure which was dimly lit by a few hanging light bulbs. He passed beyond a run of rusty farm vehicles and tractors and came upon the featured spectacular. Shiny, new, and—no longer white—the Ivory Stretch had been painted a dazzling sapphire blue! Her metallic coat shimmered and she was galactically gorgeous in her new hue.

Billy appeared ecstatic as he admired the fresh and sparkling veneer of his beloved possession. Unable to control himself any longer, he jumped behind the wheel, turned it over, and guided it out the structure.

He parked it beside the other vehicles, but not too close. He wanted her to stand alone. He vaulted from the car beaming.

"What do you think?"

Roland shuffled up, unconcerned with car color changes. He was more consumed with the predicament at hand and the latest tactics.

"Lovely."

"And Colorado plates, no less. Fine job, Max!"

"In the sun that blue sparkle like a starry night sky," Max piped.

Frenchy made a groggy pilgrimage in her rumpled Rhiannon costume and wild Halloween hair. She planted and yawned, disregarding the adventure's latest attraction. "*J'ai faim …*"

Billy was waiting on her. "Yo, Frenchy!"

"What? *Ooh-la-la,*" she reacted. "She's *magnifique …*"

"Road Scholars, I present to you, 'The Sapphire Stretch.' Come on, get in!"

Roland showed sudden concern. "You're going to drive it?"

"What do you think? I'm gonna piddle around in that piece of shit bus the rest of my life?"

"Don't say that," Frenchy objected. "The Flower bus was good to you."

"You think no one will notice it now?"

"Buys time … some anyway—"

"After Ouray then what, Billy?"

"Full of love and joy this morning, aren't you? Stay awake again? You keep forgettin' you're not a prisoner any more—"

"What's next?"

Roland craned around for support. Curiously, Frenchy stayed silent. She was no doubt deeply worried for Billy. He was wanted in two states, going on a third, and yet she remained reticent and the former prisoner wondered why and where did she stand now?

"What's next is a reminder," Billy responded. "A quote by 'Effy' Scott, Fitzgerald that is, and what he termed the 'wise and tragic sense of life.' That, 'life is essentially a cheat and its conditions are those of defeat, and the redeeming things are not happiness or pleasure, but the deeper satisfactions that come from struggle.' " My struggle, Roland. My redemption …"

"I know the quote."

"So don't be such a grump. And don't worry, I'll think of something—it is my gift after all."

There was no talking him into moderating his approach. He was convinced now that Billy was on a suicide mission. Roland would have to take matters into his own hands. What he had to do was clear—get him into custody without any further violence or law breaking while there was still a chance for a lesser sentence. He would concede to the foolishness for now.

They faded back to the cars and Frenchy gave the orange bus a peck before she opened the door to the Land Cruiser.

"I'm going to ride with Billy now," she said to him. "I may have to take over the wheel. Will you be okay?"

"I will."

"He needs me now."

Roland understood and nodded. "Be careful—"

She leaned in and kissed him softly. "*Je t'aime.*"

Frenchy climbed out and ran over to the Stretch and piled in.

An idea came to him then and Roland suddenly jumped out. He beckoned Billy and sidled up to the driver's side of the sparkling blue vehicle.

"I'll drive it. You two take the Land Cruiser …"

Billy was hesitant, but saw the wisdom in it. "You sure?"

"The only thing I'm sure of is your ass should be hauled off to the nearest precinct while you still have a fighting chance!"

"Ain't you the Seven Dwarfs' cousin, Cranky … Take care of my baby—"

Billy kissed the steering wheel and his eyes drifted to a close. "*Oof-mah,*" he chanted to prepare and purify the vehicle for his willful volunteer and friend. Then he rounded the vehicle and recovered the portable shortwave from the trunk.

From the driver's seat of the Land Cruiser, Billy offered Max a salute and then thumb-launched a shiny silver coin high in the air. Max chased after and held it up, beaming. The others waved to him and they all motored off. The Sapphire Stretch followed Billy's lead.

The two vehicles headed north on a back road due west of Durango and stopped in a camping facility in Junction Creek while careful to hide the big car behind a large dumpster. They changed out of the Halloween garb and took showers.

Billy escorted the Sapphire Stretch out of the woods to the main access route Highway 550 to the mountains, the famed San Juan Skyway, widely considered the most beautiful drive in America.

After seven-clock, darkness lifted and sunrise painted the sky in watercolors of pink, orange, and mauve. The unforgettable Skyway was more a runway to the clouds than a highway as it soared across the rooftop of the Rockies, winding its way through the San Juan and the Uncompahgre National Forests. Billy lagged miles behind now as the Stretch watchdogged the twisting terrain ahead.

Taking the popular thoroughfare was risky if not foolhardy, as if an elongated luxury car wasn't enough of a statement. Yet Billy's intelligence reports proved favorable. The manhunt was concentrated still in New Mexico and the Skyway was nearly deserted at that early hour. The local authorities could not know of the vehicle's blue color or the Colorado plates, much less a different man driving it.

The group made a coffee stop in Hermosa and Frenchy went in for the purchase. The caffeine boost picked up everyone except Roland. He'd taken a turn for the worse and mild stimulants had no effect on him at this point.

The cars cut through the San Juans and arched over the stretch of the Skyway known as the "Million-Dollar Highway," a moniker that denoted the area's mining history as well as its scenic splendor. The highway traversed along jutting snowcaps, rivers, and verdant valleys— truly spectacular. Billy phoned in to warn of avalanche chutes that funneled down, fifty-nine in all.

Nearing eight-clock, the cars swung past Silverton, an old mining town caught in a time capsule of former days. Victorian houses were painted in vibrant yellows, violets, royal blues, peaches, mauves, and pinks. Frenchy took particular notice as these colorful constructions were depicted in her recurring dream of the white lions.

Ouray was situated on the other side of the breathtaking Red Mountain Pass and the going was slow. They were fifteen miles from their destination, but this winding passage required twice the time.

As the vehicles gained in elevation the temperature plummeted and coolness chilled the windows. The massive mountain peaks were covered in snow. Roland checked his watch; it was almost nine-clock. His eyes were burning and achy, his nose running, eyelids twitching, fading, and bouncing. The man was effectively slumped at the wheel.

An animal suddenly shot from the undergrowth before the limo, a badger crossing the road. The sighting forced him to swerve and nearly careen off the cliff. The surge of adrenaline revived him. He was too dazed to recall the creature's medicine, but thanked the animal just the same for offering it.

He received another call.

"Congratulations, Roland," Billy barked. "You are officially a One Hundred-Twenty."

"Hmmm ... Thanks."

"Even I haven't done a one-twenty! You're into your sixth day; how's it feel?"

"Terrif—" he mumbled vacantly. His eyes were half-shut.

"We're almost there—hang on!"

The man had been up five straight days: one hundred twenty hours. He'd had to do it. There was no other way.

"Beware of Riverside Chute! Knocked off countless in her time!"

He patted his pants pockets and swam through them deeply to their corners. There were no more stimulants. A haul of Frenchy's cold coffee had no effect. An index speared into the tiny hip pocket and thankfully he discovered a last survivor. He scooped it and downed it and the bug-eyed, sweaty expression soon gripped his face once more.

Sharp rocks fell periodically in Red Mountain Pass and Roland did well to avoid them. The motorway was carved into the granite mountain with walls rising straight on either side, dwarfing the Stretch.

A last looping turn swung the cars around and the landscape opened to a wide recess where rows of snow-capped glaciers converged and a tiny jewel of a town lay nestled at the bottom resembling the Alps.

"Eet's Ouray!" Frenchy gasped and chills climbed her spine.

"Switzerland of America darlin', here we come!"

Up ahead and below, the Stretch negotiated the hairpin switchbacks winding down to the valley. Billy phoned and instructed his friend to pull over to the shoulder and follow his lead from there on in.

The Stretch slowed. As Roland waited for them, he scanned the call register of his new phone and saw Margaret had called twice and Adele six times. He was too consumed to play the messages. He hoped they weren't fearing his disappearance.

"*I'm OK*," he texted them both.

The Land Cruiser passed and the Stretch fell in behind. As they were about to enter town, Billy suddenly veered off twisting back around past surging falls and onto an ascending dirt drive that penetrated high into a forest of towering pines. The uneven track led to another offshoot, an even bumpier road to an abandoned mine. Beyond that and two-thirds of the way to the mountaintop, Billy slotted the Cruiser before a thick, wide, and evergreen canopy. He hopped out and guided the Sapphire Stretch beneath the chosen cover.

"Now take that in," he harked, drawing a deep breath. "Fill your lungs ..."

The cool, clean, and crisp wind expanded their lungs and resuscitated them, bringing smiles to weary faces. Even the struggling Roland could appreciate the aerating.

"That peak back there? Molas Pass, elevation 11,000 feet. Considered the cleanest, purest air in the U.S. and this here is ten miles away. This is what your environmental movement is all about." He sucked in another chestful. "Preserve that you preserve life."

Frenchy helped transfer the duffels and sleeping bags to the Land Cruiser along with more surveillance equipment. They all piled into the single car. The Stretch was left hidden under a thick forest blanket.

They descended the dirt track back down the mountain and it wound around all the way depositing them in town. Like Silverton, Ouray had a long history of mining settlements that had given birth to another Victorian-styled village. Main Street featured century-old buildings and the Ouray Hotel in particular had been marvelously restored.

Deer roamed on smaller residential streets uninhibited, even big-antlered bucks. For such a gentle and timid creature to be unafraid in public locales was curious if not odd.

"What are they doing in town?" Frenchy questioned aloud.

"I don't know," Billy said offhandedly, an uncommon admission. He was stumped for an answer a second time now, Roland noted.

At the far side of town they spotted a secluded chalet-styled motel located on a rushing mountain stream. The Cruiser pulled in.

Roland was now entertaining inconsistent, fragmented thoughts and spikes of paranoia. He was no longer able to trust his instincts and asked Frenchy to help him check in. He let her do the talking.

From the car, Billy spied four lummoxes leaving a shared room. They were loaded down with rifle packs strapped to their backs and that combined with the camouflage clothing indicated hunters. Deer season was in full swing.

The motel was a sturdy, rustic place made of oak post-and-beams. The proprietor was amiable and spoke in that rounded and cheery Colorado vernacular which complimented his split-logged establishment. Frenchy asked for two rooms and Roland laid down cash to pay in advance.

"No doubles, but I have a cancellation on a big suite. Hunters or honeymooners?"

"Hunters, *Mon Dieu*," she said, aghast.

"It's the season, most of the rooms are taken. You like hiking?"

"We hike, yes."

"Wear proper clothing. Don't want any accidents up there—"

"Does that happen?"

"More often than I'd like to think."

"Maybe we won't hike—"

"Great trails, just wear fluorescents. And don't miss the hot springs just up the road. You don't even need the car."

The man handed her keys and retreated upstairs to his living quarters.

"Mélodie?" Roland pushed feebly.

She noted his sickly pallor and clutched both of his hands.

"You're so cold. Tell me, baby—"

"Promised myself ... to get you out ... o' here ... things got dangerous," he stammered. "Feel now's the time ..."

"You know I can't go. I can't leave him."

He drew in a deep one which made him cough. He looked terrible.

"He won't listen. To me." His teeth were grinding and buzzing. "Badger ... what's that?"

"*Amour*, what are you saying?"

"The badger. I saw it—"

"Well, the Badger is Aggressiveness. Its medicine is to take action. Or more action. If you're being too shy ..."

"See?" He was frazzled and stuttered more through it. "Shy ... we need action ... to take it ... I should know ..."

"There are many ways to take action," she cast gently. "We've seen the deer which is Gentleness and it says to go with the flow. You can't take the medicines so close to heart."

"Want to turn him in ... but don't want ... to betray him ..."

She guided him over to the oak-posted sofa and sat him down, rubbing both of his chilled, trembling hands.

"He won't go back to prison. Would be torture for him. Haunts him more than the crimes," she said. "He told me he knows who did it."

Roland's burning, twitching eyes widened briefly.

"Said he's known for some time."

"But ... w-w-why ... didn't he go after *him*? The real ... killer?"

She shrugged and said resolutely, "That's Beelly ... being Beelly.'" The emotion was coming up in her now.

"Maybe doesn't ... know ... but thinks so. He thought I did it ..."

"I fear, baby," she said, her eyes suddenly flooded, "you have to let it be. We have to let it be. Best we can do is stick by him."

"He resists they'll shoot ... to kill ... a cop, Phoenix, told me—"

"I don't have answers," she said wiping her face. "You must go with your instinct. Instinct tells me going to prison for Billy is—"

" ... tell me ..."

"Worse than," she paused reluctant to say the word. "That little room, a spirit crushed—*destroyed*." Her eyes were awash again. "Such a beautiful spirit, isn't it?"

Roland eyed her steadily. His eyes were buzzing, snapping away the fleeting focus. Then his face folded to a mask. She placed his frigid palm to her cheek and kissed it. "You lovely, lovely man ..."

He wondered whether to speak or not. Or if he could.

"We met in the forest," he said jumbling words, "remember?" Her face smoothed briefly. "And it's your ... you're here, a reason ... your medicine ... for Billy ... I believe it ... Havasupais taught me." His teeth were clicking. " ... give it to him ..."

"Give him what, baby?"

He hacked loudly, his eyes running. "Your song ... Mélodie ..."

"I will, baby. I will." She smiled weakly, a graceful show. As he shivered before her she embraced him close. "You're so cold."

42

The group piled into the spare rustic room referred to by the owner as a "suite." They collapsed to the beds. Billy seemed to fall into a deep sleep. Frenchy drifted off soon after—but not Roland.

The suffering man had another prolonged seminar with the beam work before he rose up from where he lay. He stumbled onto an upholstered chair that fronted the beds and coiled there. He was an observer to their slumber, the passive voyeur once more and he mused over the last days of his incredible odyssey; all the experiences he'd lived through and past, individual moments as well. The faces conjured unforgettable memories. He'd never been so close to any group, family included.

Lastly Roland framed him alone—the one responsible for it all.

Billy Six was nearly a figment of the imagination. A figure so dynamic and explosive, he was like a bomb going off in a fireworks factory. Brilliant also, he was so much more than a manic and wacky jack-in-the-box. A teacher and artist, he burned with mighty heart and soul.

The essence of the man had been revealed to him over time, inconsistently and confusingly. Billy was a contradiction. Yet only as his own valves of sensation unlocked could he fully appreciate the man's greatness. At Havasu Falls, enveloped by the towering sandstone walls of the ancients—and surely prompted by the surging power of crystal waters—this beautiful but tortured personage let it pour of his interior like a rushing waterfall of his very own, a personal gush of humanity. You didn't have to agree with his vision to admire it, the vital embrace of life, love, and nature. He possessed integrity and courage and his coals burned for a better showing by mankind and for a better future for all.

He loved Billy Sixkiller. He was a warrior, a man battling his demons, desperately so, in a war he could never win, but fighting fiercely. He made use of each moment and cherished every breath. Oh, how he burned so.

Roland draped a leg over the armchair his rumination concluded. In the peace and stillness of that motel with the rooms emptied out and the hunters off for a day's bloodlust, the man's face was a wash of memory and sentiment.

Billy awoke in an hour, his only real repose in days and he immediately noticed the missing party. He quickly stepped outside in search of his friend.

In the misty distance behind the motel he spotted a figure hunched by the stream. "Hey!" Billy called out.

The piled man gazed blankly at the clear icy water passing over rocks. His face pale, lips purple, his teeth were again chattering. He was out of sorts enough to confront the severe elements in the first place.

"Too hot," he said to the oncoming presence. "That room … Came out … for sun … Warming me," he trailed off, shuddering.

Billy could see he was delirious. "Let's go in, brother."

"Hear something?"

"What do you mean?"

"The radio … they know?"

"Does who know?"

"Where we are?"

Billy helped his friend stand. "What do you say about some hot springs? Do you some good—"

His mouth was quivering. "They got 'em … up the road …"

*   *   *

Frenchy was disturbed by the clusters of deer prancing across the highway in families of twos and threes. She knew the creatures were fleeing the forest to avoid being gunned down and the thought of it pained her in the abdomen.

"Stay here!" she warned. "They look so frightened."

As the three marched to the natural spa, a firecracker blast resounded in the mountains and echoed past.

"No!" she cried. "How far away was that?"

"Few miles," Billy said. "Glaciers create state of the art acoustics. Put on your ugly hats—"

Frenchy immediately crowned herself and her man with the DayGlo orange crushers. He was hosting full surges of delirium and she steadied Roland's uneven gait with an arm at his waist. "What about you?" she posed to Billy.

"Fluorescents? Gone too far to draw attention now ..."

"Ours include you anyway."

"Not if I run."

The hot springs were located a few hundred yards from the motel. As they approached, they could see steam rising steadily with clouds of vapor hovering over the large outdoor pools. Though the facility was man-made, the water flowed from natural springs deep to the earth while the towering glaciers hovered over imposingly, a glorious setting.

They chose to soak in a medium-hot pool. The couple wore their hats with the brims mashed low and she clutched Roland close.

"You okay, baby?"

"Better," he said, his teeth still clacking. "Heat ... is good."

He'd turned nearly white with bluish lips, but the intense heat thawed him soothingly, bringing a smear of color back to his face. Frenchy kissed him softly though he remained immobile. They were enveloped by glaciers on all sides, one of the most beautiful spots in America and everything Frenchy had hoped for and more.

The springs were located right along the 550, the "Million-Dollar Highway," the main artery through town. Roland peered over and caught sight of a lone Town of Ouray police car as it swung past on a slow coast. The officer driving never ventured to look upon the spa.

Roland twisted sharply at Billy who had already spotted the vehicle.

" 'Ouray' was the name of a great Indian chief," Frenchy tendered.

Billy looked to her, impressed. "How did you know that?"

"I've studied this town. I had family here."

"In Ouray? You never told me that."

She eyed him squarely when she said it. "I know." She carried on before he could make issue of it. "Chief Ouray was the head of the Ute tribe. Married to the most beautiful woman, Chipeta."

"What was their story?" Roland posed it. He was feeling better.

"Same as all the rest," Billy interjected. "The story of the American Indian. Befriended, mistreated, and betrayed. Then forgotten when his usefulness was over."

Frenchy cleared her throat and Billy respected her cue to refrain from interrupting.

"Chief Ouray was one of the greatest of all the chiefs. Others like Geronimo and the Sitting Bull were better known because they took up arms and were made famous by the movies. But Chief Ouray was a great leader, a very wise man. He knew no Indian nation could win wars against the white man with few guns and weapons. But he was determined to keep his people on their land as long as possible. And he did it. By negotiation."

A strangely pleasant smile grew on Billy's face. "I hear you, Butterfly. And I'm so damned proud." And he blew a kiss her way. She blew one back.

"No wonder it's such a peaceful place," Roland added, on delay.

"Look up there—" she called out. "It's a man on a cliff. See him?"

The figure was dangling halfway up the glacier hanging from a rope.

"… Oh yeah …" Billy acknowledged. "Ice climber."

Frenchy redirected to her man who was thawing and she took his hands and guided him along in the water. They faded to a distant corner and she pretzeled him and they soon became mere shapes hidden by rising steam and the brims of orange hats.

From the other direction this time the singular prowler glided past on the road above and adjacent.

Roland sighted it first, but couldn't tell if Billy had or not. He was equally obscured at the other end of the pool behind veils of vapors and mists.

*   *   *

The black, deep maroon, purple, and blood red walls surrounding Ouray rose thousands of feet and were composed of rock strata tilting at thirty-degree angles. The glacier hues changed with each layer reflecting eons of time. On that day the enveloping geological theater was soaking up the noon sun and heating the tiny town in the valley like a sauna. The soothing warmth inspired Frenchy to change into a T-shirt.

The glorious day was crisp and cloudless and the sun's intensity was enhanced at the town's altitude. The group decided on a hike into the glaciers. Roland advised against it, but Billy was insistent.

After a quick grocery stop, they motored the Land Cruiser up a challenging four-wheel route. They were headed to a wide clearing up the southern glacier known only to Billy, the one labeled the amphitheater. The climb was rugged but steady in the all-terrain vehicle, and they reached the picturesque setting, a hollowed recess beneath towering pinyons. There they spread sleeping bags and did their best to relax for a picnic. They supped on fruits and cheese and shared a bottle of rosé too while basking in the potent sunshine.

Another *CRACK!* Rang out and echoed hauntingly, bouncing off successive walls of the amphitheater. The blast was more menacing and dramatic than in town, intensified by the surrounding geological formation that acted as a sound funnel. The hunters were making their presence known. The rifle fire seemed close as it had erupted from the near side of the mountain.

43

Moments earlier, at the opposite end of the amphitheater and around the mountainside, a forest ranger spotted a glint of chrome reflecting off sunlight through tall trees above Ouray Falls. Upon investigating, he came upon a strange sight, a shiny blue limousine abandoned curiously in the woods—the Sapphire Stretch. The Arizona State Police were notified immediately as were the other designated authorities crucial to the case. Helicopters set off from Phoenix to transport Sheriff Graves and his Task Force of sharpshooters and riflemen to Durango. They would join a fully coordinated effort with the Colorado States amassing already in Ouray.

Police had sealed off both ends of Highway 550, the only access routes to Ouray. At present they were surrounding the town. The special Task Force, armed with high-powered rifles, had assembled cautiously and was now in position awaiting word to advance and take further action. The authorities implemented the blockade, fearful of innocent civilians getting caught in any potential crossfire as the target of their police net, Billy Sixkiller, an acknowledged psychopath, was considered heavily armed and extremely dangerous.

The only other person of interest to be identified was Mélodie Charlebois said to be originally from France. Roland had not been named. Billy's precision in the planning, skillful execution, and deft maneuvering in between had proven effective until that point. Just reported, however, a New Yorker had been taken at gunpoint in New Mexico and forced to his trunk, the victim claiming Sixkiller and "the kidnapped writer" had held him up. The news flash though had not been substantiated or corroborated by the police.

State Police and Task Force members were ordered to stay off the shortwave networks for communication as Sixkiller had an uncanny capacity to pinpoint their whereabouts. He'd countered their efforts, consistently positioning himself to the voids. They were to use private cellphones. They'd assumed, and rightly so, that he had no satellite cellular intercepts.

High up in the range's amphitheater the targeted man was focused and vigilant. He'd been wearing his earphones monitoring activity, though radio pick-ups had gone nearly dead, an ominous indicator something was perhaps afoot. The shortwave silence kept him on edge. He would not alert the others something might be afoot to avoid causing alarm. He didn't divulge his strategy or let his behavior give

anything away. Billy would spare them the danger and the worry at all costs.

After the picnic, the couple curled in a sleeping bag. The effects of Roland's final stimulant pill had worn off. He had nothing left. The hot springs had warmed and rejuvenated him, softening muscles and soothing extremities, but also relaxed his frame. He was preparing for certain and long-overdue sleep.

Frenchy kissed him and pet his head as she lay beside. Though she feared for Billy, she was experiencing a special tranquility, an inner peace, poised in the mountain town. She'd never achieved any personal harmony with her environment or a sense of belonging anywhere, really; she'd been uprooted her whole life. She'd existed forever in limbo, transient, and rootless. But surrounded by the tall rock mountain walls and bathing in its gentle warm clasp she felt protected. The mountains of Ouray seemed right. In a very short time she felt it viscerally and deep to her core that she was meant to be there. There was business to take care of too, and she planned to conduct it later in the day. She'd decided it and had transferred her suitcase from the Stretch to the Land Cruiser for that purpose.

The hot springs and wine at supper had made her sleepy. The young woman wasn't habituated to the frenetic pace, the lack of sleep, the all-night pushes and treks. What had kept her going was youth, but youth now needed a rest and she drifted into a doze.

As Frenchy lay there, her old partner and companion crept silently up and took in her peaceful countenance. The thought came to him then that she possessed wings all right, but not those of a butterfly. She appeared angelic to him and he knelt to kiss her forehead. He smiled partially, mindful of the memories—a lifetime's worth—the places, the laughs, the drama, the nicknames, and now the fruits of it all: the beautiful person she'd become. "The Perfect Egg" too, he mused. Roland's lids were closed, but an eye was twitching as he stirred regularly for repositioning. He seemed awake still.

Billy checked his watch and whispered so only his friend could hear, "One Hundred Twenty-Six—damn. You're in your own *league*."

"Huh?"

"Gonna take a little walk …"

" 'Kay. Be careful," he said so faintly that it was never heard.

Billy bent low and kissed Frenchy once more on the cheek. Then he stuck the handgun in his belt and maneuvered stealthily beyond the clearing. He would climb above to secure a better lookout post. His instinct and sensorial awareness approaching that of an animal's in its acuity had designated it time to make his move.

He negotiated an ascent scaling adroitly hand-over-hand on jagged rocks high up to the crest of the amphitheater where he could survey the valley below. His suspicions were confirmed. Tiny Main Street was clogged with law enforcement vehicles perhaps three dozen in all. The 550 was blocked to all traffic at either end of the town and troopers were scurrying around taking positions.

No doubt the hunters had arrived though he was the only creature being hunted now. A trifle exciting to him too, he was at heart a gamer. He hiked and climbed the glacier further up and the Hoodoos were in sight, towering peak formations that resembled tall clay figures. They'd been sculpted over time smoothly, but crudely, and offered the appearance of monks in robes. Billy gave welcomed thought to the Hoodoos in the Superstitions revered by the Apaches and the Thunder Gods blasting booming voices with lightning flashes to the valley below. The thought comforted him.

Sheriff Graves had received new information and was briefing his squad of Arizona riflemen poised on standby at the ready. Reportedly, Sixkiller had been accompanied by a man in a gray Toyota Land Cruiser whose plates matched those of a vehicle recorded in the check-in register of a local motel. A witness had come forth who'd seen the vehicle turn up into the all-terrain vehicle chute that accessed the amphitheater.

The two assembled forces began their ascents by taking opposite flanks of the mountainside while remaining in phone contact with each other as well as their superiors. The Colorado States climbed from the west, the Arizona sharpshooters from the east.

Frenchy tossed in her sleep, her limbs atwitter, and her eyes snapped open abruptly. When she angled over she saw Billy was gone. But Roland lied beside her still, which calmed her, and she laid back again and drifted off.

Roland was still squirming in his sleeping bag, unable to reach that final frontier. The assault of stimulants had disrupted his system to such a degree that his heart beat too fast to the point of fluttering from time to time. The more he listened to the irregular beats of his heart, the more he became fearful of an arrest; and thereby, the more the adrenaline spiked his system to keep him awake. But it was a matter of time, minutes even, before he would go out.

The forces converged on Billy from the flanks as they made their way advancing through the timberline beneath the tall pines, steadily pressing and gaining in elevation.

Members of the western flank first caught sight of the pair sprawled in the clearing's recess seemingly dozing—but Sixkiller was not among them. Two armed State Troopers remained there to stand guard, careful not to wake or alarm or apprehend them yet. They didn't care to ruin any element of surprise intended for the likely armed fugitive.

Billy reached the outcrop from where the Hoodoos shot up and thrashed his way through thick shrubs and undergrowth to their base. He initiated his climb of the seventy-foot structures where within one in particular existed deep down a terrifically concealed chamber wide enough to contain a man. From there he could wait it out while giving the impression he'd escaped the dragnet. To find him, it would take a crane or professional rock climber. Entombing himself as such had been his plan, years in the making.

"Climb the rock, control the clock," he repeated, amusing himself.

He shimmied up using vines and the tiniest crags, fissures, and spires for footing unseen to the naked eye. The climb was nearly an impossible challenge, but he managed, skillfully scaling the backside of the Hoodoo wall, hidden from view. Billy was feet away from disappearing completely from sight when he heard suddenly, a sound inconsistent to the quiet surroundings—a sharp crackling of a twig, not the movement of small furrieds or deer, but something more deliberate. The disturbance had weight and dimension like his own— yet it was not his own. His head twisted around and back, his eyes firing to and fro combing the landscape.

Back at the clearing, the grip stimulants were holding on Roland released him at last and the man's eyelids sealed. The eyeballs reversed, the whites spun back in their caves, he was submitting finally, a first time in a hundred thirty hours with nothing to revive him further when a booming—*CRACK!*—blasted out from the mountaintop, bone-chilling and thunderous, taking everyone by surprise, the police and sharpshooters included. The deafening *CRACK!* produced potent echoes like lightning, a sound trail that reverberated and rippled not only through the immediate amphitheater, but the entire three-hundred-sixty degree wall of glaciers encircling tiny Ouray.

There was no mistaking it—a fresh rifle blast from one hell of a high-powered instrument.

Reacting instantly to the violent explosion, Roland's eyes clapped, his torso revolted with a cardiac jerk, and he screamed at the top of his lungs. He assumed he'd been shot through the head, a threat promised him consciously six days prior, the threat processed and trapped in his subconscious still, hot-wiring him with that terrifying sensory memory. There it was, the time had come, the horror he'd been programmed for—his assassination delivered at the time of sleep.

And he rejected it. "*NO!!!*" he roared out in abject terror.

He reoriented himself with place, time, and circumstance and spotted Frenchy bolted upright and frenzied. She'd heard the gunshot coupled with Roland's terrorized release and the fact that Billy was gone—missing—it became clear what may have happened.

"Where is he?" she shrilled. "Where's Billy???"

But Roland was already charging up the mountainside. "No!" he yelled forward.

"Hey you!" a State Trooper called out. "Stop right there!"

"I'm unarmed!" he shouted back and quickened his clip fearing the worst. "No, Billy—no!!!" he bellowed up ahead to thwart any further melee. "Don't shoot!"

Frenchy also ignored the Troopers' warnings too and followed Roland's path on a dash. The two, armed Troopers gave chase.

"Billy!"

"Ro—"

The panicked man tried to echolocate the frail delivery.

"Over here …"

Roland reached a small clearing where three Arizona State Troopers were clustered, chatting away on cell phones. One officer chimed, "Not good, one to the chest. 'N he fell sixty feet down—"

The earpiece blasted static and undisciplined barking.

"Don't know! No one from the Task, tell you that!"

As Roland came upon them they converged and apprehended him.

"Let me see him! Let me see my friend!"

"He's going fast. No point …"

The officer holding him angled one to another who bounced a nod and Roland was quickly frisked. "Clean—"

"Eddie! He's coming through!"

"Roger!" fired back through the two-way handset.

Roland fended his way through the thicket and yanked back branches, getting whipped by others as he pushed through.

Billy Sixkiller lay there flat on his back and the sky reflected white off his eyes. A wide scarlet splat could be seen to the left center of his chest. When the felled fugitive located his friend, he produced a twisted grin, his grill twitching uncontrollably. "Damn, you made it …"

"How bad?" Roland snapped at the attending Trooper.

The officer's expression cascaded grimly. "Copter's on its way—"

"Can we have some time?"

"Guess, don't move him. I'll be right here, so—" And the Trooper trailed off and faded back.

"No Meddie needed, Billy-boy's good-time gone …"

"Stop it, they're coming—"

Roland settled close and removed his own pullover, propping Billy's head with it. "How's it feel?"

"Like shit … but it's warm …" He coughed and bright maroon flows painted his lips. "You look like hell, Rollie …"

"No thanks to you."

"You'll be able to sleep now …"

"Billy—tell me—when did you know?"

He tried to clear his throat. "First day."

"Why didn't you set me free and go get your man?"

He stuttered through it. "Y-y-yours was the better journey."

Roland knew what he meant; better to bring a man back to life than to kill another. "Look at all you've done for me."

Billy's eyes rolled high involuntarily and he pulled them back with sheer will, grittily drawing on reserves. "Ain't that generous—"

"Thank you, brother."

"No, thank you. Was on the wrong Road. Medicines met. I needed yours, 's'much as … you needed mine. Was lost …"

He gagged and could feel his lungs filling up.

"Bringin' you back brung me back. Found my Walk—'gain … I'm grateful." He hacked sharply.

"But who told you it was me? *Who?*"

"*Oof-mah,*" he let loose. " 'Member what Big Elk said? 'Member? '*Death comes* …' "

" '—*And always out of season,*' " Roland finished for him.

Billy looked upon him pridefully, but bleary and glossy-eyed.

"Tell me, Billy. You must!"

He coughed hard again and it shot his head forward, hurting him.

"Hell … don't blow it … all the work we done … Gettin' justice for me? … fool idea …" He had to speak several words at a time as energy came to him. "Lemme see that picture—"

"Which?"

"One you been hidin' …"

Even at death's door the man never ceased to amaze him. From his wallet Roland drew a photo he'd never mentioned, yet Billy knew of it.

"Ah, yes … beautiful boy …" The photo slipped from his pinch and fell to his wound, smudging the image. "Know who to look for … now—keep him comp'ny. Tell 'im … the man of action … his daddy become." He gasped too.

"We found him, Billy."

"You done … At last …"

A tender, fragile silence held until they heard steps advancing. Billy gripped his friend's wrist. "Take care o' my girl …" Roland clasped the fading man's trembling, cold hand warmly.

Frenchy burrowed through the thick brush.

"Beelly!" She plopped beside him and they both flanked him in close. "God bless you, baby," she said, trying to control her emotions.

"Don't know about 'bless' … He'll do somethin' … can't have no opinion … on me … know that much …"

They all broke across through tearing eyes.

Their smiles provided the strength he needed to lift his eyes skyward. "Thank you, Great One … for bringin' 'em … to me … on my Walk. Guide me to … the next'n." His gaze fell back slowly. "Damn … done in by a hunter …"

"Is that who shot you?" Roland pressed urgently.

"No hatski … musta took me for a deer … The medicine, Frenchy?" His words were rushed, coming in spurts. He knew to get them out.

"Deer is Gentleness," Frenchy said soothingly. She eyed Roland speaking softly. "Go with the flow, let it be—"

"Damn good eulogy ..." His body released the tension toxic to it and he framed her tenderly. "Little Mistral ... we made it—"

He'd indulged too much and had paid the price. The exertion forced a deep blast from his lungs and his chest heaved. He had perhaps one left in him.

"I know ... Ouray ... *Merci, mon petit*—"

"Don't want no ... froggy send-off now ..."

She cracked a laugh only to break down.

He uttered it hoarsely. "Pocket—"

She checked his pants and in a palm full of coins she found his recent creation from Cerillos, a handmade figurine—a turquoise maiden with butterfly wings dangling from black-waxed twine.

"Didn't know what to ... but she has wings ... Angel-butterfly ... so fly, Butterfly, fly ..."

She flooded. "I will, baby. *For us.*"

"Find letter ... for hot shot ... Frenchy—?"

"Tell me—"

He winced. "That ever'thin'?"

"Easy baby," she said and kissed him adoringly.

Drowning from within, he was short of breath and chopped words.

"Known for ... days now ... you'd be here ... was a comf—" He hacked loudly—deathly. The blood surged up and he was losing control. Finally he was "going fast," having defied the Troopers' previous pronouncements. But of course, they hadn't known Billy Six.

"When it's time ... hold me ... in your arms—"

He'd recognized her medicine long before had been for this—to deliver him—his body to Mother Earth, his soul to Father Sky. He wouldn't apply animal medicine entirely to her for this reason, as it was incarnate and of the Earth and didn't incorporate the heavenly beings.

He'd known it a long time. Frenchy was his angel.

"You know I will, my love."

Water crept down Roland's cheeks and the failing man motioned him. Roland pressed his ear to Billy's mouth to listen as droplets fell from his chin to the gaping redness. Roland nodded and pulled back briefly then whispered a response. Billy acknowledged it—their tacit agreement.

"Was close ... wasn't I?"

"Not close, you're there ..."

"Did I show it?"

"More heart than I knew existed—"

"Was I ... was I ... *Joe?*" he forced out only to scrutinize desperately his friend's face; it was that important.

"You're Ali, you're Joe. You're champion twice. You just—"

Billy clutched his friend's shirt with a last burst. "Don't hold back!"

"You just burned brighter—"

"Too bright, right?"

Roland's voice split apart. "No, you burned beautifully. Like—"

"—Tell me—"

"Billy, you burned like *magic* ..."

The man broke, but held it and Billy lifted a powerless limb and brought his friend's head to his chest.

"No," he whispered. "We. *We* were magic—"

Roland felt the shuddering ribs as the dying man's head bobbed in place.

"Betting on you ... double-downed ... Write the one ... the one ... they *fear* you're gonna write ..."

Roland rose and Billy dragged dimming eyes upon her—a signal. She shifted beneath and held him tightly. His face had gone from red to violet. He was shivering and both Roland and Frenchy each clasped a hand.

"Whoa," he mumbled. His biology was raging. "Never felt ... so alive ..." He was cold, but wouldn't let on. " I fly ... the crimson ... cross ..."

"Yes, you do," she sobbed.

" ... Feelin' ... kinna Confederate ..."

"That's all right, baby; that's what you *are* ..."

An overwrought Roland craned around and witnessed the foggy mist that had silently rolled into the amphitheater. The enveloping cloud reminded him of the sweat lodge when water was tossed to the hot coals of antiquity and steam and vapor rose up. He envisioned this freshly spreading mist belonging to the ancient ones. Billy's blanket was ready, the one to carry him to the Heavens. His friend prayed then and the dying one initiated it in spoken poetry, the first verse.

> "Bye-bye baby ... been a sweet love ...
> Though this feeling ... I can't change ..."

The two carried it along supplying the tune and notes, singing it to his pauses and pace.

> *"But please don't take it so badly,*
> *Cause Lord knows I'm to blame,*
> *If I stay here with you babe,*
> *Things just couldn't be the same,*
> *Cause I'm as free as a bird now …"*

Billy paused in mid-lyric his mouth on a contented curve and his eye snagged the sky mirroring the blues and whites and he saw them fluttering. He told them and thought they heard him, but he wasn't sure. But he spoke it articulately and effortlessly the way he had in life.

"They're dancing … the butterflies … 'n the children 're happy …"

A sudden smoothness took hold of his face and eyes. He had a look of calm and quiet, but mostly peace—the one which had eluded him in life—and he froze then. His body drifted serenely in their arms. And he was dead.

The man's fading senses heard them. The song continued, performed by his Top Two, a throaty chorus pushed through the wetness celebrating an uncommon man of bedazzling and vital medicine, a medicine they were forced to acknowledge was all they had left.

> *"And this bird will never change,*
> *Oh won't you fly high freebird!"*

They wept on the mountaintop at the base of the Hoodoos, the secret hiding place to their cherished one. Whatever it was, wherever it was. The heat pressed on their backs and they felt the warmth in their hearts and bones. The soupy mist enveloping them hovered and rose and continued to rise until it disappeared and brilliant sun poured immaculately down again. It was a beautiful day.

Billy Six had been right one last time. Had he made it the rest of the way, they never would have found him.

Six Months Later

44

The Meeting

Denunzio's, located on McDowell in Scottsdale, was considered one of Phoenix's more upscale, elegant restaurants. When Roland stepped into the bar area he was immediately recognized by patrons. He'd become that type of post-millennium celebrity only scandalocity and Information Age media feeds could produce. He wore a blue blazer over jeans and was met by Rafaelo, the overly polite maître d', a true Tuscan gone local Arizonian. Rafaelo escorted him to a prominent table, a stylish low-lit banquette tufted in deep burgundy leather.

Sheriff Graves was seated already, his weathered, craggy face charged with sunburn. His eyes locked in alertly at the advancing man. His overwhelming carriage rose to greet him and the Capítan held out a hand. Roland slid into the banquette instead from the other side.

"Glad you could make it," he snapped crisply. "How was New York?"

"Father's not well so I put in a visit."

"You two get along?"

"Things are better now." Roland angled up and met the slanted and deliberate golden eyes bearing down on him.

"Guess the official determination on the case doesn't sit too well. Was the word came across my plate."

"A fair statement."

"That's why I asked you to lunch. Always good to air things."

"Sir?"

"Don't like the fact you're upset. Though I did look the other way on that weapons charge." He patted him like a barfly crony as well.

Roland nodded sparely which took some doing. "Thanks."

"Known your family a long time. Maybe I can help. There's the official story and there are details not made public. For any number of reasons."

Roland inspected the fancy tablecloth, its shiny weave glinting silvery in its whiteness. "Name one," he spouted without raising his chin.

"Protection—and—privacy. That's two."

The thin, mustachioed waiter stepped up for a drink order. Graves decided on a vodka gimlet while Roland chose mineral water.

"Anything you want to ask? Off the record?"

"With pleasure. Why would Gus Griffiths go to Billy? This stuff about gangland ties sounds like some made-for-TV drama …"

Without relinquishing eye contact, Graves drew a small black book from his jacket pocket and slapped it down on the table. "Have a look—"

Roland thumbed through it. "Names … with phone numbers …"

"Names, the Mediterranean kind," he stated pointedly. "Some South American. Google any one. Each a known organized crime figure in the Four Corners region and their contacts in the big cities."

"And?"

"Not a nameless, faceless group—we know who they are."

"So you know who approached Gus? And who killed him?"

Initially it had been reported that Adele's brother Gus Griffiths, a known drug addict and offender, had committed suicide by overdose in Jerome. But an autopsy revealed he'd been murdered with a tablet of strychnine placed in his rectum—a gangland method employed to thwart traceability. Adele had phoned Roland repeatedly during his trip to Colorado to deliver the news. The official police report concluded Gus had been behind the plot to abduct Roland. Adele had paid out the ransom money albeit unaware her brother was the perpetrator.

"Got some leads. We're working with the FBI. They've taken over the case."

Roland nodded neutrally. "And why would Gus go to the trouble of staging a kidnapping to get a piece of his inheritance?"

"Wasn't going to get it the easy way—from your wife. And the pressure was on him …"

"He could have threatened her directly."

"He knew she'd come to us which she did—initially. But not when it came to the ransom."

"Why not?"

"Ask her. Maybe she thought we'd take risks and you'd get hurt."

The big Sheriff dragged a fork down that shiny weave and appeared suddenly detached, even wistful. "Hell, Frank and I were friends, but I don't know how highly Adele thought of me. Or us. The Department."

Of all the man's declarations, this one rang truest. Frank Griffiths had warned his daughter about the Sheriff though Roland always suspected there was more to it, that her father had never divulged the whole truth about their history. He couldn't have done, as it would have incriminated him personally too much.

"Gus felt he had to do it anonymously."

"Why not use a heavy to threaten her? If he was in deep to the mob it should have been easy for him—"

"Let's face it, Gus was none too swift," Graves said coolly, reclaiming his bravado. "He was a fool, an embarrassment. Why you think the old man left him out of his will?"

Roland fidgeted with his valet parking stub.

"But he never even tried to sue her. He threatened it, but never followed through. To jump from that to kidnapping? There are easier ways—unless—he had an accomplice. That's the question here. How does a man and five million dollars just disappear?"

"Take a read of any city paper—"

"But vanish into thin air? Along with some 'deer hunter' in the Colorado woods with cops smothering the place?"

"Prolly on a Caribbean cruise together," the old man jested.

The drinks came and the Capítan reached for his. There was a rim of sweat along the white band to his forehead where his high hats rested and produced the tan line. "So then, what'd you learn up in Jerome?"

"Same old. Gus was a wreck, addicted to pills."

"No shocks there. And the last time you saw him?"

"Two years ago. But he'd taken a turn for the worse apparently. He'd attempted suicides … and had an obsession with poltergeists."

"The legendary ghosts of Jerome—"

"Gus Griffiths was unglued, unstable, and weak. To put together a scenario like this was too bold. Beyond his reach …"

"Vegas boys are no pansies. I'll show you the black and whites."

"He made one trip to Vegas in the last four years—"

"Doesn't mean they weren't knocking on his door—"

"I mean, how did he even know Billy would let me go?"

"He didn't. And didn't much care once he got the money. There was no love lost between you. He resented you, Polsonby. You were enjoying the fruits of his family 'n he wasn't."

Roland let out a gust of enduring, troubled wind. "Every answer invites another question. It doesn't add up."

"Let me tell you something," the Capítan began and he reclined back easily. If there'd been an ottoman there his flat and wide simian feet would have been rested high upon it.

"Don't want to get too sappy in my final days, but hell—I love America. I mean it. But more than that, I love Arizona. This place has something you can't find in the rest of the continental U.S. Now, I never been to Alaska or Hawaii, but I am going to Kauai next winter after I'm through and done with. But Arizona is special. The skies, the colors, the people. The desert is what it is. For two hundred years, white folk been coming here for whatever reason to find not necessarily fame, but fortune. Maybe they think Arizona folk're a little slow, baked down by the heat and they can take advantage of the situation. But men been flockin' here since the mining days, a little bent, outright thieves, gunmen, con men, convicts, chicken ranchers, murderous cults, mobsters in witness protection, *bandojeros*, drug traffickers, human traffickers, border vermin—they all congregate here. Where they think life is simpler. And easier. *To get away with things.* To plunder the poor gal. And yes, she gives it up; she's a generous gal. And she spreads her legs more than she should. Until of course she puts the bite on you. I've made ten thousand arrests in my time ..."

The Capítan sighed and let his belly expand to full girth. "Used to be metals, the copper and gold—"

"The Lost Dutchman's Mine?"

"That may be legend, but you get the idea."

"Sheriff, five million dollars did not get buried in the Superstitions. That's real money, there's a real criminal behind this, and one if not two killers on the loose—"

Graves dug his elbows in, especially aroused with that sparked and menacing glare. He wore that signature look, the look of Yellow Eyes, the one the Mexican girls feared and despised. "Lemme ask you, what's your stake in this?"

"Sir?"

"Isn't your life on the mend? You were chasing ghosts for years, you've come a long way back—"

The remark was an unsettling reference to his boy and Roland didn't take kindly to it.

"If I didn't know any better I'd say—" he paused, still beaming harshly.

"What?"

"—You're taking on someone else's ghosts. What Billy Six left behind ... his obsession. And we all know what it done to him."

"Perhaps."

"Easy to see; you want to return the favor."

"Excuse me?"

"You wanted to save him. Like he saved you. But you couldn't. Feel you let him down, just like you let your baby boy down."

Roland stiffened. His eyes went hard and narrow, his body rigid.

"Is that a healthy way to go?"

"Are you referring to my mental health?"

"I'm referring to *you*. You got a lot o' life left. Sorry 'bout the divorce, but everyone gets divorced these days. Personally I think you're better off—"

"That's none of your business," he snapped.

"Perhaps not, but I know the family. There's history there that's not all that savory and who knows about that karma stuff folk talk about, but we are in the desert, in the lands of enchantment. What are you gonna have?"

Roland took a haul of water, too unnerved to even consider food.

"Know the menu by heart, great for rib eyes ..." The Capítan eyeballed him no less carefully. "You a meat-eater?"

He spoke eventually. "Depends."

"Me? Can't live without it, need it three times a day. Sausage and eggs in the morning, good steak at night."

Roland calmed himself barely enough to peruse the card.

"You like pasta? They have an excellent dish, their specialty ..."

He told him he did "on occasion."

"This one's a little different. Noodles are black."

Roland angled up, but not sharply. His crown moved as if a crane was doing the lifting, an inch at a time. He proffered it flat and deadpan. "Squid ink pasta ..."

"Right you are. You had it?"

His pulse began to race and his cerebral circuits flooded. He recalled their first meeting in the college bar and that night atop the mesa. After he'd said prayers for loved ones he saw it; the yellow eyes reflecting the moonlight, sending it back like dot lasers from the blackness—the reverse Coyote. The Trickster's medicine taught one to be vigilant, that someone in the midst may be attempting to trick or deceive and he remembered it then.

"No," he steadied back.

"It's all natural," he boosted. " 'Cause the black ink comes from the iodine in the squid. But damn, it's tasty—"

"Really," his guest returned like deadwood.

Graves noticed a shift in the man's behavior. He'd faded back suddenly and his withdrawal sucked the energy from the table.

"I recommend it highly," he added and Roland muted himself anticipating Grave's next pronouncement. "And if you have it, lunch is on me."

Roland cleared his throat to stall his response and smooth out his delivery. His interior was raging.

"An offer hard to resist. But I thought lunch already was on you," he threw for levity's sake.

"Course. You're my guest. Nobody leaves unhappy with that one."

"Tell you what, Harlan. I'll have it—"

"—Good—"

"—If you have it too …"

"If I have it? I'm having the New York steak."

When the Sheriff looked up he scoped the man's intent expression. Not knowing why, he was strangely attracted to it. "Iodine isn't good for me, but hell. Once in a while isn't goin' to kill me."

Roland tossed Graves a few questions to show he was still at the table. He mentioned the "irrefutable proof" Gus had provided Billy concerning Roland's alleged conducting of the Randall slayings. He deemed Billy too intelligent to fall for such an obvious stretch. The Sheriff cited the members of the Manson-like cult who'd been imprisoned and testified as to Roland's participation and guilt. Though they'd been the masterminds of the plot, their testimonies indicated he'd carried out the crimes as an initiation rite. Roland had seen copies of their depositions in Billy's apartment, a veritable library of scientific and academic texts on every subject imaginable; language books, periodicals, pop culture rags, and travel magazines—and no passport. Billy had been entirely self-taught and he'd never even ventured beyond the borders of the continental United States—one more thing for Roland to marvel about.

The Sheriff's guest refolded his napkin and nodded often to keep the chatter flowing, to conclude their "airing" properly as hoped.

When the steaming ink pasta dishes were served Roland had a taste for politeness's sake, but complained of stomach pain that was true. The pressure had nothing to do with his intestinals; rather, the musculature knotted in his abdomen. Graves, on the other hand, wolfed down his entire plate. Then he excused himself to the bathroom citing in all sincerity that the black noodles tended to discolor teeth and he wanted to rinse out his mouth.

When the Capítan returned to the table the check had been paid. After all he'd gotten his guest off on the weapons charge. Besides, Roland knew Graves had just saved him a lot of time and perhaps considerable expense and he actually enjoyed seeing the irrepressible dark stains left on the big man's white caps for what would be the rest of the afternoon.

The guest covered the check for those reasons. Gladly.

One Year Later

45

The Final Flight

The retirement gala for Sheriff Harlan Graves was held a year after his lunch meeting with Roland Polsonby, eighteen months to the day after the death of Billy Sixkiller.

The celebration was an affair to remember as all of Phoenix came out; politicians, local celebrities, star athletes, fellow law enforcement figures from the Four Corners, and former colleagues old and young. Graves had given fifty years to the city and the city tried to say thank you as best it could. Adele was even on the Banquet Committee and had arranged the entertainment and catering.

Roland silently disapproved of Adele's involvement, but had gone along with her decision. They'd finalized their divorce, but he was helping her adjust to a new life. She'd found a new assistant as Fernanda and Gonzalo had bought a small horse farm in Oak Creek Canyon near Sedona and moved there.

Frenchy had taken on her real name Mélodie. She'd been released months before from her year in prison. Roland left the banquet early the night of the event to join her after congratulating the man they called "El Capítan" on a long and prosperous career.

Harlan Graves the citizen was leaving town for good. He hadn't made it known to many people where he was going. He'd alluded to it once during their lunch so Roland had an idea, but few others did. He dashed off inquiries claiming he would travel for the first time since the Vietnam War. He had no aspirations other than to get away, play some golf, and have as little contact with people as possible, especially people he knew.

The Capítan kept his word on that.

Several days later a commercial airplane carrying Harlan Graves touched down on the island of Kauai, the last of the Hawaiian chain. He'd stopped overnight in Los Angeles to buffer the long flight and recover from his community send-off several evenings before when he'd put away no less than a dozen vodka gimlets. On this day, he'd flown first class and indulged in several more.

The big man sidled up to the luggage carousel and collected his bags which included golf clubs—a retirement gift from colleagues— and the baggage handler carted them to the circular drive which served the boutique airport. Awaiting at the drive's curb was a young man dressed in dark slacks, a white shirt, and chauffeur's cap and wearing aviator eye-shields. He was planted there dutifully raising a "Graves" placard and standing beside a long white car.

The car's driver smiled when Graves caught sight of the sign and then him.

"What have we here?"

"Your car for the week, sir."

"The week? What am I gonna do with a boat like that on an itty-bitty island like this?"

"Whatever you wish. Compliments of the folks of Phoenix for your trusted and dedicated public service …"

The Capítan threw out his proud chin and spied the elongated shiny off-white chassis. He broke heartily as the man loaded his bags.

"In my day never spent no tax money on limousines for no ex-cops I know that. But tell you what, I'll take it!" he barked almost musically in his West Texas rubber band twang.

The young man held open the door for him and the passenger climbed into the rear. The interior was impressive, upholstered in red velour, elegantly furnished and appointed. The passenger admired the sumptuous look and feel. "Now ain't that soft," he remarked. "Party car if I ever seen one."

The driver got behind the wheel. "There's an open bar with ice and a choice of snacks."

"Hell, at my age, always room for one more cocktail …"

The imposing man leaned forward and swirled himself a drink as the car eased out of the circular drive and onto the main access road from the airport. Harlan Graves put on his sunglasses, gave a quick taste of his vodka martini, sat back, and counted his blessings.

At the conclusion of a short triumphant reverie, he focused on logistics. "Don't suppose you know where I'm headed—"

"Beachnut Lane in Hanalei, correct?"

"Hell, how you know that?"

"Your broker let it slip."

"—Woody," he scoffed.

"When we informed him of the surprise, he couldn't resist."

"Uh-okay," Graves sang through it with more amused capitulation. He raised his tumbler and sipped it, watching the tropical charms of the island pass by; the tall palms, the lush jungle-like foliage aflutter from the breezes, all splashed with indomitable sunshine. The northern part of the island received more precipitation than any other part of the world, but not that day. Kauai was more remote and less traveled than its sister islands in the chain. Graves had chosen it as his retirement locale for this reason.

"Beats the Maricopa Freeway with a stick."

"Kauai is very pleasant in June."

The driver's voice was soft and soothing, almost feminine, and pleasant to hear after a long voyage. From the passenger's vantage point the young man appeared to have a delicate facial bone structure. Graves thought it likely he was a Mary, cowboy slang for a homosexual.

"How does retirement suit you?"

The big man winded one loose before speaking. "Only a week into it, but it's been pretty close to heaven. No more calls in the middle of the night, no more bad news to deliver, you have no idea …"

"I think I do, perhaps."

The car hadn't gone more than a few miles when it pulled into an empty parking lot behind a boarded-up beverage distributor and came to a stop.

"Just referring to my map here," the driver informed the passenger.

Graves nodded cheerfully though he was surprised the driver didn't know his way around a small island, but thought little more of it.

At that moment, the right rear door was splayed wide and a man piled inside leveling a steady handgun on the unsuspecting passenger. Double sets of automatic door locks immediately snapped shut serving as punctuation to the intrusion. The gunman was flanking him in an open-faced sandwich and the passenger was so shocked he didn't fight or put up a struggle. He removed his sunglasses to get a better look. "Polsonby?"

"Afternoon, Capítan."

The passenger's head twisted sharply from Roland to the chauffeur who no longer resembled a man. With additional scrutiny, Graves noted the driver's dirty blonde hair was tacked, wound, and coiled in the cap, and Mélodie was now waving a semiautomatic weapon of her own for him to see.

"What's this about?"

"Easy," Roland said. "Plenty of time to talk—"

The intruder eyed the big man directly and saw the animal; the deceitful yellow eyes beaming forth from above, the creature's mouth frozen and agape showing the discolored side row of teeth stained from coffee, tobacco, and a few thousand lies. He was Coyote in the flesh—the Trickster.

"Left wrist first," Roland commanded and relieved the man of his beverage. With two guns facing him Graves steadily raised his meaty paw.

Roland spread the silver inlaid cuff and closed it on the big man's log of a wrist. "And the right—" The procedure was repeated and the Capítan was now held by Billy's treasured antique manacles.

"What the hell you think you're doing?"

The intruder provided it calmly. "It's your time."

The car sped onward and Roland leaned in again and extended the prisoner's drink. After a pause, clanking mitts reclaimed it.

As the Capítan gave further thought to the notorious white car, it struck him the fate that had befallen him. He sipped on his martini and wrestled with it in mind for several silent minutes, more like ten. Surprisingly, that was all.

Deep down, the Sheriff sensed Polsonby had been on to him. He'd postponed his fade to the private sector for a year and a half. He'd made sure everything had been taken care of, that there were no loose ends and those that were less than taut and there were only several, had been neatly knotted; but evidently not tight enough.

Not long into the incursion, Roland launched into a rendition of the facts. Harlan Graves had been handling his duties as Sheriff of Maricopa County while on the take since the early seventies. He'd provided the father-in-law Roland never knew, Frank Griffiths, with every possible opportunity to increase his power, land holdings, and personal fortune. The Sheriff had used his badge and influential position in the community to orchestrate and carry out the graft and he profited handsomely from it as well. Graves secured advantages any citizen could want—money and the law to preserve it—a potent combination yielding a power index that would not recede with time.

This stronghold gave the Capítan the ability to prosper to the tune of no end in sight. The history was known.

Roland surmised Billy's father Jack Randall had uncovered the illicit activity going on between Griffiths and Graves and threatened to turn them in. In turn the corrupt partners asked him to join their exclusive little club, with incentives, but Randall declined. This revised account directly contradicted the version Graves had given Roland in that college bar substituting Randall for himself as the embittered-'Nam-vet-turned corrupt cop.

When Randall spurned the offer to join ranks, Frank had the Sheriff do the dirty work by murdering Randall and his wife, parents to a young boy, in their home in the middle of the night.

Graves then arranged for the Randall boy to be sent to a reform school in New Mexico under the name of "Dennis Roy," the generic name given to identityless orphans, to be never heard from again. When the young man showed resilience and resurfaced at Graves's doorstep some year's later intent on finding the murderer of his parents, the Sheriff knew he had a problem. Billy Sixkiller was unpredictable, manic, and relentless in his pursuit, all of which made him a dangerous threat. The Sheriff had to act.

Roland then accused Graves of supplying Billy with the false lead that deceived him into punishing the wrong man, though it appeared the kidnapped man had motive. The victim was a legitimate adversary of Randall's whom the officer had arrested and sent away for drug trafficking. But the botched abduction got Billy locked away, removing any threat to the Sheriff. The Sheriff could have gotten rid of Billy himself, but by the time the young man was released from Telschor, he'd already had such a damnable record with professional opinions cited and filed deeming him certifiably imbalanced, Graves merely needed to nudge him into criminality to let him hang himself. The plan would save the Sheriff from spilling more blood. *For the time being.*

Because the Sheriff wasn't done.

Graves had always been envious of Frank Griffiths. Adele had attributed the Sheriff's grumblings of her father shortchanging him to the resentments of a jealous man. But Frank had, in fact, owed Graves a lot of money from their corrupt dealings which he never made good on. The Sheriff was determined to get his slice one way or the other.

And after Frank's death, Graves hatched his strategy to recoup his share.

The Sheriff approached Frank's estranged son the disinherited and embittered Gus Griffiths to carry out his devious plan. Like the Sheriff, Gus felt shortchanged by Frank Griffiths, his father. The destitute man's pleas to his sister for financial assistance had long since fallen on deaf ears. In this way the Sheriff sold them as two kindred spirits united in a common cause, to exact revenge and lay claim to money they felt was rightfully theirs—even if the proceeds came in the form of a ransom. In Gus Griffiths, Sheriff Graves had found the perfect pawn. And patsy.

Graves supplied Gus with uncontestable proof that his brother-in-law, then-young Roland Polsonby, member to an "extremist desert cult," had murdered Billy's parents while high on LSD. The subsequent drug overdose had sent Roland to a Tucson hospital. Gus then provided the evidence to Billy, which set the second abduction precipitously in motion with Roland serving as the ransom bait. What the Sheriff could not have known was that bringing these two people together, Roland and Billy, would change everything and not in his favor.

"Here," the captor said, handing a tight stack to the old man, the merciless golden-eyed glare all but absent from his face.

The prisoner perused Roland's credit card statements and receipts from that fateful night twenty years before, his hospital bill included. Roland had unearthed the material in a storage facility in New York City. The Sheriff was holding the proof he had had the hospital records altered to make the date of Roland's emergency room visit link up with the late night Randall slayings.

Having pieced the plot together it was no great leap for Roland to conclude that Sheriff Graves himself was the unknown accomplice of Gus's who'd absconded with the ransom money.

In the Capítan's warped mind of course the ransom money served as a just collection of past and overdue debts from the Griffiths family as well as his retirement and severance package. With respect to his accomplice, Graves knew Gus to be a wild card, his nerves shot from years of substance abuse. The Sheriff feared the unstable man was too fragile to hold up if ever questioned or interrogated aggressively which he would have been. Therefore, as soon as the ransom was secured,

Graves terminated Gus with the fatal rectal dose and made it appear like a mob hit.

Roland also determined the Capítan had tapped one of his boys, a top sharpshooter equally talented with pistol or rifle to throw on hunter's clothing and shoot to kill when he came across Billy high in that Colorado glacier amphitheater; then change back into uniform and blend in with the rest once he'd carried out the mission. After all, the Task Force had license to do whatever they saw fit with a man so "crazy," "dangerous," "unstable," and "psychopathic," the terms strategically used to paint Billy for years. Graves could have had his assassin do it in uniform, but it would have been risky. There would have been witnesses and under the pressure of lawyers, judge, and jury, the outcome would not have been certain.

Roland brought his charges and the big man didn't protest, not an inch of it.

The Capítan knew now what lay before him. He'd come to the end of his road. This was his final ride. And moments later, the cornered coyote finished his drink, poured himself another, and quietly confessed to it all. He even added color and detail; how much he'd resented Frank Griffiths and how this young marksman reminded him of himself when he was a green ambitious rookie on the force.

"Don't believe Frank ever intended to make good on his debts to me. He warmed to me and became my friend, but all the while he'd been using me. Didn't figure it until it was too late and we both were too far in. Personally, he had a low opinion of me and as I became aware of it I coiled red from within."

A rim of water had silently filled the man's lids. Piled deeply in the car's plush interior, the Capítan suddenly appeared diminished and very old.

"Was it all about money?"

"Is it ever for people like us, Polsonby?" he sent back. "The fact of the matter is, I was every bit the man Frank was and I showed no less valor on the battlefield. I was his equal, if not his superior, as a soldier and as a man. Before both of us fell to hell. The difference was, and I confess it is no small detail: he won his war and I did not. When push came to shove, America didn't respect the soldiers who fought for the flag in the sixties. Treated us like dog shit when we came home—and Frank Griffiths was no different.

"He certainly would never have had his daughter get involved with any man who'd been part of that losing effort, no matter how many Purple Hearts or Silver Stars he boasted."

Roland first learned of it then—this corrupt old man had been in love with Adele Griffiths, his wife, for all these years.

"The one he'd sequester away from me, the one he assumed was too good for me, the one I wanted to take out all my resentment of him and the United States government from the war years on—if I ever could.

"So, to the victor go the spoils. The wife of social stature, the beautiful daughter, the clubs, the life—Frank had it all. I was left a functionary of the city—a janitor with a carnation—while he became a billionaire. If you watched it unfold from afar you could see how it could make a man resentful about any number of things."

The water seeped into the crags of his face and disappeared, not reappearing again until the droplets reached his chin and dove off.

"No one could have known the extent of my burn nor could anyone. My wife Etta never knew. Poor gal was the lady I had to settle for. I did not give her my all, that's for sure. And this life I had to settle for, with a badge on my chest, in the old West. Oh, there was plenty of burn, all right.

"Old Frank always knew I'd been pinin' for her … Woulda made my life complete, a woman like that, the woman you married Polsonby, even though she was plenty years younger."

A peaceful stillness came over the Ivory Stretch as it rose and dipped on the ribbon-like coastal road. Roland was mindful of the haunting secrets stacked within the frame of this despicable old man, a revenge he was still pursuing, ancient betrayals still chewing away at him, even in that white limo which had effectively become his hearse. The smoldering eyes, the pressure in the prisoner's voice, the pride coming through his words, the man was still burning. Roland remembered also the man's comments on chasing ghosts. Harlan Graves, a figure so embittered, vengeful, and ruthless, had been relentlessly pursuing ghosts of his own in the same way Billy and Roland had.

Reflecting long and hard Roland reasoned that he was not personally taking on the bewitchings of others. As his good friend said, their medicines met, Billy's Walk had crossed his own and they'd shared in each others' destinies, part of his friend's Walk becoming his own. In the same way he'd crossed Walks with Mélodie, encountering and learning from her medicines, and their destinies became intertwined and commingled as well. Now they were together as one.

Since the death of Billy, the silence of Roland's heart—and Mélodie's as well—had been disturbed and their Earth Walks impeded. Yet both were certain they were on the right Road now. He'd seen the Coyote and they'd needed to take action, the medicine of Badger even, to continue their journeys on the Earth Mother and move forward with their Walks. For these reasons they would abandon temporarily the laws of men. That was the decision they'd reached.

The Ivory Stretch glided along the two-lane highway on route to the hippy village Hanalei on the island's northern tip. The captors and their prisoner remained in each other's company respectfully and silently. The pair had been patient, apprised fully of what had happened back in Phoenix, of the Sheriff's blatant misconduct in the line of duty as he'd used his position in most dishonorable ways. More significantly, they knew he was responsible for the murder of their cherished Billy Six. So the Stretch glided along undeterred, the emboldened abductors bent resolutely on their prisoner's destruction at the time of sleep just as Billy had threatened Roland as punishment for the deaths of Jack and Diane Randall all those years before.

The justice was pure, it was perfect—the way their friend would have wanted it. They were his soldiers now, Billy's soldiers, fueled by a profound love and guided by the Great Spirit.

"*Oof-mah,*" the captor released to ward off the evil spirits and to praise his friend who taught him so many things.

"You got it all on tape, right? To make it a suicide—"

The Capítan's question hung there idly and was left to the wind. And somewhere, in some way, the Mexican girls were rejoicing—Tania the Guadalupe girl included—that their prayers had been heard and their God had not deserted them after all in the mystical lands of enchantment.

"Wanna let you know, I knew it all the time."

"Well, you're a cop."

"And a s-s-soldier—" the Capítan could barely finish as the utterance hit him harder than the rest and he wept right before them. "Wasn't right what they done to us …"

With no available hand the man raised a shoulder to his wet eye and wiped it. He said it eventually. "Polsonby?"

The captor angled over again at the withered, shrinking man.

"Been curious about something pretty mundane for a bad man being put to pasture. On that mountaintop. One o' my rifle boys witnessed an exchange between you and the troubled one. What was it he whispered to ya as he lay there dyin'?"

Roland knew exactly what he meant. "He said, '*I don't like the blue— paint it white …*'"

"That's what he said?"

"That's what he said." Roland nodded too. "That was our agreement. Part of it anyway."

And they carried out his request. They repainted the Stretch ivory white.

"Shit," the man said with a tempered smile his face no longer folding from within. He appeared suddenly younger, appreciably so.

"You know, Sheriff," the captor mentioned casually, "Hanalei is home to a marvelous geological formation—a mountainous peninsula rising from the ocean and its slope is sculpted perfectly in the shape of a dragon's head. The brow, the snout, and fire-breathing nostrils are clearly visible. Surfers working the break off it nicknamed it 'Puff.' The formation was written about in a well-known folk song, I bet you know it—"

In saying it Roland recognized he'd been channeling someone and Mélodie the songstress took the cue and initiated a delicate chorus.

> *"Puff the Magic Dragon,*
> *Lived by the sea,*
> *And frolicked in the autumn mist,*
> *In a land called Honah Lee—"*

"How 'bout that?" the old man mused.

For the second chorus the prisoner even joined in. He smiled freely too, the most liberating release he'd had in half a century. In between verses the old man's two hands raised a glass. "Cheers," he said.

They returned the toast and resumed singing together the delightful folk tune, the one which made Peter, Paul, and Mary famous, *"Puff the Magic Dragon, lived by the sea …"*

At the conclusion of the performance the old crook of a man gazed out the window and nearly articulated what he had in mind, but held off. *It's a good day to die*, he thought, the purest reflection he'd had in many years.

The Ivory Stretch continued gliding along, rising and falling on that ribboning island road, appearing and fading, until it was never seen to rise up again—disappearing forever.

Four hours later, the figure of the Capítan lay there lifelessly and inert, his casing drained completely, his brain rhythms long since calmed. The rain came down hard at an angle as a final winter storm unleashed her fury on the little island and the rising tide surged over the top of him as he'd wished and it swept him away. No one ever found his remains as they'd endured a thunderous and pounding surf that evening and he was whisked away by the gentle clasp of the Pacific, back to his regiment, back to his boys, the ones whose dreams had been shortened and he returned to it; a punishment too good for the likes of him.

Old Yellow Eyes was gone forever.

The only witness to this nocturnal vanishing was the resourceful Sonoran tarantula native to the dry wilds of the Apache Trail; a creature which had escaped death in the predator-friendly desert and was taken away on, one might say, a phantasmagoric flight into freedom and destiny as it lived for eighteen months in the mechanical entrails of the Ivory Stretch while feeding off neglected foodstuffs left since the pilot's final flight and subsequent demise.

The eight-legged wonder became lost in the labyrinth of that elongated marvel of modern machinery having taken a swat to the feelers by Billy himself, somersaulting and spinning end over end beneath the seat and finding a pathway to the inner chassis at the base of the motorized partition window. The arachnid remained there, seemingly trapped forever until the rescued vehicle was shipped to the island of Kauai of the Hawaiian chain. Eventually, after concerted daily efforts to escape—a year and a half's worth—like a prison inmate lacking sufficient mental faculties to go insane and aided by the Great Spirit, the creature found its way, emerging from a dark-tunneled tailpipe into the bright yellow sunlight to a place with fewer predators and the most rainfall of anywhere in the world; a Secret Beach abounding with a fresh variety of morsels of nourishment and cool breezes, heavenly Pacific breezes, a paradise.

Spider had found a home.

Roland himself had spied the creature as he returned to the car earlier that day after fulfilling the duty to his friend, ascertaining how it had gotten there and registering its exact positioning which had been from the front. A philosophy was underscored to him then to not get caught up in one's tiny web of life, to not blind oneself to the fresh and the unseen and all that possibility which may be laying outside of the pattern, as was the medicine of Spider. The savvy Sonoran tarantula was the proof it would seem; the creature had practiced the medicine it had preached. And he noted it.

Roland thought of his good friend then and how he'd overheard him contending that the tarantula, though an arachnid, did not qualify as a true spider and therefore, its medicine was still yet to be identified. His heart warmed all over just to think it. He considered then his own medicine and where he would bring it now on his Walk of Life and what remained of it—to make him and his little boy proud.

It had become his purpose.

46

Epilogue:
The Dolce Vita Diaries VII

On our way to Colorado we passed through Monument Valley where they made the John Wayne movies and "Thelma and Louise." We stopped in Telluride, a nice mountain town, but done very much for tourists.

We didn't stay in the same motel in Ouray, either.

It is an idea strange to me and modern and even I have difficulty believing it, but that was what they decided up there in the mountains. It was Roland's idea, the second part of their agreement, and I believe it was the last joy Billy felt.

And I will do it—he is my family of course, but more because that was what Billy was about, life … And it will be one last canvas for him, one last creation, one last way to express himself in the living—his living art, our living art—perhaps; and we will bring that part of him back.

It's "the explosive DNA" Roland spoke of, the "vital pulsations" Billy spoke of; it will be my song and Billy's enlightened spirit and to see it firing from a new little being would be the magic. And Roland would enjoy the honor, to be a father again, guardian Earth Father of Billy's child to guide him on his Walk, and the idea of a completeness to our family brings tears to my eyes. To be described as a Perfect Egg is flattering, but a lot to live up to. It will be my most challenging task, with its own reward, I believe—the illumination in life I have always been searching, searching, searching, yearning for …

We will make beauty one more time.

All of us.

I spread my mother's ashes on September 6th on the tallest mountain that overlooks Ouray, saying prayers to the Great Spirit and to Jesus Christ our Lord, my mother's choice of faith. I hope she can be in peace in the part of the world she felt closest to, but could never reach. It was her request in the letter to me and I know she is happy now. Grace the shaman told me she would be.

I will write, it has become my passion, but not this way. The work on Diaries is finished, the Dolce Vita days are over. They were the sweet life as we were together, but they are no longer. Life moves us on, but the magical dolce memories will never fade.

I am enclosing Billy's final letter—written to our friend Genesis Giones—as the last page of the Diaries. The message is so beautifully Billy, I had to.

Dear Genesis,

I thought I should send a line, to give you a heads up on things that may come your way. There's a better than fine chance I'll be gone when you get this so it's with care and sincerity I'm informing you, even alerting you, before things get out of hand and I'm no longer around to do it proper.

In my time I was a mean and wild twit-wit punk who raised a lot of hell and wanted to tear the world in half if for no reason other than it didn't seem to be to my liking. Sure I had my reasons, all of them "good" ones, seemed so anyway. But you can only blame others for a while and then you realize the problem isn't with the setup, or the cards dealt, or anyone else. There's nothing dope or boss or badass about going to prison—it hardened me to the point where I couldn't listen. And let go. Life is a goddam hurricane and letting go could have changed things and helped me get through it. I'm not saying you shouldn't take action, but there are times to be bold and gutsy and times to take a deep one and think of ways to avoid the bigger conflicts. It's coming on 2016 and there's never been this many jackasses riding the planet with this type of global intensity, everyone fighting over beliefs and ever-shrinking resources. So you have to be extra sensorial, which means not only using your brain, but your eyes, hands, ears, and mouth—all the senses you got—to get through it.

It's going to be nasty on Earth for a while, more challenging than when I was here; the Golden Age of Aquarius is coming, but it's still a ways away. So be aware—and be prepared—it's gonna get worse before it gets better, but it will get better.

I want you to read a copy of a letter I've kept for many years, one I refer to when I need a proper perspective on things. I call it "The Ballad of Al and Frankie" ...

August 2, 1939

Albert Einstein
Old Grove Road
Nassau Point
Peconic, Long Island

F. D. Roosevelt
President of the United States
White House
Washington, DC

Sir:

Some recent work by E. Fermi and L. Szilard, which has been communicated to me in a manuscript, leads me to expect that the element uranium may be turned into a new and important source of energy in the immediate future. Certain aspects of the situation which has arisen seem to call for watchfulness and, if necessary, quick action on the part of the Administration. I believe therefore that it is my duty to bring to your attention the following facts and recommendations.

In the course of the last four months it has been made probable—through the work of Joliot in France as well as Fermi and Szilard in America—that it may become possible to set up a nuclear chain reaction in a large mass of uranium, by which vast amounts of power and large quantities of new radium-like elements would be generated. Now it appears almost certain that this could be achieved in the immediate future.

This new phenomenon would also lead to the construction of bombs, and it is conceivable—though much less certain—that extremely powerful bombs of a new type, may thus be constructed. A single bomb of this type, carried by boat and exploded in a port, might very well destroy the whole port together with some of the surrounding territory. However, such bombs might very well prove to be too heavy for transportation by air.

The United States has only very poor areas of uranium in moderate quantities. There is some good ore in Canada and the former Czechoslovakia, while the most important source of uranium is the Belgian Congo.

In view of this situation you may think it desirable to have some permanent contact maintained between the Administration and the group of physicists working on chain reactions in America. One possible way of achieving this might be for you to entrust with this task a person who has your confidence and who could perhaps serve in an unofficial capacity.

Yours very truly,

Albert Einstein

Which brings me to my last point. I remember you sounding off once about becoming a rapper and joining up with one of them Phoenix gangs, the Boiled Scorpions did you say? Well let me tell you, you could do a lot better than getting lost in that kind of action. As you can see from the above, be careful what you wish for, you might get it—and Al was no dummy.

I'm not talking about the hot shits making good sounds and kicking good ass, I'm talking about the dead-enders, the hangers-ons, the punks, the ones robbing liquor stores, doing the drive-bys, maiming, and worse. They're not smart. Or funny. Or brave. Or original. They're not even happy. Most of them hate their lives, but they don't know where else to go or what else to do, and that's what makes them mean, and that's what makes them bastards. It also makes them useless because there's already an oversupply of mean useless bastards in this world. This is no way to go and I know a little about breaking the law, but you can raise hell like a banshee without getting caught up in that crap.

What you have to do is find your own niche, your own special talent and take that as far as you can. And how do you find that special talent? School. Because education will get you your freedom, freedom to choose a vocation, to find what you are good at, maybe the best ever at. And that gives you freedom to do everything else— like travel to all those places you've been dreaming about, the ones I never got to see. You can raise hell when you want and back off when you want, because you've got some place to go. And you'll leap over all those desperate dopes, creeps, and useless bastards who don't have that place, the ones who took the path of worshipping someone else's scene without developing their own. You gotta make your own scene, Genesis, don't depend on others for it, believe me, double-downed.

I'm not saying you can't get drunk, finger girls, or fist someone in the grill who's got it coming. And I'm not trying to be some tight-ass camp counselor, church rector, or highway cop, the type of authority figures I've fought against all my life. I'm telling you one man to another; it's you the real hot shot from here on in. And your decisions should be reflecting that.

And whatever you do, don't blow it the way those pathetic punks the Boiled Scorpions surely will.

Straight up.

Now get out there and kick some wild ass for me, make your tick-tocks on this rock count. I'm betting on you—double-downed. And of course, I'll be watching ...

Okay, hot shot, signing off.

Until we meet up again. To manufacture nonsense in the Big Sky, of course.

Your good friend,

.

Also by

Coerte V. W. Felske

for

The DVP

coertefelske.com
thedolcevitapress.com

Cover art, calligraphy, cover photograph of Alessandra Ambrosío and back cover
photograph of Ana Beatriz Barros, Alessandra Ambrosío, and Irina Shayk by
Peter Beard shot on Giant Polaroids in New York City, 2009, produced by CVWF

Cover design by Christian Toms for Red & Jacket or chris@redandjacket.com
and CVWF for The Dolce Vita Press
Cover concept and design by Jackie Merri Meyer for MeyerNewYork@aol.com
and CVWF for The Dolce Vita Press

"Tom Wolfe rewrites *American Gigolo*."
— *Kirkus Reviews*

"Crass, slangy, egotistical, and reeking of sun bronze, and the turnover of fleshy delights makes the narrator's decision to become an aging roué instead of responsible adult seem like an admirable choice. Felske writes like a gigolo and treats seduction as a dirty sport."
— James Wolcott, *Vanity Fair*

"Model citizen. Nick Laws, who narrates Coerte Felske's amusing first novel, proves that the unexamined life is worth living. Nick detests the beach but this novel is perfect for it."
— *The New York Times Book Review*

"Felske spins a clever tale of the narcissistic world of fashion modeling. Nick is so perfect he's hilarious. *The Shallow Man* is fun, flash, and filigree—a sexy, witty, spoof of the 90s."
— Digby Diehl, *Playboy*

"Tight prose, smooth dialogue, captures characters' gloss with a smart shine of its own."
— *Publishers Weekly*

"Shallow waters run deep. The quick-witted prose makes a case for the unexamined life."
— *Esquire*

"Spiked with original Nickspeak and hilarious dialogue. Very clever."
—*People Magazine*

"Felske's novel *The Shallow Man* turned the fashion world on its head—and introduced the term 'modelizer' into the collective consciousness. Refreshingly moral-free."
— *Detour*

"Deep thoughts from a hand model, fans of McInerney and O'Rourke should be amused."
— *Glamour*

"Make no mistake, Felske's literary Lothario, the Shallow Man, is no ordinary ladies' man. He's an uberstud for the '90s, otherwise known as a model hound, beauty junkie, or, **modelizer**."
— *Details*

"The *Shampoo* of the 1990s."
— *The New York Daily News*

"The *Bright Lights, Big City* of the 90s."
— *Buzz Magazine*

"Generation X's answer to *Less Than Zero*."
— *Sydney Morning Herald (Australia)*

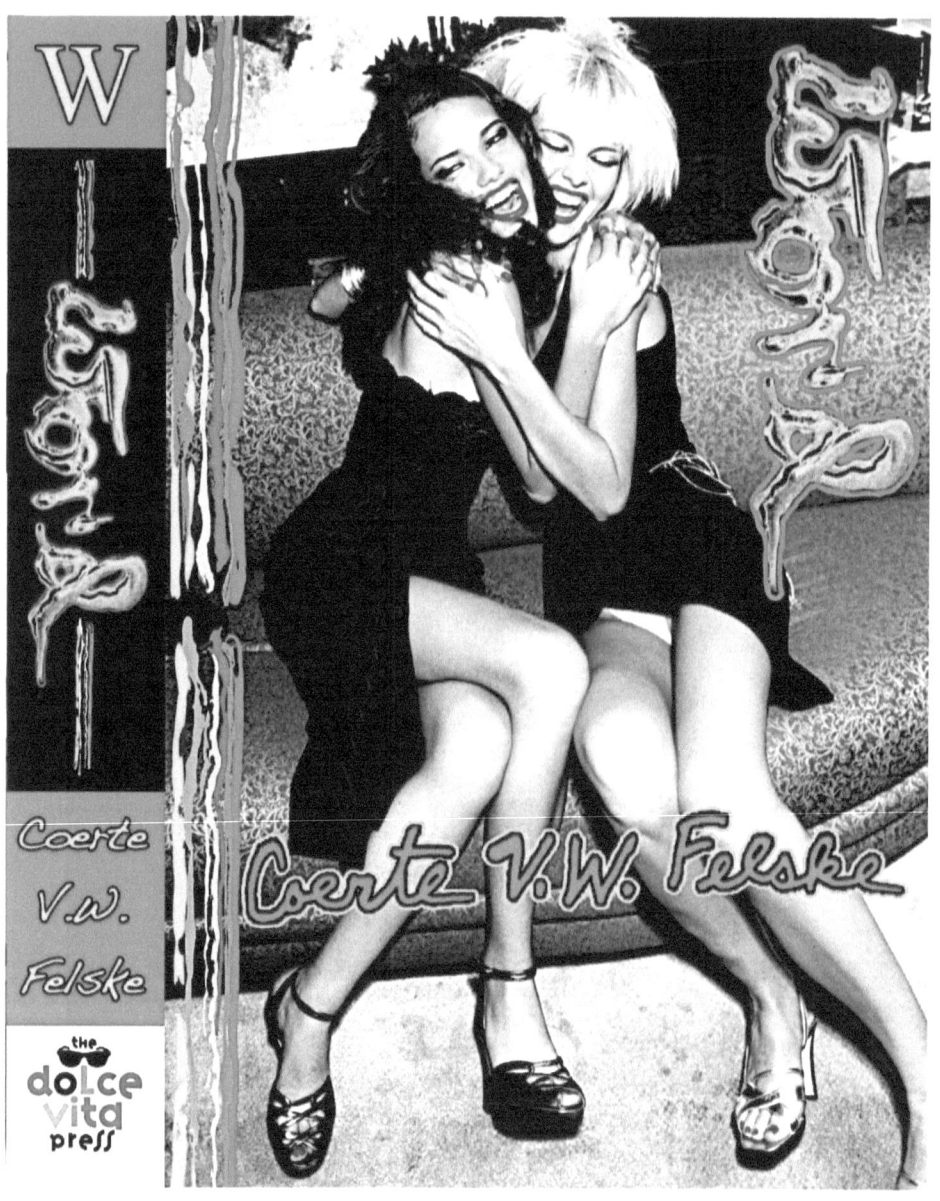

Front and back cover photographs of Adriana Lima by Ellen von Unwerth
Calligraphy by Peter Beard and Chris Toms

Word 2014 cover design Cover design by Christian Toms for Red & Jacket or
chris@redandjacket.com and CVWF for The Dolce Vita Press

Original cover concept by Jackie Merri Meyer for MeyerNewYork@aol.com and
CVWF for The Dolce Vita Press

"**Chandler for the 90s: (*****)** *Word* is pure 40s cool and paragraphs swing with voiceover rhythms that put Harrison Ford's *Blade Runner* monologues to shame. Beautiful babes, New York wasps and sleazy zillionaires flit through *Word*, larger than life and twice as interesting."
— Carrie O'Grady, *The Guardian (England)*

"A torrent of L.A. buzzwords and insider cynicism unmatched since Odets and Lehman's *Sweet Smell of Success* took on Manhattan. The Hell-A hypechat will flick all of your fuses."
— *Kirkus Reviews*

"Flashy and dark, this energetic Nathanael West retake offers a rich Hollywood menu of pandering, ambition, power, and retribution."
— *Publishers Weekly*

"**Magnificent Obsessions:** *Word*, the book Bret Ellis didn't write, is Felske's satire of Hollywood, i.e., 'Star Camp,' and he does a great job with female movie colony characters."
— *Playboy*

"*The Shallow Man* turned fashion on its head bringing the term 'modelizer' into the collective conscious. With tough-talking *Word*, Felske is back, red-eyeing it over Tinseltown's turf."
— *Detour*

"By page 3 of this sharp send-up of all things Hollywood, you'll be patting yourself on the back for having discovered *Word* before *Variety* announces its arrival at a theater near you."
— *Marie Claire*

"**If We Gave Out Book Awards:** Edgiest Boy, *Word*.. Felske's anti-hero hilariously manages to find some beating hearts inside the hippest Hollywood hyphenates."
— *Glamour*

"*Word* belongs to the growing genre of Hollywood novels in which idealistic filmmakers experience disillusionment and con artists and charlatans occupy the positions of power."
— *USA Today*

"*Word* is winningly told, with often ferocious humor, including a fresh, funny argot. Recommended for fiction collections."
— *Library Journal*

"A vicious story of the movie-driven anathema of depth that is L.A, Felske's tale about aching for success and the price of achieving it will remind you why you live in Northern California."
— *San Francisco Metropolitan*

"*Word*, is a jazzy, ironic appreciation of writing, filmmaking, and chasing skirt. In two of those arts, at least, downtown novelist Coerte V.W. Felske seems more than passingly adept."
— *New York Magazine*

"The word on *Word* is all good."
— *"Page Six," The New York Post*

Front and back cover photographs of Alessandra Ambrosío by Raphael Mazzucco
Calligraphy by Peter Beard and Chris Toms

The Millennium Girl 2014 cover design by Christian Toms for Red & Jacket or
chris@redandjacket.com and CVWF for The Dolce Vita Press

Original cover concept by Jackie Merri Meyer for MeyerNewYork@aol.com and
CVWF for The Dolce Vita Press

"**How to Catch a Man at the Century's End:** A face-to-face with 'diggers,' women who troll resorts in search of millionaires. We know that women like this exist, but until now we didn't have all the gory details. Bo is charming and the book is hilarious and sympathetic."
— *The New York Times Book Review*

"*The Millennium Girl* skillfully takes us through the marriage market of the new millennium. Felske is the real thing: He knows his territory, and he writes about it with wit and style."
— *Vogue*

"The resourceful Felske's latest topic is gold diggers, the sweet lovelies more shark-like than Anita Loos's or Truman Capote's and the author laces every page with a masterful cynicism."
— *Kirkus Reviews*

"Based on a magazine article Felske wrote about young women hustling in Aspen, *The Millennium Girl,* is snappy fun, a box of candy wrapped up with a black latex bow."
— *Booklist*

"A strong follow-up to his previous, *Word*, Felske uses his trademark insight and detail to peer into the lives of sassy, sad women and their encounters with the richest. A complete hoot, sexy, hard to put down, it's 100 percent fun, and recommended for all fiction collections."
— *Library Journal*

"In *The Millennium Girl*, pulse-of-the-Zeitgeist author Coerte Felske sets his sights on 'Diggers,' the globe-trotting hotties on the hunt for 'Walletmen,' the ultra-rich men of their dreams."
— *Detour*

"Who are these lit It Girls?*The Millennium Girl*. 'I'm not a hooker but I do live off men,' says Bodicea. I wanted to hate her, but she was too shameless and too hilariously over-the-top."
— *Mademoiselle*

"Felske's cleverly describes the art of the gold-digger and the folly of their prey. Bo invents cute nicknames for the Diggers and acidic jibes at upper-class hypocrisy, good for chuckles."
— *Publishers Weekly*

"Great fun and more than a racy rehash of *Pretty Woman*, Felske covered the 'digger' scene in an article for *Esquire* and clearly knows the turf. Female empowerment, a having-it-all ending, a pampered husband-hunter, and a flaming gay sidekick perpetuate these pages."
— *Entertainment Weekly*

"*Breakfast at Tiffany's* for the year 2000. A totally titillating read."
— *Woman's Own*

"Bodicea is possessed of a wry sense of humor and eye for detail and she sympathetically picks apart her own insecurities and those of fellow Diggers. Once again, Felske expertly maps the morally dubious interiors of characters who live on a razor's edge of scruples."
— *The Southampton Press*

Cover art, calligraphy, front and back cover photographs of Irina Shayk by
Peter Beard shot on Giant Polaroids in New York City, 2009, produced by CVWF

Cover design by Christian Toms for Red & Jacket or chris@redandjacket.com
and CVWF for The Dolce Vita Press

Original cover concept by Jackie Merri Meyer for MeyerNewYork@aol.com
and CVWF for The Dolce Vita Press

Scandalocity

Author Coerte V.W. Felske's fourth novel, *Scandalocity,* comes on the heels of his highly acclaimed "dolce vita fiction" trilogy: *The Shallow, Man, Word,* and *The Millennium Girl.* Zeitgeist for the Information Age, the book is set against the backdrop of the starry lights and glamorous nights of New York City. Defined as "The speed at which scandal, measured in velocity, can turn you into a star," *Scandalocity* is a sexy, ADHD psychological thriller, and the master of guilty pleasure prose takes on our technology-driven, media-consumed, and celebrity-obsessed culture in a taut, explosive narrative. Protagonist Harry Starslinger is a neurologically disordered online gossip columnist who becomes embroiled in the police investigation of his girlfriend's murder. Like Dostoevsky's *Notes From Underground,* the book takes off in roaring first-person as we ride Harry's spontaneous, insightful thoughts. One of the most connected men in the City, where his high-profile position as a purveyor of celebrity gossip offers him access anywhere, anytime, "Slinger" finds it difficult to founder life-sustaining connections in a rocket-paced world of IMs, iPods and e-mails, social networking sites, and hand-held techie toys. The story unfolds in parallel between the ongoing murder investigation and the burgeoning romance with the victim in the past. There's more murder, a manhunt, and Harry becomes the hunted one. A pulsating page-turner, the novel combines the scalding thematic tones of Odets and Lehman's *The Sweet Smell of Success* with the suspense and dramatic twists of Kasden's erotic cinema thriller *Body Heat.* Felske's fourth installment in his "dolce vita fiction" series, *Scandalocity* crackles with razor sharp vernacular and a lexicon's worth of bleeding edge phraseologies, hallmarks of the author's inimitable life-in-the-fast-lane literature.

Three Sleeps to Double Happiness

Coerte V.W. Felske

Three Sleeps to Double Happiness

In the tradition of Herman Hesse's spiritual journey of self-discovery in *Siddharta* and Santiago's "Personal Legend" in Paolo Coelho's *The Alchemist*, Coerte V.W. Felske's *Three Sleeps to Double Happiness* sets the imagination afire in an exhilarating allegorical tale of love, loss, vindication, and triumph. Written in hauntingly spare prose TSDH is the story of an unlikely hero, Gonzalo, an alternatively-abled albeit functional Spanish boy who travels to India to seek out a legendary tiger in order to achieve what he has theorized to be "Double Happiness." The tale is told primarily in flashback as "the young teen of indeterminate age" perches in a Dhok tree in India's Sariska jungle and awaits the appearance of the Great One for "three sleeps," his term for days, at the territorial beast's waterhole. As the boy waits and unwittingly fends off aggressive lemurs and the menacing leopard, his pinwheeling, Kaleidoscope mind conjures disjointed reminiscences of a devastating childhood in Spain. Abused mercilessly for perceived disabilities by kids and adults alike the boy, along with his sister, the beautiful and exceptional Aravella, live north of Barcelona in the coastal town Llavaneres with their mercenary foster father. Not only has the greedy Tuko adopted the two for government subsidies, he sells hashish and procures women for the notorious drug lord Don Pepe whose sprawling *finca* overlooks the town. Still, the siblings form an unbreakable bond and the sacrificial Aravella, Gonzalo's Sister the Angel, teaches him Spanish, biology, religion, folklore, even the Chinese love fable Double Happiness. Gonzalo's best friend is the Old Man, Santoro, a local spice farmer who offers the boy paternal guidance and recounts fantastic adventures traveling the world. Gonzalo marvels at Santoro's trip to India when he came face to face with Zephyrles a thirteen-foot Bengal tiger. The Old Man, stricken with cancer, laments he hadn't offered himself to the tiger to die an honorable death rather than to rot ignominiously in a field shack. After the Old Man passes, more misfortune and tragedy beset the boy. In a harrowing sequence Aravella is killed defending her honor against Don

Pepe while Tuko's corruption catches up with him. The boy is left to fend for himself. In his sweetly configured, contemplative mind he decides on a plan to go to India to confront the Great One and discover the meaning of Double Happiness. Back in the jungle the boy entertains a rush of memories; he gets a job on a pleasure yacht and cruises the Spanish coast, then is offered work on a hashish farm in Morocco before taking the overland train to India. He recalls the physical abuse of classmates and his foster father, sexual abuse by Father Miguel, witnessing his sister's murder, the raping of a Dutch girl, as well as making love to Sofia. But the boy who only sees the good in people finds his mind to be repairing itself. He gains the capacity to process the teachings taken in these years, allowing him to understand the world and identify, decipher, and evaluate all the love and cruelty he has encountered. With this fresh clarity of thought, if not raised level of awareness, Gonzalo is emboldened to carry out his mission to offer himself for what he processes now to be that noble death of which Santoro spoke. After his third sleep, Zephyrles the Great One appears and the boy must decide on his own ultimate fate. The tale is a scalding treatise recounted in a simplistic, meditative, almost poetic style, the prose so beautiful, it sings. Unintentionally the quintessential "green" novel, at once mystical and magical while no less brutal and unforgiving, TSDH excites the imagination long after the boy's final "Celebration" attended by a very special guest concludes.

Chemical / Animal coming Summer, 2018

Completed Works

of

Coerte V.W. Felske

coming soon from

The Dolce Vita Press

Chemical / Animal

A Touch of Noir

the
dolce
vita
press

The Dolce Vita Press Presents The Complete Works of...

Coerte V.W. Felske

To purchase Coerte V. W. Felske titles,
request signed or review copies, write to the publisher
or author, or for news, updates, and descriptions
of upcoming releases and an in-depth biography,
please visit the author's Web site at:

coertefelske.com
thedolcevitapress.com

Coerte V.W. Felske was born in New York City and grew up in Manhattan and Quogue, Long Island. He attended Bronxville High School and received his Bachelor of Arts degree from Dartmouth College. He did his graduate work in film directing and screenwriting at Columbia University. *The Shallow Man*, originally published in 1995, was his first novel. His second novel, *Word*, came out in 1998 followed by *The Millennium Girl* in 2000. In 2010 the independent online literary imprint The Dolce Vita Press was founded in conjunction with Amazon.com to publish and distribute Felske's books. The imprint's inaugural publication was *Scandalocity* published in 2012. Special author's cut anniversary editions of both the acclaimed *Word* and *The Millennium Girl* were released in 2014 followed by *The Shallow Man: 20th Anniversary Edition* in 2015. Felske's southwest psychological drama *The Ivory Stretch* was released in 2016. *Three Sleeps to Double Happiness*, Felske's sixth original novel, is slated for a summer, 2017 release accompanied by a book reading and signing tour in in the U.S. and Canada.

The Dolce Vita Press was established to enhance contact with the readership as well as offer the author the creative freedom to incorporate the talents of top photographers, graphic artists, and book jacket designers. The DVP label derives from the Italian term "dolce vita," which translates to the "sweet life." Felske was influenced by Federico Fellini's cinematic masterwork, *La Dolce Vita*, which tells the tale of a carefree, decadent group of seemingly glamorous partiers, nightclubbers, and exotic women as they navigate their way through Rome's high society, all pursued by a dashing playboy paparazzo. The author has often referred to his literature as "dolce vita fiction," stories about nightclub impresarios, serial womanizers, fashionistas, fortune hunting women, entertainment business hopefuls, and scandal sheet writers entrenched in a similar dolce vita circuitry; in essence, characters living modern versions of that illusory 'sweet life' depicted in Fellini's film. In addition to the summer 2017 release of *Three Sleeps to Double Happiness*, the author has two more works completed and coming soon. Felske's *Chemical/Animal*, his second written in first person as a woman, will be released in summer, 2018, followed by the hard-boiled Los Angeles 1940s thriller *A Touch of Noir* in 2019. All Coerte V.W. Felske titles for The Dolce Vita Press are available at the author's Web site coertefelske.com, thedolcevitapress.com, Amazon.com, BN.com, independent bookstores and e-book distributors worldwide. To contact The DVP, request a review or signed copy, or write to the author or publisher please visit the author's Web site at coertefelske.com.